Pirate Freedom

BY GENE WOLFE
FROM TOM DOHERTY ASSOCIATES

Pirate Freedom

GENE WOLFE

A TOM DOHERTY ASSOCIATES BOOK
New York

PIRATE FREEDOM

Copyright © 2007 by Gene Wolfe

Illustrations © 2007 by David Grove

Edited by David G. Hartwell

A Tor Book
Published by Tom Doherty Associates, LLC
175 Fifth Avenue
New York, NY 10010

www.tor.com

Tor® is a registered trademark of Tom Doherty Associates, LLC.

Library of Congress Cataloging-in-Publication Data

Wolfe, Gene.
    Pirate freedom / Gene Wolfe. — 1st ed.
        p. cm.
    "A Tom Doherty Associates book."
    ISBN-13: 978-0-7653-1878-7
    ISBN-10: 0-7653-1878-4
    1. Priests—Fiction. 2. Buccaneers—Fiction. 3. Caribbean Area—Fiction. 4. Time travel—Fiction. I. Title.
    PS3573.O52P75 2007
    813'.54—dc22

                                                                            2007014348

First Edition: November 2007

Printed in the United States of America

0 9 8 7 6 5 4 3 2 1

This book is dedicated to
SIR HENRY MORGAN, WILLIAM DAMPIER,
ALEXANDER O. EXQUEMELIN, CALICO JACK RACKAM,
ANNE BONNEY, and MARY READ.
Most of all, it is dedicated to
BEKAH ROHRIG
by its grateful author.

Every normal man must be tempted, at times, to spit on his hands, hoist the black flag, and begin slitting throats.

—H. L. MENCKEN

Pirate Freedom

Preface

WE DO NOT usually hear confessions, but I heard several by special appointment last Saturday. Tonight one man came to the rectory to ask whether I remembered his. I said that I did not.

"Then you've probably forgotten what you told me after you heard my confession, too."

I shook my head. "I recall that perfectly. I told you I'm a murderer myself."

He looked a little stunned, and I invited him to sit down. "The housekeeper's gone home," I added, "but I can make tea for you, or instant coffee." I pointed to my glass. "This's ice water, something I can never get enough of. We've lots of that, too."

He said, "I told you what I did."

I nodded. "I know you must have. I advise you not to repeat it."

"I won't. I don't even want to. That felt so good! I shall owe you for that as long as I live."

Of course I said that was nice and asked, politely, what he wanted.

"I want to know what you did." He sighed, and grinned as soon as the sigh was finished. "You don't have to tell me. I know that. You don't owe me anything. But . . ."

"Confession's good for the soul."

"Right, Padre. It is. Besides, I very much want to know. I'll never tell anyone, and no one would believe me if I did. Will you? As a favor?"

"For my sake," I said.

"Mine, too. I think it might help me."

"And you told me, even though I've forgotten. I won't ask whether you'll forget this. I know the answer."

The smart thing was for him just to wait, which is what he did.

"I was on a ship. A certain man there had insulted me. Over and over, and in a way that threatened to do a lot of harm."

My visitor nodded.

"We had been in a big fight with some other people—he and I on the same side. There were a lot of other men on both sides. Fifty or so. And one woman on ours—I nearly forgot her. This man had a hammer in his belt, positioned so that he could pull it out with his right hand. He'd been using it as a weapon."

"I'm most sorry, Padre. I shouldn't have asked."

"It's okay." Now it was my turn to sigh. "This is only one instance. There are a good many others, I'm afraid, depending on just how God judges these things."

I sipped my water while I pulled myself together. "This man I spoke of— the man who had insulted me—came up to shake hands with me when the fight was over. I'd been using an oak bar with an iron tip as a weapon. It was about this long."

I showed it the way fishermen show the length of a fish, and my visitor nodded.

"Four and half feet, maybe. Maybe five. About that. It would have been heavy even without the iron tip, but the tip brought its weight toward that end. You know what I mean?"

"He wanted to shake your hand," my visitor said.

"Yes. Yes, he did. Everyone was shaking hands with me then, and he wanted to be one of them. I accepted his hand and held it so he couldn't get to his hammer, and I swung the bar I had been leaning on overhand with my left hand."

"I see. . . ."

"When he was lying unconscious on the deck, I hit him again, harder, swinging the handspike with both arms. I've never been quite sure why I did that, but I did. A friend of mine picked up his feet, and I picked up his shoulders. His head was a mess—I remember that. Together, we threw him over the gunwale into the sea."

My visitor had a great many questions after that, but I answered hardly any, just telling him over and over that the answers were too complicated to explain unless we sat up all night. I did not add—although I could have—that he would not have believed me. Finally I promised I would write everything out and mail it to him when it could do no more harm.

Now I am going to take a long walk and do a lot of thinking. When I return to the rectory, I will begin.

I

The Monastery

SOMETIMES IT SEEMS that I spend most of my time trying to explain things to people who do not want to understand. This may be more of that. My evenings are free once I have locked up the Youth Center. Maybe I should have written semi-free. I read whenever I can, the lives of good and decent men and women who sought God and found Him.

I am not like that—either I have never lost Him or I have never sought Him. When you read this, you can say which. I have already confessed many times, but I think someone ought to tell my story. I am no autobiographer, just the only one who knows it.

I was ten, I think, when my father and I moved to Cuba. The communists had lost power, and my father was going to run a casino in Havana. Some monks had reopened an old monastery outside the city, and they were trying to start a boarding school. After a few years, my father signed me up. I think he must have given the monastery fifty thousand or so, because nothing was said about payment in all the years I was there—nothing I remember.

A year seems like a lifetime at that age, so three or maybe four lifetimes passed before I went from being a student to being a novice in the order. You would think I would remember something like that better than I do. All that I recall is that the Novice Master called us together one day and explained that the abbot had given up the idea of a school. The parents who did not want their sons to enter the order would come and take them home.

Most of my friends left after that. My father did not come, so I became a novice.

I see I have gotten ahead of myself, which happens a lot whenever I try to talk in public. I should tell you first that up to then I had gone home for holidays. Not all of them but some, like Christmas, and for eight weeks in the summer, every summer until then.

After that, my father never came for me again. I talked to my confessor about it, and he explained that being a novice was different. My father could not come anymore. He could have written letters, but he never did.

It was still like going to school. I helped Brother Ignacio herd our pigs and weed the garden, and there were novenas and mass and vespers and whatnot. But we had always done those. We still had classes and grades and all that. Now I know the subjects we studied were just the ones various monks could teach, but they knew a lot and it was a pretty good education. Most of them were from Mexico and most of the kids from Cuba, so we spoke Spanish in the monastery. The kids' Spanish was a little different, but not a whole lot. Mass was in Spanish at first, Latin later on.

A lot of what I learned there was languages. We did two at a time: Spanish and Latin for a year, French and English the next year, then Spanish and Latin again the year after. Like that. I had picked up quite a bit of Italian from my father and his friends, English was what we had spoken at my school in the States, and I had gotten a good bit of Spanish just living in Havana before I went to the monastery. So I did not do too badly. I was not anybody's star pupil in languages, but I was not at the bottom of the class in any of them. Or even close to it.

Besides the languages we got a lot of theology, like you would expect, and liturgy, Bible studies, and so forth. I guess all of us thought we would be priests eventually, and maybe the monks did, too, or some did.

We took biology every year. We called it biology, but a whole lot of it was about sex. If we became priests as well as monks we would have to hear confessions. Some of them would be the confessions of other monks, but two or three of our priests went into Havana almost every Friday and Saturday to help out in various parishes, and one of the things they did was hear the confessions of the laity. Not just men, but women too. I used to daydream about having this beautiful woman come into the confessional and say, "I know it's wrong to lust after a priest, Father, but I can't help myself. It's Father Chris. Every time I see him I want to tear off all my clothes." One time I told my confessor about those daydreams, but he just laughed. I did not like it, and I like it even less now. I pray that God will strike me down before I ever do that to anyone.

We learned about all the perversions, or at least about all those our teacher knew about, and that was a lot. Some were pretty funny, but some were just horrible. There was a lot about homosexuality, how bad it was, and how we must love the sinner but not the sin. That stuff was one reason I left the monastery. I will get to that soon.

Math was my best subject. We got arithmetic, algebra, trigonometry, and geometry, plain and solid. Most of the kids griped about math, but I loved it. Pretty soon I caught on to what Fr. Luis was doing for tests. He would assign certain problems in the book for homework. The problems he had not assigned would show up on his tests. I got wise and worked all the problems. I got quite a few hundreds on my tests, and hardly ever had a test come back lower than ninety-seven. Fr. Luis used to brag about me when I was not around. Two or three of the other monks told me about it. I can never repay Fr. Luis for teaching me math—geometry and trig, especially. I know he is in Heaven.

Those were the main subjects we took, but Fr. Patrizio had a telescope and used to point out all the stars to us, and tell us about them, and how you could see the Southern Cross once you crossed the equator. He was from Argentina, and he must have been lonely for the stars he grew up with. So we did not actually study astronomy—nobody thought we would have to know it—but I found the stars beautiful and interesting, and I picked up a lot from him.

We took music, too. I like music a lot, but I did not like or even understand the things we studied in music, and I always wanted to play faster than I was supposed to.

After a while the old kids were mostly gone, a few new ones had come, and nobody wore wristwatches anymore. (I noticed that.) Mass was in Latin instead of Spanish, and everybody seemed a little calmer. Fr. Patrizio was dead or gone or something. I missed some of the old kids and some of my old teachers. But basically I liked it better.

One day the Novice Master came into music class to take me to the abbot. I had heard his homilies two or three times, but I am not sure I had ever spoken to him until then. On feast days we were at one end of the table and the abbot was at the other, so we never talked. There were at least two abbots while I was there. Maybe three. I remembered my father saying abbots brought you down, and I was sure I was not going to like him and that it was going to be bad news.

Which in a way it was. I did like him, though, and by the time we were through talking I liked him a lot. By then I knew I had hurt him, too, and felt bad about it.

He was a lot shorter, and pretty old. I remember the lines on his face, and how shy his eyes were. Now I think he must have known right from the start that I was looking to lie to him. (Sometimes I have wondered what he thought about me, this skinny gringo kid who was going to sit there and lie to him. Some other times I have been glad I do not know.)

He said that it was time my novitiate was over, that I had to decide now whether I would take my solemn vows at Easter. He talked a little about his own life outside the monastery. His father had been a cobbler and had taught him the trade. Then he talked a lot about his life as a monk, how he used to mend sandals for the other monks, and all the monastery had meant to him. He talked about God, and devoting your life to Him. He asked a lot of questions about me, too. What the monastery had been like for me, and what my life outside had been like.

By the time he asked for my decision I had already thought it over, though perhaps it was not really thinking but only what kids call thinking. I said that I was not ready yet to take my vows. That I wanted to go home and see my father and have a chance to talk things over with him and with myself.

The abbot sighed, but I do not think he was surprised. He said, "I comprehend you. Will you promise me something, Crisóforo?" (Everything was in Spanish, but I might as well translate for you because I do not remember the exact words we used anyhow.)

I said it would depend on what the promise was.

"A very small thing, Christopher. To make an old man happy?"

I said I would try. By then I was pretty sure it was going to be about sex, probably to keep away from women.

For a minute or two he sat there studying me. His eyes had probably been sharp once, but they were too kind to be sharp anymore. "I would like a better promise than that," he said at last, "but I shall settle for that one, since I must. I want you to promise that you will never forget us."

I said, "Wait, you don't understand. I'll probably come back," and I talked a lot about that, going on and on and repeating things I had said already. Lying.

Finally he cut me off. He said I was free to go. If I wanted to say good-bye to people I could stay that night.

I said, "No, Reverend Abbot, I want to go right now," and after that he called for Brother Ignacio.

Brother Ignacio took me to the gate. He never said a single word to me. Not one. Only when I turned back to wave good-bye, he was crying. There have been times since then when I thought I understood how he felt.

I had taken off my habit and put on the clothes I used to wear back when I went home for the summer, my T-shirt and jeans. They were way too small for me now, but that was all I had. I started walking down the road dressed like that, and carrying my little holiday bag. I should have known right away that something was wrong, but I did not. Not even when the farmer came by in his wagon and gave me a ride.

It was an old wagon pulled by an old horse. I thought there would be cars and trucks whizzing past us, but there was not a one. After a while it came to me that the road ought to have been asphalt. Not a good road, potholes and all that, but asphalt.

It was just dirt. For a while I leaned out of the wagon watching for tire tracks, but the only tracks were from horses, and wagons with wheels like ours—wooden wheels with iron tires.

I started talking to the farmer then. I was supposed to be trying to find out what had happened, but I talked a whole lot more than I listened. I told him a lot about the monastery, trying to make it as real as I could. Because I felt—I do not know why—that it would not be there if I went back. When I had gone out the gate, waved to Brother Ignacio, and walked to the road, I had ended something. I did not know what it was then, but I knew it was over and I could not go back. Not for a long time, and maybe never. Later on the *Santa Charita*, I prayed to God that He would change His mind and put me back there. But as soon as I had said the amen I knew He would not.

Anyway, the farmer did not talk much, and when he did I did not learn much from it. *Camión?* Oh, yes. A big wagon with four horses. It goes to Matanzas, you pay to get on. *Habana?* Yes, a big city. Very big. Many people.

But when we got there, it was not. It was a town, and not a big one either. There was a big stone fort, still being built in places, and some stone churches. Just about everything else was wood, and pretty rough. A few streets were paved with rocks, but most were just dirt. There was garbage in them and horse shit. Lots of both. When we got to the market, I helped the farmer set up and said good-bye.

There were refreshment stands in the market, and the food smelled wonderful. I went off looking for our house, hoping my father would be home and thinking about ways I might be able to get in if he was not. It had been east of the city, but when I got there it was not there. There were no houses at all, just fields of corn and sugarcane. I was sure I had gone wrong, so I went north as far as the beach, and south quite a way, and so on. You can imagine.

And it was not there. I decided then that there were two Havanas, or maybe the city had changed its name and this little town had taken it over.

By then I was about starved. I went back to the market and stopped at every stand, saying I would be glad to do some work if the man or woman who ran it would give me something to eat. It was no at every stand.

Finally I stole some food. It was a little loaf of Cuban bread, still warm from the oven. I grabbed it and ran as fast as I could, which was pretty fast even back then. When I got into an alley that had a good hiding place, I ate it. I have never eaten anything better in my whole life than that little loaf of Cuban bread. Cuban bread is about like our Italian bread but sweeter, and for me it was like I was in Hell and a fresh loaf from Heaven had fallen and I had caught it. Right then I should have thought seriously about the Eucharist, but I did not.

What I thought about instead was sin. I knew that it was wrong to steal and that I had stolen the bread, but I had learned enough moral theology to know that when a hungry person steals food it is only a venial sin. I had committed quite a few venial sins already, like lying to the abbot, and I figured God was not going to send me off to Hell for venial sins anyway. That night I slept in my hiding place in the alley, and I did not like it.

The next day was not much different, except that I stole a chicken. There was a woman in the market who roasted them to order on a spit, little skinny chickens that would have made my English teacher make jokes about friars. Without letting on that I was paying attention, I watched her pretty carefully while she was roasting one. When it was done, the customer who wanted it spread a rag on the table, and the chicken-stand woman laid the hot chicken on that. There was a little time—a few seconds—when nobody was holding it. Then the customer wrapped it up in her rag and put it in her basket and paid.

So I waited for the next customer, figuring I would grab the chicken out of her basket while she was paying. Only the next customer had a basket with a lid, and I saw that my idea was not going to work. She would put it in there and close the lid, and start screaming while I was getting her basket open. What I would have to do instead was grab the chicken as soon as it was put down on the rag.

I tried to, but all I got was a whack from the chicken woman's stick, a stick I had not even noticed she had. It hurt like the devil and I was afraid I was going to get caught, so I ran.

It made me mad, too. Mad at her for whacking me, and mad at myself for not grabbing the chicken. I knew it was going to be a lot tougher when I tried it again, so I waited until the sun was nearly down and some of the stands were closing. That made it easier for me to see from a distance when she had a customer, because there were not as many people. For a while I was afraid she would not have any more.

Finally somebody came, a man. I think he meant to eat his chicken as soon as he got it, because he did not have a basket or anything to carry it in. She got a chicken for him from the wooden cage and showed it to him. He nodded, and she twisted its neck, and plucked and gutted it faster than you would have thought possible.

While it was cooking, I worked in a little closer. And as soon as she had it off her spit, I had it out of her hand. She got me again with her stick and it hurt pretty bad, but I grabbed her stick with my free hand before she could get it back up and got it away from her.

She thought I was going to hit her with it then, but I did not. I just dropped it and ran off with her chicken.

Maybe it tasted as good as the bread. I do not know. All that I remember is how scared I was that I was going to get caught before I finished it. How scared she was too—that short fat woman cowering with her arms up, afraid I was going to brain her with her own stick. When I thought of her just now, that is how I remembered her.

When I had eaten everything and sucked the bones—it did not seem like much—I found another sleeping place, not so near the market and the docks. And when I was lying there thinking about the chicken and getting hit twice with her stick, it came to me that if the lanky man buying the chicken had grabbed me from behind, it would have been all over. I would be in jail, was what I thought. Now I think they would probably have tied me to a post and beaten the merda out of me, then kicked me out. That is how they usually punished people when I was then.

After that, I started thinking about the monastery. Really thinking about it, maybe for the first time ever. How peaceful it had been, and how just about everybody there tried to look out for everybody else. I missed my cell, the chapel, and the refectory. I missed some of my teachers, too, and Brother Ignacio. It was funny, but the thing I missed most of all was the work he and I had done outside—helping milk sometimes, herding the pigs, and weeding. Collecting eggs in a basket like the ones I had hoped to steal out of, and carrying them in to Brother Cook. (His name was José, but everybody called him Brother Cook anyway.)

Then I got to thinking again about the rules, and what they had meant. You could not go into anybody else's cell, not ever, and the cells had no doors on them. You got told when to take a bath, three novices at a time, and there would be a monk there watching the whole time, generally Brother Fulgencio. He was older even than the abbot.

Those were rules I had not thought about at all when I was little. I took them in stride, like I had taken the rules at our school in the States. But when I got older and we learned about being gay and all that, I understood. They had thought we were, and they had not cared as long as we did not actually do anything with another kid. Once I had realized what was going on, it bugged me a lot. I did not want to spend the rest of my life thinking about girls and knowing that the people around me were thinking about boys, and thinking I was, too.

It was that last part that really got to me. If it had not been for that, if there had been a way I could have proved once and for all that I was no leccacazzi, I think I might have stayed.

That got me to thinking about how it was outside. It seemed to me Our Lady of Bethlehem had been a good thing, a good idea Saint Dominic had a thousand years ago: a place where people who did not ever want to fall in love or get married—or felt like they could not—could go and live really good lives.

But it seemed to me, too, that the world outside the monastery ought to be about the same, only with falling in love and maybe having kids, a place where people liked each other and helped each other, and everybody got to do what he was good at.

That has never changed for me. When you read the rest of this you're not going to believe me, but I am writing the truth. We have to make it like that, and the only way we can do it is for each person to choose it and change. I chose it that night, and if I have slipped up pretty often God knows I am truly sorry about every slip.

Sometimes I have had to slip. I ought to say that, too.

2

The Santa Charita

I AM NOT going to tell you much about the next few days. They are not important and run together anyway. I asked various people about another Havana, and they all said there was not one. I asked about my father and his casino, but nobody had heard of it. I walked down every last street in town, and I talked to priests at two churches. They both told me to go back to Our Lady of Bethlehem. I did not want to do that, and I did not think I could even if I tried. Now I hope things are different, but then I was sure I could not. I tried to find work, and sometimes I did get a few hours' work for a little money. Mostly it was around the docks.

Then Señor heard me asking about work. He said, "Pay attention, muchacho. You got a place to sleep?"

I said no.

"Bueno. You need someplace to sleep and meals. You come with me. You got to work and work hard, but we'll feed you and give you a hammock and a place to sling it, and when we get home you'll get some money."

That is how I got to be on the *Santa Charita*. English sailors talk about signing articles and all that, but I did not really sign anything. The mate I had talked to just talked to the captain, and the captain wrote my name in his book. Then the mate told me to make my mark beside it, so I initialed it and that was all there was to it. I think the mate's name was Gómez, but I have known a lot of people with that name and I may be wrong. We said Señor. He was a little man with big shoulders, and smallpox had given him a really tough time when he was younger. It took me two or three days to get used to the way he looked.

I got a hammock in the forecastle, like he promised. The food was not good except when it was, if you know what I mean. I had never drunk wine before, except just a sip of the Precious Blood at mass sometimes, so I did not know how bad the wine was. Or how weak it was, either. We had been loading cargo for Veracruz, a lot of it live pigs and chickens in cages, and the deck was a mess to the big. We would clean up one side, then the other, then back to the first one. We pumped water out of the harbor and squirted it out of a hose, mostly, and when we were not doing that, we pumped the ship. It leaked. Maybe there are wooden ships somewhere that do not leak, but I have never been on one.

You could go ashore when you were off watch. I did that just like the others, but I could not have gotten drunk or hired a whore even if I had wanted to. (Which I did not.) The Spanish sailors were not nearly as bad about getting drunk as some I have known since, but they were worse about women. The night we sailed they smuggled a battery girl on board and hid her. When we had gotten the anchor up and the pilot was taking us out of the harbor, the captain and Señor pulled her out of the hold and threw her over the side. I had seen something of her by then and had not liked it, but I would never have done that. It was the first thing that made me really understand what kind of a place I had landed in.

The second thing came three or four nights later. When we got off watch and went below, two guys grabbed my arms and another one pulled my jeans down. I fought—or thought I did—and yelled my head off until somebody about knocked it off. You know what happened after that. So did I, after I woke up. The only good thing that came out of it was that my old jeans got ripped so bad that I had to have new pants, and I found out you could get them from the bosun. He took care of the slop chest. He charged too much against my pay and my new canvas pants were too big, but I was so glad to get rid of those tight jeans I did not care.

About then I started going aloft, making sail and taking it in. Vasco and Simón told me I would be scared to death and dirty my new pants, but I told them they had better be scared, because I was going to grab them if I fell and take them down with me. I meant what I said, too.

The weather was calm with just a little bit of a breeze, you stood on the foot rope and held on with one hand, and I was not scared at all. Besides, you got a great view from up there. I did my work, but I sneaked looks every chance I got. There was the beautiful blue sea, and above us the beautiful blue sky with a couple of little white clouds, and I kept thinking that the earth was a beautiful woman, and the sky was her eyes—and thinking too how the sea and the sky would be there when everybody on our ship was dead and forgotten. I liked that, and I still do.

When we were down on the main deck again, I kept hoping the captain would want to take a reef in the topsail, but he did not. Only by then I knew that we furled all sail at night and lay to. (And I thought all ships did.) So I would get my chance for sure before we went off watch.

Here I ought to say that we were the starboard watch, which meant the one that Señor bossed and the one that did just about all the work. There was a larboard watch, too, which was a lot smaller. The larboard watch could sleep on deck if there was nothing for them to do, and sometimes they shot craps. Our ship was a brig, a bergantin was what we called it. It means that it had two masts the same size, both square-rigged. I was a foremast man then, not that it matters.

While I am filling you in, let me say too that in those days I knew a lot more Spanish sea talk than English, although all the other sailors knew a whole lot more than I did. They would not tell me what they meant, either, just saying that it was a comb to smooth the water or a dildo for a whale or whatever. I had to figure out everything for myself, and I got laughed at if I was even a little bit wrong.

Another thing I did not know then was that our handy bergantin was one of the kinds of ships pirates like best. The others are Bermuda sloops and Jamaica sloops. They are both bigger than most sloops, and a lot faster. The hulls are pretty much the same, and the difference is in the rigs. Everybody has his own tastes, but I always liked the Bermuda rig, myself.

When the sun was on the horizon, we went aloft again and furled the sails, the mainsail first, then the topsail. The stars were coming out and the wind picking up a little, and I remember thinking that sailors were the luckiest people in the world.

As soon we slid down to the deck, we were dismissed and went below and they jumped me again. This time they did not catch me completely off guard, and I fought. Or anyway, I would have called it fighting if anybody had asked. They beat and kicked me until I passed out and they got what they wanted. I did not know then that it was the last time.

I would not call what I did that night fighting, or what I did afterward sleeping, either. Sometimes I was conscious and sometimes I was not. I prayed that God would send me back to Our Lady of Bethlehem. I threw up a couple of times, and one time was on the deck. The larboard watch made me clean that up, although I was so bad I fell down two or three times while I was trying to do it.

The next day el capitán saw how bad I was—both my eyes were swollen just about shut, and I had to hold on to something to keep from falling over—and put me on the larboard watch myself. He did not try to find out who had beaten me or even ask me to tell him. (I think I might have.) He just said I was larboard watch until he changed it, and sent me below. It meant my old watch had to do the same work minus one man, so that was their punishment. When we came on watch about sundown, I made up my mind that they would get some more punishment from me as soon as I felt better.

(All this comes back to me with a vengeance tonight, because of what happened yesterday evening. I made four of our boys in the Youth Center quiet down, and they waited for me to come out at ten. They were all good-sized and pretty strong. Tough, too, they thought. They got in each other's way, and if there was only one of me, every kick and punch did real damage. They finally knocked me down and knocked my wind out. When they had kicked me a couple of times they beat it, practically carrying Miguel. I caught up with them after about three or four blocks.)

Larboard watch was easy, and it was a good thing it was, because I was still coughing a little blood now and then. I just rested, and slept when I could, and when we were off I stayed awake most of the time, keeping quiet in my hammock. It was nice, just a gentle rocking like a cradle, and I got to thinking I would kill everyone on board and have the whole ship to myself with nobody around anymore to do what they had done. I knew I would not really do it, and that I could not have managed the ship alone. But it was nice to think about, and I did. Later that helped me understand Jaime.

One of the things I did on larboard watch was be lookout. That was the same as starboard watch, but I had never gotten to do it on starboard watch. After I had been on larboard watch for a couple of days and my eyes were not so swollen I got tagged for it. It meant I climbed up the foremast and stood on the topsail yard, holding on to the masthead. It was a job nobody wanted, because it meant you had to stand or squat there for hours, and the roll was a lot worse at the top of the mast.

I loved it. One of the great things about my life has been that every so often I have really enjoyed something everybody else hated, and that was one of them. First off, I was all alone up there with nobody to hassle me. Another was that I could look up at the sky and way, way out to the horizon as much as I wanted. It was what I was supposed to be doing. That night there was no chop at all, just a greasy swell, and a million stars looked down at me. I saw the Angel of Death one time. (Maybe I will tell about all that later.) His robe is black, just like they say. But it is spangled all over with real stars, and when I saw it I knew that dying is really not as bad as everybody thinks. I still did not want to die, but I knew that if I did it would not be the worst thing that ever happened to me, and that afterward I would not have to worry about it anymore, ever again.

One of the pigs had died that day, so we had roast pork at supper. Whenever one of the animals died, we ate it. It was warm where we were, just like Cuba, so we ate it ASAP. Probably we would have eaten it fast anyway. The captain and the mate got the best cuts, and the rest of us got the rest. I do not think we ate the guts, but I know we ate the stomach and the head. And the heart and the liver, and all that. And hollered for more, and cussed the cook for holding out on us.

So I was a little bit sleepy up there, but naturally I could not sleep and would have fallen if I had. I would shut my eyes just for a minute, and feel myself starting to go, and grab on and wake up. About the third or fourth time I saw something way off to starboard when I woke up. There was no moon that night, but I thought I saw something white above the black bulk of it, and a dark line going up that might have been a mast. I yelled down that there was a vessel out there with no lights, and the rest of the watch woke the mate.

I expected him to be mad, and maybe he was. He asked where it was, and when I had told him, he asked eight or ten questions I could not answer. Eventually they unshipped the boat and rowed over for a look. It was a long time before they came back, and when they did they would not tell me anything, not even when we went off watch. I still felt bad, and I was pretty tired by then, so I just slung my hammock and turned in.

Pretty soon the rumble of our guns woke me. I got up and went up on deck to see what was happening. There was a little breeze, and we were making maybe two knots. The captain had the whole starboard watch pretending they were loading the guns, then running them out for real. That had made the noise. Once they were out they pretended to shoot them, ran them back in (more noise), and did the same thing all over again: the wet swab, the imaginary powder charge, the imaginary ball, run them out, and slow match to the touchhole.

We mounted five guns a side. They were small—four-pounders I found out later—but I had never paid much attention to them, and I had never seen slow match. So I found it all pretty interesting.

After a while the boat went out with a big empty box. It floated pretty well when they dropped it off, one corner up and maybe two-thirds underwater. Then each gun was loaded for real, one at a time, and the slow match lit from the galley fire, and each gun crew on the starboard side got to take a shot at the box.

I watched the whole thing, knowing I would not be able to sleep anyway, and when the boat went out again with an empty keg for the port guns to shoot at, I was pulling one of the oars.

3

Veracruz

———————

IT TOOK ME longer than it should have to connect the dark ship I had seen with the guns, but eventually I did. It was in the air, if you know what I mean. I overheard people talking and so forth. Everybody on that ship had been dead, and their ship drifting. Maybe Spain was at war with England again. Maybe not. Nobody knew, but they might know in Veracruz.

It means "true cross"—you probably know. It was bigger than I had expected, and rawer than I had expected. Once we had unloaded all the cargo, the captain let us leave the ship if we wanted to go. Our ship was tied to a pier, and the mate stayed on board with a couple of other men. We had to promise to come back that night, each of us promising before we set foot on the gangplank. Everybody except me wanted to sit around in cantinas, tell jokes and lies, pinch girls, and maybe get laid. I wanted to get out where I would not have to look at their ugly faces, stretch my legs, and see the town.

And I have got to say that there was a lot to see. They were building a fort to defend the harbor, plus three churches—all four going up at the same time. It was about noon and really hot by the time we got the *Santa Charita* unloaded, and just about everybody was having a siesta. The big stones kept moving just the same, one after another lifted up, swung carefully around, and set down on the mortar, then pried until it was lined up just right. It was done slowly, you bet it was. But it was always slow.

Those stones kept moving because slaves were doing the work, and they got it with whips if they quit working. In one way it was not much different from being a sailor. We got hit, generally with a rope with a knot at the end, if we did not work and work hard. And I knew by then that we could get flogged, too, if we did something really serious. The difference was in the faces and the eyes.

We had come aboard because we wanted work, and we would get paid when the ship got back to Spain. We were loose now in Veracruz, and if we wanted to walk away there was nobody to stop us. (I was thinking a lot about that right then.) The slaves were not going to get paid, or even get enough to eat. They were chained together in gangs because they were going to run away the first time they got a chance and everybody knew it. The guards sat in the shade with muskets in their laps, and yawned and tried to scratch under their armor, and once in a while one said something to someone else. But they did not sleep. They were soldiers, I found out later, and besides their muskets they had the long straight swords that soldiers call bilbos. The slave drivers were civilians, guys who knew (or were supposed to know) how stone walls ought to be built.

The slaves were mostly indios, what in English you call Native Americans. The rest were black. I want to say Afro-Americans, only later at one of the churches I tried to talk to one and he did not know any English. Or much Spanish either.

The fort was the first thing I had gone to look at, because I had seen it while we were unloading. It was only later that I went around to the churches. I had gone to the market hoping to steal something to eat. Let me be up-front about that. Pretty soon I saw a man unloading a wagon and helped him, and when we were finished I asked for one of the mangos we had been unloading, and he let me have it. So I walked around some more, peeling it and eating, and wondering where the heck I was and what had happened to me. And two of the churches were right there at the sides of the market, so I sat down in the shade to watch the slaves finish the tower for the bells.

Pretty soon a priest came out with water for them. He was forty or fifty and pretty fat, but he went out into the hot sunlight where they were and let them each drink from his jug until the water gave out, and talked to them a little. He had a wooden crucifix, pretty big. He would point to it and talk. Then he would go back into the church. And by and by he would come out with more water.

He was sweating a lot, so after I caught on to what he was doing I followed him back inside. I found him in the patio, sitting in the shade and fanning himself with his big hat. "Padre," I said in Spanish, "why don't you rest here awhile and let me do that?"

"Would you, my son? It would be a most noble work of charity."

I said sure and that I was a sailor, and I gave him the name of my ship. After that, he showed me how to hook his jug to the well rope. You could not give it too much rope, because it would float and come unhooked until it got quite a bit of water in it.

When I went out with the jug I saw a scrap of rope, so I pulled off a strand and stuck it in my pocket. After that I climbed the scaffolding to where the slaves who got the stones in place were. I let them drink until my jug was empty, and talked to them a little, and went back inside. When I went to the well the priest wanted to know what I was doing, and I showed him how I could close the hook with a couple of half hitches. He shook the hook to see if the jug would come off. Naturally it did not, so we lowered it and pulled it back up when it was full.

"My son," he said, "you are an angel of God, but I should not have permitted you to do my work even once. It is my duty to bring the knowledge of Christ to those poor souls."

I said, "Well, I tried to do that too, Padre. I know I'm probably not as good as you at it, but I told them that God loved them so much that He had sent Jesus so they could be His friends again."

After that we sat in the shade and talked awhile. Then he took the jug out again. When he came back, he shut the hook the same way I had. It took him longer, but he did it. While the jug was filling, we sat down and talked some more. I said the slaves ought to be free, that nobody ought to be a slave.

"I agree, my son. But what benefit would they have from their freedom if they did not know God? They would not save their souls, because they could not."

"Maybe they could find God better if they were free to look for Him," I argued. "Besides, they wouldn't have to work as hard, and they could eat better."

"That last would certainly be true, my son, if they enslaved others as they themselves have been enslaved. The men who own them are free to look for God, I would say. Do you think they have found Him?"

I shrugged.

"Answer, my son. Do you?"

I had to admit that it did not seem like it.

"Can you free their slaves, my son?"

I shook my head. "It would take a cartload of reales, Padre, and I don't have any."

"No more can I, my son. But I can show the overseers and the guards, and the slaves themselves, how a Christian ought to act toward his fellow men."

After that he told me about another church a few streets away, and I went over and had a look at it. I did what I could there, and when I went back to the ship I was pretty tired.

Señor had stayed on board, with the bosun and Zavala, one of the old guys from the larboard watch. They made me come over and sit with them so they could kid me about girls and so on. I just grinned and shook my head, saying I had not even met any. Which was the truth.

When they saw they could not get me mad, they talked about other things. That was how I learned that Veracruz was a treasure port. A galleon would be coming to take the treasure back to Spain, and we were going to wait for it and sail back with it.

"To have the kindness of fifty guns" was how Señor said it. I wanted to hear more about the treasure house and find out where it was. I knew nobody would tell me if I asked, so I just kept quiet and kept my ears open.

A few more sailors came back, all pretty drunk. Señor let them sleep on deck or go into the forecastle, which was fine with me. After a while, I just lay down on the deck myself, and went to sleep listening to them talk.

Way too soon, the bosun shook me awake. I remember I did not feel like I had slept long at all, but the moon was up and pretty high, too. The captain had come back, there were more sailors sitting around talking, and Señor, the bosun, old Zavala, and I were going ashore to round up as many as we could.

So I ended up going to all the cantinas and talking with a few girls there, too. Some of them were pretty nice, and some were the pits. And just about all of them kidded me more and worse than Señor and the bosun had. "You come back alone, and we'll show you things you've never seen." "Sit with me and I'll straighten out that crooked nose." "Yes! It will stand tall and proud." With a whole lot more, some of it pretty dirty. Italian is a real good language to talk dirty in, but sometimes I think Spanish must be the best in the whole world. Those girls had a great time teasing me, laughing at me and anything I happened to say, and enjoyed themselves so much that I told them, "Listen up! You owe me, all of you, and one of these days I'm coming to collect."

The next day the captain put me back on starboard watch. We worked until it got hot, cleaning up the ship and replacing some of the rigging that was getting worn, and then we got to go ashore again. This time I knew that most of the men who promised they would come back did not mean a word of it and would not come back until somebody came and got them.

Which I was not about to do again. At first I thought I would just find a place on shore where I could get some sleep, maybe in the church where I had gotten to know the priest. Then I decided that the thing for me to do was to sneak back on board without Señor's seeing me. If I could do that, I could come back early, sling my hammock in the forecastle the way I always did, and crash. That would be a lot better than sleeping in a hiding place in some alley—I had done that a lot before I joined the crew—and I would not be breaking my word. I had not promised to report back to Señor, or any such thing. Just that I would come back to the ship that night.

The first thing I did, though, was to strike up a conversation with somebody in the market and find out where the treasure house was. It turned out it was behind where the fort was being built, and I had been pretty close to it without knowing when I had watched the slaves work there.

I went there to see it and hung around looking at it, and pretty soon I had a real piece of luck. Mules and soldiers came—there must have been a hundred mules—and the big doors were opened. Those mules had been carrying silver bars, each bar heavy enough to make a pretty good load for one man, and I got to see the soldiers unload them and carry them inside.

The treasure house was not very big, or very high either—not even as high as our little chapel at the monastery. The walls were thick just the same, the doors were big and heavy and bound with iron, and the top of it looked like the top of a castle, with openings between the big stones for soldiers to shoot through. I was not thinking of getting the silver or anything like that then. But I saw right away that if somebody was, the thing to do was to get it while it was still on the mules.

After that, I went back to the harbor for a look at the *Santa Charita* before sunset. There I got lucky again. A big galleon was making port, and I got to watch the whole thing. It was about five times the size of our ship, with crosses on all the sails and a lot of carving and gilding on the stern.

It tied up at a different pier, and I went over there for a closer look and so I could see who got off. It was a pretty good show, too, with trumpets blowing and soldiers with red pants and polished armor escorting the captain. I jumped up and touched my forehead the way you are supposed to, and nobody said a word to me.

Walking back to the quay, I could see the starboard side of the *Santa Charita,* and I got an idea. If I could get something that would float that I could stand on, I could reach up and grab the edge of the anchor hawse, pull myself up, and climb in through the hawsepipe. That would put me on the weather deck, where the capstan was, forward of the foremast and right over the forecastle. Señor and whoever he had with him would be in the waist where they could watch the gangplank. If I stayed low, I could keep an eye on them over the edge of the weather deck. When they were busy with something, I could hold the edge of the deck and swing myself down into the forecastle. All I had to do was wait until it was good and dark, and borrow a boat to climb up from. I found a nice shady spot to sit in, and dozed off for a couple of hours.

WHEN I WOKE up I went looking for the kind of boat I needed, one small enough that I could manage it by myself but big enough that it would not capsize when I stood up in it. Of course it had to be a boat nobody was watching. Once I got into the hawsepipe, I would let it drift away. The owner would probably be able to find it without too much trouble unless the tide carried it out to sea. Still, he would not like what I was going to do, and I knew it.

That was a pretty tall order, and I had hardly started prowling through the hot, dark night when I spotted a boat in the harbor with two men rowing and another in the stern who seemed to be looking for something too. I thought they were probably soldiers or night watchmen or something, so I strolled along like I did not have a care in the world when they seemed to be looking my way. Out toward the end of one of the piers, I stepped on a round piece of something—probably a boat pole—that rolled under my foot. I just about went into the water, and I yelled, "Oh, shit!"

As soon as I said that, the man in the back of the boat sang out, "Ahoy there! You speak English?"

He had a British accent and was a little hard for me to understand, but I waved and yelled, "Sure!"

The other two rowed him over and he jumped up on the pier. I am taller than most people—my father told me once he got me engineered that way—and I was taller than he was by quite a bit. It was too dark to see a lot, but it seemed to me that he had more hair on his face, even though he did not seem like he was a whole lot older than I was.

"Say, this's luck! We've been hours tryin' to get our bearin's. None of us speaks the lingo, you see." He held out his hand. "Bram Burt's my name. Midshipman Burt that was, late of His Majesty's *Lion* and these days skipper of the *Macérer*."

He had a good handshake. I could tell the name of his ship was French from the way he said it, but I did not know what the word meant. I gave him my name, called him sir, and explained that I was just an ordinary seaman from the *Santa Charita*.

"Bit of an accent there, eh? You're a Day—You're Spanish?"

I said, "I'm from Jersey, but I speak Spanish."

"That explains it. Have to, on a Dago ship. Parlez-vous français?"

I told him I did, a little, saying it in French. Then I started trying to tell him about the monastery.

"Belay that. Bit too quick for me, eh? You'd be a handy sort to have 'round, though. Half my bloody crew's French. See here now, the dear old *Macérer*'s markin' time out there, eh? Outside the roadstead. They goin' to get huffy if we make port tonight?"

I explained that some of the guns were up in the fort already, said I would not try it, and showed him where he could find the harbor master in the morning.

"What do you think our chances are of gettin' a cargo here? Sold everythin' in Port Royal, eh? No cargo for us there, so we're lookin' about. *Saint Charity* havin' much luck?"

I shrugged. "They say we'll load tomorrow, Captain, but I don't know what it is."

"That's interestin'." It was too dark for me to be sure, but I believe he winked. "Gold doubloons, hid away ever so snug. Put it in kegs marked BEER, eh? They're shippin' gold back to the Spanish king like 'twas sand, we hear."

I shook my head. "I'm sure it's not that, sir."

"'Cause of that big lad?" He pointed to the galleon.

"Yes, sir, the *Santa Lucía* there. She'll carry the treasure."

After that he asked me what treasure I meant, and I told him about the treasure house and seeing the mules unloaded there. I offered to take him to see it, and he thanked me.

"Interestin', I'll be bound, but my duty's to my ship, eh? Got to get back to her. I'll go sightseein' tomorrow, it may be."

"In that case, could you run me by the *Santa Charita*? It won't take you much out of your way, and I'd like to get aboard without being seen."

He laughed and clapped me on the shoulder. "Slipped off, did you? I've done the same once or twice. Got a masthead for it once, too."

I jumped from the pier into his boat and sat in the bow, as he directed. When we lay against the hawse of the *Santa Charita,* he whispered to the rowers to ship oars and join him in the stern. That raised the bow a foot or more, and it was no trick to pull myself into the hawsepipe, or to slip into the forecastle as I had planned. The next day I looked around the harbor for the *Macérer* without finding her, and I soon forgot Capt. Burt and his ship in the work of stowing cargo.

It was mixed, as they say. There were big bales of leather, box after box of dried fruit, and crates of terra cotta cookware. There were also seven parrots in cages, a private investment of Señor's. They had to be carried out of the hold in fine weather and set on the weather deck, and carried back to the hold at night for fear they would catch cold.

The rest of the crew hated them because of the extra work they made, and their noise and dirt. I thought they were cute and did my best to make friends, talking to them and scratching their necks the way Señor did. After one died, I was assigned to water and feed them, clean their cages, and take care of them generally.

It brought me closer to Señor, and that soon paid off in a big way. He would come out and shoot the sun at noon every day, check the logbook just like the captain did, and calculate our position. Then he and the captain would compare their results, and go over their calculations, too, if the results were too different. About the time we went through the Windward Passage, I started asking him about it.

I had been taking care of his birds and talking to him about them, and we were pretty good friends. He was still Señor to me, and I still touched my forehead and all that. But I had showed him he could relax with me and I would still jump when he gave an order. So he answered my questions when there were not too many, and showed me how to work the astrolabe. Basically what he was doing was measuring the angle of the sun at noon. Once you know that and the date, you know the latitude. The farther north you are, the farther south the sun rises and the lower it is at noon in the winter. If you know the date, the table gives you your latitude. Certain stars can be used the same way.

There are a bunch of problems with this system, as you can see. For one thing, it is hard to get a good measurement unless you happen to be standing on a rock. When the sea is calm, you take three measurements and average them. When it is rough, you can forget the whole thing.

And that is not all. In dirty weather you cannot see the sun, so no measurement. On top of that, your compass is pointing to magnetic north, not true north. There were tables for compass deviation, too, but you had to know your position to use them. So what I used to do (now I am getting ahead of myself again) was check the compass bearing against the North Star. If this is starting to sound complicated, you have no idea. I have just given the high spots.

When you have found out your latitude, you still need your longitude, and for us the only way to know that was to measure our speed with the log, and record it in the logbook, which we did every hour. The log is on a line with knots in it to measure speed. You throw the log off the back of the ship, watch the little sandglass, and count knots.

Of course if you are in sight of land, it is all different. You take bearings from objects on the chart, which gives your position—if the chart is right, and if you have not picked the wrong island or mountaintop or whatever.

By the time I had learned even half this stuff, we were a long, long way out from Veracruz. So good night!

4

Spain

———

WE CROSSED THE Atlantic with the galleon, which meant we had to match its speed. In light airs, it would hardly move, so we spent days and days creeping along under reefed topsails. When the wind whistled in the rigging and spray came over the side, the old slowpoke *Santa Lucía* turned into a racehorse, setting sails in places most ships do not even have and creaming the sea for a mile behind her. We had to do our best to keep up, all plain sail set and the deck so steep you couldn't walk on it without holding on to something. I do not know how close we were to capsizing, but I would not want to come an inch closer than we came a dozen times a day. When we finally split up—us heading north to Coruña and the *Santa Lucía* east for Cádiz—we were all praising God and blessing the Virgin. It was the only time I ever saw the whole crew smiling.

We unloaded at Coruña and were paid off, each of us going up to the captain one at a time and having the book explained to us before we got our money. That was when I found out that I had worked for a week to pay for two shirts and two pairs of pants.

I will stop here and explain that I still had the little bag I had brought from the monastery, but there was not much in it besides one pair of slop-chest pants and a slop-chest shirt. I had lost my sandals in Havana, kicking them off so I could run faster, and my T-shirt had been worn to rags and thrown away. You know what happened to my jeans.

When the captain had explained everything and paid me, he told me it would probably be a couple of weeks before the next voyage. He would see his family while the ship went into dry dock to get her bottom scraped and so on. But when she was ready to go again, he hoped I would come back and sign on. That made me feel good. I thanked him for it, and I meant it.

After I had been paid, Señor asked me to help him take his parrots to the bird seller. I said sure and off we went, him carrying three cages and me carrying three. The cages were wood, woven out of sticks and tied with twine that the parrots kept picking at with those big strong bills parrots have. They were not heavy, and I had carried and cleaned them many a time.

The bird shop was interesting, and I had plenty of time to look around in it while the bird man and Señor argued over prices. There were three parrots there already, gray ones from Africa that would talk to you and do everything they could think of to keep you with them. They were all hoping to be let out of their cages, but they did not know how to say that. It seemed to me then that it was about the only thing they did not know how to say, and I decided that if I ever had a parrot of my own, I would not cage it. If it stayed with me, fine. If it flew away, that would be fine, too.

Then a young lady came in, wanting to buy a bird. She saw Señor's and got him to take each of them out so she could see it better. The bird seller kept explaining to her that they were new birds who had not been around people much and might die before long, could not talk, and so on. I got one of the redheaded green ones to say, "Pretty miss! Pretty miss!," cocking its head. It was something I had said to all of them sometimes. After that, she had to have that one. She asked Señor how much, and he told her a lot more than he had been trying to get from the bird seller. So everybody argued about that for a while—the lady and an old woman in black who was with her, and Señor.

While all the palaver was going on, her maid and I were looking each other over. She would peek at me, and I would get embarrassed because I had been staring and look away. Then she would look away and I would start staring again. She had been carrying three packages and a shopping basket when she came in, but she put them down and got out her fan, and fanned herself, and looked at me over the top of it. I kept thinking of how it would be if the two of us were out on a little boat of our own, sailing far away to someplace wonderful.

Finally the lady bought the parrot she wanted, and told the girl to take the cage, saying they would go home now.

"Oh, Señora Sabina, I can't possibly carry all this and that heavy cage, too! Couldn't this sailor carry them for us?" So I ended up with the parrot cage and the shopping basket, walking behind the maid. She was round in all the right places, and it was a nice view. We got to the lady's house a lot sooner than I wanted to, and she smiled and thanked me and gave me a little money. The maid gave me a wink, which I liked a lot better.

I went back to the bird shop thinking about a whole lot of things, including a few I was pretty ashamed of. Señor was still there, and eventually we went off to a cantina together, got something to eat, and drank wine. I was scared the whole time, thinking he might want me to pay for us both. Do not get me wrong here. I would not have done it. But he was a ship's officer and I was just a common sailor, and I was afraid he might make trouble for me.

It turned out that I did not know him as well as I had thought. He paid for everything when we split up. He had drunk most of the bottle, but I had drunk a good bit myself, and eaten every bit as much as he had. They had been cooking some kind of fritters in that cantina, and those were the best things I had eaten since the mango in Veracruz.

Probably I do not have to tell you what I did after we split up. I went back to Sabina's house and hung around outside hoping to see her maid again. Finally I went to the door, very polite, and told the manservant who answered it that I was looking for work, any kind of work, and that I had carried things for Señora earlier that day. He said there was nothing and shut the door in my face.

When you read this you will probably say I should have gone away at that point, but I did not. I went around to the back and hung around there some, and finally I saw her looking out of a window. All the windows had iron grilles over them, and big shutters that could be closed over the grilles, too. But the shutters were open, and she blew me a kiss through the grille. I blew her a kiss back, and she went away.

After that, I knew I would not see her again that night. I ran into Vasco and Simón, and asked them where they were putting up. They told me about their inn, saying it was not too big and about as cheap as anything decent and had good food and wine. So I went there. They were splitting a room. I told the innkeeper I wanted a room to myself, but a cheap one. As cheap as I could get it, as long as it was clean. He said fine and put me up in a *guardilla*, a little attic room with one window high above the street. I would not have wanted to sleep in that room in the winter, and it was up three flights of stairs. But when a man has gotten used to climbing the mast four or five times on his watch, stairs do not bother him. It was quiet and cool, too. I have stayed in better places, but after the forecastle it was just plain wonderful.

In the morning I noticed there was a little church near the inn. I could see a lot of steeples from the window of my new room, and that one looked really close. So after breakfast I went in there and sat down, trying to think things over. When I finally got up, I saw this Spanish priest sitting at the back. He said, "Would you like to talk to someone, my son?"

So I sat down next to him, and told him I was from Cuba, and that I felt like I had left God behind me there.

"You have not. If you had, you would never have come here seeking Him."

I said that did not make sense to me.

"It makes sense to Him, my son. Our foolishness is His wisdom, in this and many other things."

He did not look like the priest in Mexico, or even remind me of him much, but I said I did not have much to do that day and would do some work for him around the church if he wanted me to.

He shook his head. "I cannot pay you, my son."

"I've got money, Padre. Not a lot, but some."

After that we talked a lot more. I told him about being an altar boy, not saying it was at Our Lady of Bethlehem, and he wanted to know if I had ever learned to play the organ.

I said sure.

"Really? Would you play for me, my son, if I find someone to pump for you?"

So he got his servant to pump and I played three or four pieces I knew by heart, trying my best to keep them slow. After that he showed me a lot of church music. The notation was a little different, but he explained that, and I played a couple of the easy ones. That made him really happy, and he made me promise to play for his mass next morning.

"It is a shame, my son, that you cannot play strings as well. You might play and sing beneath the window of the señorita you speak of. It is how women are won here, more often than not."

I said anybody could play the guitar, but that my voice was not much. Which is the truth.

"You err, my son. Few can play a guitar as well as you play this organ. It may be you underrate your voice as well."

After I left there, I looked at guitars in some shops. I did not want a cheap one, and even the cheap ones cost a lot. The good ones cost more than I had, and if I had bought one I would not have been able to eat or pay next day's rent. That night I went back to the house and around to the alley, and waited for three or four hours, hoping to see the girl I had carried the parrot for. I never did, and when the lights went out I went back to my room.

Next morning I got up early and went to the padre's church. The padre sang the mass, his servant pumped, and I played whenever the padre told me to. After mass he heard confessions, mine included. You already know everything I confessed to. When he had given me my penance (which was not much) he asked me to wait until he had finished.

I did, of course, and when he had heard the last old lady he wanted to know whether I had a guitar. Of course I said I did not.

"I have my father's. It is precious to me."

"Sure," I said. "I'd love to have anything my father owned."

"But you do not? There were many children?"

I said no, but I did not want to talk about my family. I knew he was about to ask if my father was dead, and I did not want to have to say he had not been born yet, which by then I was pretty sure was the truth.

"Very well, my son, I will ask no more. Will you play my father's guitar for me? I would like very much to hear it sound again."

It was out of tune, which I expected, and I had to tune it by ear. But it was a good one, with a good, rich tone. I played some songs that had been old when I was a kid. He sang a couple of the songs his father used to sing for him and his mother. The tunes were pretty easy, and I could play along without much trouble.

That night I was walking past a cantina when I heard somebody playing a really good guitar inside. So I went in and got a glass of wine, and sat around and listened. He played a song all the customers knew, and they sang it. A lot of them could sing pretty well—more than I would have expected.

After that he passed the hat, and just about everybody put something in. He was a gypsy, and played gypsy style, but I did not know that then.

The next day I played at mass again, and when it was over I asked the padre to loan me his guitar, just for that night, promising to return it the next morning. He would not, and would not even speak to me after that, just going into the confessional and shutting the door.

After that I wandered around quite a bit, wondering how I could get him to lend it. So after mass the next day I waited until he was through hearing confessions. Then I showed him my money—not all of it, but most of it. I said that was all I had, which was pretty close to the truth, and said for him to keep it until I brought his father's guitar back, which I would the next morning.

"I do not want your silver, my son. I want my father's guitar."

"But I want my money, Padre. It's all I've got in the world."

It took a long time, but he finally agreed. I felt guilty as heck, knowing he would be worried to death. But I took the guitar that had been his father's just the same, and played at the back of the house, and sang a little. A fat cook looked out at me, then closed the shutters. I kept playing and sang a little, Spanish and Italian songs.

Finally the girl I wanted looked out of a different window, one up on the third floor, and smiled, and blew me a kiss, and closed the shutters. And I went away feeling absolutely wonderful.

After that I went to three cantinas where nobody was playing, and played and sang in each of them. (Mostly I just played, though.) I did not get as much as the old man had at that one cantina, but it was enough for me to eat next day and pay my rent. I felt like I had done pretty good—and learned a little, too, because when I went into a cantina and somebody good was playing there already, I just sat and listened.

The next day was Sunday. I went to the early mass, just like I had before, and played the organ. But when I tried to give the padre his guitar back he just asked me to play for the next mass, too. Which I did.

There were four that day, and I played at all of them. Then I said, "If you want your dad's guitar, you'd better take it, Padre. If you don't, I'll take it with me."

He smiled, but his eyes were full of tears. "Leaving all your money, my son?"

I shrugged. "I've got some more now. Not a lot, but some."

He pointed to the poor box. "Put the smallest coin you have in there, and I will return your money."

I did, and he gave me all my money back. When I had counted it, I tried to return his father's guitar again.

He would not take it. "Keep the guitar, my son. My father wanted me to give it to my own son. I do so now."

It just about had me crying, too. I swore that when I had enough to buy a good guitar for myself I would return his, and that was where we left it.

After that there is not a lot more to tell about the time I spent in Spain, and I do not enjoy telling what there is. Every morning I played the organ for morning mass, and I generally brought along the padre's guitar so he could see it was okay. (I was also afraid that it would be stolen if I left it in my room.) Then I would go back to the inn and sleep awhile like everybody did, because I would have been up late the night before playing in cantinas. A little after sundown I played for the girl I have been telling about. After a while she started talking to me through a first-floor window, and we held hands through the grille. I told her I was a sailor and I used to live in Havana. One night she came outside to talk to me. She danced when I played—she was a really good dancer—and we kissed and so on.

The next night the fat cook came out. "Master's been screaming to the sky, and Señora has been beaten to a rag because of you. Estrellita, too! Worse, and she can hardly walk. Get out!"

That was that. In the morning I gave the padre his guitar back and went down to the quay. The *Santa Charita* was out of dry dock and fitting out, and the captain took me back like he said he would. I was glad of it, because I knew that if I went back to my room in the inn I was going to jump. It was four floors up and cobblestones down below, so it would probably have killed me. I had needed a knife before, and I bought a regular sailor's knife with the money I had left—a big folding knife with a straight edge for cutting rope and a folding marlinspike. Every time I looked at the wooden handle of it, I would think of the padre's guitar. They were not really the same, but I did. I lost it when they chained me up on the *Weald*.

It took us another ten days to finish fitting out and load cargo. The cargo was mostly tools for carpenters and blacksmiths and so on, but there was a lot of classy stuff too, bolts of China silk and good clothes.

We felt pretty classy ourselves, with fresh paint on all over, the ship re-caulked, new sails, and new rigging. We shook out for a couple of days to make sure everything worked. I got seasick in the forecastle and got knocked down for it, and when I felt better I had it out with that guy. I was younger and faster, I had more reach, and I meant to kill him. He was stronger and maybe forty pounds heavier, and he just about killed me. Eventually I got him down, and pretty soon he begged for mercy. When he did, I let him up. It takes a lot to make a sailor beg.

5

Pirates!

ABOUT HALFWAY ACROSS the Atlantic we ran into a storm. Some of the
other guys said they had been in worse, and my guess is they were telling the
truth. That one was plenty bad enough for me, and I know the captain thought
it might sink us. For three days and three nights, it bounced us around and
rolled us like a ninepin. One time there was green water three feet deep in the
waist. We lost a man overboard, and just about lost another one—the other
one being me. Nobody could have slept on that ship, we just passed out when
we got into our hammocks. We were dripping wet, but it did not matter because the weather deck was leaking water onto us anyway. Sometimes we got
an hour or two of sleep before somebody yelled, "All hands!" Most often it was
more like fifteen minutes.

We were under bare poles, but things kept breaking or blowing loose.
Whenever a sail came loose, we had to try to furl it again before the storm
tore it up. Sometimes we got it in, and sometimes we did not. All the standing

rigging got soaked, which made it longer. That meant all the stays were loose, and we might lose one or both our masts when she rolled. We had to try to tighten everything up, working in the dark even when it was daytime, with the rain driving in our faces and breakers coming over the rail. I do not know how hard that wind blew, but when it got hold of anything you just saw it for an instant before it disappeared forever.

I did not pray then—I was too busy and too tired. I would have let the storm kill me, if it had not been for the other men in our crew. I did not like most of them, and those I liked I did not like much. But there was no time to think about that. We were us, and if our ship went down we would die.

When the storm finally ended in warm weather, blue skies, and sunshine, it was half a day before any of us had energy enough to bring out our hammocks and spare clothes so they could dry. We just slept on deck. That evening we got the first hot food we had seen in four days. It was the best the cook could do, a hash of fresh beef, salt pork, ship's bread, onions, and tomatoes, with a lot of garlic. There was wine, and I remember old Zavala grinning at me over his. He had lost about half his teeth.

A lot of things may have happened between then and the next time I remember, but they cannot be important things or I would be able to think of them. We worked on the ship all watch, every watch, trying to fix up as much of the damage as we could.

One night somebody shook me awake and yelled at me to get out on deck. There was another man with him who had a cutlass in one hand and a lantern in the other, and I did not know either of them. All I could think about was where they might have come from.

Outside, they made us line up. Like I said, I have forgotten a lot that happened between the storm and that night, but I remember that night as well as anything that has ever happened in my life. It was overcast, no moon and just one or two stars peeping though tears in the clouds. A little swell to the sea and the *Santa Charita* rolling to it just enough to feel alive. Five or six or maybe eight or ten lanterns lit, one run halfway up the mainmast and one on the quarterdeck railing and looking like it was going to slide off any minute. Pirates holding the rest, a lantern in one hand and a cutlass or a pistol in the other.

I had gotten into line and everything before I saw there were two bodies on the deck. One was old Zavala. I kept staring at the other one, trying to figure out who it was. His face was turned away from me, and he was not wearing anything but a long shirt.

Somebody—a voice I did not know—said, "Let's have another light over here," and I kind of jumped. That was because it seemed to me that I *should* know it, and because the words were in English.

"There's many a one would cut your throats," the man who spoke English said. Then another man said the same thing in Spanish and louder.

"You've been lucky. Very lucky. You've fallen into the compassionate hands of Captain Bram Burt. Any man who disobeys or lies to me will lose his life a damned sight quicker than a court would kill him. But the ones who obey and tell me the truth will live, and some of them will even get a chance to grow rich while they're still young enough to enjoy it."

When the Spanish translation came, all of us were looking at each other. Before that I had been looking at him, trying to remember where I had seen that round face and long blond mustache before. If you read this far, you will have gotten it a lot quicker than I did.

He pointed to the dead man in the long shirt. "This was your captain. I know that because he came out of the captain's cabin. What other officers are there on this ship? Watch-keeping officers."

Señor took a step forward. He looked scared enough to faint, but he sounded brave when he said, "Only I."

Capt. Burt unhooked a pistol from his belt, cocked it fast and easy, and leveled it at Señor. "You had better call me 'Captain.'"

Señor touched his forehead. "Sí, Capitán."

"You can navigate?"

"Sí, Capitán."

"Who else can?"

Señor's mouth opened, but nothing came out.

I raised my hand and said in English, "I can, a little bit, sir. Nobody else."

"En verdad, Capitán. Nadie."

Capt. Burt was looking at me and paid no attention to Señor. "You—put down your hand." He raised his voice. "Now I want every married man to raise his hand. Don't lie to me. Every married man."

After it was said in Spanish, most of the hands went up, including Señor's.

"I see. You married men stay where you are. Single men, over to the starboard rail and sit down."

We did as we had been told. There were only four of us. Two pirates watched us there for what seemed like an hour.

While we sat there, the other pirates were getting the boat into the water and getting the married men into it, with a keg of water and a string of onions. We could not see the boat until it pulled away. When it did, it was just a sort of darker shadow on the sea, but I knew it had to be jammed full of men and ready to sink the first time the sea got rough. There had been sixteen men in the starboard watch and eight in the larboard watch, plus the captain and Señor, so twenty-six men. Two had been killed that I knew about, and I think that was all. We four had stayed on board. So twenty men jammed into a boat I would have thought could not carry more than a dozen.

"Listen to me," Capt. Burt said when he got back to us, "and listen sharp. You may join my crew if you wish. If you do, each of you will take an oath, and your lives will be forfeit should you break it. When you've taken that oath, you'll share in our gains just as these men do. You'll eat and drink with us and be accounted a full member of our crew. If you don't, you'll be put ashore on the next deserted coast we reach. Now I want every man willin' to join us to stand."

He stared hard at me while the other man was repeating what he had said in Spanish, but I did not get up. The others did, but I did not.

After that they tied my hands, and I sat there for hours. I asked the guard if I could lie down. He said yes, and I was about asleep when they got me up and brought me to the captain's cabin.

Capt. Burt was in there. So was his sea chest and all his stuff, which was a lot. There were two chairs, and he told me to sit down in the empty one, which I did.

"You're the Jerseyman I talked to in Veracruz, ain't you?"

I mumbled that I was.

"Thought so." He took a silver snuffbox out of the blue, brass-buttoned coat I was to know so well, took a pinch, and said, "You know my name, but I've forgotten yours. What is it?"

I told him again, calling him Capt. Burt.

"Right. You speak good Spanish."

I nodded.

"French, too. Quite a bit of French."

I answered him in French, saying that I did, but that no one was likely to take me for a Frenchman.

"You can navigate?"

"A little. I never said I was an expert."

"I want you, Chris. I've got three already, but I'd be glad to trade 'em for you. What would it take to get you to join?"

I tried to think whether there was anything.

"Your own ship? You'd be captain, reporting to me. I'd claim a captain's share of anything you took on your own, but the rest would be yours."

I shook my head. "It's stealing, Captain. Stealing and murder. I won't do it."

Burt sighed. "You're a gentleman, Chris, whether you know it or not. Give me your parole, and I'll cut those ropes. Givin' your parole means you won't try to get away, 'pon your honor."

I nodded. "Cut me loose, and I won't try to get away, I swear it to God."

"On your honor."

"Right. I swear it on my honor."

He pulled out a dirk and showed it to me. "My ma gave this to me when I joined His Majesty's Navy."

I said it looked like a good one, because it did.

"It is." He used it to cut the rope around my hands. "Sheffield steel, and this black handle's ivy root. The mountin's are silver. We weren't rich, you twig? My pa's a grocer. I know it must have cost my old ma every penny she had."

I was rubbing my wrists.

"Why do you think she did that?"

"Because she was proud of you." It hurt me to say that, but I did.

Capt. Burt nodded. "She was. She was proud of me 'cause I was goin' to fight for my king and my country. It's your country, too, Chris."

I knew that it was not, but it seemed better not to say so.

"And that's what I'm doin'. Ever been paid half of nothin'?"

I did not understand what he meant, but I shook my head.

"I have. A midshipman's pay's the kind of money you'd throw to a beggar. You don't join for pay, eh? You join for prize money, and if you're lucky it can be rum quids. My ship was laid up and me put on half pay. Meanin' half of nothin'."

I said, "What did you do?"

"You're seein' it." Capt. Burt grinned. "I did this."

He jumped up. "Listen here, Chris. Spain hates us and we hate Spain. The only reason we're not at war with 'em is that we're not strong enough to fight 'em yet. The only reason they're not at war with us is that they've all they can do to hold down the savages over here. My men and I rob Dago ships and Dago towns. How long do you think we could keep it up if His Majesty were to tell the governor of Jamaica to clap me in irons?"

I did not know and said so.

"Per'aps a year. Not a day more than that, and it could be a lot less. Hear me now, Chris. Back before Cromwell, Spain set out to conquer us. Their king sent the biggest bloody fleet anybody's ever seen, and we only beat 'em off by the skin of our teeth. If things had been just a bit different, if Drake hadn't been around, or certain others, they'd have beat us."

I can still see him standing there staring at me, his thumbs hooked into his wide belt, and two big guns hooked on to it too. If he had been an inch taller, he would have had to stoop a little under the deck beams, and he had the look men get when they have killed people they have talked to and drunk with. (Maybe I have it, too, since I have done those things. I do not know.)

"The gold I take from the Dagos is gold they stole from the savages."

I nodded. I did not want to, but I did.

"I don't know everythin' you've been taught, or how much of it you believe. But that's the way the world is, Chris, and that's the way it's goin' to stay. Well by God, I can play the game as well as any Dago. No, better. And I've proved it."

All of a sudden he smiled. "Let's have a drink on that. Your captain had some decent canary."

He got out the wine and poured a glass for each of us. "You're a gentleman, Chris. So'm I, and a king's officer, eh? Even if he won't own to me out loud. We can be pals without agreein' on everythin' under the sun, can't we?"

I said, "Yes, absolutely."

"So drink up. Want to join us? No, I can see you don't. Per'aps you'll change your mind later though."

He sipped his wine, smacked his lips, and chuckled. "Want to know what happens at Westminster? The Dago ambassador comes to the king and complains about me. The king and all his ministers look grave as parsons and say I'll be dealt with severely, and as fast as they can lay hands 'pon me. When he's gone, they have a good laugh and another drink."

He drained his glass. "We'll sell the cargo of this ship in Port Royal, and we'll sell it cheap because sellin' it anyplace else would mean a long voyage.

My men'll spend their share of the price we get there, too, or most of it. A lot of that will end up in London as taxes. So what I do helps England and hurts Spain. How many nights' sleep has the king lost tryin' to dream up a surefire way to rein in Bram Burt, do you think?"

I said, "None, I guess."

"Exactly right."

Capt. Burt sat down again. "I said the men spend their takin's in Port Royal. Mostly it's wagered and wagered again till it's lost. I fancy a girl and a glass as much as any other man, Chris, but I don't gamble unless I feel sure I can win. I've chests buried on two islands, and one fine day I'll dig 'em up, put a bit more with 'em, and turn my prow to England, a rich man. Squire Burt, eh? Me and the old'uns, we'll live in a house with thirty rooms and servants, and every maid in Surrey will set her cap for Squire Burt, the man that brought home a fortune from the West Indies."

I did not know what to say, so I nodded.

"I won't ask you to join us, Chris. I've asked twice already, and I don't ask most men even once. But anytime you change your mind, sing out. I'll keep you here on my ship for a bit so you can see how it's done, then we'll see about gettin' you a ship of your own. You've a hammock in the fo'c'sle? And a seabag?"

I said I did, a small one.

"Fine. Fetch 'em both. You're my prisoner, so I can't have you minglin' with my crew. But I don't want to clap you in irons, 'cause I know you'll come 'round. Stay close, so you get an education, eh? Stay close and stay awake."

I said, "Aye aye, sir."

"You'll answer to 'All hands,' but won't stand watch. Keep your eyes open and your mouth shut, 'less you want to feed the fish."

SO THAT WAS how it was for a while. Capt. Burt slept in the captain's bunk, I in my hammock, slung on the other side of the cabin, which was not very large by landsmen's standards. I hung around him, ran errands when he told me to, and tried to learn. Once or twice I was pretty badly tempted to join, but I never did.

Here is the thing. The clothes were different, the talk was different, and even the guns and rackets were different, but he wanted me to be a wiseguy.

I did not know much about wiseguys, and I do not know much now. But I knew enough, even back then, to know that I did not want to be one. I do not think my father wanted me to be one either. That was why he sent me to Our Lady of Bethlehem in the first place, or I think that it must have been.

In a minute I'm going to tell about pirates, but there is not any real difference between pirates and wiseguys. One is at sea and the other is in cities. A big part of it is money, and money is just another way of saying freedom. If you have money, you can do pretty much whatever you want to do. (If you do not believe me, look at the people who have it.) You eat what you want to eat and you drink when you want to drink. Can have two or three women at the same time, if that is what you want. You can sleep late if you want to, and you do not have to work. If you want fifteen suits, you can have fifteen suits, and you can travel if that's what you want. If you like a certain kind of work, you can do it. But nobody can make you.

That is not exactly how it is for pirates or wiseguys either, but it is close. And that is why they do it.

You take a pirate ship like the *Weald,* which was the new name they gave the *Santa Charita.* Twenty-six of us had done all the work. But when we left Port Royal we had almost a hundred on board. Capt. Burt explained to me that he needed to have men enough to work the sails and man all the guns at once. And of course he was right, and it meant there were a lot more hands to do the work, so no one had to work very hard. Somebody who worked too slow might get yelled at, but he never got hit with a rope or anything like that. If he was really goofing off, eight or ten others would jump him—I saw that happen to a guy named Sam MacNeal, and I will tell about him pretty soon if I have time—but nobody could just stand there with a rope and give it to him.

There was a lot of drinking, and there was one man in the crew who was pretty drunk all the time. Everybody just let him alone. They said he did it about once a year, and it would stop when he could not get any more. He would be sick then for about a week, and after that a good sailor and one of the bravest men on board. They called him Bill Bull, and that may have been his real name. We all stunk but he stunk worse, and anytime I get tempted to drink a lot (which does not happen much) I remember Bill Bull and how bad he smelled.

In Port Royal, after we sold the cargo, the money got split up according to rule, which was basically one share for every man on board except me.

Capt. Burt did the splitting and got ten shares, and if he put a little extra into his own pocket, I would not be surprised. It always seemed to me like he had green eyes. Still, every man got a lot, and in Port Royal he could buy anything he wanted.

And I mean *anything*. If it was for sale anywhere in the world, it was for sale in Port Royal. Things that were not for sale anywhere else were for sale there, too.

There is another thing I ought to say about pirates. Last night I saw a movie on TV about us, and it got a lot wrong. The worst thing was ages. Everybody on that pirate ship looked like he was at least thirty, and a lot seemed ten or twenty years older. Real pirates are not like that. Pirates are just about all young. A lot of our men were sixteen or seventeen, and I do not believe there was anyone on the *Weald* as old as thirty.

Capt. Burt did not put her into dry dock, but we had carpenters come aboard, and a sailmaker and so forth, and he made a lot of changes. When we put out again, we had bigger guns and more of them and the mainmast was fore-and-aft-rigged instead of square. It meant the ship would not be as fast before a following wind, or as easy to handle with a wind like that either. But it would be easier in general, it could turn a lot handier, and it could sail closer to the wind.

There is a lot more that I could tell, but I think most of it will be better and clearer later on. Let me just say here that having no money I stayed on the ship most of the time and tried to take care of things there, which Capt. Burt appreciated and thanked me for. And that when we put out again there were two carronades on the quarterdeck, and Capt. Burt and I shared the captain's cabin with a long nine.

There was more trouble about MacNeal, too, and when we came to a little island pretty close to Jamaica that had a few trees on it and no people, we just put him ashore there and left him.

6

Captain Chris

AFTER I SAW what they did with MacNeal, and how he begged, and how they did it anyhow, I thought sure that was what was going to happen to me. I knew that if I was left on a little island like that with a bottle of rum, my seabag, and a pistol, I would probably die. Not because I would shoot myself like they thought MacNeal would—I would never do that—but from hunger and thirst. I would try to fish, and dig up shellfish if there were any, set out shells to catch water when it rained, and hold on as long as I could. But if nobody picked me up in a week or two, I would die.

I said to myself, "All right, I'll die. But I won't beg, and I won't murder." It sounded good, but I was not sure I could really keep to it, especially the part about not begging.

Then we sighted a ship. "Dago, by the look of her," Capt. Burt said. And he had a couple of men get out the signal box and run up 'WARE PIRATES in Spanish. I told them how to spell it.

After that they wanted to talk, the captain shouting at us through a megaphone, and us yelling, "No tan aprisa! Qué? Más despacio!" and so forth. When our side lay a half cable from theirs, we ran out the guns and told them that if they surrendered their lives would be spared.

They started to run out their own guns—three small pieces on that side—and we gave them a broadside. I do not mean that I helped fire those shots. I was with the foremast men, but I was part of the crew when they were fired. There is no getting around that. And I helped Capt. Burt with the Spanish.

Our broadside did quite a bit of damage and killed most of the gun crews. They surrendered and we boarded. Capt. Burt told me to come with him, and I did. I do not mean that he made me. He just gave the order, and I did it. I am not going to lie about it, not to you and not to myself.

She stunk. The whole ship stunk something terrible. I said something about it, and Capt. Burt said she was a slaver and they all stunk like that.

When I heard there were slaves on board, I went below. The men were chained on platforms about two feet apart, layer after layer of them. They could not get off. The women were loose in the hold, some of them with babies. (Later we found Azuka hiding in the captain's cabin.) The shit and piss and vomit and everything else went down into bilges, some of it. And some stayed right where it was.

I came up feeling sick, and when I got on deck, I chucked over the side. After that I tried to tell Capt. Burt how it was, but he would not listen. He made me listen to him instead. He was going to talk to what was left of the crew, and he wanted me to repeat what he said in Spanish.

I did, and there was not a whole lot of it. He said he would have spared everybody if they had surrendered. ("Struck their colors" is how he really said it.) They had not, so he was going to kill half of them and let the other half go to tell people ashore what happened to people who did not surrender when we ran up the black flag. First he wanted to know which ones were married.

It was not as many as there had been on the *Santa Charita,* but it was all but two. He separated the groups, and told the single men they could join our crew if they wanted. Nobody who joined would be killed. It was a Spanish sailor and a grometto, and they did.

After that, he divided the others into two groups—three in each group—by pulling out men one at a time and tying their hands. Three pirates were counted off, and each cut the throat of one of the men whose hands had been tied. The bodies were thrown over the side, and the rest rowed away in the jolly boat.

By then the *Weald* and the slave ship had been grappled together, pirates on the *Weald* throwing ropes to others on the slave ship. The slave ship was the *Duquesa de Corruna* when she was captured, but afterward I changed her name to the *New Ark*.

I see I have gotten ahead of myself again. Here is what happened. I buttonholed Capt. Burt and said I had to talk to him about the slaves.

"Stow it," he said. "I've got to talk to you about 'em first. Find out where the chains are fastened, and fetch up as many as are on one chain. I want to look at 'em. We'll jaw about the rest later. Take Lesage with you."

I started to say something, but he ordered me to get moving. I know now that he was afraid another Spanish ship might show up while the *Weald* and the slave ship were tied together.

Lesage and I grabbed the men who had joined, and asked how we could get the slaves loose. The keys were in the captain's cabin, and we found them without a lot of trouble and found a slave woman hiding in a wardrobe in there. The men slaves were chained in bunches of eight on that ship, and we unchained the bunch nearest the hatch and brought them up on deck. There was no trouble from them.

We told them in English, Spanish, and French that four slaves were wanted aboard the *Weald,* their chains would be taken off, and they would get better food. Three seemed to understand, so we unlocked those, sent them over, and brought up another bunch. Capt. Burt picked one who seemed to be in good shape and looked smart, and sent him over, too.

After that, he had the pirates on both ships come up on deck, and had me come up on the quarterdeck with him. "We're free Brethren of the Coast," he told them, "free to elect as captain anyone we want. I plan to send this prize to Port Royal, and send it there as fast as I can. If you know anythin' about the business, you know that two or three slaves die every day on a slaver, so it's best it go direct and fast. I'm puttin' Chris here in charge. He can navigate, and he's got a good head on his shoulders. He'll take no prizes, but sail straight to Port Royal and sell the slaves and the ship. Six hands ought to be enough to handle her, so I want six men willin' to vote him captain. Who wants to go?"

I do not remember how many came forward—a dozen or so. Capt. Burt chose six and told them I was their new captain. After that, we cast loose and got under way.

The first thing I did was to set a course for Port Royal. After that I had the women and children brought up on deck, with one of the bunches of men. Chain gangs, I guess you would call them. That gave us a chance to hose down their shelf with seawater, and hose down the bilges, too. Of course all that had to be pumped out after that, along with all the filth. It was a lot of pumping, and the men said the slaves ought to do it. I agreed, and we picked out four strong-looking ones and set them to work.

I gave the first gang an hour on deck, then sent them back down and brought up the second, and so on through the day. By nightfall I was getting dirty looks from some of the men, so I walked up to Magnan and cold-cocked him.

He went down, but he bounced up pretty fast and tried to draw his cutlass. I got there first, got it away from him, and threw it up on the quarterdeck. (Lesage left the wheel for a minute and got it for me, though I did not know that then.)

We went at it again, and pretty soon somebody threw Magnan a dirk. He cut me a couple of times before I got it, but when I had it I pinned him and put the point up his nose. I told him, "If I have any more trouble with you, I'm going to stick this big shank in clear to the guard, capeesh?" Then I slit his nose, just on the one side. It is done sometimes to punish slaves, both sides. I did not know that when I did it.

When I stood up, I was bleeding pretty freely. I told the other four pirates that I was not going to try to find out who had thrown Magnan the dirk, but I was going to keep it. I said I wanted the sheath, too, and that if I did not get it they were going to have serious trouble with me.

I went into the captain's cabin after that. I had seen medical supplies in there when Lesage and I were looking for the keys. I got them out and tried to bandage my cuts. There was no disinfectant, but there was brandy in a decanter, and I splashed a lot of it on the cuts. I had bandaged my side and was trying to get a bandage to stay on my right arm when somebody knocked. It was a soft little knock, like the person was scared, and I could not even guess who it might be.

I opened the door, and it was the slave girl we had found in there. She had the sheath and gave it to me, and said that the other masters had given it to her and made her knock. I say she said that, but about half was gestures. She knew a couple of hundred words of Spanish, I would say, and her pronunciation was so bad I had to get her to say some words over and over. I asked her name, and she said Santiaga. After she finished bandaging my right arm, I got her real name out of her. It was Azuka.

She went over to the bunk and got ready for what she thought was coming next. When I said she had to go out, she cried. The other women had beaten her, she said, and made fun of her because we had killed her man. It was mostly making fun, I think, because I could not see that she had been badly hurt. No swollen eyes or cut lips or anything like that. Anyway, I told her that was her problem and they would get tired of it pretty quick.

Then she wanted to know if it would be all right if one of the other masters became her new man.

I said sure.

What about the one at the wheel?

I said that would be okay, but she would have to wait until he was off duty—until his work was finished.

She smiled and went out.

My cabin was right under the quarterdeck, like they usually are, and the chains ran down the aft bulkhead, so I could hear just about everything they said. She could not speak French and Lesage could not speak Spanish, or very little, but it took them about as long to understand each other as it would take me to tie one shoe. Azuka was naked and that probably helped.

When it was over, I put my new dirk into its sheath, stuck it in my belt, and had a good look around the cabin. The arms locker was under the captain's bunk, and the key was on the bunch we had already found. Except for four muskets, it was nearly empty until I put in the things that had been picked up off the deck after the fight. My guess is that most of the cutlasses and pistols had been issued to the crew as soon as the ship got to Africa. On a slave ship, there is always a chance that the slaves will try to take over.

I had been thinking a lot about that for two reasons. The first was that some of the crew said these slaves would try to when they were brought up on deck. I limited that to sixteen men—two bunches—at a time because I was afraid they might be right. I said that if sixteen unarmed men who were chained together could beat seven armed men who were not, they deserved to win.

The second was that I had been thinking about taking off their chains some night and telling them to go to it. In a lot of ways I would have loved to do that, but there were five big problems with it.

Five!

Number one was that there was not enough food and water on the ship for us to sail it back to Africa. Number two was that I could not talk to them. Even if I could have, they might not have followed my orders. As it was, they could not even understand them.

Number three was worse: they were not sailors. Unless the weather was good all the way, we would not make it there and everyone on board would die.

Number four would have given me fits if the first three had not been so bad. The crew had made me captain. (Capt. Burt had put on board only men who would vote for me.) If I unlocked the slaves, those men would die, not just the one whose nose I had cut, but Lesage and all the rest of them.

You will have guessed number five already. I would be stranded in Africa, and if Capt. Burt ever got hold of me I was dead meat alla grande.

So no. It sounded good, but that was out.

I kept worrying about it just the same. Suppose we just landed them on the coast of Mexico or South America someplace and turned them loose? In the first place, I did not think I could talk the crew into doing it. They would mutiny as soon as they caught on. In the second place, the Spanish would round up the slaves I freed and they would be slaves all over again. So that was out, too. I was going to have to take them to Port Royal and sell them, because there was nothing else I could do.

Praying to God only brought me back to that priest in Veracruz.

Looking around the cabin, I found a Toledo hanger. It was good and sharp. I had been needing something like that, so I put it on. There were a couple of whetstones, too, oil, and some other stuff.

Out on deck, one of the kids had fallen overboard. If we had been going fast it would have been bad, but we were still loafing along under topsails. We threw him a rope, got him back on board, bent him over a gun, and whaled the merda out of him.

After that, I went looking for Azuka. Lesage had chased her off the quarterdeck, and she was not all that easy to find. I had her get the mothers to line up the kids. More or less together, we explained to them that anybody who fell overboard in the future would be left to the sharks. I did not think I would really have the guts to do it, but I knew the pirates would. And if I did not hear about it until it was too late, nothing I did then would help the kid who fell off.

Pretty soon the watch was over, and Lesage asked if it would be okay if he took Azuka to the first mate's cabin. I said sure, he was first mate until I said different. I took the wheel myself, and ordered my watch—three men—to make sail. We set fore, main, and mizzen, one mast at a time. She did not exactly fly after that, but our speed went from one knot to three. I remember it because I cast the log myself, as well as making the entry.

(It was that logbook that really got my head straight about what had happened when I left the monastery. The entries were dated, of course, and the years were wrong. Years were supposed to begin with a twenty, and these did not.)

Lesage had been doing the same thing—tying the wheel, casting the log, and writing in the book. He had been turning the glasses, too, and he had rung the bell to signal the end of the watch.

That and seeing how tough it had been for my watch to make sail made me realize how badly we needed more men. In a gale, I would call for all hands. When I did, I would have six men. Two men per mast, in other words, and I had seen how fast a gale can come up. Landsmen think the wind rises gradually. I know, because I have talked about it with them. It does not. It comes at you like an eighteen-wheeler and you had better do something ten minutes ago.

Pretty soon the men came to the quarterdeck rail. Red Jack spoke for them, pulling his cap and saying we were all shipmates, he was quartermaster now, and by the Custom of the Coast there should be no trouble about it if they spoke their minds.

I said, "Stay polite, and there'll be no hard feeling here, Jack."

"Cap'n, we can't make sail proper, nor take in sail neither with so few as what we got."

"You did the best you could, Jack. Did you hear me yelling at you? You didn't. I didn't say a word."

"I know, Cap'n, and we take that kindly. Only we're askin' that all hands be called to make and take."

Ben Benson said, "Or else we furl fore and main, and run so."

I had been wanting to look over the slaves anyhow. I did it then, and shook my head. "We'd lose too many, and it's money out of our pockets.

We've got to get them to Port Royal as quick as we can before the water runs out."

Red Jack nodded to that. Magnan never said a word the whole time. (He was the man whose nose I had cut.)

I had them take down the slaves who had been on deck and bring up a new bunch. One was big and looked strong, so I had Ben take the wheel and tried to talk to the strong slave. He did not know any language I knew, but there was another slave on the same chain who knew a little French. I told him he could join my crew if he would swear loyalty to me. He could not wait, so I got the keys and unchained him. He knelt and swore in his own language (bowing to me about twenty times while he was still on his knees), and I gave him one of the cutlasses. His name was Mahu, only later Novia and I called him Manuel.

After that I went back to the big man I had picked first, scribed a line on the planking with the point of my hanger, pointed to Mahu, and indicated that he had been on that side, where the slaves were, but that he had crossed over to my side. The big man nodded to show he understood, and I had Mahu ask whether he wanted to do the same thing.

He nodded a lot, talking in his own language, and Mahu explained that he agreed and would obey me as his captain. He got his chains taken off too, swore, and got a cutlass. His name was something I could not have remembered for five minutes, so I told him his new name was Ned. Big Ned was what we called him, and is the way I remember him. He generally looked like he was mad enough to kill somebody. The funny thing was that he did not mean it—that was just the way his face was. He hardly ever smiled, but he had a big booming laugh. I would not have wanted to fight him.

When the larboard watch came on, I got the whole crew together and told them Big Ned and Mahu were part of the starboard watch now, it would give us more hands when we needed them, and it was up to everybody on board to teach them seamanship. Nobody disagreed, so I told Red Jack that as quartermaster he was in charge of the larboard watch, and turned the one that had been mine over to Lesage.

You can guess what came after that, and so did I. The larboard watch said they were even more shorthanded than the starboard watch had been and wanted me to let them have a couple of slaves, too. I frowned and pointed out that freeing so many slaves was going to cut into our profits. They said we had better than two hundred on board, not counting women and children, and two gone would not matter. Finally I said we would have a meeting next day and vote on it. It was pretty hard to keep my face straight through all this, so I went into my cabin and slammed the door before I got to giggling.

Here is the way I saw it. There was a good chance of trouble with the six pirates I had gotten from Capt. Burt. Any four of them could have voted me out, to begin with. Magnan would vote against me as sure a gun. Lesage would probably vote for me unless they were going to make him captain. If they were, that was two against me already—two more and they could vote me down. Or one of them might just waste me. There was not a one of them who would not as soon kill a man as eat alongside him, and if somebody had a grudge and thought he could get away with it, why not?

All right. But the slaves I had freed were bound to think that with me gone there was a swell chance they would get chained up again—and wind up grinding sugarcane on somebody's plantation, too. They would not take kindly to anybody knifing me, and if it came to a vote I would have five right there, my four grommettos and me. If we could win over one pirate we would be a majority.

The downside was that they might try to free some of their friends and take over the ship, but that was really an upside for me. The pirates would think of that, too, and they could not help seeing that if we did not stick together we would not stand a chance.

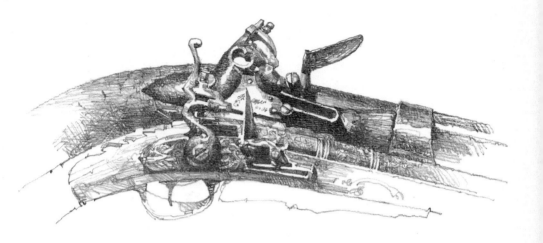

7

The Windward

WITH TWO WATCH-KEEPING officers, I got to spend a bit of time in my cabin, and one of the things I did there was play around with the pistols and muskets in the arms chest. My father had two guns. There was a big one he wore when he went out of the house, and a little one he wore all the time, even when he was sitting by the pool. Both of them had laser sights—you squeezed the grips, and the laser jumped out to show you where your bullet was going to hit. I knew about those because he showed them to me one time, but I was just a kid then and he would not let me touch the guns.

The pistols and muskets in the arms chest were not like those guns at all. There were no laser sights, and they were single-shots, all of them. They had flints in their hammers, and there were more flints in a bag, with wrenches for opening the hammer jaws and putting a fresh flint in. (There were tools for knapping the flints, too, but I did not know what they were for then.) You cocked the hammer and made sure it stayed back with a safety catch. Then you pointed the muzzle up, and poured in gunpowder from a brass flask that measured it for you. The big flasks were for the muskets and gave a big charge. The medium flasks were for the pistols. After that, you got a ball, set it on the muzzle, and tapped it in. Once it was in, you could ram it down with the ramrod, a big wooden rod with a brass tip that was fitted under the barrel.

When the ball was down as far as it would go, you still had to open the pan and put in fine powder from one of the little flasks. Close the pan again, take the catch off the hammer, and you were ready to shoot.

I have learned since that somebody who has had a lot of practice can do all that faster than you would believe, but back then it took me about ten minutes to load one of the muskets. I fired it out an open window of the cabin, and of course that had half the crew pounding on my door. I told them I was having a little target practice and not to worry.

I had expected the musket to kick a lot, but it was too heavy. I never did find out how heavy those things really were, but if they had been any heavier one man could not have carried them around.

The pistols were the same way. I said my father had a big gun, but it could not have been half as heavy as they were. The barrels were closer to two feet long than one, and I thought they would be better if the barrels were shorter. Later I found out how handy those long barrels could be once you had fired the one shot in the gun. I loaded one and stuck it in my belt, but pretty soon I took it back out. It was too heavy to tote around all day, as far as I was concerned.

We ended up with four gromettos, like I had planned, which gave us a big enough crew to set the spritsail under the bowsprit and the topgallants—everything she had, in other words. There were topgallants for the foremast and mainmast. The old *New Ark* was no greyhound even when she was carrying all that canvas, and we had to take in some anytime there seemed to be the slightest chance of a blow. Mahu was scared to climb a mast at first, but we got him over that.

There were two ways to sell slaves in Port Royal. The fastest was to sell everybody to one buyer. The other was to wait for the next slave auction, and auction them off one by one there. The advantage of one buyer was that we would get the money quick. Wait for the auction, and we might get more.

There were disadvantages, too. As soon as I sold everybody to one buyer, the crew would expect some money, and that would mean no crew when I tried to sell the ship. I wanted crew so I would have a crew to clean the ship and fix it up, like we had the *Santa Charita*.

That is why I decided to wait for the auction, which was only a few days off. The crew griped about it, but I got them to working hard, and kept them at it.

There was another advantage to waiting that I had not figured on at all. I could get all the slaves up on deck, and get them better food, too. (I sold a few things off the ship, piecemeal, to buy the food.) Just a few days of that, and they were all looking a lot healthier. One more was that Lesage wanted to buy Azuka. I did not want to sell her right off, because I was pretty sure the rest of the crew would say I had not charged him enough. I would have had to give her to him on credit anyway, since he would not have any money until we paid off. That would mean that the rest of them would have wanted to buy slaves on credit, too.

So we waited, and I got fruit for everybody. Fruit is full of vitamins, and oranges and limes were pretty cheap. We were afraid some of the women and kids would jump into the harbor and swim for it, but nobody did. Of course I had two men with muskets watching them all the time. That was the easy duty, so I gave it to the ones who had been working hardest.

Another problem with waiting for the auction turned out to be that some of our slaves did not sell—five men and four kids. I turned that into an advantage. I paid the crew. (They were wild to get ashore and spend it and would have smoked me if I had not.) When they were gone, Lesage and I fixed up the ship some more with the men and kids we had left.

Lesage was still on board because we had not auctioned Azuka yet. I put her up at the next auction, and he bid on her and got her. Lesage had killed one of the men, but I put up the other four and all four kids with lower minimum bids, and sold them all.

After that I sold the *New Ark* to a man who had already been on board looking at her. I named a price just a little bit higher than his latest offer, and he took it.

After that I had a lot of money, because the ship brought more than the slaves had. It takes two or three voyages to pay off a slave ship. But before I tell about that, I ought to cover the distribution. Things went by shares. Each man got one. The captain (me) got ten. The quartermaster (Red Jack) got seven. The mate (Lesage) got five. If there had been a barber-surgeon, he would have gotten four. A bosun, a carpenter, or a sailmaker would have gotten two. Capt. Burt got ten, too.

There were four pirates originally, not counting the two officers. Add the four gromettos, so eight shares there. Seven, five, ten, and ten made thirty-two more, so forty in all. That was how I split up all the slave money. I gave everyone his fair share, and I bought a soft leather money belt that I could wear under my clothes for my share and Capt. Burt's. For the gold, really. I just put the silver and change in my pockets like everybody else.

The ship money was different, because I had to buy a sloop for us to go back in, fit her out, and provision her. I did, too. Her name was the *Windward,* and I did not change it. She had the Jamaica rig, meaning a short mast and a long boom. I did not change that, either, but I had seen a Bermuda rig in the harbor, and it stuck in my mind.

Before I go on, I ought to say that sloops are always pretty small and always one-decked. Flush-decked is what they say. Sloops are boats, not ships. If a boat like that has one mast, it is a sloop. Two, and things get complicated. Say the second is shorter than the first. If it is forward of the stern post, the boat is a ketch. Aft of the stern post, and the boat is a yawl. Is that clear? If a flush-decked boat has two square-rigged masts the same size, she is a brig. Same thing for a ship—two square-rigged masts the same size make her a brig. (The *Santa Charita* was a brig until Capt. Burt put a gaffsail on her main. Then she was brigantine. A brigantine is not a little brig, it is a brig with a four-and-aft main.)

If the first mast is smaller than the second, it is called the foremast, like the first mast of a brig. We called a boat like that a sloop or a two-stick sloop, but it is a schooner now. The *Windward* had one mast, so she was a sloop for sure.

When she was ready to go, I would need a crew. So I braced each man when he came for a share of the ship money. Most of them did not want to ship on her—they had money in their pockets, and they wanted to spend it. Lesage was the only one who hung on to his ship money, which told me something about him I had suspected already. He said he would stick with me if he could bring Azuka along. I said sure, so that gave me somebody to take care of the boat when I was ashore.

I had quite a bit of money myself, as you will have figured. I went ashore then, looked around more than I ever had before, and bought a dagger, a pretty big one with a good, big guard and an ivory grip. I had some long, hard looks at the girls, too, and to tell the truth I did not like them as well as I had the girls in Veracruz. Some of those Veracruz girls had been trouble, and you could generally see it right off. I do not think there was a single English girl I saw in Port Royal who was not trouble, although some of the black girls might have been okay. On some it was easier to spot than others, but when you talked with them a few minutes, you knew they were trouble.

Another thing was that I could hardly understand most of them. I have spoken English since I was a baby. I speak Spanish so well that a Cuban or Mexican will think I am from his country—of course I am dark and have black hair, which helps. English is still my native language. Capt. Burt had a British accent, but I could understand him fine. I could not understand some of those Port Royal girls for beans.

One by one we got more men. Red Jack and Ben Benson came back, and so did Big Ned and Mahu. Some new men joined. When I had eight, not counting me, we put out. Nine men could barely have handled the *New Ark*, but it was a lot more than I needed for the *Windward*. I only shipped that many because Capt. Burt had said to bring back more than I brought, if I could. I had brought six, and I was afraid he might not want Ned and Mahu. If he would not take them, at least he had not lost men with me.

Azuka cooked for us, cleaned up, and turned her hand to just about anything we asked her to. She had clothes by then (and some junk jewelry), but there was a fight just the same. Lesage did not kill that guy, but he hurt him so bad he might just as well have. With nine men and a woman on that sloop, we were living in each other's armpits. I had the only cabin, and it was like sleeping in a closet.

I have told already how much I like the sea and the sky, the peace and beauty of it and how near to God I feel when I can just drink it in. Now I have to talk about something more—the thing behind my whole life, which is the way it seems to me now. It was the first watch and the sun was low, all orange and gold behind clouds. That was Lesage's watch, and he had a man on the pump and Ben at the wheel. I told him I would take the wheel myself, which would give him another man.

Pretty soon it got too dark to work, and everybody except me sat down or lay down, and most of them went to sleep. Finally I decided there were only two of us still awake, the *Windward* and me. We were on course for Tortuga, the big mainsail was drawing pretty well, and the sea so calm it seemed like it was sleeping, too. I knew that all sorts of things could go wrong.

There could be trouble with the men, we could founder in a gale, Capt. Burt might not get to Tortuga for a month, and so forth—more trouble than you could get from ten girls in Port Royal. But the sea was calm, the weather was good, and the boat was alive under my hands. I felt I could count on Lesage, Red Jack, Ben Benson, Big Ned, and Mahu—which made it five to four, even if the rest turned against me. We would go where I said to go, and anybody who did not like it would have a long swim. There was no novice master to worry about, and no feds. Just about everybody on earth was chained up, even if they could not see their chains, but I was not. I could breathe in a way most people never get to breathe. I stayed at the wheel like that for the whole watch, and I cannot tell you how wonderful it was.

The next day, I did it again. It looked like we might be in for a little blow, and I thought that with me at the wheel Lesage's watch would be able to handle the sails without my calling all hands. It was not bad at all. We set the spritsail, the main filled fit to bust, and we sailed along pretty good.

The wind was singing in the rigging, and after a half hour or so it came to me that it was trying to tell me something. That was one of the things—just about the only thing—I had gotten out of music class: listen to the words and notes of hymns and chants and see what they are saying. I shut my eyes for a minute, and it seemed to me I could hear Fr. Luis. No words, but the sound of his voice. I was outside the classroom, and he was lecturing at the blackboard.

When I opened my eyes again, I saw that I was standing in one of the drawings he used to make for geometry. The mast was a line, the mainsail a plane, the boom another line, and the shrouds that braced the mast were lines, too.

And I could change that drawing.

I had been thinking about the Bermuda rig I had seen, and wishing we had that instead, because I felt sure it would be faster. I could not change over the *Windward* to a Bermuda rig, because I did not have a taller mast to step in her. I could have shortened the boom—we had a saw and a few other tools—but I needed a new mast, and I did not have it. What I understood then was that I could change other things.

During the next watch I made some drawings for myself on a blank page of the logbook. I put letters at the corners, the way we did in class. The back-stay ran up from deadeye "A" to "B," the head of the mast, and so forth. I will not give all the rest, but the end of the bowsprit was "I."

After that I got Lesage and Red Jack to look at it, and drew a three-cornered sail set on the forestay just as if it were a mast. One corner was the top of the mast, one was the end of the bowsprit, and one was cleat "J" on the deck that we would have to put there.

"The stay's as stiff as a yard," I said, "because it's so tight. So why couldn't we do that?"

Lesage pointed out that we would have to cut a square piece of sailcloth cattycornered, and half of it would be wasted.

"It won't be wasted," I told him, "it will be a spare J-I-B sail."

Lesage did not think my J-I-B sail would work, but Red Jack wanted to try it. So did I, and I was captain. We did not have a real sailmaker, but it was pretty simple and a couple of hands cut it and sewed the edges in one watch. We put cleats on each side a little forward of the waist, bent our new sail, and it worked so well we almost stopped using the spritsail.

THE *WEALD* WAS already there when we got to Tortuga. Ned and I launched the little jolly boat that was the only boat our sloop had, and he rowed over to her. I told him to wait in the boat for further orders and went aboard. There are things about my life I cannot explain, and one is why I remember certain things clearly when I have forgotten a lot of others. One that I remember very, very clearly from those days is telling Ned I did not think I would be long, turning away, and grabbing the sea ladder. I never set foot on the *Windward* again—or saw some of her crew again either.

Capt. Burt shook my hand, took me into his cabin, poured me a shot of rum, and asked for my report. I gave him the works—everything that had happened. At the end, I pulled up my shirt, took off my money belt, and counted out his shares of the ship money and the slave money.

He thanked me and slapped my back. "You're a captain now, Chris my lad."

I nodded. "I know it."

"The sort I look hard for and seldom find, eh? I'm glad to have found you. We've had better prizes than the *Duquesa* since you've been gone. Much better. Add your sloop and your men to what we've got already and we might have a shot at a galleon." He stopped, waiting for me to say something.

I thought hard before I spoke. I knew what I had to say, but it was hard to get out because I wanted to do as little damage as I could. "You told me you liked me once, sir. I like you, too, and I hope anything you try works out. The men I brought are yours, and so is the *Windward*. But I won't take part."

He had his hand on the butt of his pistol by the time I finished. He never drew it, though, and I've always remembered that about him. All he said was "I knew it was comin', eh? Still, I tried."

He kept me chained in the hold for three days after that. They did not always remember to feed me, but when they did the food was decent. On the third day, the man who brought it told me the captain was going to maroon me, which is what I had been figuring all along.

Where I had been wrong was the size of the island. I had been figuring on a little one, one that might take a day to walk all the way around if I was lucky. This looked like the mainland—mountains rising out of the sea, all covered with the greenest trees in the world. Capt. Burt and I sat in the back of the longboat, so I got a good look before she beached.

We got out, just the captain and me, he unlocked my chains and tossed them to the cox'n, and we walked up the beach a ways. I was barefoot, in a slop-chest shirt and pants to match. He had that blue coat with the brass buttons that he never buttoned, and he was carrying a musket. I thought it was probably because he was afraid I might jump him.

"Know how to use one of these?" He took it off his shoulder.

I said, "I can load and shoot one, but I'm no great shot."

"You will be, Chris. This is yours now." He handed it to me, and the pouch with it.

I stood the musket on its butt and opened the pouch. There was big powder flask, a little flask for priming powder, half a dozen bullets, a bullet mold, flints, and some other stuff, like the wrench you use to tighten the hammer jaws and the little piece of soft leather that lets them get a grip on the flint.

I had been too busy looking at the island to notice that he was wearing my dagger, but he was. He took it off and gave it to me. "This was yours already."

I tried to thank him. I knew he was a murderer and a thief, and those things really bothered me back then, but I tried anyway.

"This is yours, too, eh?" He opened up his shirt and untied the money belt I had bought in Port Royal. "Your share's all there, every farthin'. Count it if you like."

Since there was no point in not trusting him, I did not. I just took off my shirt and put on the belt. I kept that one up until the time the Spanish robbed me.

"This is Hispaniola," he told me. "There are wild cattle here—quite a lot, apparently. Wild Frenchmen, too. Boucaners is how the Frogs say it. They shoot the cattle, dry the beef, and trade it to ships that stop here to buy it." He grinned. "Make first-rate pirates, the buccaneers do. I've a dozen or so, and I'd take another dozen if I got the chance. They'll cross your bow before long if the wind holds."

He surprised the heck out of me when he held out his hand. As soon as we had shaken hands, he turned as serious as I ever saw him. "They're dangerous friends, Chris, and foes hot from Hell. Make friends if you can, but 'ware shoals. If they see your gold, you're as good as dead."

If I had loaded as fast as I could—I mean, as fast as I could back then—I might have gotten a shot at Capt. Burt as the longboat took him back to the *Weald*. I thought of it, but what good would it have done? When your only friend is a murderer and a thief, those things do not seem as bad as they used to.

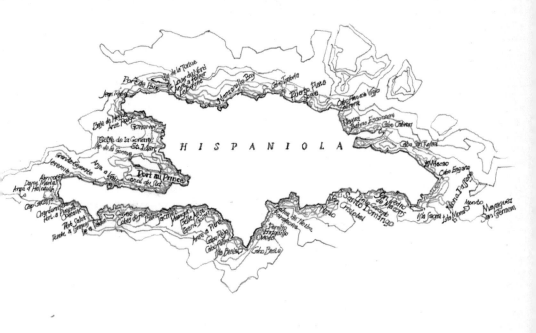

8

How I Became a Buccaneer

THE BUGS WERE bad. That is the first thing I have to tell about Hispaniola, because if I do not say it right up front, Hispaniola is going to sound like paradise. The bugs were terrible. There were stinging gnats so little you could hardly see them. There were red flies that went straight for your face every time. Where they were bad, you had to break off a branch and wave it in front of your face for hours and hours. Worst of all were the mosquitoes. There were a lot of good things about Hispaniola, but there was not one day there when I would not have been glad to go back to the monastery or the *Santa Charita*.

I did not know about the bugs when Capt. Burt left me on the beach. There was a fresh wind blowing, and when there was a wind the beaches were clear of bugs. What I did know about Hispaniola was that it was not a desert island. There were people who lived there all the time, just like Cuba and Jamaica. I thought the best thing for me to do would be to find some and try to get them to help me. There had been Spanish maps on the *New Ark*, and I had spent a lot of time looking at them. The big town on Hispaniola had been Santo Domingo, and it had been on the south coast of the island over toward the east end. I did not know whether I was toward the east end or the west end (which is really where I was), but I could tell from the sun that I was on the north coast.

If I had been smarter, I would have walked east, following the coast. What I tried to do instead was cut across to the south coast, walking south-east so as to be near Santo Domingo when I hit it. If I had known more about Hispaniola, I would have known how dumb that was.

When I started out, I was hoping to see some of those wild cattle Capt. Burt had told me about. I thought I would kill one and cook some of the meat. By the time I had been walking an hour or so, I just wanted to get away from the bugs. I finally found a place that was clear of them, up on one of the mountains. It was rocky and wide open except to the west, but there were no bugs and that was where I spent the night. The next morning I found a spring, drank as much water as I could hold, and started walking again. I did not have a clear idea of how big the island was or how far I could walk in a day, and thought I could probably cross it in three days, and maybe in two. Just for the record, Hispaniola is about seventy-five miles across, and a hundred or so the way I was going. Walking the way I was, navigating by the sun and working my way through rough country, ten miles would have been a really good day.

Just for the record, too, I did not just look at maps after that. I studied them. There were maps on the *Magdelena*, good ones, and by the time I was through with them I could have drawn them myself.

Now it seems to me like it was forever, but I think it was probably the second or third day when I met Valentin. I came out of the rain forest onto a chip of prairie, and I saw a naked man over on the other side. I yelled "Bon jour!" and he was gone as quick as that. I went over to where I had seen him and started talking all the French I could lay my tongue to. I said that I was lost, that I did not want to hurt anyone, that I would pay somebody to help me and so on.

Pretty soon somebody said, "You are not French." He said it in French, of course, and he sounded scared.

"Non," I yelled. "I just speak it a little. I'm American."

"Spanish?"

"American!"

"Not Spanish?"

"Italian! Sicilian!"

"You will shoot me?"

I wanted to say heck no, but I was afraid I would screw it up. So I just said, "Non, non, non!" and laid my musket down. Then I held up my hands, figuring he could probably see me even though I could not see him.

There was a lot more talking before he finally came out. He was about my age, had not had a shave or a haircut in a long, long time, and wore nothing but a strip of hide in front. There was another strip, pretty thin, around his waist that held up the first one, and his knife hung from that, too, in a sheath he had made himself. I gave him my hand and said, "Chris." After a minute, he took it like he had never shaken hands in his life and told me his name. Pretty soon his dog came out. Her name was Francine. She was a pretty good dog, but a one-man dog. She never did trust me a lot.

From the time I had eaten on the *Weald* until the time I met Valentin, I had eaten nothing but a couple of wild oranges, and by then I was plenty hungry enough to eat Francine. I asked Valentin whether he had anything, and he said I had a gun and he would show me where there would be good shooting.

We walked another three miles or so before Francine flushed a wild pig. I shot at it and missed, but Francine got out in front of it and turned it back toward us. It went past us faster than I would ever have thought a pig could run, but Valentin cut it with his knife as it went by just the same. Francine went after it, yelping now and then to let us know where she was, and we listened for her and tried to follow the blood trail the pig had left.

Pretty soon Valentin stopped me and pointed. "In there." It was thick cane, but I listened for a minute and he was right. I could hear Francine growling and a *click-click* noise I did not understand back then. When I had reloaded, priming the pan and all that, I went in with the safety catch off, trying to keep the muzzle down all the time and reminding myself that if I shot his dog, Valentin would probably go for me with his knife.

Francine was keeping the pig busy, dodging the pig's short rushes and trying to get behind it. When I fired, I was so close I could almost touch the pig with the end of the barrel.

I do not think I have ever been more aware of the delay between the time I pulled the trigger and the shot than I was right then. It is only a little piece of a second, but that was when I began to understand that little piece of time is the key to good shooting. A man who thinks his gun is going to fire when he pulls the trigger is going to miss. Pretty soon I learned to wait for the hammer to fall, for the powder in the pan to flash, and for the gun to fire. It is fast, sure. But it is during that quarter second or so that the man who pulls the trigger has to have his sights right where he wants the bullet to go. When I had trained myself to do that every time I was a good shot.

So I was not, but I was lucky with the pig. I was trying to hit its shoulder. My idea was that if I could break something in there, the pig could not run. I missed the shoulder but I just about hit the heart, and the pig went down. It did not die, but lay there shaking until Valentin stabbed its throat.

We pulled it out of the canebrake then and butchered it. I had my dagger, but I did not know how to butcher. Valentin did and worked five times faster. We gutted it, and gave Francine the heart and the liver, plus whatever else we threw away that she wanted. We cut off the head, too, cut off all four feet and skinned what was left. Then we used strips of pigskin to tie the rest to a sapling we could carry on our shoulders. I got my bullet back, and while we were drying the meat, I held it on a rock and tapped it with the little flint-knapping hammer in my pouch until it was round again.

Before I did that, we built a fire. Valentin told me that making fire was the hardest part of living in the rain forest like he did. He had to make a fire by scraping the back of his knife with the right kind of a rock to make sparks. He tried to save fire when he had one, but usually it did not work—it was just ashes and charcoal by the time he needed it again. Since I was there, we made ours by putting a little priming powder on a piece of tinder and snapping the lock of my musket.

We roasted meat and ate, and Valentin showed me how to rub pig fat on the places the mosquitoes like best to keep them off. It was messy and got to smelling bad, but you had to do it or they would eat you alive. Even with a lot of pig fat on I still got bitten, but nowhere near as much.

After that, he taught me how to build a rack of green sticks so we could smoke the rest of the meat. Boucaner is what the French say. After that, we had to keep the fire going without getting it too high. That was pretty tough, because pig fat kept running down and burning, which meant that the hotter the fire was already, the hotter it got. We had to keep pulling it apart with sticks and pushing it back together.

We had time to talk just the same. It was in French and I do not remember Valentin's exact words, but I asked him how he got where we were.

"I was a servant on a big farm in Languedoc. I signed a paper, so the company would take me across the ocean. I was to serve three years, then I would be free. I meant to claim land and farm it for myself.

"When I got here the company sold me to Lesage, a hunter and a cruel man. He told me he had bought me for five years. I said, no, three, and he beat me. After that, he beat me often. He did not feed me or give me clothes, though the paper I had signed said I was to have good food and clothes from my employer. My clothes wore to rags, and I lived on what I could find when he was away hunting, and what I could steal. Sometimes other hunters gave me something. Sometimes they would not. Some of the other hunters had servants, too. Some were treated badly, but all were treated better than I. When we had meat to smoke for our employers, I ate some if I could. If I was seen to eat it, I was beaten.

"The rack burned through, and some meat fell into the fire. I knew I would be beaten to death for that. I took some of the burned meat and this knife I had been given to cut the meat and ran into the jungle. Francine followed me. She had been one of Lesage's dogs. Perhaps it was because I petted her sometimes, perhaps only because I had the meat.

"I have lived here ever since. It is not as good as home but better than being starved and beaten. There are many wild fruits here that can be eaten. I know them all. I throw my stick at birds—some are very good to eat. Sometimes the hunters shoot the wild horses for sport and leave them to rot. I wait until they have gone, and eat. Horseflesh is good food. There is more food along the shore, but I do not go there often. I am afraid Lesage will see me, or that others will and take me back to him."

I am not sure anymore how long Valentin and I stayed together. Two weeks is probably about right, but it could have been three or even four. When we heard shots, we got out of that area. I think that happened twice. We stayed away from the places where the red flies and mosquitoes were worst, or tried to. Valentin said there were a lot of farms on the southeast end of the island, where there was more flat land. We did not go there.

There were a few farms on our end of the island, too. They grew tobacco, mostly, and had a few cattle. Valentin told me that the farms on our end were French, those on the other end Spanish. The Spanish farmers tried to chase the French out sometimes, he said. They had more men, but the French were better fighters.

We hunted birds sometimes. I had no birdshot for my musket, only round bullets about as big around as my thumb, so I had to shoot them sitting and try not to spoil too much of the meat. There were ducks and wild geese, and a big bird Valentin called a turkey, although it was not. Those big birds were the best. The ducks and geese were so fat I used to be afraid they would melt away to nothing. When I shot them on water, Francine would swim out and get them for us. It was pretty safe, because waterbirds would not land on water that had crocodiles in it. When Valentin told me you could not shoot crocodiles because the bullets would not go in I tried to shoot a couple, and he was right. On Hispaniola you wanted to stick with clear water all the time, so you could see the crocodiles if there were any.

Mostly we hunted wild cattle and wild pigs. The pigs were dangerous, because they would try to kill you. If there were lots they would probably scatter, but they might try to mob you. If there were only a few, they always scattered, but one might rush you just the same. They had tusks and clicked them together when they were mad—that was the sound I had heard the first time we killed a pig.

So the cattle were safer to hunt, but it was not easy to get a shot at one. It always took a lot of stalking, and three times out of four you came up empty. I got two while I was with Valentin, and one more pig. We always had plenty to eat, and meat to smoke, too.

Storing it was the problem. If it got wet it would rot like any other meat, and there were wild dogs that would take it if we were not around to protect it. What we did at first was hide it in a dry hollow in the rocks, and put a big flat rock on top to keep out the dogs. Later Valentin told me there was a dry cave we might be able to use.

We went to look at it, and there were bones in it, the bones of at least a hundred people. I wanted to know who they had been, and he said sauvages. Native Americans, in other words. They had hidden in that cave, but someone had found them and massacred them there. We dumped the bones at the back of the cave, and left our dried meat in there. Before we left we piled rocks in front of the mouth to close it. It was not very big, but the cave was a lot bigger inside. I told Valentin I was surprised there were no bats in it, but he said it was too low for them, they liked to sleep a lot higher up. I said it was too low for me, too, because I had never been able to stand up straight in there, although Valentin could.

The next day I think it was, I shot the wild bull. It chased us up on the rocks, and that gave me a chance to reload and shoot it again. Altogether I shot at it five times. I know that, because I counted my shots. When we butchered it, I had hit it three times. So that was pretty poor shooting.

After that I got to worrying about what would happen when I ran out of powder. I could get my bullets back, sometimes, and use them again. But when all the powder was used up I would be out of luck, and sooner or later I was sure to lose my last bullet, too. I thought about making bows and arrows. I was pretty sure we could do it, but I did not know anything about shooting with a bow. And if it was as good as a gun, why did people stop using them when they got guns?

So while we were cooking our dinner, I started asking Valentin about the hunters again. I said that it was all right, living like this in the rain forest, but the hunters probably lived better than we did. They could get powder and bullets from the ships they sold meat to, for one thing.

"Rum, too, Christophe. Needles for sewing, and the coarse thread for sewing sails. That is what they sew their clothes with. Money, and they go to Tortuga to be drunk and lie with women."

"Then why don't we join them? We can hunt."

"They would return me to Lesage, and he would beat me until I died."

"Not if they didn't recognize you. Aren't there different groups? The captain who left me here told me there were lots of buccaneers on this island."

"Oh, yes."

"Then we can go with a different bunch, and if Lesage sees you, I'll get you away from him. How long has it been since he saw you last?"

Valentin shrugged. "A year, perhaps. Two."

"It sounds to me like your time might be up already. Did you have all that hair on your face back then?"

He shook his head.

"Fine. You don't shave it off, just trim it up. You give them a new name, and if somebody says you're the guy who ran away from Lesage, you say he's lying to get you into trouble, and you saw him murder another man while you were living out here. Valentin, this is all kindergarten stuff—my father taught me this stuff when I was a little kid."

"They will not take me unless I have a musket. One must have a musket to hunt."

That was when I understood why Capt. Burt had given me a musket in the first place. I thought about it, then I said, "Okay, here's what we'll do. I'll go alone. There's muskets for sale on Tortuga?"

"I suppose. I have not been there."

"There have to be. The buccaneers' guns must wear out and break like anything else. I don't like getting drunk, and there's probably not one sow there I'd want to screw. So I'll buy a musket for you when I get more gunpowder and bullets for me."

I got a new idea. "I'll buy scissors and a comb, too, and a little mirror. Maybe some clothes. I'll leave all that stuff in the cave with the meat we smoked. The next time you go there, you'll find it. Then you and me will be goodfellas again like now."

"I would be able to go home. . . ."

"Right! Save some money instead of blowing it on Tortuga. Then you'll be able to book passage back, or maybe we could find you a ship going back to France that needs a hand." It took more talking than that, really, but I finally got him to liking the idea.

If you get this far you will be wondering about Lesage by now, and believe me, I was wondering ten times as much. I tried to get a description of his Lesage out of Valentin, and he said strong, shorter than me but taller than he was, big nose, mean face. It could have been a hundred guys. My Lesage had been a pirate, his had been a hunter, and I had the notion that Lesage was a pretty common name in France. So I did not know, and the only thing I could do was keep on wondering if they were the same man.

After that we found a buccaneer camp, and I walked in alone. I thought I was going to get a load of questions and had my answers all worked out, mostly lies. They were not big on questions, though. When I said I had been left on shore by a ship, I thought they would ask why the captain did not want me anymore. They did not. They asked whether I had hunted before. I said I had killed two pigs, a cow, and a bull while I was looking for somebody, and smoked some of the meat. (I showed them some.) That was that. I was not French, and they must have known it, but I had been talking with Valentin for two or three weeks by then, and some of them spoke pretty bad French, too. There were five hunters, a pack of dogs, and a couple servants. The servants kept fires burning to keep off the mosquitoes while the rest of us slept.

Next day we went hunting. I got a good, clear shot at a bull and missed. At the end of the day, we had a calf, two cows, and a bull, none of them mine. We cleaned the carcasses and carried them back to camp, where the servants skinned them about as fast as I can write it, and started cutting up the meat to smoke.

I asked whether we were not going to save some for dinner, and the man I asked spat at my feet. His name was Gagne. He missed them and I think he meant to, but I did not like it. After that, one named Melind explained to me that by the Custom of the Coast no one could eat unless the hunting party killed at least as many animals as there were men in it. I just about ate some of the smoked meat I had brought with me that night when everybody else was asleep, but I did not.

We got six the next day, none of them mine. When we were back in camp and the servants were cooking for us, Gagne asked to see my dagger. I drew it and handed it to him. He looked at it in an admiring way and asked for the sheath. When I gave him that, too, he stuck my dagger back into it and put it in his belt.

When I asked him to return it he just cursed me, so I knocked him down, kicked him a couple of times, and took it back.

About the time I did that, the others grabbed me and told me we had to fight, Gagne and me. Melind explained that it would be a fair fight, which it was, with muskets.

Here is what we did. Melind paced off twenty paces for us just outside camp. We stood there, twenty paces apart, and fired our muskets into the air so we would each have a fresh load to fight with. After that we reloaded, pouring powder down the muzzle, ramming a ball, priming the pan, and so forth. Gagne was a lot faster than I was, and stood with the butt of his musket on the ground and the barrel in one hand while I finished. Melind made me stand like that, too.

"Now I'll count to three," Melind told us in French. "At the count of three, you're free to fire. If you both miss, you can reload and fire again if you choose. When one draws blood the combat is over."

It meant I had to win with my first shot, because I had seen that Gagne could reload a lot faster. I figured he would be a lot faster to aim and shoot, too. So here is what I planned. I would shoot first, very fast, drop my musket, and run. It was almost dark, everybody was tired, and I figured I would have a good chance of getting away. I would get my musket back when they were

89

asleep if I could. If I could not, I would live in the rain forest like Valentin until something else turned up.

Melind cleared his throat. I was not looking at him. Neither was Gagne. We were looking at each other.

"Un." It seemed to take forever. "Deux." I was ready—so was he. I could see the hate in his eyes even twenty paces away. I knew what I was going to do.

"Trois!"

I jerked my musket up, pointed it at Gagne, and shot. My musket jumped up and back, but for some crazy reason I held on.

For a second or two, I lost Gagne in the smoke. When I saw him again, he was bent over. He had dropped his musket, and all I could do was stare at it. I was the one who was supposed to do that.

Melind went over to him and squatted down beside him. After a minute or two he stood up, told us Gagne was dead, and said we ought to eat now and get some sleep. Gagne was the first man I ever killed, and I prayed for him that night.

The next morning he was still there when we went out to hunt. I downed a bull with one shot that day although Joíre had to shoot it again, in the head and up close, to finish it. By the time we got back to camp, the servants had done something with Gagne's body. I never did know what.

After that I hunted with the buccaneers for a couple of months. I made some good shots and missed some easy ones—if you are a hunter, you will know how that is. By the time we went to Tortuga, I was pretty good friends with all four of them.

It was a shantytown there, huts made out of whatever they could cut down roofed with palm fronds. You could buy just about anything, and that included white servants like Valentin had been and black slaves. People told me that the slaves got better treatment, usually. That was because you had the slave for life. If you bought a white servant for three years, and he died after two years and eleven months, why should you care? Look at all you had saved on his food! I watched some auctions, thinking that if there was a big price difference between Tortuga and Jamaica somebody could turn a quick buck. Prices were a little cheaper, maybe, but pretty much the same.

I bought a musket for Valentin, too, with a musket bag. And a pair of pants and a shirt. We wore leather, mostly, but I figured Valentin would not want to look like he'd been on the island a long time, so this was better. I wanted to get him a copper powder flask like mine, but they only had horns. The big end had a plug in it that you pulled out to fill it, and the little end had a little one you pulled out to pour the powder in the gun. That was what all the other buccaneers had. The bad thing about those horns is that you have to guess at the right amount or use a separate measure for the powder.

I asked about priming powder, and the shopkeeper had small horns for those. But he said you could just use the coarse powder and maybe grind it a little finer in the pan with the end of your finger. Nothing metal, because it might spark. So I just bought the big horn. It was too big to go in a musket bag. You just slung it over your shoulder on a cord.

By now you may have guessed what I almost forgot. It was not until the morning of the day we were going to leave that I remembered. Then I ran off quick and got a mirror, a comb, and a pair of scissors for Valentin.

I had been able to buy everything (and more besides, because I bought stuff for myself, too) from what I had made hunting. My money belt was still under my shirt. I had never let anybody see it, and I never touched the gold. When we were about ready to go, the others came to me one at a time, asking to borrow a little for things they really needed. Mostly it was powder, and lead to cast into bullets. They had gone through all the money they had made in months of hunting in just a few days—drank it, or gambled it away, or spent it on women. All three for most of them. I lent each of them a little because I wanted to get in good with them, but I kept the amounts small. They promised to pay me back before we went Tortuga again.

But to tell the truth, I was not sure I was ever going. Pretty soon a ship I liked that needed another hand was going to come by to buy our smoked meat. That was how I was thinking then. I kept thinking about the *Windward,* and how nice that had been. I was a good sailor by then, and I knew it.

So we paddled back to Hispaniola, me thinking to get a good berth and them just thinking to do more hunting as far as I know. We did hunt for a few more days, but before I get into that I ought to say that we had a piragua, a big boat made by hollowing out a tree, Native American fashion. They are very handy boats, those piraguas, although they do not have keel enough for you to put a mast and a sail in them. Or at least, a sail will not work very well unless the crew keeps its paddles in the water to stop the piragua from drifting too far to leeward.

The same day we got back to our camp, I went inland and found the cave, way up on a mountain, that Valentin and I had hidden our smoked meat in.

I left the new musket and that musket bag there for him, and the mirror and so on. I left him my big powder flask, too, because by that time I had got to liking the horn so much I wanted to keep it. If you had asked me then, I would have said Valentin would be joining us in a few days. He never did, and pretty soon I was glad he did not. Now I wish he had.

It was not more than a day or two after we got back that the Spanish men-of-war came. There were three, one of about sixty guns, one of about forty, and a flushed-decked three-master of twenty. At first we thought they wanted to buy from us.

The officer who came talked to us in Spanish with the Castilian lisp. I could understand him, but nobody else could, and I played dumb. After that he used French about as bad as mine.

"This is the island of His Most Catholic Majesty," he told us. "You are here without his permission, which you will not receive. You are to depart it at once. If you do not, your lives are forfeit."

Melind asked, "Who is this who will kill us, Monsieur? You?"

The officer shook his head. "His Most Catholic Majesty."

"He must be a fine shot, Monsieur, to fire so from Madrid."

We laughed, but the officer frowned, and the men who had rowed him ashore looked like they were ready to kill us. I counted a coxs'n and twenty-two at the oars of the longboat, and it looked like every man had been issued a pistol and a cutlass.

"His Most Catholic Majesty has long arms," the officer told us. "This you yourselves will see, perhaps. He is a good and a humane king, however. Thus he sends me to warn you. You are to depart his island of Hispaniola by the couching of the sun, all seven of you. You are not to go to His Most Catholic Majesty's island of Tortuga when you quit this place. Nor are you to go to any other place in his domain. Other than that, you may go where you please. Depart, and you will not be molested. Remain, and you will be killed, or taken for slaves should you give yourselves up."

Melind started to say that we were doing no harm and had resupplied many Spanish ships, but the officer cut him off. "I will not dispute with you, as it would be without point. His Most Catholic Majesty has made the decision, not I. You will die or be enslaved if you remain where you are. You have been warned."

"We will not go," Melind told him, "and we will kill anyone who tries to force us to go."

A real Frenchman would have shrugged. The officer turned up his palms instead. There was more talk, but I have written everything that mattered.

As soon as he got back into his longboat, I started backing away toward the rain forest. I motioned for some of the others to come, too, but nobody did.

The longboat went back to the big galleon, and I watched the officer go up the sea ladder, and the crew go up, and the longboat hoisted back aboard. The galleon squared around and the hatches of the gunports went up.

I yelled for the buccaneers to scatter and get down then, but nobody did much of anything until the guns were run out. Then Melind shouted for everybody to get back.

Nobody had moved more than a couple of steps when the broadside went off. I had been on Capt. Burt's *Weald* when she fired her broadside at the *Duquesa,* but that had been smaller guns and a lot fewer. Besides, I had been behind them, and that makes all the difference. This was thirty big guns on two decks. For a second it was like being in a hurricane. Trees and limbs were falling, water was jumping up out of our little bay, and the noise was terrible.

As fast as it had come, it got quiet again.

One of the buccaneers was dead and so was his servant. I cannot remember the buccaneer's name now, but the servant was Harvé. He only had three or four months left on his contract, and used to talk a lot about raising pigs. He knew more than I did about it, and I knew a lot. Joíre's arm had been taken off, too. We did what we could for him, but he died that night.

The worst thing for me was the dogs. We had about a dozen, and four were dead or hurt so badly that we had to kill them, all of them good hunting dogs. We pulled back into the rain forest that night, and buried Joíre the next day.

After that we went back to hunting, but we kept away from the beach and had the other servant watch the sea. He was supposed to tell us when a ship came.

What really came was more buccaneers, forty or fifty of them paddling down the coast in piraguas. They said there was a Spanish army on the island. They had fought and lost, and they were going to Tortuga until things quieted down on Hispaniola. They had not been able to bring the beef they had dried and had nothing to eat.

We fed them, and everybody talked a lot that evening. I said we ought to go inland and hide in the mountains. Melind told me it would not work. The Native Americans had tried it, and look what had happened to them. We might be all right until we ran out of powder, but when we did they would slaughter us.

"Like shooting the horses to see them die," I said, but nobody got it.

Finally we bedded down, all of us having decided we would go to Tortuga in the morning.

9

How I Became a Pirate

IT WAS THE middle of the night when I woke up. I sat up, thinking I had heard a shot. All the dogs were barking. There was another shot, and I rolled out and grabbed my musket.

That was about as bad a fight as I have ever been in, and I have been in some bad ones. It was dark, and you could not be sure who you were fighting. I heard Melind yelling and recognized his voice, and ran over and helped him out. After that we called the rest over, shooting at just about anybody who did not answer in French. The sky got gray, and the shooting got better, everybody hiding behind trees and popping out to shoot. There seemed to be six or seven of them for every one of us, and they drove us toward the sea and finally out onto the beach.

That was bad, because they could see us better. But it was good, too, because there were rocks and driftwood we could hide behind, and they were afraid to follow us out into the open. One or two tried, and they were shot the minute they stepped out from behind their trees. I figured the ships would come back, and then it would be over for us.

What really happened was that they hollered for a parlay. They swore they would not hurt anybody we sent to talk to them, but they would not send anybody out to talk to us. There was a lot of jawing back and forth about that because nobody on their side could speak much French and Melind could not speak much Spanish.

That was when I did one of the dumbest things I have ever done in my life. I told him I spoke Spanish better than he did, and I would translate for him. So before long Melind and I left our muskets and knives behind and went up the beach and into the edge of the rain forest to talk to them.

There were two, a Spanish officer and a Spanish farmer. From what I saw, the officer had about ten soldiers and the farmer maybe a hundred other farmers. Once they got us into the trees they grabbed us and searched us for weapons, and of course they found my money belt and kept the money. Melind protested and I yelled my head off, but it did no good. Before long they told us they would kill us both if we did not shut up about it.

That was when I tried to jump them. A farmer standing pretty near me had a big knife in his belt, with the handle sticking out. I grabbed it and went for the Spanish officer. I would have killed them all then and there if I could, and I have never hated anybody in my life the way I hated that guy. That was my money, I had earned it with worry, hard work, and tough decisions, and they had sworn we would be okay if we left our weapons behind and came over.

I got that officer in the side, before somebody hit me. When I was conscious again (and feeling like something scraped off a shoe), my hands were tied behind me, and so were Melind's.

What it came down to was that we had to go—get in our piraguas and go off the island. If we did that, they said, we could leave in peace. If we did not leave, they would hold us where we were until more men came. They had sent for them, they said, and they would be there the next day.

We pretended not to believe them, but we did. I did, and I know Melind did, too. They were too happy about it for it not to be true. (It is pure hell to see somebody you hate happy. I found that out then.) Parties of soldiers and farmers had been searching the island for the past few days, and now that this one had found us the others would join it. They agreed to let us bury our dead and fill our water bottles, then we had to go. I would guess it was about noon the next day when we left, twenty or thirty men in four piraguas, but I was still feeling rocky, and I do not remember a lot about it. We camped that night along the coast, and made Tortuga the next day.

The shantytown was gone. The Spanish had blown it apart with their ships' guns, then landed and burned what was left. A lot of people were left just the same. They had run off into the woods when the Spanish guns opened up. Melind got a bunch together that night and talked to them.

Only first, he talked to me. I told him the truth. It was the first time I had told anybody the truth since I had talked to Capt. Burt in his cabin on the *Weald,* so maybe that knock on the head had done me some good. I told him I had been a pirate, could navigate, and was a pretty fair sailor.

I do not remember everything Melind said when he made his speech. Besides, it was in French and there were some things I did not understand. As close as I can come, it went about like this.

"My friends, we have been driven to the wall. If we remain here, they will come again and kill us. If we return to Hispaniola, they will hunt us down and butcher us like cattle. Can we return to France in piraguas? You know that we cannot.

"Every man must choose to live or choose to die. I choose to live, and here is how I propose to do it. With a few friends to whom I have already spoken, I shall follow the coast to San Domingo. Not until very late will we enter its harbor in our piraguas. We will show no light and fire no shot, boarding a likely vessel before the cowardly curs know we have come. As silently as any ghost we will sail out of the harbor, and once we are at sea—well, my friends, I pity anyone who tries to prevent us from going wherever we choose.

"Those who want to accompany us must be ready in the morning. Some of you will not want to come, for whatever reason. We wish you well, and ask only that you pledge our success when next you drink. There remains plenty of water on this island."

When we left next morning, there were seven piraguas in all. I would guess each held ten men. It took us a lot longer to get there than I had expected. It might have been two weeks, but I think it was nearer three. Whenever we came to a Spanish settlement, we robbed the people. We had to, or we would have starved. A few fought, and some got killed while they were begging for their lives. We tried to stop it whenever we could, but I could not be everywhere, and neither could Melind.

In one way, all that time was valuable. We got to know each other, and who could do what. When we were so close we knew we would reach the harbor after sundown the next day, Melind divided us into two crews, fighters and sailors. My crew was the sailors, and that was half a dozen men plus me. Melind had the fighters.

They would board whatever ship we picked first and take care of the crew, killing everybody who did not give up. My crew would come after them, leave the fighting to them, and get her under way as quick as we could, cutting the anchor cable and running up sails. I would take the wheel and do my best to pilot her out of a harbor I had never seen, at night.

The whole thing scared the heck out of me—I would say it scared everybody—but that was the part that scared me the most. I knew we had a good chance of grounding on a mud flat or whatever, and we would be dead meat if we did. If the ship had a kedge anchor, we could try to kedge off before the guns in the fort blew us to splinters, and dear, dear Saint Barbara, please pray that the nice gunners get a real good sleep.

Next day off we went, all of us knowing that there was a swell chance we were seeing our last sunrise. I had picked out two men to cut anchor cables, and four men to make sail. I told them to set the mains as quick as they could, and we would worry about the rest afterward.

I have seen plans go right and plans go wrong. That one went crazy. Melind and I had said we would look over the ships in the harbor, and try to take the one that looked easiest. Fine, except that there was only one, unless you counted the little fishing boats.

What was worse, I recognized it the minute I saw it, even by moonlight. It was the little flush-decked three-master, the smallest of the Spanish Navy ships that had come into our bay to tell us we had to go. I do not know whether Melind recognized it, too. He may have. He went for it anyway.

So we followed, seven men in the smallest piragua of the bunch. We had planned to wait until the fighters were on board, but we did not. Melind and his bunch climbed over the rail, there were two or three shots, and up we went.

The two I had assigned to cut the anchor cables both went to the bow cable and cut it. I had to cut the stern cable with my dagger, which meant I had to stop cutting and fight twice before I got it cut through. My dagger was sharp, heck yes. Try cutting a thick, tarred rope with a good sharp knife and tell me how it goes.

The worst part was that there was not enough wind just then to bother a candle. My boys set the foresail and the spanker, but there was no wind to fill them.

So, did we do it? By the grace of God, we did. Two things saved us. The first was that the crew was not armed. After that I asked about it, talking to a guy who had been in the French Navy and later to Capt. Burt, who had been in the British. Both navies were so scared of their own men that they kept all the weapons locked up and did not issue them until they thought their men might need them.

The Spanish were the same way—more scared of their own crew than they had been of us. Most of the soldiers had gone ashore, and some of the sailors had, too. The only men on board who had swords, pistols, or anything like that were the officers and a couple of soldiers. My father told me one time that a good lawyer means a lawyer who is more scared of you than he is of the cops, and it seems to me that if somebody is more scared of his own men than he is of the enemy, he ought to go home and go to law school. Those Spanish sailors fought, but it was with belaying pins and handspikes. That sort of stuff. We had our muskets and our knives.

The other thing was the tide. By God's grace it was going out, and as soon as I cut the other anchor cable it started carrying us out of the harbor. We had not paid a bit of attention to the tide, but we should have paid it more attention than anything. Saint Brendan was with us on that, a real stand-up guy.

We had some bad luck, too. Melind had gotten hit in the head with something, and he would not come to. We took good care of him until he stopped breathing, which was four or five days later, I think. It could have been a week. I know it seemed like a long, long time.

I had been his right-hand man, and everybody knew it. I took charge just like on the *New Ark,* only I was a lot more confident. We did not have many sailors, and I was the only man on board who could navigate, so I had the job. I headed for the Guadeloupe Passage because the wind was fair for that, and I figured we ought to make tracks away from Hispaniola for a while. Also I kept thinking here we had a Spanish Navy warship, and why should I not get some of my money back?

Because that was what we had. A little warship, sure, but a warship. With ten guns a side, no way were we going to slug it out with a galleon. But except for galleons, there was not much that could stand up to us. Her name was the *Magdelena.* I liked it and never did change it.

Up to now I have not said anything about the Spanish captives, and there is a reason for that. Once I get into all that it will be a long time before I come out, and I thought you ought to know the other stuff first.

There were only five of them, four men and a boy was what it looked like to me. I had them brought up on deck once the sun was up and talked to them. It was in Spanish, but this is the drift of it.

"We don't like the king of Spain or any of his people much on this ship, and if I listened to my crew the way I ought to, you'd be taking a seawater nap this minute. It would be murder and I'm not crazy about that, but I don't mind it too much either. I see one wounded man. Anybody else wounded?"

Another man edged forward. "Me, Señor. I am." His right arm had been torn up, I think by a musket ball. He was holding it with his left and had a rag wrapped around it.

"Okay, you're out. So is the other wounded man. That leaves three. If any of you three want to join us, we'll take you. Come over here if you do. Stand by me."

The boy did. Nobody else. I had said what I did because I knew that most of the men I had knew about as much about sailing as that priest who let me use his father's guitar. I was hoping to get the two able-bodied seamen, because I knew we were going to need them.

"All right, here's one. Join us, and you'll be full members of this crew. Nobody's going to jump you because you're Spanish. Anything we get—anything we find on board this ship, for example—we'll share out according to the Custom of the Coast. You'll get your full share just like Clément over there. How about it?"

They looked scared, but they shook their heads, both of them. The boy whispered, "I must speak with you alone."

I nodded a little, figuring there might be treasure on the ship. He would know where it was.

Out loud I said, "Okay, the four of you get the jolly boat. Hispaniola's that way." I pointed behind us. "Row hard, and you might make it. Or maybe some other ship will pick you up."

We put all four of them in the boat, and I told the boy to get them a little ship bread, figuring he would know where it was. He had a bottle of water, too, when he came back. As he handed them to me, he whispered, "I must speak with you, Crisóforo."

I nodded again, had the boat lowered into the water, and told the four men in it, "Captain Chris has saved your lives. You tell them that, if you make it."

10

He Was a Woman

AFTER THAT, THE boy and I went into the captain's cabin to have a look at Melind. My idea was that it would be a private place to talk to the boy, and afterward I would have him nurse Melind. I had been doing most of the nursing myself up to then and had been too busy to do it right. So I started with that.

"Out there I told those guys I was the captain," I said, "but this is the real captain. He got hit in the head, and he's been out ever since. I've tried to get him to drink, but I can't. Maybe you can, and I want you to try. Keep him warm and clean, and stand by. That's about all you can do. How did you know my name?"

"He will die, I think." The boy's voice was so soft then that I ought to have known right off. I did not, and I am not going to lie about it. Or about anything else here. I have told a lot of lies in my life, mostly because I had to. I never have liked it or really gotten used to it. I have met people who did it all the time, as natural as breathing. Maybe that is good, at least for them. But I have never wanted to be one of them.

"You are the captain" was one of the things the boy said to me. At least I still thought he was a boy when she said it.

"I'm acting captain," I told him. "This is the real captain, like I said, and as soon as we can we'll get him to a doctor."

"I knew you would be a captain when I found you."

That got me thinking, and after a minute I said, "You're somebody I met in Port Royal, right? How come we're talking Spanish?"

She laughed, and my jaw dropped.

"My laugh betrays me, I know. This is the first time I have laughed since putting on men's clothing. Would you like to take away my shirt?"

I did not say anything, just reached over and pulled off her cap. I expected a lot of long hair to fall out, the way it would have done on TV. So that was one of the really dumb things I have done. Her long, shining hair was braided in back—one thick black braid that did not quite reach her waist. A lot of sailors wear their hair like that.

"I will not undress for you until I have bathed. But do you not recall Coruña?"

I guess I gulped. I know it took me a minute to catch my breath. "Estrellita! You're Estrellita!"

She did not answer, just kissed me. After that I usually called her Novia. It means sweetheart. That is what I am going to call her here.

WHEN WE WERE through kissing, I left her in the cabin with Melind and went up on deck. Shore people use gallons and gallons of fresh water for a bath, twenty or thirty liters, maybe. Enough to fill a small bowl twice is what it really takes, and there was plenty of water in the captain's cabin—soap, a sponge, and more. I showed her where everything was and heard her bar the door behind me.

We did not have many real sailors, like I said before. Besides me, there were only three who were really good, three men who had been in my piragua. I got them together, asked how old each of them was, and made the oldest first mate. The next oldest was second mate, and the youngest third mate. My second mate could not read or write, so I got another man who could to help him with the logbook when he was on watch. I told him and the men that he was quartermaster, and the second mate—his name was Jarden—would teach him how to steer while they were on watch. A quartermaster ought to know how to steer.

Then I sat them all down and said, "This ship is a lot slower than she looks. Why aren't we making more speed?"

It had to be because the bottom was foul—they all agreed on that.

"Okay. We've got two choices, the way I see it. We can go to Port Royal or someplace else like that, put her in dry dock, and pay somebody to scrape her and tar her again. There's two problems with that approach. One is that we don't have the money, and the other is that we're liable to lose half our crew while we're getting it scraped and tarred. Anybody want to argue?"

Nobody did, or at least not much.

"We could fix it by knocking over a few Spanish ships first. That would be swell. Pay the crew a lot of money, and they'll have fun instead of hooking up with somebody else. We can pay for the work on the ship, too. Or maybe we take a ship we like better with a clean bottom, though I wouldn't bet on that one. The problem is that to take a ship we've got to find one and catch it, and we'd need a fast ship to do it."

Rombeau said, "We must scrape and tar it ourselves, Captain. We have plenty of men." He was my lieutenant, and when he said that, I knew I had picked the right guy.

I nodded. "That's what I was getting at. Has anybody here ever done it? I haven't."

Nobody else had either. So we got to talking about ways we might be able to do it, and after an hour or so we came up with a pretty good plan.

NOVIA AND I were not really alone that night; Melind was there, too, but he could not see or hear us. She had opened all the windows, and the wind was soft and carried the smell of flowers on some island far away. I blew out the lantern—moonlight and starlight were plenty for us. We must have kissed a thousand times, but I cannot remember hardly anything we said. She said I must have had a lot of women, I do remember that, and I told her the truth— that I had never done it with even one. She called me a liar, but she was just teasing me.

She had been with a man before, she said, but only one man. "Once I loved him. Now I hate him. I would have killed him, Crisóforo, but I was afraid. I was a great coward when I left him."

And she said, "I do not want clothes when I am alone with you." It was not exactly what I had imagined some girl saying in the confessional, but plenty close enough.

I DO NOT remember how long it was after that. It could have been the next day, or two or three days after. All I really remember is that I was leaning on the stern rail listening to Jarden teaching the quartermaster how to handle the wheel when one of the men came up and said the boy in the cabin wanted me. I said okay, went down into the cabin, and Melind was dead.

We buried him at sundown, sewing him into a spare hammock and weighting it with a roundshot. Maybe I should not put it in here, but we never did make anybody walk the plank. I never knew pirates to do that and I was one. But when Melind was in his hammock we laid him on a plank, and when we had finished the service (the crew singing a couple of French hymns, me saying the Our Father and Hail Mary in Latin) six men picked up the board, held the foot over the rail, and raised the head so Melind slid off the board into the Caribbean. I cannot forget how I leaned over the rail and watched the water swallow him, clear water at first, then light blue, then darker and darker until I could not see him anymore. Someday I was going to die, too, and I felt like I was watching myself go down. There are worse graves than the one poor Melind got, a lot of them.

But there are no better ones. None at all. May he await his resurrection in peace. God grant him rest is the prayer of his friend.

He was a Norman, big and strong, and pretty close to blond. Not much older than I was back then. He had a smile you wanted to earn, and he could do tricks with his voice, private and friendly one minute and booming out like those speakers on police copters the next. He was a good shot and a real good tracker, and he used to talk about his mother and sister when we had eaten all we wanted and drunk a little wine, and were just sitting around the fire. That is all I know about him. I never even knew his first name.

When the service was over, I told the crew that by the Custom of the Coast we would have an election to pick a new captain. I said we would hold it in the morning so as to give everybody time to think things over.

As soon as I said that, a guy named Yancy piped up. He wanted the election right now, and he wanted everybody to vote for him. I said, no, it was not decent. We ought to be thinking about Melind now, and all of us ought to have a little bit of time to think about who would make the best captain.

He argued until I told him to shut his mouth or I would shut it for him.

Here is one of the places where it is hard for me to be completely honest. I did not really want to be captain, or anyway, not much. There was too much responsibility. If it had not been for the other thing, I could have given in to Yancy pretty easily, or had the crew vote on picking a captain that day like he wanted.

Here is the truth. The other thing was that I wanted to be able to spend the night alone with Novia, who was drawing little pictures of me while she waited for me in the captain's cabin. We had done it quite a bit by that time, but it was still new to me and I was wild to get at her again. It meant we would have to have the cabin or one of the mate's cabins, and I did not want to take the chance that night. So I told Yancy that in the morning would be plenty soon enough. I do not think he liked me anyway, and he sure did not like that. I got my way just the same.

That night, while she and I lay together on the wide bed we had made for ourselves on the floor—two blankets I think we had between us and the boards—I said, "How did you live on this ship without anybody finding out you were a girl, Estrellita?"

She grinned at me. "I couldn't be flogged. Men are stripped to the waist for flogging, so I had to be good. I hoped that if they punished me, I would be bent over a gun and beaten as the other boys were. The trousers were on for this, but I was never punished at all. How did you become captain, Crisóforo? You were a common seaman when you sang at the window in Coruña."

"I may be again after we vote," I said. "I'll tell you all about that later. You came looking for me?"

"Of course. He would not let me see you and you went away. I thought I would be a sailor on your ship. You would know, but no one else. It was not easy for me to leave the house. When he ceased his vigilance, I fled. I bought sailor's clothing and changed in the bedroom of a friend. Your ship was gone, but I learned where. When I found this ship which was going to the West Indies also, I joined its crew. They thought me a boy and gave me silly tasks that need no skill. If we fought, I was to bring up powder to the guns."

She laughed. "I know something of powder, but I did not tell them so. Really, Crisóforo, it was not difficult. We slept in our clothing."

I said, "Sure. Everybody does. You never know when you might have to go on deck, and it's four-hour watches."

"Sometimes two. I did not rouge, spoke and walked like a boy, and kept to myself. Kept silent, so that it is a great relief for me to speak with you like this. There was but one lantern in the forecastle, you understand, and it an old and smoky one."

"Sure. I've slept in one."

"Thus you know. Always I had to wait until night to relieve myself, and that was difficult. We will not speak of it."

"All so you could find me."

She kissed me. "Now I will say something. I am a willful woman. Bad! Very bad!"

"I've got it."

"I am sick of playing boy. I will wear women's clothes for you as soon as I find some. Your crew—everyone—will know I am a woman."

I said, "I think some do already."

"Good! Do not be afraid for me, Crisóforo. I have my knife." She jumped up and showed it to me, one of those big, rat-tailed Spanish folders. "And I will stay here in our cabin unless I go with you. My hands will be soft again for you. I will grow round again, as a woman should be. Are you afraid for yourself?"

That made me feel better, because it had seemed to me her face and lips were too thin. I said, "No, I'm not. But what if I lose in the morning? What will we do then, Estrellita?"

"We will leave this ship in a boat, like those others. If they will not give us one, we will take it."

I admired her guts, and I have ever since. I have seen whole ships full of men with a lot less guts than she had in a curvy little body I could have picked up and thrown.

NEXT MORNING I got the crew together like I planned. I asked whether there was anybody there who wanted to be captain, and Yancy jumped up. I told him he ought to tell everybody why he was the best for the job, sat down, and let him talk.

He did for a long time, mostly about things that he had done before: what he had done in France, why he had come over, and so on. Finally they made him shut up and sit down.

I got up again and asked if there was anybody else. There was not so I said, "Okay, I know you're sick of listening so I'll make it short. I've been doing the job since Melind got hurt. You know what kind of captain I'll be. We all want to go to France."

That was not a lie. I had never been there, and I thought it would be interesting.

"But we don't want to go back there as beggars. Or anyway I don't. I want to have quite a chunk of money. Maybe some of you would like to hear people say you went to the West Indies to make your fortune and came home with nothing but the clothes on your back? Speak up, if that's you. I'd like to hear about it."

Nobody said a word.

"Fine. We all feel the same way. The Spanish owe us."

A lot of them agreed with that, some pretty loud.

"If I have my way, we're going to get what they owe. I've been a pirate. Some of you know that already and know that I know how it's done. I'm going to do it again if you'll choose me. The king of Spain is going to hear about us again—" Here I had to yell. "And he's going to be sorry as hell he ever heard about us the first time!"

Three voted for Yancy, counting him. All the rest voted for me. About an hour later, he challenged me to fight it out. He was big and tough, and I know he thought he would kill me.

Jackson on the *Weald* had told me how pirates handled that, so that was how Yancy and I did it. I had thought we would fight with muskets, but somebody must have told him about Gagne and he would not go for it. I pretended to be really unhappy about that, but finally gave in: "Okay," I said, "cutlasses."

After that, we had to find an island where nobody would interfere. It took two days, which gave me plenty of time to think back to things my father had said about knife fights. (A cutlass is just a long, heavy knife with a big hand guard, really.) I had found a little money in the captain's cabin, and I left the gold with Novia and put the rest in my pocket—all the copper and some silver.

We got in the longboat together, Yancy in the bow and me in the stern, and the crew rowed us out to a little bit of an island where nobody lived.

The quartermaster got us to stand ten long steps apart just like I had told him. "When we have gone, shipmates, you must settle things between you. Only one of you will return to the ship. We will remain within hailing distance. When the winner halloos, we will come back for him."

I nodded to show I understood. Maybe Yancy nodded, too. I do not know.

When they had pushed out the longboat and gotten on board it again, I said, "Look, Yancy, I'm your captain whether you like it or not. You're a tough fighter and I'm not looking forward to losing you. What do you say we call it off right now?" My left hand was in my pocket getting the money while I said all that.

The longboat's crew started backing water on one side and rowing on the other to turn it around, and he rushed me. I threw the coins in his face and stuck my cutlass clear through his chest. Back when we took the *Magdelena*, I had seen a Spanish officer do that with one of their straight swords, taking a long step forward with his right leg. I did not do it as well as he had, but I did it good enough and I caught Yancy's wrist with my left hand.

By the time they got the longboat turned so that the bow was toward the ship and the crew facing me, Yancy was lying dead on the sand at my feet. I yelled for them to stop where they were, and I would wade out and climb in.

Probably I should have prayed for Yancy that night, since I had been the one who did for him. I meant to, but I got busy with other things, kissing and tickling and all that, and I did not. I have prayed for him since, though, and I will say mass for him today.

He was about as tall as I was, and probably a hundred pounds heavier. Maybe he really was a good fighter, too—I know he thought he was. I have fought quite a bit in my life. I do not think I am a real good fighter, only a pretty fair one. Just the same, I have learned two big things about fighting and I will pass them along. The first one is that if you rush somebody you have to make good on it. Rushing works best when the man you are fighting does not expect it. If he knows you are coming, maybe you better think of something else.

The second one is even more important. It is that if everybody knows you are a good fighter, you do not have to do it much. People who go around picking fights do not want to lose them. It means that every fight you have is more important than it looks. You want to win it, and you want to tear the other guy up so everybody knows who won and there is no doubt about it. Never listen to guys who talk about fighting fair. Half the time they are just trying to tie one hand behind you. If you box or play cards or shoot dice, you ought to play fair. Those are games. A fight is not a game.

Now it is late and I ought to lock up the Youth Center and go back to the rectory, so I will just tell you what my father told me about knife fighting. The one who wins is the quick one with something in his other hand. It can be just about anything—keys he can throw like I threw those coins, a rock, or a stick. His coat. Anything. He uses it to get the other man's attention just for a quarter of a second. If you can make a long cut without getting cut yourself, you are going to win. If you can get your knife in deep without breaking the blade, same thing.

I HAVE BEEN hearing confessions. It is something we do not do here any-where near as much as we did in the monastery, even though the people here have a lot more to confess than I ever had when I was there. So I would have more confession if I could, but I am not the pastor.

Of course we cannot talk about anything we are told, but a British accent I heard today reminded me of Capt. Burt. There are not many Catholics in England and we do not get a lot of English people in this parish, which is more Latin than anything else. So I listened as much to the way this person talked as I did to what this person told me.

Capt. Burt never got to go back to Surrey like he planned, and I used to think that even though he was dead he had been better off than I was, be-cause I had no Surrey to go back to. Not really. But I heard a girl waiting out-side the confessional laugh at something some guy in the line had said, and that was when it really came home to me that I do. My Surrey is not a place, but a person. I am going back to her, no matter what.

So I should say here that when we had been together a few days she said something that should have bothered me a lot more than it did. I have writ-ten it in this, and later on I will talk about it more.

THERE WAS TROUBLE about the pool table again, and I had to make it clear to everybody that I am not Fr. Phil. I am Fr. Chris, and if you push me I know how to push back hard. I always forgive the boys, but I have found that it is better to knock them down first and forgive them when you help them up. They need to bounce off the floor if they are to repent.

The boys' fights about the pool table are a long way from Capt. Burt and the Caribbean, so I will stop here and not talk about the maps at all. If you ever read this, maybe you will wonder what happened to those coins I threw at Yancy, whether I picked them up. I did not. To tell the truth, I never even thought of it then. I left him lying there on the beach, with coins all around him in his blood and on the sand.

II

The Island and the Auction

I HAVE BEEN on a good many islands, some of them nice and some not so nice. The one we picked to scrape the bottom was never my favorite island, although it was okay. Just the same, it has my all-time favorite name. It is Fat Virgin Island. We never think of Mary the Mother of God as being fat; but it is entirely possible she was, in later life particularly. Fat Virgin Island is there to remind us that fat women can be good women, and often are. It is one of the things God knows that we should know too.

Fat Virgin Island welcomed us. We found a nice little bay on the east side of the island that had a creek of sweet, clear water. There was nobody around and no sign that anybody had been. The beach looked great, so I said that was it.

Getting the guns out of the ship and up on shore was the hardest part. Guns are heavy, and no matter how heavy you think they are, they are heavier than that. You can take them out of their carriages but the weight is in the iron barrel, so that does not do a lot of good. Ours were only twelve-pounders, but they weighed a lot just the same. It could take a couple of hours just to get one into the longboat. Then it had to be lifted out of the longboat with a crane we had rigged up, and after that it had to be dragged up the beach far enough to get it out of the way. The *Magdelena* had twenty of those guns, plus two long nine-pounders, one forward and one aft. The long nines were not as bad as the twelves. They were worse.

About the time we had most of the guns out, a farmer rode up to see what we were doing. Right then is when I ran into the language problem. He spoke Dutch, and nobody in our crew knew it. The map said the island was British, so I spoke English and tried to tell him we were English privateers, figuring I could fake up a letter of marque if I had to. I am not sure he ever understood, but he drank a couple of shots of brandy with Rombeau and me. The part he did understand was that we wanted food and would pay for it. When he left, we ran up the Cross of Saint George just to play it safe.

Pretty soon we had him and another farmer bringing things they thought we might want to buy—a couple of steers, fruit, and so on. (That was when I wished I had picked up the coins I had left scattered around Yancy.) We did not have a lot of money so we bargained hard, but we ended up buying both steers and a lot of oranges and limes. Later we got rum and tobacco from the same two guys.

Once the guns were out, everything got a lot easier. We dumped our water and floated the empty barrels to shore. We could float the tar casks, too, the extra spars, and a lot of other stuff. Nothing else was nearly as hard as the guns.

After that we took down the yards, waited for high tide, and hauled the ship up the beach far enough that we could get at the whole larboard side. We had known it would be foul, but it was worse than we imagined—worse than I had imagined, anyhow, and Jarden said it was worse than he had thought it would be, too. Every square inch had to be scraped, and all the damaged planks fixed as good as we could fix them. Once it was done, we re-caulked her and tarred her, floated her out again at high tide, turned her around with the longboat, and hauled her back up so we could start over on the starboard side.

That was where we ran into a big problem. We had used up more than half of our oakum and tar already. We could unravel old cordage to use in place of oakum, but there is no substitute for tar. You have got to have it, or the sea worms will be in your planking as soon as you have your ship back in the water.

Our maps said there was a place called Spanish Town on the west side of the island. I did not like the idea of going around in the longboat, but I picked the steadiest men I had and took Jarden and the quartermaster with me to keep an eye on them and the boat when I was away from it.

Novia was the problem, and a big one. She would not say she was afraid to stay behind, but she was and I do not blame her for it one bit. I had been trying to keep her under wraps (which was not as easy as it sounds), figuring out of sight out of mind. There was no way to do it in the longboat. The crew all knew she was a woman by then, and they got a good look at her while she was sitting in the stern beside me. She had her knife open in her lap the whole way, but there was not one man there who would not have tried to take it, and most of them would have pulled it off, too. I took her with me—you bet I did!—when I went into town to buy supplies.

It meant we had to buy three different kinds of cloth, needles, thread, and so forth so she could make herself gowns. After that, more paper, wax pencils, and pens, so she could draw. We had to buy those things first, and arrange for them to be delivered to the longboat.

Which turned out to be a good thing, because a nice Englishwoman came into the shop while we were in there looking at various kinds and sizes of paper and told me about a man named Vanderhorst who might have tar and oakum.

If the town had been bigger, we would have been lucky to find Vanderhorst at all. Spanish Town was as small as a town can be, with houses that told you right off that most of the people there were really Dutch, and it took us about an hour to run him down anyway.

When we did, it was the farmers all over again. I tried English, and he just shook his head. Spanish the same.

Finally I said, "If you know any language besides Spanish, give it a try, Estrellita."

She knew a few words of Italian (which I should have thought of myself) and got nothing. Catalan did not work either, although she knew a lot more of that.

Finally I broke down and tried French. I had not wanted to let anybody hear me speak French because I had been pretending we were English.

He did not understand French either, but he brightened up when he heard it and seemed to be trying to tell us that he would take us to somebody who talked like that.

The three of us got into his wagon and rode out to his house, maybe a couple of miles outside of town. By then I was wishing I had sent the longboat and its crew back to the ship, but once we were in the wagon there did not seem to be any way of doing it. I was nervous about it and talked a lot, telling Novia about the monastery and Brother Ignacio, how good he was and how I had talked English with him sometimes.

Vanderhorst had a nice house and a big garden, fields, and three blond kids. We met his wife, a blonde quite a bit bigger than he was who could not speak anything but Dutch, and she went back into the kitchen and brought out a slim black woman with a bandana over her hair. She had on a faded housedress and was wiping her hands on her apron like she had been washing dishes. If it had not been for those things, it would not have taken me nearly as long as it did.

But I looked at her, and she looked at me, and both of us started to say something and stopped. And after that we yelled names and hugged, and she started talking bad French faster than I could follow her. It was Azuka, and it was really, really good to see her again.

Well, her French was not a whole lot worse than mine, but her Dutch was not much better than mine, either, and I did not know even a little bit. We finally got our point across, though: we wanted to buy tar and oakum, and did Vanderhorst have any?

Yes, it was in town in his warehouse. Did I maybe also want to buy Azuka?

Nope, I said, I have no interest in that. She looked like she was about to cry when I said it, which made me feel bad. Novia held me tighter, though, and that felt good.

I wanted to find out what had happened to her—why she was on Fat Virgin Island working in this guy's kitchen—so I kept on talking about her, with her interpreting to him. I said we were hard up for money, and I knew a fine girl like Azuka would cost a lot, and so forth.

That was too bad, he said. He had three men slaves, another woman, and Azuka, and he was going to auction them on Saturday, but meantime he had them working around his farm, and Azuka had been helping his wife. He got *auction* across to us by pretending to be an auctioneer with a hammer. There was a bunch of stuff like that, but I am not going to write it.

Well, I said, I have hardly any money and we have to buy the tar and oakum, but it might be fun to watch your auction just the same. What time?

Azuka smiled big enough to light up the room when I said that, so I was not fooling her for a minute. To tell the truth, I do not really think I was fooling Vanderhorst, either. I was going to buy her if I could, after I got the stuff we had to have.

Azuka and his wife fixed a swell dinner for us. There was chicken pie with a yam crust, which I had never had before, fried bananas that made me think of the monastery, homemade bread with butter and three kinds of cheese, and a lot of other stuff. When we had eaten we went back to town and bought a new jolly boat and as much tar and oakum as we needed. The quartermaster wanted me to buy more, so we would have some on the ship, but I said no. The Spanish captain's money was about gone, and by then I had the feeling I was going to need what was left on Saturday.

When we got back to the *Magdelena,* I had to tell Novia all about Azuka. You bet I did! I explained over and over that she had belonged to Lesage, nobody else could so much as touch her, and I had not wanted to anyway. Novia tagged me a couple times before I got her knife away from her. After that I showed her I could break her arms easy if I wanted to. Then I kissed her, and once we got the bleeding stopped we went on from there, trying a few new positions. I have never thought she really wanted to hurt me. I would have been cut a lot worse if she had. It was just her way of showing me that she was dead serious when she said she loved me. In a way, she was right. I never had exactly believed her. Not all of it. I mean, who would love a guy like me? But after that I did.

WITH THE NEW tar and the new oakum, I had been hoping the ship would be ready by Saturday. When I remembered that we were going to have to put the guns back, I knew it would not. It would have been nice to figure out some way to postpone the auction. I worked on it, but none of my ideas seemed like good ones, even to me.

All our men had muskets already, and we had a pretty fair number of Spanish cutlasses, too. When we went back to town Saturday morning, I wore the Spanish captain's sword, a long one with a fancy silver hilt, and his boots. With two pairs of stockings on and some thick wool we had cut out in the shape of a footprint, they were a pretty good fit. (After that I wore the sword and the boots just about any time I needed to impress people.)

"Crisóforo, darling, look at these."

It was a fancy case we had taken off the ship with the other stuff from the cabin. Inside it was a pair of little brass pistols, right hand and left hand. There were powder flasks, bullets, and so on in the case, too. I had found them myself when we first took the ship, but I had not paid much attention to them. I had a good pair of iron pistols, big long-barreled pistols that would really get somebody's attention.

"May I have them, Crisóforo? I need them much more than do you."

I said sure, and taught her how to load them. After that, I took her away from the beach half a mile or so, and let her shoot each of them a couple times. That may have been the first time they were ever fired—they looked that new. I checked the flints, and they were in real good shape.

Those pistols had belt hooks, so when we went back to town for the auction, she had them hooked in her belt. I had my pistols, too, but mine were in canvas slings I hung off my shoulders. Every man in the longboat's crew had his musket and a cutlass. I had left the crew with the boat the first time, and I had made sure they would stay there. This time it was the other way. I left the quartermaster to watch the boat, and led the rest to the square. We tramped through that little town like an army, and you could hear the shutters closing and locking as we went by. The auction had not begun when we got there, which gave me plenty of time to get my men into position and make sure they understood their orders.

This was not Port Royal by a long shot. There were only five slaves—three men, another woman, and Azuka. I went up to the auctioneer and told him to take Azuka first. He did, and announced a minimum bid of one guinea.

I yelled "A guinea!" and drew my pistols.

In the silence that came after that, I could hear the musket hammers going from half cock to full cock. There was no other bidder.

I was supposed to pay Vanderhorst then and get a signed paper saying I was Azuka's new owner. I admitted that I did not have a guinea and gave him a gold Spanish doubloon instead. He did not like that, but I pointed out that I had been a good customer already and promised to trade more with him the next time we got to Fat Virgin.

He still would not do it, so I said, "Sign it. Sign it now. That will save a lot of bloodshed." It was in French and he did not understand it, but Azuka interpreted for us like she had before and pulled her finger across her neck. When she did that, he signed.

I borrowed his pen and wrote across the bottom of the paper that as Azuka's new owner I freed her. I wrote that in French, signed it, and read it to her.

"I am free?"

I said, "You sure are," and handed her the paper.

"But where will I go, Captain? What will I do?"

"You're a free woman," I told her. "You can do whatever you want to, and go wherever you want to."

"Then I go with you," she said, and took my arm.

I yelled, "Estrellita, don't!," because she was pulling one of the little brass pistols off her belt. I do not believe just yelling would have stopped her, but I caught hold of her pistol and that did.

"What are you going to do now?" she yelled. "Flog me?"

I kissed her instead, and took my time about it.

Pretty soon after that all of us walked back to the longboat. I got everybody together and explained that Azuka had been in the crew of a ship I had before, and was one of our crew now. Anything she did willingly with any of them was between him and her, and I made sure everyone understood that. Then I explained that if anybody forced her, the rest of us were going to be very, very unhappy about it.

"We're all one family," I said, "the Brothers of the Coast."

That got nods and yells.

"We're brothers, and I'm the capo, the head of our family. Part of my job is seeing to it that my brothers treat each other the way brothers ought to, that nobody gets cheated and nobody gets picked on. I'm going to do that, and it would be good for everybody to remember it. It doesn't just protect Azuka here, it protects every person on board our ship."

Nobody wanted to argue, but Griz wanted to know what she was going to do.

"She'll be working with Estrellita," I told him, "and that means the two of them will do whatever I tell them to—fight, cook, make sail, nurse the wounded. Whatever I say."

Simoneau said women could not fight, and both those little brass pistols were pointed at him a lot faster than one had been pointed at me.

I yelled, "Hold it! We can't start fighting among ourselves like this. We're toast as soon as it starts. You know how I fought Yancy. If you two want to fight like that, we'll find you a little island—there's a hundred of them around here."

When I said that, Simoneau muttered something about not fighting a woman and turned away, and the whole thing blew over.

The funny thing was that the two women got to be friends, but they were always jealous of each other. Men can do the same thing, I know. Sure, they like each other, but there is a certain rivalry. I think Azuka may have made it with some of the guys in the crew, and I know with Jarden, who was pretty good-looking. I also know Novia did not, that I was the only one she ever slept with.

Or anyway, that is what I think.

12

Our First Capture

SUNDAY AFTERNOONS ARE always slow at the Youth Center, probably because kids who have not touched their homework all weekend are trying to catch up. That was yesterday, and Fr. Phil offered to Phil in for me. (His joke.) That gave me a chance to poke around the library for a few hours. Writing about Novia and Azuka the way I did on Saturday got me to wondering about women pirates, sailors, and so forth. I thought maybe we were the only ones who ever did that, and I wanted to see.

It turns out there were quite a few. Mary Read and Anne Bonney are the famous ones, but there were others. Her captain called Mary Anne Arnold the best sailor on his ship. Grace O'Malley and a mysterious Chinese lady known as Mrs. Cheng were pirate captains, both of them. Some pirate crews had a special rule—NO GIRLS—just like a bunch of little boys playing in a tree house. When I read about it I wanted to say, "Oh, grow up!"

Well, I had two of them, just like Calico Jack Rackam. Back then I thought I knew how Novia had come on board, but I was as curious as anybody would be about Azuka. When I asked whether Lesage had sold her, she said he had and cried. I let a few days pass and tried to find out what happened again, and she cried just like before. So you can say, if you want to, that I never did find out.

In another way, I did. I wanted to know whether Lesage had sold her because he got tired of her or because he had to have the money. But it had to be both. A man who loved a woman would never sell her, no matter how badly he needed the money. And a man who owned a woman and was tired of her would always find out he needed the money sooner or later. Mostly it would be sooner.

Since I have been ordained, I have spent quite a bit of time counseling people. I would say offhand that it has been about forty percent men and boys, sixty percent women and girls. Even if that is not quite right, there have been plenty of both. A man cannot sell his wife, and a wife cannot sell her husband. But I have talked to a good many husbands and wives who would if they could, and cheap. Teenage girls would buy certain boys, too, if they could. And the teenage boys would let them, pretty often for a paper clip and a stick of gum. They do not say that, but when I have talked with them once or twice I know.

The pirate books I found in the library are not as bad as I had expected. They do not tell you what it was really like, but they cannot be blamed for that, since the people who wrote them did not know. I know what it was like for me, and that is why I am writing this. (You have to know to understand why I murdered Michet.)

Things I have seen on TV have not been nearly as good. One thing I have noticed particularly is that the pirate ships look like big navy ships and fight the same way. I never saw a pirate ship as big as a Spanish galleon, and we never opened fire on a Spanish ship unless we had to. Once the cannons open up, ships get trashed in a hurry, and a lot of people get killed. We never wanted the ship we were taking to get smashed up. We wanted to sail it someplace and sell it. Getting our own smashed up would have been ten times worse, especially when it was the *Magdelena*, which was poison fast once her bottom was clean, and just the right size.

We did not want people killed either—not us and not them. There was always a chance that a Spanish ship would have people we could use on it, a carpenter, a surgeon, or whatever. If they had hidden their money, they could be scared into telling us where, but only if they were still alive.

You take the *Rosa,* which was the first ship we took. She mounted ten little guns, about four-pounders. We were flying the Spanish flag, and I hailed her in Spanish. When we got close, we ran out our guns and ran up the black flag. I told her to surrender, or we would blow her out of the water.

Which is what we would have done as soon as her gunports opened.

She surrendered, and we grappled her and boarded. I had more than fifty men, and every man had a musket and a cutlass. That was the minimum. Most of them carried the big butcher knives they had used on Hispaniola, too, and some had pistols. I had two pistols, my dagger, and the long Spanish sword. But all that was just for show—I knew I would not have to use them. They had twenty-one counting the captain. What chance would they have had if they had fought us?

I got them all together and told them the truth—we were buccaneers, and their king had treated us like dirt. We could not make an honest living anymore, so we were doing this. Since they had given up without a fight, I would let them take the boats. I would even let them take food and water, if they would tell me where the money was.

They said they did not have any, and there were too many to go in the boats.

I said, "In that case the boats will sink. I don't care because I won't be on them. The rest of you can lighten them by joining us, maybe. Anybody want to apply for a job?"

For a minute it looked like nobody did. Then somebody in back said, "Captain! Captain!"

I thought he was talking to me, but he meant the Spanish captain. He was a black man, average size, who looked like his life had been pretty rough lately. He said, "Me stay ship, Captain? One not in boat."

The Spanish captain said no.

I asked the black man if he was the captain's slave, and when he said yes, I explained that he was free now. We had taken the captain's ship, so everything he had belonged to us. That made him our slave, and we freed him. If he wanted to join us, he could.

The Spanish captain looked like he wanted to kill me, but had sense enough to keep his mouth shut.

"You make joke?"

I shook my head. "You want to be a pirate? Fine!" I slapped his back. "Welcome to our crew." I took one of my pistols out of the sling and handed it to him. "You're a pirate."

He took it and turned. He must have cocked it as he turned, because it was very quick—turn and bang! He shot the Spanish captain, so that was two fewer in the boats.

When the rest of the Spaniards were gone, we held a meeting and decided to sail the prize to Port Royal, sell it, and split the money. I made Jarden prize captain and kept the black man on the *Rosa*, since he knew how she sailed already. His name was Mzwilili, but I generally thought of him as Willy and sometimes I called him that. A lot of guys look tougher than they are. Willy was tougher than he looked, something you do not see a lot of.

"You sent him away because you were afraid he would take me," Azuka said, and pouted. She was supposed to be helping with a new dress.

I shook my head. "That's between you and him."

"Also the sea. Much sea between us, because of you."

"Okay, I'll send you over in the jolly."

At that, Novia laughed and stabbed the cloth with her needle.

"I will not have you to protect me there, Chris."

"Willy will protect you."

"He is new man." Azuka giggled. "All will be against us."

I sat down and grinned at her. "I can see you're worried sick."

"I am not worried, because you will not send me away. I can make you happy every day. Estrellita will not do that."

Novia said, "There are knives enough on this ship for both of you." She had not looked up from her sewing.

"Sure," I said. "I've got one already."

The sewing dropped into her lap. "For your backs, imbéciles!"

"That does it," I told Azuka. "I'm sending you over tomorrow morning. Now get out of here."

In the morning the *Rosa* was nowhere in sight. I talked it over with Rombeau and Dubec. Both of them said she was probably ahead of us. Rombeau said that Jarden was the impetuous type and had probably sailed harder that night than he and Dubec had. Dubec thought Jarden was probably going to try to beat us to Port Royal, sell the *Rosa,* and split with the money. Both of them said we ought to set more sail and catch up.

I thought it over and ordered all sails furled. I had two good reasons, and I have generally found that if you can think of two good reasons for doing something you ought to do it.

The first was that I wanted to make one of my jib sails for the *Magdelena* like we had on the *Windward*, only bigger. It had worked fine and given us more speed, and I could not see a single reason why it would not work on *Magdelena*, too. As unhandy as our crew was, I did not want to have a lot of sailcloth laid out on deck and half the watch working on that while we were under sail, but this would give me a fine chance to get one made and bent.

The second was that I knew that even without a jib, the *Magdelena* could sail rings around the *Rosa*. *Magdelena* was built for speed and had a clean bottom now. *Rosa* was built to carry freight and to sail with a small crew. If *Rosa* had fallen behind us, she would catch up in three or four hours, tops. If she had gotten ahead, well, we were still a couple of days out of Port Royal. Maybe more. We could wait until noon and still get there before *Rosa* did.

The sea was not dead calm, as I remember, but you had to look for the chop to notice one. I explained my jib design to Rombeau and told him how well it had worked, and he got his watch to making one. Dubec pointed out that there was a stay on the mainmast, too. If the jib worked on the foremast stay, what about putting a sail on the mainmast stay? I said that was a great idea—which it was—and promised we would try it.

Sure enough, here came the *Rosa* about the middle of the morning. When she was close enough, Jarden hailed us and said there was somebody on board I might want to talk to. Should he send him over?

I said, "No, I'll come over myself, and you'd better furl all sails so as not to get ahead of us."

This time I had four reasons for deciding the way I did. If you ever read this far, you will have guessed the first already. I wanted to take Azuka over before she and Novia really got into it.

The second was that I wanted to talk to Jarden about keeping up and hoisting lanterns and so forth. And the third was that I wanted to give the watch time to finish my jib.

The fourth was probably the most important of all: I wanted to find out what was going on. We had let the Spanish crew have all *Rosa*'s boats when we had captured her, so how was Jarden planning to send anybody over to me?

When we got there, there was a boat bottom up on the forward hatch. Jarden had a guy I had never seen before up on the quarterdeck with him. He was short and stocky and had a bristly gray beard and the look of a man who had done quite a few things in his life. "This is Antonio," Jarden told me. "He says he is not Spanish but Portuguese. He wants to make one with us."

I shrugged. "Maybe we can use him. Where'd you find him?"

"He was in that boat you were looking at, Captain. There were five others in there with them, all Spanish. They were out of water. I got them on board and gave them some."

I asked Antonio whether he understood French, and when he said, "Un peu," I asked him to talk some Portuguese.

He did, telling me where he was from and his family and so forth. I do not know Portuguese, but it was near enough to Spanish that I could guess at most of it. And I could certainly tell that it was not some made-up gibberish but a real language he knew well.

So I said, "That's Portuguese all right. Now let's hear your Spanish."

His Spanish was not as good—better than his French, but I could tell he had not grown up talking like that. After that I asked Jarden where the rest of the Spanish were, and he said he had killed them and thrown them over the side.

I felt bad about it and I still do. I had just been hit with one problem, and now I had two. The new one was that I wanted to give Jarden what for in a mild and good-mannered sort of way—you know, three Our Fathers and five Hail Marys. I could not do that up on his own quarterdeck with Azuka and eight or ten of his men in earshot.

The other problem, about five seconds older, was that I wanted to talk to Antonio quite a bit, and it was pretty clear that I was going to have to talk Spanish to him if I wanted to learn much. It would not be too bad for Jarden to hear me rattling away in Spanish, but I did not want his crew to. If they got to thinking I was really Spanish, they would get that across to my crew pretty quick. When they did that, I would be in the soup.

So I told Jarden I wanted to talk to him and Antonio in the captain's cabin. It turned out to be one of the worst ideas I have ever had, but that is what I did. If I had it to do over again—well, I could use up lots of paper writing about that, but what is the use?

We went into the captain's cabin and sat down, Jarden and me on chairs and Antonio on the bunk. Azuka wanted to come in, too, but I chased her.

I started on Antonio, asking my questions in French then switching to Spanish for things he did not understand. There is no use writing down all that. Here is the gist.

"You and some Spaniards were in one boat when Captain Jarden picked you up?"

"Sí, Captain."

"What happened? How did you come to be there?"

"We were taken by pirates, Captain. They spared us, putting us into that boat, but gave us only one small keg of water. We had been at sea four days and three nights when Captain Jarden took us on board."

I turned to Jarden. "Why did you take them on board if you meant to kill them? You must have known they were Spanish."

He sighed. "I need seamen, Captain. The men I have must be shown everything. I hoped some would join us, as this one did."

"The rest refused?"

He nodded.

"They would tell you nothing?"

"Nothing of value, no."

"Did any of them speak French? How did you question them?"

"Through Antonio here. I told them quite directly that we would kill them unless they gave us the information of good and engaged with us. I do not think they believed I would do it."

"I wish you hadn't. I might have gotten something from them." I returned to Antonio. "Did they believe him? What do you think?"

He shook his head.

"Did you?"

He fingered his beard, which looked as stiff as a brush. "No, Captain."

"But you joined us anyway?"

"I thought he would return them to the boat, Captain. I had sat enough in the boat."

"You were their leader." It was a guess, from his age.

"No, Captain. Captain Lopez was."

"Who might have told us a lot. Merda di cane!"

I took a deep breath, leaned back, and made a steeple of my fingers. "Let's start at the beginning. What were you doing on a Spanish ship?"

"Working, Captain." He spread his hands. "I had no ship, and this one paid. Not well, but enough."

"Where did you come aboard?"

"At Lisboa, Captain. That is my home. The *San Mateo* unloaded cacao there. I came looking for a berth, and we agreed."

The way he said that had given me a hint. "You were one of the mates?"

"No, Captain. I was Sailing Master."

I had not heard of that, but it sounded good. I said, "What can you do, Sailing Master? What are your skills?"

"On a ship, Captain? Everything."

"Carpenter?"

"Sí, Captain. If there is no carpenter aboard."

"Make sails?"

"If you have no sailmaker, Captain."

Jarden asked, "What of treating wounded men?"

Antonio shook his head. "No better than you, Captain."

"You cannot do everything in such a case."

Antonio shrugged. "I have done it, but I have seen other men do it better."

I asked, "Can you navigate?"

He smiled. "Sí, Captain. I am a skilled navigator."

"Can you teach others to navigate?"

He rubbed his beard again. "It is long since I have done that, Captain. But yes. Where there are instruments, I can."

Jarden told me, "You can navigate already."

"I know," I told him, "but Rombeau can't, and neither can you. I could teach you as much as I know, but Antonio here may know more than I do. For sure, he'll have more time to do it than I will."

"I ought to be on deck," Jarden said. "Are you about finished?"

"Almost." I motioned toward the door. "Go ahead if you want to." Actually I wanted him out. With him gone I could have spoken straight Spanish. I knew that better, and it would have saved a lot of time.

"I shall wait until you finish in that case."

"Swell. Antonio, did you offer to join the pirates who took the *San Mateo*?"

He shook his head.

"Why not? You were willing to join Captain Jarden here."

"Captain Burt wanted only young men, Captain, and wanted no married men. I am married and no longer young."

I had hardly gotten past the second word. "Wait up! Captain Burt was the one who took your ship?"

"Yes, Captain. He was."

Jarden said, "Do you know him?"

I nodded. "He's an old friend. I'd like to hook up with him, if—"

Right then is when they started shouting out on deck.

13

Escape, Murder, and Reunion

DO YOU KNOW the joke about the turtle getting mugged by two snails? When the police ask what the snails looked like, the turtle says, "I . . . don't . . . know. . . . It . . . all . . . happened . . . so . . . fast. . . ."

That was what it was like. It probably took fifteen or twenty minutes really. But Jarden, Antonio, and I were running around like crazy, yelling at people and trying to get things done, and it seemed like the whole thing was over before it started.

When we got out on deck, there was a Spanish galleon making for us, all plain sail set and heeling to a quartering wind. Jarden's crew was loosing the sails as fast as they could, which was not very fast, and trying to get *Rosa* under way. Azuka was screaming at nobody, and the first thing I did was to make her shut up.

The second was not much different. The lookout who had not spotted the Spaniard until she was on top of us was still yelling from the masthead. I laid aloft and told him to shut the hell up and get down and do some work. After that I helped with the mainsail.

Magdelena had more sail set than we did—Rombeau had a heck of a lot more men—and was firing her stern chaser. The Spaniard's bow chasers started answering as I watched, and the men at those guns were faster than ours. I would have tried to get *Rosa's* stern chasers into action if she had any. She did not.

I wish I could say now that we went flying down the wind. *Magdelena* did, and was out of range before long. If God had blessed us with a handy crew and a whole lot more luck, we might have gotten away, too. As it was, we did not have either of those things. There at the end, I was just hoping that the Spaniard would chase *Magdelena* and let us alone.

It did not happen like that. I was on the quarterdeck trying to surrender when the Spaniard fired her broadside into us. It killed two or three men and knocked down the mainmast. After that, the Spanish captain accepted my surrender. I could have kissed him. You can laugh at that all you want, but a second before he did it I was certain we were all going to die in the next five minutes.

It would have been nice if I had been brought before him for some witty conversation. That was how it happened in one pirate movie I watched on TV. It was not like that for us, and I never even learned his name. We were boarded by what seemed like a hundred Spaniards and roughed up quite a bit. Then the Spanish officer, a young guy who was probably some kind of junior officer, had our hands tied behind us.

That was when Antonio yelled that he was no pirate, he had been captured on the *San Mateo* and so forth. I got close enough to tell the Spanish officer it was the truth. I told him I was the pirate captain, these were my men, and Antonio was our prisoner. I was hoping, of course, that Antonio would help us if he were free. I got smacked hard enough to knock me off my feet for my trouble, and Antonio was thrown into the hold with the rest of us.

I have had worse moments in my life, but that was a bad one. They put the hatch cover on when we were all inside and battened it down. Once it was closed, that hold was as dark as the inside of a cow. Somebody began cursing in French. He was pretty good at it and kept it up for a while before he started repeating himself. Finally I told him to shut up. My jaw still hurt, and I was not real nice about it.

"You are no longer captain! You are food for the gallows bird. We are all food for the gallows bird!"

"That's right," I said. "That's what I'm hoping to fix. If you want to hang, keep on cussing and I'll see to it as soon as possible."

He started calling me names, but he had not gotten very far with it when a woman's voice whispered, "Would you like me to put your knife in him, Chris? I have it."

"Azuka?"

"Who else?" She kissed me. "Am I still so black? Down here?"

"I never saw anything wrong with black. Cut my hands loose, will you?"

She tickled my chin. "Let me stab him for you first. It will teach him a lesson."

Jarden must have overheard us. He yelled, "Be silent, Michet!"

"Who cares what you say, gallows-food?"

I told Azuka, "I want you to kiss him on the cheek for me, and make two cuts there afterward. Deep scratches is all, because we're going to need him. A cross, okay? It doesn't have to be perfect. Can you do that? His feet are loose, and he may try to kick you."

Her voice got louder. "If he kicks I will stab him no matter what you say."

After that it was as still in that hold as I have ever heard it. Sure, there was a little chop to the sea. Maybe the timbers creaked, and you could probably hear the slap of waves on the hull sometimes if you listened for it. But everybody seemed to be holding his breath, and the silence was so thick you could feel it pressing on your face.

"I have done as you told me." Azuka was back. It seemed like an hour later. "The right cheek."

"He didn't kick you?"

"I would have killed him. He knows that."

"Or make a noise when you nicked him? I was listening for some and didn't hear any. He's got balls, that Michet. A real soldier. Now cut me loose."

My hands were numb by then, but I felt my arms move as Azuka started working on the ropes. She said, "I could cut off les couilles, if that would make you feel better."

"Nope. We're going to need them."

She stopped sawing my ropes. "Azuka saves you, Chris. Are you going to marry me?"

"Cut rope. I marry." (That was Willy.)

"I have a good offer. You must say at once. Will you marry me, Chris?"

"What about Estrellita?" The ropes seemed looser. I was trying to work my hands out.

"Marry her, too. Such men as you have many. I will not object."

Jarden said, "Free me, Azuka, and I will marry you and shoot that sponge Michet."

Azuka said, "We will be most happy together, Chris darling." She sort of moaned it, rubbing her hip against me and having the time of her life.

By that time I knew I was going to get my hands loose. I could feel the life rushing back into them. It hurt, but that was fine with me. I said, "I wish you two well, and I'm going to give you a swell present as soon as we have the ceremony. Only we need Michet. We need every man."

Michet started ordering Azuka to cut him loose right about then. She did not pay any attention, and neither did I. I was too busy rubbing my hands.

By the time my fingers worked again, she and Jarden were whispering, which made it easy to locate them. I did, slid my hand down her arm quick to locate my dagger, and took it.

"You—you rital!" I suppose she had picked that one up from Lesage, along with the rest of her French.

"That's pronounced wop," I told her. "This is my dagger and I took it back, that's all. You can be mad at me, but I'm not mad at you. I owe you a lot. Everybody here does."

That got the rest of them to begging for somebody to cut them loose, too.

She was quiet for a minute, which gave me time to start wondering what else she might have.

Jarden said, "Give me the knife. I will free my men."

"I'll do it," I told him. I found somebody and started in. It was not Michet, but I am not sure who it was. Louie the Bull, maybe.

Azuka said, "You're going to fight the Spanish?"

"Sure," I said. "How did you get down here, and how did you get my dagger?"

"You will be angry, Chris."

"Try me. I'd still be tied up if it weren't for you. Did one of the Spaniards give it to you?"

"I took it from you when you would not let me go in. I saw how some men were looking at me. You would not be with me. Neither would Paul. I left the sheath in your belt and took the knife. When the Spanish came, you struck me so that I would not cry and I hid here."

"I'm sorry I slapped you," I said.

"Sometime I will slap you. Or slap your child, the child I shall bear. How are we to get out?"

"I don't know. Jarden, are you untying somebody?"

"Aye, Captain. Is Azuka mine or yours?"

"Yours, if you want her. Have you any idea what the cargo is?"

"Chain, what I have seen of it. I had only a moment to look, you understand."

Somebody said, "It is in crates, Captain."

"Marked chain?"

"I broke one open," Jarden said. "It was chain."

Somebody growled, "We can fight with chain."

One of the others said, "We should break open more. There may be other things."

"I'm for that," I told him. Groping in the direction of his voice, I touched his face. He turned, and I put the dagger blade to work on his ropes. That dagger was pretty sharp, but the ropes were tough and tarred. Some people have said since that I am cracked on sharpening knives and cutlasses. Maybe it is true. If it is, I got cracked when I cut the *Magdelena*'s anchor cable and got darn near broken down in *Rosa*'s hold.

It was easy to say we ought to open more crates. But without tools, that was not so easy. After a few crates we found some tools, though. There were saws and hammers and even a couple of hatchets. And brackets and those iron doodads with spikes you stick candles on. It was ironware, in other words. Some of it was useful and some not.

The Spanish had battened down the aft hatch good, but the forward hatch was pretty sloppy. Three men pushing on the hatch cover got it up far enough that we could get at the ropes with saws. The problem was that the boat was on top of it, and we were afraid it would make a racket when we moved the cover. We took it slow and careful, and no one heard us—or if they did, they did not think anything was wrong. It was dark by the time we crawled through the hatch and out from under the boat, and I am pretty sure most of the Spanish prize crew was asleep.

I have never known how many there were, but there were more of them than there were of us, and they had better weapons—ours were hammers and the hatchets, except for me. Mostly I used my dagger, but toward the end I got a handspike. That is a long wooden bar with an iron tip you use for prying. On a lot of ships, handspikes double as capstan bars, too.

When the fight was over, I had the men come up to Jarden and me one at a time. I shook hands with each of them, told them how well they had fought and how much I appreciated everything they had done, and got Antonio to clean out any wounds and bandage them.

Antonio himself was next to last, because he had been busy with a couple of wounded men. I had Simoneau and Yves holding lanterns so he could see what he was doing. I shook his hand like I had everybody else's and told him he was a full member of our crew now, a made man. "If you want or need anything, if you've got any kind of problem, you come to me, capeesh? You'll get a hearing and fair treatment." I was leaning on the handspike when I said that, and to tell the truth I was just about tired enough to fall down without it.

Michet was last. There was a cross of dried blood on his cheek, and that is something I can never forget. I had thought he might give me trouble, but he had his hammer stuck into his belt where he could not get to it with his left hand. I shook hands with him like all the rest, but when I got his I held on. "It's about respect," I told him. "I'm the captain, and to be captain I've got to have respect."

I brought the handspike up and over with my left hand when I said that, and to tell the truth I do not think he even knew it was coming. The first one knocked him down. I think the second one killed him. I used both hands for it.

After that, Jarden took the feet and I took the head, and we threw him over the side. He was not what anybody would call beefy, and weighed down by the hammer in his belt he rode pretty low in the water and was out of sight before long. I would have liked to throw in the handspike, too. It had killed Michet and the Spanish officer, and I felt like it had done enough. But you cannot just pitch things you might need later when you are on a ship, and I did not.

Do I feel bad about offing Michet? Yes, I do, but not as bad as I do about certain other things. To start with he was a pirate. The Spanish would have tried him in about half an hour and hanged him five minutes afterward, and from their standpoint they would have been dead right to do it. At sea, the captain is the only law you have. Sure, Jarden was captain of the *Rosa,* but he took his orders from me.

I had been hoping the Spanish would settle Michet for me. We lost two or three men to them—I am not sure now exactly how many—but Michet was not one of them. That was just the way the dice came up, and as it turned out he died in the same fight. So what is wrong with that?

But the main thing is that I had to do it. I did not really have a choice. If we had been a regular merchant ship, I could have had him flogged and that would have been plenty. On a pirate ship you cannot get away with flogging people, or much of anything else. I have confessed to erasing Michet and I wish to God it had not been necessary, but He had plucked me out of my own time and plopped me down where He did, and if I were back on the *Rosa* again, with Michet coming up to shake hands, I would do it over again. I would have to.

Jarden and I flipped a real to see who got to sleep and who had to stand watch, and I won. I told him to wake me up if anything happened, went into the captain's cabin, and sacked out in the bunk the Spanish officer had been sleeping in. It was still warm. Maybe that should have bothered me, and maybe Michet should have. Maybe they did, but I know I was sound asleep almost before I lay down.

Jarden woke me to go on watch. He said, "I did not wish to disturb you, Captain, but there is a large ship to starboard."

"Spanish?"

He shrugged. "Who can say?"

I went up onto the quarterdeck and had a look. It was not as big as the galleon and showed no lights. That was enough to spook me or anybody, and it started bothering me that I had nothing to fight with except my dagger. Then the man at the wheel said, "She has been closing with us since I came on, Captain."

That did it. I grabbed Cicatrice and told him to find all the stuff the Spanish had taken from us. "I want my cutlass," I told him, "and any spare pistols you can round up. Give the rest back to the men who lost them."

After that, I sent men aloft to let out sail. The other ship did the same, and did it so fast I knew the watch there had not been asleep on deck.

It was quiet, too. If anybody had been yelling at those sailors, I would have heard it. Faint, sure, but it would have been there. And it was not.

There was something else that bothered me, too. I scratched my head and rubbed my eyes, but after that it still bothered me. When I ordered the watch to load the guns, they told me they were already loaded. The Spanish prize crew had done it before they went to sleep, it seemed like—loaded them, but not run them out.

I stationed men with slow matches at every gun on the starboard side, and told the watch they had to be ready to run them out any minute. Five little four-pounders that was, and one of the men located a swivel gun and stuck the swivel in the quarterdeck rail. By then the other ship was about half as far as it had been when I came on deck.

The sea was calm, with just enough wind to fill our sails. So I jumped up on the quarterdeck rail myself, next to the gun, waved, and yelled in English, "Ahoy the *Weald*! Captain Burt on deck there?"

14

Thousands of Miles

"THE SPANIARDS KNOCKED off the mainmast," I told Capt. Burt when we sat in his cabin, "and cut away the wreckage after they took the ship. All that's left is the stump. I'd say she's making two knots with the foremast and the mizzen. If the wind freshens a bit she might make two and a half."

He was whetting his dirk and gave it a couple of good whisks across the stone before he spoke. "Rig a jury mast, eh?"

"With the men we've got now, we'll be in Port Royal before it's ready."

"I've a hundred and nine aboard. Suppose I lend you a dozen?"

"If they're good seamen, sure. Why not?"

"Ever done it before, Chris?"

I shook my head.

"Pity. I have, and there can be complications. Stick with it, though, and you'll get through. Port Royal, you said?"

"Sure, that was where we were going to sell the *Rosa*."

"And this other ship of yours, the *Magdelena*? Bound for Port Royal as well, is she?"

I had to think about that one. "She was, Captain. Our idea was to sell *Rosa* and get the men some pay. Without the *Rosa* to sell . . . I don't know. I can't guess what Rombeau might do."

"Your guess'll beat mine, Chris. You know him and I don't. Will he try to retake *Rosa*?"

I considered it. "You know, he might. He might do exactly that, or try to."

Capt. Burt wiped the blade and tested the edge with his thumb. "Loyal to you?"

"I think so. Of course, if the men would elect him . . . They'll want to get the *Rosa* back, though. They were counting on the money. Some of them will have friends on board, I'm sure."

"Then they'll try. We can be sure of it from what you say. If this Rombeau won't do it, they'll vote him out and put in some chap who will." Capt. Burt stood to get a map from the cabinet at his elbow. The captain's cabin on the *Weald* was a small room by shore standards, but a big one to sailors, a low room of varnished oak with wide windows. In movies, the pirates hold their maps open by pinning them to the table with their knives. Capt. Burt and I held down the far end of his with a brass inkstand.

"Here's our present position, Chris. Here's Jamaica, there's the Spanish Main, and right here's the Yucatan Channel. They're watchin' for me there, as it happens."

"The Spanish?"

"None other. Been up to my old tricks, eh? Gulf of Campeche. That's where the money is these days, never doubt it. Gold out of Peru, eh? Up the Pacific Coast, then overland to the mint at Veracruz. Galleons to pick it up. Three at least. Split up the gold between 'em. Treasure fleet, eh? What's troublin' you?"

I pointed. "Look at this port here, Captain. Panama. They could unload here and cross where the land is so much narrower."

He chuckled. "They could, but I doubt they've been thick enough. On the other side, eh? Can you read that? I'll get you a glass."

I did not need one. "The Gulf of Mosquitoes."

"See any ports there?"

I shook my head. "No, I don't, Captain."

"'Cause there ain't any. Not a one, eh? Nothin' closer than Portobello, and it's a hellhole. If you went west of there, you'd soon come flash—no safe anchorages, and the most fever-ridden coast on earth. Not to mention the bloody mosquitoes. So the treasure ships put out from Callao and sail north to Panama, which is decent enough. The gold's loaded onto mules at Panama and sent overland to New Spain's capital—Mexico's its name—or straight to Veracruz."

Capt. Burt paused, looking up from the map; slowly and deliberately he said, "Three hundred pounds, Chris. That's a decent load for a Spanish mule. Three hundred pounds of gold. Rum quiddies, eh?"

I could not imagine that much gold. I suppose it showed.

Capt. Burt fished in a pocket of his blue coat, and dropped a bright gold coin on the table. "Here's a guinea. Ever see one before?"

I shook my head.

"Worth a bit, that is. Slap it down in an inn and they'll treat you like a gentleman. Twenty-one silver shillin's, that's what it's worth, and there's many a good man in London who don't earn a shillin' a day. How much would you say your guinea weighs?"

"It isn't mine," I said. "It's yours, Captain."

"I'm givin' it. Pick it up and get the feel of it. How much?"

I thanked him and tossed it in my hand. "It's not as heavy as a musket ball. Half that, or less."

"How much?" Capt. Burt repeated.

"Well, we get fifteen balls from a pound of lead, so they're around one ounce. That would make this a little less than half an ounce."

"Not bad." Smiling, Capt. Burt went back to his whetstone. "I've weighed a few guineas, and they're a quarter of an ounce or a trifle over. Sixteen ounces to the pound for us, eh? Won't bother with Troy. So sixty-four guineas struck from a pound of gold. Let's call it sixty."

I am not terribly good at mental math, but I am better than some people. "Six thousand guineas from each hundred pounds of gold, eighteen thousand guineas from every mule-load. How many mules?"

He shrugged. "Varies. Thirty, sometimes. Sometimes a hundred. Like a spot of sherry?"

I nodded, and he fetched a decanter and poured for both of us. "Crew's got to be paid, eh? Custom of the Coast. Ten shares for you, as captain. Think your ten would come to six thousand guineas?"

I thought about it. "Say that we had a hundred shares, with ten for me and extra shares for mates and so on."

"Ten for me, too, Chris."

"Right. But say a hundred in all. If there were thirty mules, that's nine thousand pounds of gold. One share would be ninety pounds of gold . . ."

"Go on."

I had not touched my sherry, but I swallowed. "It comes to five thousand four hundred guineas, Captain. One share comes to that."

"Buy a manor in England for that much, Chris." Capt. Burt sipped. "Bit of land with it, too, and change to the bargain. Collect your rents, put the change in the Funds. Should fetch five percent or better. Set for life, eh?"

I nodded.

"That's one share. You'd have ten, Chris. So'd I. You're from Jersey? You told me so once, if my memory's not playin' tricks."

I nodded again.

"Thought so. So's George Carteret. He's got a place in the forties. New Jersey, he calls it. A thousand guineas might take the whole colony. Wouldn't be surprised."

I felt my heart jump. It seemed like a long time before I could say, "You've been there?"

"Aye. While I was still Navy, eh? Not much there—small farms and so on. Now looky here, Chris." Capt. Burt leaned back, his hands forming a steeple. "I want that gold. So do you, and there's three ways a man might get it before it's safe in Spain." He held up his index finger. "First way. Take the galleons. With force enough it might be done."

"Not by me," I said. "Not even if I had *Magdelena* back."

"Nor by me," Capt. Burt acknowledged. "I've five besides this *Weald,* and I still couldn't do it. Nor by both of us together."

He raised his middle finger. "Second way. Take Veracruz. They coin some gold there before they ship it home, eh? All the better so. Mules come in—under heavy guard, of course—and the gold's put in the treasure house there. Minted, it goes back there. Most secure place, eh? Take out a few bars, mint 'em, put the doubloons back in the treasure house. So take Veracruz, break into the treasure house, and off with the gold before the galleons put out from Spain."

I said, "I suppose that might be workable."

Capt. Burt nodded. "I've been thinkin' 'bout it for a year now, Chris. Five hundred men might do it, if we took 'em by surprise. Trouble is, we can't. They're on to me. Strengthenin' the forts, eh? More men and more guns. Dago men-of-war patrollin' the Gulf of Campeche. So no. That's out, for a few years at least."

He raised his ring finger. It had a ring on it, a wide band of bright gold. "Third way. Take the ships after they put out from Callao. Drake sailed 'round the world, Chris. Almost a hundred years ago, that was, in the *Golden Hind*."

TIME IS GETTING short, and I have been thinking about all this and why I am writing it. I did not write anything yesterday, because of my interview with His Excellence. I had seen him before, but this was the first time I ever sat down with him and talked man-to-man. He looked older than I remembered. There was something bare and cheerless about his cluttered study, although it took me ten minutes or more to put my finger on it: there was no comfort there. The lamps were for reading and writing. The books were such as a bishop might require—no novels or travel books, no biographies that I could see, save for those of a couple of popes. The chairs were dark wood carved with the arms of the diocese, without cushions. A crucifix on the wall, but no pictures.

We shook hands well before I began these speculations, of course. He greeted me, sat, and invited me to sit as well. "I receive only good reports of you, Father."

I said, "Thank you, Bishop Scully. They must be very different from those I give myself."

"I'm sure they are. How old were you when you were ordained?"

"There were two priests in my class who were older than I, Bishop Scully. Much older. I was twenty-six. I'm twenty-eight now."

"Tempus fugit, Father. Those older classmates of yours were widowers, both of them. Men in their fifties who have lost their helpmates and nobly chosen to devote the rest of their lives to God. It's not quite the same for a man of twenty-six, is it? Or twenty-eight."

"I have no direct experience of it, Bishop Scully, but it seems to me you must be right."

"You were married, too, Father. Your wife is dead?"

I nodded, and did not say that she had surely been dead now for hundreds of years.

"All young men feel the temptations of the flesh, Father. I did myself at your age."

"They are among the least of mine, Bishop Scully."

We watched each other then, and at last I let my gaze wander the room.

"We have seven deadly sins, Father." The bishop's voice was hardly a whisper. "Lust is one of the worst, but not the worst. Pride is worse, the worst of all. No doubt you are troubled by it."

I shrugged. "No doubt I am, Bishop Scully. I am not sensible of it, but that may mean its grip is tighter."

"You're a tall, strong young man, Father. The young men at Saint Teresa's stand in awe of you. So Father Houdek reports, and I find it easy to believe. Have you no pride in that?"

"Strength is good only when it's used for good, Bishop Scully. Strong men—I've known many stronger than I am—soon learn how little strength they really have. As for my height, I've spent my nights sleeping on the floor or in beds that were too short for me. I'd be shorter if I could."

He nodded, his thumb and forefinger stroking his lower lip. "Saint Teresa's is a large parish, Father."

I nodded and said I knew it.

"A large parish, and a most difficult one. I would like to give the best priests the best parishes. Staffing is a persistent worry, and I do not have that luxury."

"I understand," I said.

"A large and difficult parish, but that is not the sole reason Father Houdek has two assistants. Two?" The bishop shook his head. "Two, when priests are so few? When so many parishes have none? I trust that you are learning from his example, Father."

I said I tried to take advantage of every educational opportunity that came my way—something of that sort.

"You have given thought, I am sure, to your conduct when you have a parish of your own."

"Not as much as I should, perhaps, Bishop Scully. That day seems very remote."

He smiled, lips tight. "Give more thought to it, Father. It may come sooner than you think."

There is so much to write, and I may have little time in which to write it. I am losing patience with this pen, wishing I could kick and whip it, like a donkey. Where are the jibs for a ballpoint pen advertising a funeral parlor? Where are its studding sails?

VERY WELL. I left Capt. Burt and returned to the *Rosa* with the men he had given me. The wind was rising, and the *Weald,* which had planned to remain in our company until dawn, was quickly lost to sight. Ships menace one another in a high wind, and night was coming on, which would make the danger worse.

So that was how it began. Capt. Burt and I had agreed that Rombeau would not come so long as the *Weald* was in sight—it looked Spanish because it had been. He loaned me a dozen good sailors, all English save for O'Leary, and we shook hands and agreed to meet at the end of September.

That night, as the *Rosa* rolled and pitched and every timber groaned, I explained as much as I thought wise to Jarden and Antonio—and to Azuka, too, because Jarden had brought her and I did not want to send her away.

"There are a couple of points that worry me," I told them. "One is Rombeau. Captain Burt thinks he'll come back once *Weald's* gone. So do I, or I think he'll try to. But Rombeau can't navigate. We need to keep a sharp lookout every moment of the day and night, and get close enough to take a good look at every sail we see."

Antonio fingered his beard. "And if the sail proves to be a Spanish warship, Captain?"

"We'll be flying the Spanish flag," I explained. "That won't bother Rombeau—he'll expect it."

"We cannot outrun them, not even with a jury mast."

"Which we do not have yet," Jarden added.

I shrugged. "We won't try to outrun them. You speak a good deal of Spanish, Antonio, and I speak good Spanish. We're the *Santa Rosa,* out of Havana. We're in trouble and we need help."

Jarden said, "What if they offer to provide it, Captain?"

"We'll accept it, of course. And thank them with tears in our eyes. But they won't. The worse our setup looks and the more help we ask for, the more they'll want to get away."

Jarden rubbed his hands. "Ask for water, Captain. Every ship needs it and no one wants to give it."

Antonio nodded. "And medicines. A physician, if they will be so good as to lend us one."

"Right," I said. "A doctor and medicine, and we'll swear we have nothing infectious on board. The more we swear, the less they'll believe us. We'll keep most of the crew below—the fewer men they see, the better."

Azuka said, "What is needed? Ask for that."

"I am," I told her. "I will, just in case they give them to us."

Antonio said, "Two things troubled you. The other?"

"We'll have to sail down the coast for thousands of miles and 'round the Horn. What if the men won't do it?"

Everybody got quiet, but I was so busy thinking myself that it did not bother me.

Finally Jarden said, "I cannot navigate either, and I have been considering what I might do, were I in Rombeau's plight. Do you wish to hear it, Captain?"

I said, "Sure, go ahead."

"Very good. I am Rombeau. I cannot navigate, but I can read. I have the logbook. In the logbook I have the last position. It is your custom, Captain, to compute the position each morning and each evening. Thus I, Rombeau, know the point at which my ship separated from this one."

Azuka looked puzzled. Antonio said, "He might guess at the direction of the gale, east or northeast. Knowing that, and the direction in which he fled the Spaniard, he might achieve something. Or might believe he might."

"I might," Jarden agreed, "but I would not know where to stop."

"True."

"I will seize a Spanish ship," Jarden told us. "A rich ship would be good luck, but any ship larger than a piragua. There will be someone who navigates. It must be so, unless he was killed in fighting. Perhaps I will put the others in the boats. Perhaps I will kill them. But him I will keep. You must guide me to this place, I will tell him. From it, you must set a course for Spain. If we find the *Rosa*, I shall free you. If we do not, your life will be forfeit."

Azuka asked, "Is the entry in your book the same as that in the other book, chéri?"

Jarden shook his head. "The final entry will have been made before we seized this ship, but it will be near it."

I said, "I remember what my last entry was. That will be better. We'll sail back there."

Antonio said, "This Rombeau will sail but slowly, if he is of sagacity."

I agreed. "Either that, or turn back and retrace the last half of his route."

Azuka asked, "Those men? They must be told?"

Jarden said, "Told what? That we're hoping to find the *Magdelena*? Yes. Of course."

I said, "About Captain Burt and the treasure fleet from Peru—the thing I was worried about telling them. I see what you mean, Azuka."

"You must sharpen their hunger, Chris. Say the gold. The galleons. Later, Veracruz. More later, the mules of Panama. We will go south along the land to be rich. Do not say how far."

I agreed, and that is what we did—or tried to do.

15

A Woman Hiding

FR. HOUDEK IS well liked here, but we get fewer at mass every Sunday. That is how it seems to me. The people like him, but do not come. This morning, I said the ten o'clock mass. Until today, I have been careful to speak out as little as possible, keeping my homilies brief and talking only about the gospel for the day (or the bazaar). Today I was brief, too, but I talked about marriage, the sacred character of it and the need for repentance. Without it there can be no forgiveness.

Where there is no repentance, forgiveness is only permission by another name. I hope I said that.

The human heart is like a bird, I said. It flutters from this place to that—then back to the first as often as not. Poets say we must follow our hearts. Anyone who reads their lives will soon see where that leads and where it ends.

The people were not smiling when mass was over. I shook their hands as

I always do, standing in the blessed winter sunshine outside the doors. I hate doing it, but it is my duty and I try to do it well. Usually someone says how hard my hand is. No one did that today.

Maybe it would have been better if they had smiled.

SOON, VERY SOON now, the communists will fall. Then I will begin the long voyage back to her.

RETURNING TO OUR old position meant sailing against the wind, and that meant tacking this way and that, in a ship without a mainmast. I would be lying if I said we gained with every tack we made. Often enough we gained nothing, and sometimes we actually lost, thrown back by the wind. Half the watch was putting up the jury mast, a poor stubby thing but the longest spar we had. It is no easy matter to tack a square-rigged ship, so we put a gaffsail on the jury mast. Tacking means sailing as close to the wind as possible, and one always wishes to sail a little closer. Another point, half a point. I prayed for both of those.

We made long tacks, of course, an hour this way and two that way. With our crew we had to, and Antonio proved his worth once and for all. Jarden and the quartermaster wanted to throw half the cargo overboard. That would have hurt more than it helped, I think. Riding deep gave the keel more bite.

We saw nothing that first day, but by the end of it the jury mast was up and the new gaffsail filling, and we had a handier crew than the one that had eaten breakfast that morning. One of the good things about a gaffsail is that the gaff can reach higher than the mast. With a short mast like ours, that is a great advantage. There are bad things, too, but that good one was plenty good enough for me just then.

Sleeping was a problem. Jarden wanted to give me the captain's cabin. I would have felt like a bully if I had taken it, and if I had shared it with him he would have wanted to give me the bunk while he slept on the floor with Azuka. I ended up sleeping on the quarterdeck aft of the wheel, saying I was worried that the jury mast would not hold in a blow, and that we might pass the *Magdelena* in the dark. None of it was true, although the last came near it.

In one way my sleeping on deck like that was good, but it was bad in another. When I finally stretched out on my folded canvas, I never guessed that it was the beginning of a night I would never forget. Each night in the rectory, when I have brushed my teeth and gotten into my pajamas, I cannot help remembering that one. No other night of my life has been quite like it. Let me start with the good.

The night sky was as clear as crystal, and there was no moon. I looked out into the vast universe, saluting suns and families of suns far away, and watched the planets creep among them—bloody Mars, and Venus radiant and pure in her robe of cloud. For the first time in my life I really understood that I rode a planet like those, that Earth and I were swinging through the dark vault even when we smiled in the sunlight. All my life I had thought of Heaven as a vague place far away, a mysterious land outside the universe where God sits a golden throne. That night I realized that Heaven is not far away at all—that Heaven is wherever God is, and that God is everywhere. That every human soul is His throne room.

Hell is right here, too.

The artists of the Middle Ages painted allegories, we say. What really happened was that they saw more clearly than we do, and painted what they saw—angels and devils, beasts, and half-human monsters like me.

How long did I lie there staring up at the stars? It must have been some time, since I distinctly recall their movement across the sky. I knew then that the blessed dead see God face-to-face, and felt that I, too, had seen some small part of what they saw. It was glorious, and beyond my poor powers of description. Eventually I slept.

A woman was caressing me when I woke, and I was naked, or seemed naked, from the waist down. I thought then that I was wrong, that Novia had not been left behind on the *Magdelena*, that she was here with me on this ship. How had I come to make such a foolish mistake? Had I dreamed that she had been left behind? She kissed me and stretched her bare body on mine, and did certain other things it would be wrong for me to describe here or anywhere. It felt good. I would be lying if I said that it did not. There was clean desire in it, and love, too. Real love.

Here at the Youth Center, I have heard boys say that there is good sex and bad sex, but that even bad sex is pretty good. I have had bad sex and they are wrong. They speak as they do because they think it sounds cool. They will change their minds about how it sounds when they get older. I have had bad sex, as I said, but I had none that night.

When I really woke at last, I sat up—and lay down again at once. "Azuka," I whispered, "what are you up to? Jarden will kill us."

She giggled. "He sleeps, Chris. I tired him very, very big."

"Me, too."

"Not nearly so grand as Jarden. Nor will he kill you. I have taken your measure and his. He could not do it and would not try. Mzwilili will not care. He is honored."

So there were three of us. It took me a second or so to digest that.

"You must not tell your Novia. She will be angry with me. Tell her too much, if you enjoy this telling." Azuka giggled again. "You lie to make her jealous. That is what Novia shall think. I must be with when you tell, Chris." She kissed me. "I wish to hear everything."

"If I had any guts at all, I'd throw you over the railing." I started to stand up and discovered that my pants were still around one ankle.

"You will not do that."

I knew she was right. I liked her too much.

Okay, I loved her. Besides, she had saved us from hanging. I made her go back to Jarden, and made her promise to be quiet about it.

"I will not wake him," she whispered. "Too much you have tired me, Chris."

After that I went forward to relieve myself. The watch was snoring through the making tack, lying on deck like so many dead men. When I came back, I had a long talk with the man at the wheel. When I felt sure he would keep his mouth shut, I lay back down again and slept until the sun woke me.

I GUESS I ought to say here that *Magdelena* was lying alongside the next morning, but she was not. I know we did not sight her that day. It may have been the day after, but I cannot be sure.

When we did, she had a Spanish capture with her. That was the *Castillo Blanco,* but you could not buy hamburgers on her. Jokes aside, the *Castillo Blanco* was a galley, and maybe the most beautiful ship I ever saw, low, slick, and sleek, with two fore-and-aft masts and a long bowsprit that carried two square spirit sails. Before I go any further with this, I ought to say that she was not like the kind of galley people think of today when they hear the word, a sort of prison ship with galley slaves chained to the oars. She had oarlocks in the rails and the long oars we call sweeps, but the crew pulled them, not slaves, and although they could be very, very handy in a dead calm, they did not get used a whole lot. I had already fallen in love with *Magdelena*. You have probably seen that, if you have actually read this far. With *Castillo Blanco* it was different. I did not really fall hard for the *Magdelena* until we had her bottom clean and the jib up. With *Castillo Blanco* it was love at first sight.

Jarden launched the boat Antonio had come in, and had me rowed over to *Magdelena*. Azuka was left behind on the *Rosa*. Rombeau and Novia were waiting for me as I came over the side of the *Magdelena*. We set a course for Port Royal and told Jarden to follow us. And it was like coming home.

THIS IS PRETTY stupid, I know, but I am going to do it anyway. For the past two days I have been trying to talk myself out of telling what Rombeau said and what I said, what Novia said, how we hugged and kissed and held hands, and all that. I have been trying, but I cannot do it. Those things are too important to me. If I do not write about the things that were important to me, I cannot write at all.

The weather was great. There was a little breeze to cool us off, and the sun was low in the west. That sunset had FAIR WEATHER written all over it. The stormy season was coming, but there were not any storms yet. Or if there were, they were nowhere near us. I got one of the men to carry a chair up for Novia. The rest of us stood, or sat on the railing.

But before I tell about that—the whole crew was glad to see me, and it was something I will never forget. They came crowding around when I came up on board, and we shook hands and hugged each other and all that. I had never made a special effort to learn everybody's name, but I found out I had learned practically all of them. Mostly it was just the last name, which was what we used mainly. Sometimes it was the first name or a nickname, but I had some kind of a name for just about everybody.

Then Novia came pushing through, and we hugged and kissed for about a year, and she gave me that wonderful smile. A long time after that Rombeau got me aft and had Dubec chase the crew back where they were supposed to be, although the mizzen men were close enough to hear a lot and the man at the wheel must have heard everything.

I said, "You got someone to navigate for you, someone off that beautiful white galley. Who is it?"

Rombeau's eyes got a little wider—which I enjoyed, I admit. "How did you know, Captain?"

"It made sense, that's all. I would have done the same thing. Who is it?"

"The captain. He and his ship were all we got, but we did get him. His name is Ojeda." Rombeau paused. "He was reluctant at first. I was able to persuade him. He—all the prisoners are below, in chains. You wish to speak to him?"

I did, and we sent one of Dubec's men to fetch him. He was smaller than I expected, and stood very straight. His beard and mustache must have looked neat and cool when he stood on his own little quarterdeck. There on the afterdeck of the *Magdelena* they were just sad.

I had the idea that it might be good not to let him know I spoke Spanish. Rombeau had surely been speaking French to him, so that was what I did, too. "You were master of the *Castillo Blanco*? What are you doing here?"

He nodded. His French was really bad, and pretty often he had to make signs. I will not give all that. "We could not resist" was what he meant. "Six little guns I have. He swear our lives we have."

"I see. Was the promise kept? All of you are still alive?"

He nodded.

"How many?"

"Owner and his wife. Treated much badly, we are. Alvarez. Three seamen."

Rombeau touched my arm when Ojeda said that, and I knew something was up. I said, "Who is Alvarez?"

Ojeda was at a loss for words. At last he said, "Me oficial, Señor. He help me."

"Your mate."

He nodded, looking relieved. "Sí."

"It doesn't seem like much of a crew for such a fine ship."

He shrugged. It meant, "I am not the owner."

Rombeau had been holding the prisoners below. I called Menton over and told him to take Ojeda to the bow and keep him there. "Don't beat him unless he gives you trouble," I said. "Don't talk to him, and don't let him talk to anybody."

Rombeau chuckled when they had gone. "They cannot plot, Captain. Menton has no Spanish and the other no French."

"Does Ojeda not know any, or just pretend he doesn't?" I asked. Rombeau had no answer for that, so he changed the subject. "There is a woman hiding on board the *Castillo Blanco*. Did he tell you? I could not understand all he said."

"He said the owner and his wife, but the way he said it, it sounded like the wife was down in the hold."

"Another woman. Perhaps a man, too."

"You haven't been able to find them?"

Rombeau shook his head. "Not yet."

Novia said, "A woman only, Crisóforo. No man."

"It would be pretty hard to hide on a ship," I told them, "and that one's not nearly as big as this one."

"Yet she is there," Rombeau insisted.

Naturally I quizzed them, and here is what it came down to: there were two nice cabins on the *Castillo Blanco* and Ojeda had not been living in either one. One had been for the owner and his wife. A woman had been living in the other one. A woman's clothing was scattered around in there, there was some jewelry not in the jewelry box, and so forth. Powder and rouge left open. There was a man's baggage in there, too, but all that had been neatly stowed away.

I asked Novia why she had said there was only a woman.

"Because that captain protect her. He will lie to you. He will say there is no woman. It is most dangerous for him, my heart, and he know it. But he will do it, because she has no protector. You are not Spanish nor is Rombeau, thus you do not understand. I am Spanish and I comprehend him. There is the woman, alone, hiding on his ship. Or he think this."

16

The Accursed Galley

WE NEEDED TO talk to the owner and his wife, only not together. The question was, which one first? We argued about it, Rombeau and I saying the owner, Novia the wife. Novia was outvoted, so I had a man bring the owner up.

His hands were chained. So were his feet, and there was a chain running between them. He bowed just the same. It was pretty good, and without the chains would probably have been beautiful. "I am Don José de Santiago, Monsieur. I take it you are master of the third ship that joins us?"

I shook my head. "I'm captain of this one. Rombeau here is my first mate. You've talked to him?"

"Alas, Captain, only briefly. I am eager to serve him, but he gives me no opportunity."

"He's a wise man," I said.

Rombeau chuckled.

I said, "You have money hidden on your ship, Don José. Perhaps other things. You must show us your hiding place. If you do not . . ." I raised my shoulders and let them drop.

"We were promised our lives, Monsieur. Are you not a man of honor?"

"I am," I told him. "Please permit me to explain the situation. First, it was not I but this man Rombeau who gave you his word. No doubt he will keep it. I did not give mine and am not bound."

"Monsieur—"

"Second, my own eyes have eyelids." I blinked to show what I meant. "I've never been without eyelids, but I'd think somebody who had none might like dying a lot better."

I paused, trying to make it impressive. "You will be in a position to settle the matter for us, Don José. And third," I drew a pistol and knocked him flat with the long iron barrel. I hit him hard, but not hard enough to kill him.

Novia asked, "What make you think he has hidden money?"

"I know he has," I told her. "I hope he's not a relative of yours."

"I have never see him, Crisóforo, and it would not matter if he were my brother. But how do you know?"

I turned to Rombeau. "What was he doing here? Did he say? Why did he leave Spain?"

"Like us." Rombeau smiled a little sadly. "He has come to make his fortune, he says. He is known to the governor."

"He owns that white ship, and he has come to make his fortune?"

"A greater fortune. So he says."

Novia said, "By smiling and bowing? I think not."

"I tell you what he says," Rombeau declared. "I did not say I believed it."

"Once I had to kill time in Veracruz," I told them, "and I heard a few things. Men with money come to New Spain pretty often. Land is cheaper than dirt, and they buy a lot of it. They build a big house, and the people who used to own that land work it for them."

I kicked the Spaniard. "Get up, Don José. You're not fooling anybody. Stand up."

He did, and I said, "If you give us the money, there won't be any reason to do anything to you, capeesh? We'll put you ashore someplace and go away, and you'll be all right."

"I am poor now, Monsieur. What little I had, this man took."

"You want me to fight with Rombeau. That's smart, but it's not going to happen." It was getting pretty dark by then, and I was thinking about building a fire in a pan or something so we could heat irons in it. Brother Ignacio had branded the new calves at the monastery, and I knew how impressive a red-hot iron looks after vespers.

Novia said, "Who was on your ship when you put out, Monsieur de Santiago? We must have the names."

Hearing her French, he switched to Spanish right away and bowed to her. He must have been getting a pretty good knot on his head by then, and the way he was chained up he could not reach it. He bowed just the same. It got me to wondering whether I would have his guts in Hell. Maybe when I first checked in, I decided.

"You know me, Señora. If you would honor me . . ."

"I will not," Novia told him. "The names!"

"As you wish." (He told us about his wife, but I do not remember all his wife's names. We called her Pilar.) "My captain is Ojeda. His first name is Carlos. Our crew," he made a small, polite noise, "do not matter. Ask Captain Ojeda. He will tell you, I am certain."

I translated for Rombeau and told de Santiago to speak French.

Rombeau said, "There were also two passengers, a man and a woman. They had a fine cabin. I have been in it."

De Santiago sighed. "Very well. You have found me out. Their families— it would be better, you understand, if they did not know. Much better."

Novia stood up to whisper in my ear. "This will be a new lie."

I nodded, trying not to make it obvious.

"My friend Señor Guzman was to travel with me. With him, his wife—"

I had felt Novia stiffen and relax, and did not hear the rest of it.

Rombeau said, "They were on board when you took the sea?"

Sadly, De Santiago nodded. "They were, Monsieur."

"In that case, you lied to us," Rombeau sounded angry, and I did not think he was faking it.

"I did, for their families' sake. You see, Monsieur, my old friend Jaime had lost his fortune. When I say so, you will think he gambled. You will be right. He had owned shares in ships, a dozen perhaps. Those he sold, and had built and fitted out a ship of his own, a fine ship. He provided a good captain and an ample crew, put his own brother on it to trade for him, and sent it to Brunei to trade among the Islands of King Philip. His so-fine ship never returned."

De Santiago sighed. "It destroyed him, that so-fine ship. He was a broken man. His house—all that he had—went to pay his debts. I persuaded him to accompany me. In New Spain, I said, you may recoup your fortune. Many a man of less ability has returned rich. He agreed."

"Get on with it," Novia said. "You squander our hours with your lies."

"If you were a man," de Santiago told her, "I should meet you sword to sword. As it is, Señora . . ." He smiled. "So lovely a lady may speak as she will. I am honored by the soiled shoes you scrape upon my honor. This man with his pistols, he is your husband?"

"He is," Novia said. (We had planned to marry, so it was not much of a lie.)

De Santiago turned to me and bowed. "You will defend your wife's honor, Señor?"

I said, "Sure."

"At some more convenient time, my seconds will wait upon your own."

I shook my head. "Now. Here. Hey, Chin! Bring Ojeda back."

It took a while to get the chains off de Santiago. While they were doing that, I borrowed a cutlass for him and explained to Ojeda that his boss and I had agreed to fight, and that he was there as a witness.

"You do not lie," Novia told de Santiago. (I could see how much it cost her.) "I am the liar. I tell many, many lies. Forgive me! I implore it!"

His smile might have coaxed a dead woman from the grave. "You love your husband, Señora."

"I adore him," she said, and indicated me. It makes me feel good, even now, when I remember it.

"Thus you must wish his honor unblemished, as I wish my own. They have been sullied by a female tongue. I do not say whose. We will cleanse both his and mine."

It was nearly dark by then, and I did not realize that Novia was crying until I heard her sob. "These men . . ." Her voice shook. "These pirates. They love him. All of them. If you kill him they will kill you."

"My father desired to die with a sword in his hand," de Santiago told her. "San Martín doubtless interceded for him as he asked, but God awaited the proper time. What was denied the father is granted his son this night. Do your pirates think us cowards, Señora? We Spanish? They will learn otherwise."

If you ever read this, you will already have guessed what I wanted to do. I wanted to throw something at de Santiago the way I had at Yancy. Sure I wanted to, but there were a couple of things wrong with it that night. The first one was that I did not have anything to throw. The second one was that I did not know how Rombeau and the crew would take it. Everybody was watching by that time. Rombeau and Dubec chased anybody who tried to get too close, but there were men in the rigging and a lot of others crowding aft. I would like to say I breathed a prayer and decided to take my chances, but the truth is I ran out of time.

De Santiago knew more about sword-fighting than I did, and to be honest anybody who knew anything about it knew more than I did. But I knew more about just plain fighting than he did, I was younger and probably stronger, and I had a longer reach.

There was more, and I might as well write that, too. It had probably been years since he had fought with a sword or even practiced with one, and the swords he was used to were longer and had straight blades. Besides, it was dark and neither of us could see the other's blade very well. My night vision may have been a little better, too. I do not know.

Another thing I ought to say is that it did not last anywhere near as long as the sword fights on TV. Nobody jumped up on a table or swung from a rope or any of that. He tried to stab me the way I had stabbed Yancy. I got out of the way and cut at his arm. I remember those. Pretty soon we banged together. He grabbed the blade of my cutlass with his free hand, not expecting it to be as sharp as it was. I slugged him in the belly with my left, giving it all I had and trying to punch through him.

I do not think that punch traveled more than six or eight inches, but he doubled over. I banged him in the head with the brass guard of my cutlass. He still did not go down, so I kicked his legs out from under him.

That was when Rombeau surprised me. He grabbed the cutlass out of de Santiago's hand, and when de Santiago tried to stand up he had the points of both of them in his face.

"You had better concede, Don José." I said it in Spanish and tried to make it as polite as I could. "I'd hate to kill such a brave man, so give up and I'll get somebody to bandage your hand."

After a second or so, he nodded. "I am vanquished, Señor Capitán. What would you have me do?"

Novia said, "Tell us where the woman is," and I seconded her.

It was hard, but he managed to get up. "In the sea. Will you hear me out now, Señora?"

Novia did not answer and Rombeau was yelling for someone to stop the bleeding, so I told de Santiago to go ahead.

"It was our custom to breakfast together, Señor and Señora Guzman, and my wife and I. In fine weather, the little table would be carried from our cabin and placed on deck. You understand, I feel certain. One morning Señor Guzman was not to be found. I had the ship searched. He—"

Novia muttered. "That ship is searched very much."

De Santiago bowed to her again. "As you say, Señora. It is searched, but little is discovered. This was ten days, perhaps, from Coruña. He had thrown himself into the sea. There was no other explanation." De Santiago sighed. "His wife followed him two days ago. I have concealed this matter from my own wife. Señor Guzman's suicide was a great and terrible shock to her. She was devastated. Another suicide . . ." He let it trail away. "I have given her to think that Señora Guzman keeps to her cabin now, that she is indisposed. You understand, I am sure."

What I understood was that I was the biggest fool ever to have had Menton bring Ojeda forward. I had wanted him to see it was a fair fight. Now he had heard his boss's story, and he would probably stick with it. We got the chains put back on de Santiago and had Menton take both of them forward again.

That was when the watch changed, as close as I can remember. Then, or about then. Anyway we stood around and talked it over, Rombeau, Novia, and I. He thought it might be true. Novia said it was a pack of lies, and there had never been a Mr. and Mrs. Guzman on the ship at all—that this cabin had belonged to some other woman, and she was hiding on the *Castillo Blanco* this minute.

"Whoever she is," Rombeau said, "he would rather die than hand her over."

I pointed out that de Santiago was not dead.

"Well, Captain, he thought he was going to die."

Novia shook her head. "He thought he would kill Crisóforo. After that, who could say?"

"You understand him, too."

"You may be sure I do," Novia told Rombeau. "What I do not understand is his reason for sheltering the woman. He is not a man of the type of Ojeda. Why does he do it?"

It hit me when she said it, but I tried to pretend I had known it all along and I think I must have fooled them both. I said, "It's her hiding place. He knows where she's hiding, and that's where he's hidden the money."

They looked at me like Saint John looking at the angel on Patmos, and it felt wonderful. I wanted to say that I too was just a servant of the Lord's. It would have been the truth, but I did not.

Finally Rombeau said, "I cannot see through bricks. It is good that we have among us a man who does."

Novia touched my arm. "You comprehend all this, mi corazón?"

"I think so."

"He conceals his money in this very secret place, yet this woman knows of it, for she conceals herself there?"

"It's a little room," I told her. "Probably just big enough for two people to lie down in."

Rombeau spat. "I am still in the dark, Captain."

"I am not," Novia told him. She laughed, and just hearing her laugh made me feel wonderful all over again. "Her husband is dead. He consoles the widow."

"But his wife is on board." Rombeau rubbed his chin. "I am a donkey."

"You have not been married, I think. Crisóforo, should we go to the white ship to look?"

"It's dark," I said. "Finding her will be a lot easier by daylight. It'll be easier to go from this ship to that one, too. Let's see what the wife knows."

We had Pilar brought up after that. She was crying, and kept on crying even when we had the chains taken off her wrists. I got Novia to hug her and so on, but it took a while to get her quieted down.

"Your husband is still alive," Novia told her. "I swear it. So are you. If you tell us everything we ask, there will come a day when you are home once more, telling your friends of your capture by pirates."

Pilar nodded and tried to smile. It was full dark by then, but somebody had lit the stern lanterns and I could see her pretty well. She was years past her best, and she had been through a lot. Even making allowances for all that, I could see she had never been a treat. If de Santiago had married her for her money, I hoped he had gotten his money's worth.

"There was a woman besides yourself on your husband's ship," Novia began. "What was her name?"

Pilar nodded. "Señora Guzman."

"A younger woman, your husband said." Novia smiled. "No doubt she looked to you for wise counsel."

"Oh, yes." Pilar nodded vigorously.

"It is strange to me that a woman would journey so far alone."

"You are kind, Señora, but she was not alone. Señor Guzman accompanied her when she set out."

I said, "This is one of the people down there? Maybe I should see him."

"He is dead, Señor. Many are dead."

Rombeau touched my elbow, and I translated for him. He asked me to ask her if there was disease on board, and I did.

That started her crying again. Finally she whispered to Novia, and Novia said in French, "There is something that kills. A curse."

Rombau and I just stared at each other.

They whispered some more, and Novia said, "I have promised that she and her husband will be permitted to remain on this ship for the present."

I said, "Sure. Tell her she's got to pull herself together." I can be terribly, terribly dumb, particularly about women. But I finally had the sense to tell Rombeau we needed another chair, a bottle of wine, and a glass. Sitting down, with Novia patting her shoulder and a glass of medium-good wine under her stomacher, Pilar dried her tears and got pretty chatty. Señor Guzman had been the first to die, not long after they had left Spain. She did not know how long. A few days. The rest had been sailors. Sometimes they disappeared like Señor Guzman. Sometimes they were found dead. Her husband had not permitted her to view the bodies, and she did not know whether they had been stabbed or shot.

She leaned toward Novia confidentially. "They were frightened to death, Señora. That is what I think. Some so frightened they died, some leaped overboard rather than face the ghost. Their expressions were most horrible."

Naturally I wanted to know how she knew that, if she had not been allowed to see them.

"He told me, Señor. José told me. He saw them all. Their faces were hideous, he said."

"Only not Señor Guzman, right? He didn't see him?"

"No, Señor. He saw none of those who leaped into the sea, only those whose bodies we found."

I said, "But he must have been very worried about Señor Guzman, wasn't he? Señor Guzman was a close friend?"

"No, no! Only a friend of a friend. I never saw either of them until the day before we sailed. He was a tall, handsome man, Señor. Very strong. Muy macho. It frightened him to death even so. From this you conceive how much I feared it."

Rombeau said, "I'm surprised that Don José let him and his wife travel on his ship, a penniless couple he hardly knew."

When Novia had translated, Pilar said, "Oh, no, Señor! The Guzmans were not penniless. Far from it! They had very much gold. My husband desired to form a partnership with Señor Guzman in New Spain."

Rombeau's ears pricked up when Novia translated that.

Mine had pricked up already. We wanted to know who had that gold now.

"Señora Guzman, of course, Señors. He is dead, so his gold is hers."

We gave Pilar another glass of wine, chained her hands again, and sent her forward with the two men. After that I plumped myself down in her chair, and Novia, Rombeau, and I looked at each other.

"That liar of a shipowner told us Guzman was ruined," Rombeau said. "He will pay for that!"

I nodded. "He did, and he will. He's got guts, just the same, and you've got to give him credit for them. He wanted his stash and Guzman's, too, and he was willing to fight for them."

"Already he has lost them, Crisóforo." Novia was thinking so hard she sounded as if she were talking to herself instead of me.

"Not the way he sees it. Rombeau's promised they won't be killed. That sounds like we're going to let them go eventually. Put them ashore someplace or send them off in a boat. After that we'd probably sell the *Castillo Blanco,* or so he thought. He has friends and business connections, and he might be able to find her and buy her before the new owner finds the money."

"Or the woman will save the gold for him, perhaps." Novia went to the rail to look at the white bulk of the *Castillo Blanco,* a quarter mile away and glowing in the moonlight. "You will not sell her?"

"I don't know. I want to look her over, and I want to find that money." I went to the taffrail, too, and stood there beside Novia with my arm around her waist, a waist no bigger than a child's. Ten dozen things were swirling around in my mind then, and I could not write them all down here if I wanted to.

She leaned against me, just a little. She was wearing one of the calico gowns she and Azuka had made, and there was perfume in her hair. "Do not sell her, Crisóforo." It was a whisper.

"I won't," I promised. "Not if she's half as fast as she looks." I do not believe either of us were thinking of Pilar's ghost, monster, or whatever it was just then.

17

God Has Punished Me

FR. PHIL AND I went for a walk this morning. It was the first time we have ever done that, and was probably the last. At least one priest is supposed to be at the rectory every minute of the day and night in case someone is at the point of death or in urgent need of confession. Fr. Houdek is usually somewhere else, so Fr. Phil and I rarely have a chance to go out together.

Today was different, because Fr. Ed Cole has come to take collections for the missions. He said he planned to spend the rest of the morning reading, so off we went, a couple of young priests on a sunny Monday-morning stroll.

While we walked, we talked about a good many things. Fr. Phil is eager to get a parish of his own, but thinks it will be years. I know I may get one in the next few weeks, and am not at all eager—which is not what I said to Fr. Phil.

One of the things we talked about (maybe the only important thing we talked about) was what it means to be a priest. He is focused on the priest as leader of a little community of believers. That is what he wants from his priesthood, though he did not put it like that. I am more focused on the sacred nature of the calling. "After all," I said, "a priest living alone on a desert island far away remains a priest. Does God think less of him because he has forsaken the world of men for God?"

"You ought to say, the world of people," Fr. Phil told me.

I have used the word *importance,* but none of this was important at all. The subject is certainly important, but we had nothing of importance to say about it. And we were both right, and both quite willing to concede that both of us were right. If Fr. Houdek had been with us, he would have focused on something else, I am sure, though I am not sure what it would be. Raising money for a new school, or administering the sacraments, or any of a dozen other things.

One thing I am sure of, now that I have had a chance to think our conversation over, it is that the thing we should focus on depends on where we are. My priest on a desert island is not in a parish. Fr. Phil's priest in a parish is not alone on an island. Fr. Luis was in a third place, and so on.

I started writing about this because of what happened at the end. Fr. Phil said something I ought to have said, and felt something I ought to have felt. We were out of character (as an actor would say), both of us. But life is not a TV series, and this was a salutary reminder of it.

We were returning to the rectory when Fr. Phil stopped and pointed to the spire of the church, raising its shining gilt cross to the clear blue sky. "Look at that, Chris! Isn't it inspiring? Every time I see it, I want to cheer."

I did not feel that way. I knew I should have, but I did not. Still, there was a little tickle of memory there for me, and I knew there had been a time when I had felt like that about something. It took me hours to recall what it was. Eventually I realized that it had hit me so hard because I am at that point in this private and probably worthless chronicle—in this, the true story about me that I tell myself each evening at the hour when all or most of the kids have gone home from the Youth Center and we are about to close. It meant a great deal to me then, as it still does. It did not speak in words, however, and I know that no words of mine can make anybody—no, not even this man in black who writes it—feel what I felt then.

When Novia and I went aboard the *Castillo Blanco,* we did not set out to look for the hidden woman or the hidden gold straight off. My first concern had to be for the ship itself—how well Bouton had been handling her, and how well she handled.

He was full of praise for her, though he had less for the crew Rombeau had given him.

"You don't have a pistol," I said.

"Mine are in my cabin, Captain. I did not feel one was necessary."

"You're right. You need two. Two at least. Go to your cabin and get them. Three would be better."

When he had gone Novia said, "I have mine, Crisóforo," and I told her I hoped she would not have to use them.

"First we'll explain things to them," I told Bouton when he came back with his pistols. "If we do it right, we won't have to worry about their ganging up on us. If you see anybody goofing off, smack his ass with the flat of your cutlass. If anybody hits you or pulls a knife—or if anybody even tries it—kill him. I'll be with you, and I expect you to be with me. We kill him quick, throw him over the side, and get them back to it. Capeesh? We don't give them time to talk it over."

He got the watch up to the quarterdeck rail for me. This is more or less what I said, only I said it in my second-rate French:

"Friends, we're on our way to Port Royal to sell the *Rosa* and her cargo. When we do there will be plenty of money for everybody."

Some of them cheered.

"We're not going to sell this ship, though. She's fast, and we're going to make her faster. Handled right, she'll bring us ten times more than she'd fetch at auction. The thing is, she's got to be handled right. We can't slug it out with a Spanish galleon, not even with the *Magdelena* doing most of the fighting. So we've got to be able to run, and we've got to be able to catch. Anybody want to argue with that?"

Nobody did.

"Fine. We're going to put her through some maneuvers now. Me and Bouton are going to be jumping around yelling at you, trying to get everything better and faster. If you don't like that, I don't blame you. I've been yelled at a lot, and I never liked it for shit. But those officers who yelled at me were trying to save me from drowning. If the ship wasn't handled right and fast, we were all going to drown. That's true here on the *Castillo Blanco*, too. We handle it right or we drown. Or hang. I'm a pirate, so I've got a noose around my neck right now. You've got a noose around yours, too, every man of you. Feel it?

"Stations now! Stations, everybody!"

After that we tacked, wore ship, and so on. We took in canvas, and we let canvas out. At first we had to yell at the men to get down when she gybed, but they caught on faster than I expected. We kept them at it until the watch was over, then we went to it with the next watch while they stayed out of the way and jeered. One of the good things was that we did not have to kill anybody.

Another good thing was that I took the wheel for the last hour or so of that second watch. I wanted to see how she answered her helm, and she drove like a sports car. What a ship! I had been shouting out the maneuvers, *stand by to go about* and all that. Finally I called, "Mister Bouton! Run up the black flag!"

Although he was a big, solid man, he was back up on the quarterdeck and into the signal chest like a boy, and had the flag climbing its halyard almost before I caught my breath. We had a good breeze by then, and I stood there at the wheel looking up at that flag snapping at the masthead while the whole crew cheered. I was as happy right then as I have ever been in my life.

We ate at eight bells, Bouton, Novia, and me messing together at the little table Don José had talked about. It was a lot better food than Novia and I had been getting, and we enjoyed it. There is nothing like warm sunshine, salt air, and a stiff breeze to give you an appetite.

Looking at all that good food, I happened to think of the fat woman back in Spain who had told me to take a walk. I asked Novia whether she had been a good cook and easy to work with. Novia said no and no, but did not want to talk about her. I would not mention it here if it had not been for what happened that night.

After dinner, Bouton and I went down for a look in the sail locker. There were studding sails for every sail on the ship, sailmaker's supplies, and a lot of spare canvas. Everything was new. As I said, I had already fallen for that ship, and just looking at her stuff made me feel good. When I went back up on deck, I got a couple of men started on a jib for one of the forestays.

Maybe here I should explain that both masts were raked. That means the foremast slanted forward and the main backward, so their tops were farther apart than their bases. Raking the masts like that meant that each could carry more sail, and that the main was less liable to kill the wind for the fore with a following breeze. It also meant that there was more rigging and more complicated rigging, and things were more likely to go wrong with it. The foremast had a stay running to the top of the lower mast and another running to the top of the topmast. We bent that first jib sail on the fore topmast stay.

After that, I took the keys to the cabins and let Bouton drill the men at the guns while we searched. The first place we looked was the cabins that had belonged to de Santiago and his wife, and Guzman and his. It seemed to me that those were the most likely places for them to have hidden their money, where they could keep an eye on it.

I know I have written before about the smallness of the cabins on ships. These were smaller than that. There are rich people with walk-in closets that are bigger than those two little cabins under the quarterdeck. I had to walk bent way over in them. Novia could stand up straight, but it always looked to me like the top of her comb was going to hit the deck beams.

There were two doors, both locked and very small and narrow, down a few steps from the main deck. One went straight into the tiny cabin that had been the Guzmans'. The other went into a hall a few steps long that was so tight my shoulders rubbed both walls. It led into the back cabin, the one that had been the de Santiagos'. That cabin was a shade bigger and had two windows. (The Guzmans' cabin only had one.) When she saw it, Novia said very firmly, "This is where we sleep, Crisóforo."

I said, "Yeah, sure," and sat down, which was a big relief after all the bending over. The little table was in that cabin, with two chairs, chests, a cabinet, and two tiny little bunks. The Guzmans' cabin had not had anything beyond bunks, a matching cabinet, and four chests, and it had been crowded just with those. "When we get to Port Royal," I told Novia, "I'm going to have that wall torn out and make one cabin for us back here."

"One door, too, Crisóforo."

"Right. One door, twice as wide as those two little ones. They must go crazy getting this table out of here."

"It folds." She showed me how, and while I did it myself she went back to looking up between the deck beams. Finally I asked what she was looking for.

"A box. A wooden box for the money and fit between the beams. It is dark up there in the spaces, no? A box the same color, not so deep as the beams. Open it, and the money is in a bag so it will not scatter. That is what I would do."

"Okay," I said, "but Señora Guzman couldn't hide up there."

"We say there is a woman. I say it, too. What if we are wrong? Suppose there is not a woman?"

"Suppose there's no box, Novia?"

"You are not helping. If there is no box, the money is elsewhere. We must burn the feet of Don José." She got up to feel in a corner. "You say the woman hides where the money is. Why a hiding place so large?"

"So a lot could be hidden there, I guess. Silver bars, maybe. Or silver and good dinnerware. Something like that."

Novia kissed me. "I love you, mi corazón, but you are wrong. He would put such things in a chest."

"Then let's look in those chests," I said. We did, and found a lot of clothes and a little jewelry. After that we looked in the bunks. There was a cabinet on the blank wall between the two cabins, high and wide but very shallow, a place where you could hang a few clothes out of sight, and maybe put a spare pair of shoes.

"Señora Guzman left hers out for everyone to see." Novia was holding up a necklace. "So were we told. Did you see it?"

I shook my head.

"Nor I. One of your buccaneers took it, perhaps."

I promised to ask Bouton.

If I were to detail all the places on that ship we searched, I would be sure to leave some out. Let me just say that we searched every place we could think of, and looked in a lot of them twice. We found no woman and no money.

We did not find a ghost, a curse, or a monster, either.

The wind died toward evening, and we held a little meeting in the captain's cabin of the *Magdelena*—Bouton, Rombeau, Novia, and me. I explained that I was going to keep the *Castillo Blanco* as a second ship for us, arming her with bigger guns and more of them at Port Royal and making a few other changes. Rombeau was captain of the *Magdelena* now, and Bouton first mate of the *Castillo Blanco*. I was going to be captain of the *Castillo Blanco,* at least until we found the woman and the money, and maybe after that.

When everything was settled, we ate, drank some wine, and sat around yarning. Novia gave Rombeau and Bouton a little Spanish lesson, and we taught them a Spanish song.

So it was way dark when we collected our sea chests, got into the tender again, and started back to the *Castillo Blanco*. The sea was glassy by then, and you felt you could have touched the stars with the boat pole. Bouton took the tiller, and Novia and I sat in front of him with our arms around each other.

Back on board, we said hello to Boucher, who was being officer on, and went down to our cabin for serious kissing. We were undressing when it hit me, and I froze.

"What is it, Crisóforo? You have thought of something."

Maybe I should have told Novia everything right then, but I was not sure enough to do it. What I said was "Right. I'd meant to ask Bouton about the jewelry, the stuff Señora Guzman left out. Only I forgot."

"He is asleep now, perhaps."

"Yeah. But Boucher might know."

I pulled my pants back on, told her to get back into her dress, and stuck my head out the window. "Boucher! Come down here when you've got a minute. Bring a lantern."

By the time I had run my fingers through my hair and rubbed some of Novia's cosmetics off my face, there was a knock at the door. I opened it expecting Boucher, but it was Bouton. "Someone ought to be on the quarterdeck," he said. "I heard you and came myself."

I told him he was right, which he was, and that he would be better and asked him about the jewelry.

"I did not take it."

"Okay, I believe you. Do you know who did?"

He shook his head. "No one was to touch it, although some of us touched it when we found it. That was Rombeau's order. He was sure there was something in these cabins we had not found, and locked them until they could be searched with thoroughness."

"I've got it."

"He searched them, but he found nothing and locked them again. I gave you the keys, Captain. They were locked when you came?"

Novia said, "Oui, but no jewel." She was lighting candles from the one in the lantern.

"So we've got another mystery," I said, switching to Spanish. "But the main reason I called Bouton was that I want you to try out those little brass pistols you wear. You loaded them quite a while ago, and the charges may have gone bad. Salt spray and so forth." Back to French. "You know how that is, Monsieur Bouton?"

M. Bouton looked mystified, but he nodded.

"It's the same for me. I don't think mine have been loaded quite as long as hers, but mine may not work either. We're going to use this wall between the cabins for practice—it looks solid enough. Then we'll all have some more of that wine. Go tell Boucher not to worry when he hears a few shots. Then come back down here. You can have another drink and help us test."

While he was gone, I told Novia in Spanish what I had told Bouton in French, although I knew she had probably understood just about all of it. I did all that pretty loudly, but when I had finished I got a lot closer and whispered in French: "When I leave, count to ten, not loud, before you fire."

"As you say, Crisóforo." She looked as puzzled as Bouton.

When he came back, I had her draw one of the little guns hooked to her belt. When she started to cock the hammer, I made her turn and pointed her gun out the open window. After that I left. I was barefoot already, and I tried to make it as quiet as I could. Before that little gun banged, I had the key in the lock of the other door.

The only light in there was the starlight coming through the window. I could see her just the same, a dim black shape a lot smaller than I was. I grabbed her as quick as I could, figuring she might have a gun or a knife and might use them if I gave her a chance.

As soon as I got my arms around her, I knew she was a woman, like Señora de Santiago had said, and a young one. As I hustled her out of the Guzman cabin, down the tiny hall, and into ours, I was getting all set to explain to Novia and Bouton how smart I had been.

Then Novia screamed and the woman I had been hustling along burst into tears. Her legs went limp and I let her go until she was crouched in a sad little ball in front of Novia, whimpering and sobbing.

I had slipped up once already, and that was when I slipped up again. Novia had her other pistol out, and she cocked and fired it before I could stop her. I hit her arm, though, and the bullet went wide and into the deck. The shot made the girl she had been shooting at look up, and I saw her face in the candlelight.

Even so, it took me a good minute or more to really get it through my head. This was Estrellita.

When I sort of woke up from that, I had opened a bottle and was pouring myself a glass of wine. I took it to Estrellita instead, and told Bouton—he was standing between them by then—to get her into a chair. He did, and I got Novia into the other one with a lot more trouble.

Between sobs Estrellita said, "I am sorry, Señora. So very, very sorry. God has punished me."

"I have not even begun!" I had forgotten about Novia's big folding knife, but it was in her hand.

I made both of them shut up. "I think I understand all this by now," I told them. "Maybe I even understand more than the two of you do. We'll see."

I switched to French and told Bouton, "You don't understand any of this. There's no way you could."

He shrugged the way only a Frenchman can. "An affair of the heart? I will go."

"You will stay," I told him. "I'm not sure I could manage both of them alone, and you've already seen a lot. Are you going to talk about it?"

He shook his head violently. "Not I, Captain."

"Good. We'll explain it to you. That might be the best way."

Novia's French was not bad, she could understand most of what anybody said, although she had a lot of trouble sometimes when she tried to speak it. But Estrellita did not speak a word of French, which meant I had to translate for her until I got Novia to do it. Whenever Estrellita talked, I had to translate it into French. All this stuff would get old fast, so I am not going to write it when I get back to this.

18

This Horrible Ship

I AM NOT sure it was the first thing I did, but one of the first things I did was make Estrellita show us the catch on the inside of the cabinet. It was pretty clever, a wooden piece (the same color as the rest of the wood) that was a peg to hang clothes on, only if you pushed it sidewise it would slide about half an inch. With it like that, you could swing the big, shallow cabinet out and step through the opening. Inside was the money in two heavy leather bags, with some dried fruit, wine, a couple of glasses, bedding, and a slop jar.

I told Estrellita I was surprised she had been able to stock it before Rombeau and his guys got her, and she said the food and wine had been in there already. That was the reason it was as big as it was—Don José had it built originally as a place to store wine and food where the crew would not steal it.

One of the bags was embroidered with the letter G.

I carried them back to the table and Bouton and I dumped them out. It was beautiful—more gold than I had ever seen in my life.

"This belongs to everybody," I told him, "our whole bunch, on all three ships. We'll share it out when we get to Port Royal."

He nodded, but he was staring so hard I am not sure he had heard me.

Novia pointed to the one with the G. "That one is mine!"

"I'm afraid not," I said. "If I were as mad at you right now as I ought to be, I'd give it to you and shove you out the door. That bunch outside would have it before you got ten feet down the deck, and then they'd have you, one after another until everybody'd had his shot.

"Only I'm not going to do that, Señora Guzman. You didn't take this ship or any of the others. We did, and this is part of the loot. You're down for one share."

Novia was staring at me. "You know!"

"After you said it was yours? Heck yes. Anybody would. Sit down."

I was sitting on one of the bunks already, and Bouton made her get back into her chair. With the gold in the bags again, I said, "Okay, we'll start with you, since you left home first. What's your real name?"

"You know it." Her chin was up, and I knew she would have loved for those little pistols to be loaded again. "I am who you said."

"Señora Guzman. Sure. But what's your first name?"

She would not say a word, but Estrellita whispered, "Sabina."

Novia looked daggers at her.

"Fine. Do I call you Novia or Sabina? It's got to be one or the other."

"It is a matter of no difference to me what you call me, Capitán."

That hurt. It still hurts just to think about it. I tried not to let it show. "Okay, Sabina, if that's how you want it. You were the lady who looked at all the parrots, then got your maid to carry the one you bought. Estrellita here was the maid. Go on from there."

She only shook her head.

Estrellita said, "You came back to play for me. We held hands, and once I came out to dance to your music. For that I was beaten. Oh, most terribly!"

"I, too," Novia muttered.

I nodded. "That's what the cook said. Your husband beat you both. Why did he beat you?"

She would not speak, and Bouton offered to make her. I told him no.

"What was your husband's name?"

Still nothing.

I turned to Estrellita. "What was it? What was the name of the man Sabina here was married to?"

"It was Jaime, Señor Capitán." Her voice shook.

"He was the man who brought you on this ship?"

"Yes, Señor. This horrible ship. My husband."

We had to pull Novia off of her. It took a few seconds, and she did some damage. When I got her knife away from her, I threw it out a window.

After that I had to patch up Estrellita enough to stop the bleeding. The devil of it was that I could not have Novia do it, and if I had Bouton do it I knew what would happen. So I had to do it myself, and that was bound to be bad. I took her into the other cabin, and went back for two candles.

"It does not trouble me that you see so much of me, for I have always loved you. How many nights I have made your picture in my poor, fretted thoughts and clasped it to my heart, mi marinero!"

I made her shut up and hold still.

"Will you not kiss my wound? For me?"

When I got her back in the bigger cabin with Novia and Bouton, I sat down again. I was getting pretty tired by then and trying not to show it. "Okay, Bouton," I said, "here's what happened. If anything I say is wrong, they can sing out. Only they'd better tell the truth, or we're going to get into it.

"Jaime Guzman beat them both. I won't ask them what was going on, or what he thought was going on. Or what may have gone on before. He did what he did. Sabina wouldn't take it. She ran away."

"He beat me because I was in love with you." Sabina's voice was so low I could hardly hear her. "I can draw. Have you not seen my pictures, Crisóforo? I learned in my father's house. In my tocador in Coruña, I had drawn your picture over and over. Many pictures. He found them."

"I see," I said, and wondered whether I could believe her. I turned to Bouton. "She ran away. I don't know why she didn't go to her father, but my guess is that he'd have taken her back to her husband. She was afraid her husband would find her—"

"I searched for you!"

I nodded. "Yeah. That's what you said when you said you were Estrellita. If you lied about one thing, you could be lying about a hundred."

Bouton said, "They all lie, Capitán. I have never known a woman who did not lie, not even my mother."

"I could not make myself known!" Novia jumped up screaming. "I was a married woman! You were a sailor!"

I tried to say okay or something like that, but she kept yelling. "I watched, every night! You had eyes for my maid! Only her! I watch and envy her! Holy Mother, how I envy!"

I pushed Novia back into her chair, and she finally shut up.

"She bought sailor's slops," I told Bouton. "She's slender, and small in the chest. She tied a rag around those to keep them in and passed for a boy. There was one thing she said to me when we first got together that ought to have bothered me a lot more than it did. She said she would be my lady, wear a gown, and stay in my cabin. And pretty soon her hands would be soft for me again."

I reached over to Estrellita, felt her hand, and put it down. "Only Estrellita's hands hadn't been soft. We'd held hands, and hers had been almost as hard as mine. They're soft now because she hasn't been doing the work she used to do when she was just the Guzmans' maid, sweeping floors, washing dishes and so forth."

Estrellita's chin went up. "*I* had maids. Two! One for the house, and one for me alone."

"I've got it. Ugly girls, I'll bet. I wish I could see them. You were sleeping with Jaime."

"He forced me!"

Novia laughed. "For one real. 'How could I refuse, Mother? He gave me a real.'"

"He did! Defend me, Crees!"

I told them both to shut up. "So you lived together as man and wife, only you couldn't be the real thing. You couldn't get married, because everybody knew Guzman had a wife already. She'd run away, but he was still married just the same."

"Adulteress!" Estrellita hissed it. It does not hiss as good in Spanish, but she hissed it anyway.

"Right," I said. "She was, only he's dead now. You two couldn't marry in Coruña. Nowhere in Spain, really. Or anyhow, there wasn't any place where he'd feel safe. Some people must have known you'd been the maid, too, and that can't have been nice. Maybe he could have gotten a different girl, but he still wouldn't have been able to marry her. So you two decided to go to New

Spain, where you could play lady and he could tell everybody you were his wife."

When I had translated it, Bouton laughed. "I'd have told them to go to the devil."

"So would I, but they were his business connections, or some of them were. Besides, this was better. He'd buy a big place, build a house for her, and raise cattle and corn. Have a bodyguard of vaqueros. Any man who lived within a hundred miles would pull his hat off when Jaime Guzman rode by. De Santiago told us a fairy tale about Guzman's losing his money. He hadn't. He had a lot. What he'd lost was his wife. If he'd really lost his money, I doubt that de Santiago would have agreed to take him across the Atlantic."

"You said he was dead, Captain. Did we kill him?"

I shook my head. "He killed himself, or that's what they say. When they were a week out of Coruña, he wasn't around anymore."

"It is accursed," Estrellita burst out, "this horrible ship! Will you not take me from it?"

"Yeah, sure." I went back to Bouton. "I've got two ideas. I'll give you both of them. First idea—he really did kill himself, like everybody says. He'd beaten his wife and lost her, he was giving up his house, his friends, his country, everything. And he was giving up all that for a girl who was already cheating on him."

"That is a lie!"

I told Estrellita to sit down. "The heck it is. You were cheating on him with de Santiago."

In French, Bouton said, "It was this de Santiago?"

"Right. When I first saw that trick hiding hole, I thought both of them must have known about it. When I'd had time to think it through, I saw that couldn't be right. In the first place, de Santiago wouldn't have trusted Guzman that much. If Guzman knew, he could open the cabinet on his side and take de Santiago's money. So he didn't."

Bouton scratched his chin. "But he let de Santiago put his money in there?"

"No, of course not. He had his money in his cabin, locked up. Or maybe hidden someplace, although there aren't a lot of places to hide things in there, because it's so small. I asked Estrellita how she'd been able to put food and wine and all that stuff in there when you and Rombeau showed up, and she said she hadn't. It had been in there already. She didn't tell me, but what she really did was grab the gold—the money she thought was hers now that her man was gone—and take it with her when she hid."

"Smart girl."

Novia laughed. "She is a fool. Even I know that. I know her far better than either of you."

"She was sure a fool to start fooling around on the voyage," I said, "so you've got a point. Besides, she wasn't smart enough to remember in all the excitement that she'd left her jewelry on top of that chest. When things quieted down, she was fool enough to sneak back out and get it."

"Holy God!" Bouton had seen the light.

"That's the goods. It's what tipped me off to start with. Me and Novia had looked all over the ship for the missing woman. After we gave up, it hit me that it wasn't just the woman who was missing anymore. Now her jewelry was missing, too, even though it had been locked in. The simple explanation was that she'd popped out and taken it. That meant she was hiding in the cabin where it was, which had always been the logical place—she wouldn't have known her way around the ship."

Novia said, "In a better world, you would be an admiral, Crisóforo." She sounded as if she meant it.

I said, "Thanks, Sabina."

Bouton said, "But she would not have known about the place unless that man who owned this ship had shown it to her. I see."

"You've got it. There were blankets and a pillow in there. Two wineglasses, not just one."

Estrellita whispered, "You did not have to tell that, Crees."

I felt pretty bad right then. I have felt pretty bad quite a few times in my life, but I have always gotten over it. I said, "I didn't have to tell Bouton and I sure as heck didn't have to tell Sabina here. But I had to tell me. I need to understand what it would be like if you and I got together the way I wanted to once, and the only way I'll ever understand it is to say it out loud. Say it a lot."

Estrellita said, "I confess to you the truth. José surprised me in the dark. I was asleep. Jaime was still on deck but I think he has come back to our room. We kiss, we make love. Then he reveal himself. He is not Jaime. He is José. After that, I must do as he ask, or he will tell Jaime."

Novia made a noise that sounded like I felt.

I said, "Sure. To you, one man's just like another in the dark. I got it."

I translated for Bouton, then I said, "So as long as Jaime was around, they used the space between the cabins. She just hated it, but she lay down in there with Don José and had a little wine and ate some dried apricots every couple of days. Then Jaime jumped—I can guess why—and after that they didn't have to. They had nobody to fool but Pilar, so they could use the Guzmans' cabin and—"

Novia cut me off. "Two ideas you say, Crisóforo. One I know. What is the other?"

"It's pretty obvious, isn't it? Jaime didn't jump. De Santiago killed him. He wanted the money, and he wanted Estrellita. Jaime had them both."

Bouton said, "He would have to get rid of his wife, wouldn't he, Captain?"

I shook my head. "He might want to, but he probably wouldn't. He'd set Estrellita here up in a cute little house someplace, with enough money to keep her happy. He had Jaime's money, and he'd tell her he was keeping it for her, and give it to her in dibs and dabs. She'd keep hoping to get it all, and she'd know that if she left him she'd never see another real of it. You haven't seen much of Don José and Pilar, but Sabina and I have. He'd have about as much trouble managing Pilar as you'd have managing a cabin boy."

We said a lot more, but there is not a lot of point in writing it all out. After that, sleeping arrangements were the problem. Novia and Estrellita wanted to sleep with me, although Novia was too proud to say it. Estrellita just about begged.

I did not want to sleep with either of them—but I did not want to get them raped either. On top of all that, I was worried about what Novia might say or do if I left her with somebody like Rombeau or Jarden. She was a good-looking girl, and I knew by then how smart she was. I ended up tying Estrellita's hands and sending her over to Rombeau to be held with the other prisoners, and locking Novia in the Guzmans' cabin. From inside, it was not hard to jam her trick cabinet's latch so she could not open it. That was what I did, and I never unjammed it. That night I drank most of a bottle of wine trying to get to sleep. Eventually, it worked.

And when we got to Port Royal, those cabinets went, along with the whole fake wall. I cannot tell you how much I hated that whole deal by then.

There is just one other thing I ought to say before I wrap up for tonight. The next day I was on the quarterdeck trying to forget my headache, which was about like trying to forget that somebody had just whacked off your thumb. Boucher came up and said that one of the men had seen something funny.

It had been a man. Nothing fancy, just a man. Only this guy had seen him, and felt like he was not one of our crew but somebody he had never seen before. He had yelled at him, and then he was gone.

Boucher said this guy had seen his own shadow, and Bouton thought he might be having hallucinations. I told everybody about it just the same, knowing they would find out anyhow, and told them to keep an eye out. I think it was a day out of Port Royal.

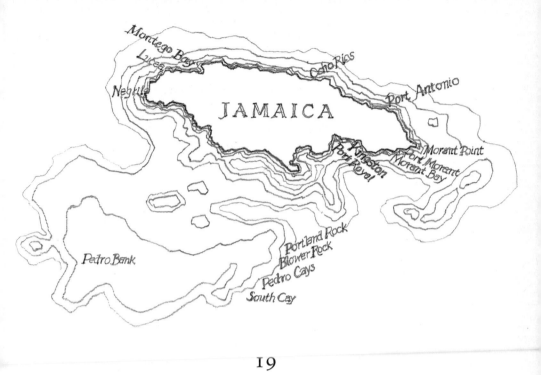

19

Novia, Estrellita, and Some Others

YESTERDAY I TALKED to a lady who has come to the U.S. from Jamaica. I asked whether she had lived in Port Royal, and she laughed and said she had been born and raised in Kingston. I said I knew it had been a bad town a few hundred years ago. That was gone, she said. It had been destroyed by an earthquake, and a new Port Royal built near the same site.

Yet I know that it is not gone. It is back there, where she is, where the hurricanes blow and lean, hard ships snap at the edges of the Spanish Main like wolves around a sheepfold.

Before I went to bed, I spent an hour or more just studying those maps. When I was at sea, I was crazy about maps. Give me a map, and I wanted no other book. I knew that many details were wrong or at least inaccurate. I committed them to memory just the same, knowing that it was better to know them than not, yet knowing that we would have to proceed cautiously always.

That was how I proceeded when we brought the *Rosa* and the *Castillo Blanco* there, getting the best price I could for *Rosa,* and making sure that the carpenters I hired to alter the *Castillo Blanco* knew their business.

First, however, I saw to our prisoners and to Novia. Capt. Ojeda and his crew I simply freed, giving Ojeda a little money, shaking his hand and wishing him well. I thought I had seen the last of him when I did that.

I let Don José write three letters explaining his fix and asking friends and relatives to ransom him. I read them before I mailed them, and made sure that he had told each of the men he had written to that the money was to be sent to me in care of a ship chandler in Port Royal we were buying supplies from. He had promised to handle the money end of the deal for us for ten percent. There were others who would do it cheaper—seven for one and five for the other—but I was not sure they were honest. This guy would take his ten percent and hand over the rest, and there would be no trouble about it.

After that was all set, I knocked on Novia's cabin door and told her I needed to see her. She came into my cabin half an hour later and gave me quite a surprise. No calico gown this time, and no makeup. She was dressed the way she had been when I had first seen her on the *Magdelena*—sailor's white canvas pants, boobs tied in and hidden under a loose blue shirt, and her hair in a long braid down her back.

I told her I was going to give her enough money to pay her passage back to Spain.

"I must walk unescorted in this Port Royal of yours. It is a bad place, you have told me."

I nodded.

"I wish a favor, Crisóforo. You owe me none, I know. Already you do me a favor, giving me money so that I may go home. I ask another. I would recharge my pistols? May I do so if I swear I will not shoot you? Please?"

I said sure, and handed her the box with the powder flasks and so forth. That was when the carpenters came to tear out the wall and the secret compartment, and cut new gunports in the gunwale. I got busy with them, and when I looked for Novia again, she was gone. The beautiful wooden case that her pistols had come in was still there on the table, with the ramrod, the bag of bullets, and the other stuff still inside. But no Novia, and no little brass pistols. Not crying can be hard sometimes. Not often for me, but sometimes. That time I tried not to, but I did not make it.

Of course, I still had my worst problem—what to do with Estrellita. There were complications. Here I am supposed to advise other people about their problems, and they just about always have complications, too. So I will list mine here. I do not want to, but it will be good for me, and I have never done enough penance. The last one was the big one.

1.   She had no money and nobody to take care of her except Don José and Pilar, and they were not going to be loose any time soon. If we kept her until they could look out for her, we might have her for a year. Two prisoners was bad enough.

2.   She had been cheating with Don José. If I handed her over to him, I would be aiding and abetting. I had met Pilar, and I did not want to do that.

3.   Sooner or later Don José would cut her loose, probably with nothing. She might be worse off then than she was now, and in fact it seemed pretty likely.

4.   He might do something unpleasant with Pilar so he could have Estrellita all the time. I thought there was a good chance he had killed Jaime Guzman. If Don José wanted Pilar out of the way, she just might have some sort of accident. My father would have said, "It's been known to happen."

5.   I had wanted her more than anything for so long. Now she looked like something the cat dragged in, dirty and chained with her hair all messed up and her eyes red from crying. Pretty soon she was going to look worse, and I was not sure I could keep from getting her chains taken off, giving her a square meal and a chance to clean up, and after that so on and so forth. From what I had learned about her, and what I had seen of her since I had grabbed her in the dark, that would be a big, big mistake.

I do not know now just how long I worried about her, walking up and down the little quarterdeck of the *Castillo Blanco* and watching the carpenters. By the time they were ready to knock off, I had made my mind up. I got Antonio to come over and keep an eye on the ship and went ashore.

I had thought it was going to be tough to find Ojeda, but it was not. Finding Vanderhorst on Virgin Gorda had been a lot harder. Spaniards hardly ever came to Port Royal, and everybody had noticed them. He and Alvarez were splitting a room in a private house, and my guess is that they were paying through the nose for it.

"I need your help, Captain, and I'm willing to pay for it." I got out a couple of doubloons and showed them to him. "You'll leave soon for Spain?"

"Sí." His beard and mustache were nice and neat now, and his face told me he wanted the money but was going to be darned careful not to say too much.

"You've found a ship that will carry you?"

"To Spain?" He shook his head.

"To New Spain, then."

"From here there are no ships, Capitán. One must take passage to your island of heresy. At times, our ships come to trade." He was watching the doubloons.

"An expensive journey, no doubt." I tried to look sympathetic. "What I ask will increase the cost. Thus I offer these." I made them chime softly in my hand. There is nothing else exactly like the mellow chink of gold. "Maybe you remember Señora Guzman?"

He nodded, his face tighter than ever.

"I'm holding Señor de Santiago and his wife. A matter of business. A man's got to live."

"I comprehend. He has friends, Capitán."

"But Señora Guzman?" I shrugged. "What am I to do with her? Her husband was ruined, and he's dead now. She hasn't a brass cuarto. I could kill her, but Rombeau objects. His honor is involved. You know how that is."

"Sí."

"You can help me here, Captain. You can take her back to Spain. These will pay her fare."

He did not actually kiss me, but I could see he wanted to. We went to the *Magdelena* together, and I got her chain off and turned her over to him. They were holding hands before they were out of sight.

Could I have done it without the two doubloons? Heck, yes. He would have paid me for her if I had pitched it that way. The thing was, I got a lot more fun out of my money than the guys who spent theirs guzzling kill-devil or hiring women nobody in his right mind would want. Also, I still had that soft spot for Estrellita. A little one, but it was there. I did not want her for myself, but I did not want her to suffer, either. With two doubloons, she and

Ojeda would be able to skip Jamaica for sure, and that was what I wanted. I felt good about the whole thing. I still do.

After that I chewed things over with Dubec awhile. He had spent more time on the *Magdalena* than I had, and I wanted to know what he thought of her sailing qualities. He thought she should be carrying a little more weight astern. He had told Rombeau, and they had agreed to try it. We planned to buy a lot more ammunition for the big guns, round shot, grape, canister, and maybe even some chain shot. They would load it aft and see what it did.

He thought most of the men would be back, which interested me. There were a few, he said, who planned to take what I had paid out already—money from de Santiago and Guzman, mostly—and head home to France. Because I knew it had been French before America got it, I asked about New Orleans. Dubec had never heard of it. There was a place called Acadia, he said, way, way up north. He did not think any of our men would go there. I thought for a while that might be another name for Louisiana, but the way he talked about it, it sounded like it was north of the North Pole.

What he said got me to worrying about manning my ships (what Bishop Scully would call staffing) although I could not do much about it. We would have two ships instead of three, which meant that Jarden, Antonio, and some of the other *Rosa* men would be on the *Magdalena* or the *Castillo Blanco*. That would be good. But we would lose men in Port Royal, too, and not just those who went home. We would lose them, and there was not one darn thing I could do about it, beyond paying out what everybody had coming when we sold the *Rosa* and telling each man, individually, how much I wanted him back.

I thought all that over while I was shooting the breeze with Dubec, and later when Antonio and I were checking out the new gunports and the other carpenter-work. I told him about the wall between the cabins I wanted ripped out, and the little compartment inside, and we went into the one that had been the Guzmans' and had a look at it. The carpenters had taken the doors off both cabins that day and started changing the frame over to make one big door, like I had told them. I stood there looking at it, and wondered why I was doing it, now that Novia was gone. The back cabin would have been plenty big enough for me, and I could have let Bouton have the other one. I told myself that I would get another woman someday—you can imagine all that I said. But I did not believe me, no matter how often I said it in my mind.

I would have a big cabin with three windows, a nice one too low for me to stand up in, and that is where I would sleep at night, stretched out on two blankets on the floor, unless I decided to sleep on deck. That night it was going to be hard to get to sleep no matter where I slept, and I knew it.

Just to change the subject, I said, "We're going back to Hispaniola, Antonio. You ever been there?"

"No, Captain. I have not. There is gold there?"

I thought, Only what they took from me, but I did not say that. "There may be men there, buccaneers. The Spanish will have driven some of them out, maybe all of them. Only I don't think so. My guess is there'll be quite a few left, and I want them. They're good shots, but they won't be sailors. Somebody will have to teach them, and on the *Magdelena* that will be— What is it?"

"We can get more here, I think, Captain. Perhaps not enough, but two came while you were away." He rubbed his chin.

"Wanting to sign on? I wish you had taken them. We could use them."

"I tried, Captain. We had difficulty understanding each other, the small one and I. The larger understood still less. So it seemed to me."

"Well, maybe they'll come back. How's Jarden coming with navigation?"

Antonio said it had been going as well as could be expected, that the quartermaster was teaching Jarden his numbers and that he could use the backstaff but still had trouble reading charts.

"He knows how to use the lead?"

"Oh, yes, Captain. He knew that already. He can count, you understand. And add and subtract, which surprised me. It is the written number that must be taught. Now we teach Captain Rombeau as well. It is easier there, because he can multiply and divide, and read and write."

"What about the quartermaster?" I asked. "He must be learning, too."

"He is, Captain. He can navigate now. Not well, you understand. But better—"

Somebody shouted, "Ahoy the white ship! Cap'n Chris aboard?" It was in English, and I just about broke my neck looking around.

There were two men on the pier, both waving. They seemed about the same size to me—medium height and husky—but I told Antonio, "Here are those guys you talked to."

He shook his head, but I hardly noticed. I bawled out, "I'm Chris! Come aboard."

We had one lantern lit already, and Antonio lit another from it while they were coming up the gangplank. Even so, it took a second or two for me to place them: Ben Benson and Red Jack. We yelled and shook hands and all that, and I introduced Antonio. They could not talk because he knew no English, and that was the only language they could speak, but everybody smiled and shook hands again. If they had been French, we would have hugged, too. They were not. Now, when I hug the kids here at the Youth Center sometimes, it seems a pity.

Capt. Burt had made Lesage captain of the *Windward,* they said. They had not liked him much and had decided to look elsewhere. I asked whether she was still in port, because I wanted to look at her again and talk to Lesage about Valentin if I could. They said she had been gone for about a week. I figured that what had really happened was that they had missed the sailing, probably because they were still drunk, maybe just because they still had money. Even so, I was glad to have them. They were sailors, both of them, and good ones.

I showed them around the *Castillo Blanco,* everything except the two little cabins under the quarterdeck. I did not say anything about Estrellita, though— that was none of their business—and I did not even think about the curse. Maybe if I had said something then, it would have been different later. It could be, but I do not really think that.

Antonio had gone over to the *Magdelena* while I had been showing them the ship, and had fetched back a bottle of rum. While the four of us killed it, I told them a bit about my plans—Hispaniola if we needed men when we left Port Royal, then raiding south down the Spanish Main. We would leave the Portuguese alone, I said. There were more Spanish south of them, in the silver country, but I doubted we would go that far. When I said it they looked a little disappointed, which was what I wanted.

And after that, there was nothing for it but to go to bed. Red and Ben went into the forecastle to sling their hammocks, Antonio and I said good night, and he went back to the *Magdelena.* When Bouton showed up to take the watch, I briefed him and went into the captain's cabin, not quite as steady as I would have liked.

My bed was already made up on the floor. I did not remember doing that before I went out, but I figured I must have. When I slipped under the sheet, Novia was there already, naked and waiting.

Afterward I went to sleep before she did, which was the way it just about

20

The Voice of God and the Santa Lucia

FROM PORT ROYAL we rounded Morant Point and made north for the Windward Passage, intending to check things out at the French end of the island. But before I get into all that there are a few things I ought to cover first.

All the changes I wanted done to the *Castillo Blanco* had been completed. I did not like the new door to the captain's cabin and made the carpenters do it over and better—a heavier door with a higher sill to keep water out, a better lock, and so on. Everything else was fine the first time.

I put a stern chaser in that big cabin, a long nine that could fire out the back window right over the rudder. My idea was to have a bow chaser and a stern chaser the same size as the main battery guns, and that is what I did. We started with three guns per side, three four-pounders. We sold them and bought five nines per side, plus the stern chaser and a bow chaser. More guns always hurt the sailing qualities of a vessel because the weight is too high, but if she is not overgunned, the harm is not too bad. With twelve nine-pounders, the *Castillo Blanco* was not overgunned.

Speaking of that bow chaser, I saw something when we put it in that I had never realized before. A ship cannot have spirit sails set and fire a bow chaser dead ahead, not unless the captain is willing to blow his spirit sails all to heck with the first shot. That made me like jibs more than ever. We took down both spirit-sail yards and stowed them in the hold. Nobody wanted them.

Before we sailed, Red Jack came back with the men Antonio had talked to, and it was Big Ned and Mahu. Mahu talked too much and Big Ned hardly talked at all, but oh my gosh was it good to see them! The *Magdelena* was anchored out in the harbor by then, but Azuka spotted them and she and Willy came over in the jolly. Everybody met everybody and we had a party.

There are really three big differences between serving on a pirate ship and a merchantman, and they explain why so many sailors turned pirate. Number one is that everyone on board is easier and more relaxed. If the crew does not like the captain, they can vote him out. He has got to maintain discipline and the crew knows that, but he cannot be unfair or he goes. I would not treat a dog the way some merchant captains treat their men.

Number two is that each man does a lot less work. That is mostly because there are so many. If a man will not do his share, he generally is not made to do it. That is a danger sign, and most of the men know it. When the petty officers stop trying to put a man to work, he knows he is not going to be on board much longer. Sometimes he will shape up and work harder than anybody then, but a man like that will hardly ever keep it up for more than a few days, and pretty soon he is as bad as ever. Then he is put ashore someplace, and if it happens to be a place without water, those are the breaks. Sometimes a man like that will be put ashore on the mainland. Nine times out of ten the Spanish nab him and he hangs.

Number three everybody knows already. The money is a lot better. Sure, a pirate risks his life for it, but the merchant sailor does, too. What if pirates take his ship? Half the time they kill everybody. Do you want to be on the winning side or the losing side? The side that makes big money or the side that gets paid peanuts?

I have been surfing the Internet looking for info on pirates, and found some, too. I also found a guy who knew quite a bit, and we have been trading e-mails. One place in which he is wrong—in which a lot of books are wrong, too—is that he thinks discipline was rougher on a warship than on a merchant ship. I never served on a warship, but I talked with Capt. Burt every chance I got, and with some others who had sailed on them. Red Jack was one, and Novia was another. From what everybody tells me, a warship was about halfway between merchant and pirate.

People today can hardly bear to think of punishing anybody for anything. A kid can kill his mother, and if he cries a little and says he is sorry, they want to let him walk. (Fr. Phil is like that.) Back when I was Captain Chris, people got the merda beat out of them for petty little stuff and nobody thought much about it. But on a man-of-war, the officers knew they were going to be out in front when it came to fighting, and their men were going to be following them with cutlasses and pistols. It made a big difference.

Also the money was better on a man-of-war, at least when there was a war. If they captured an enemy ship, they paid out shares pretty much like we did. (If we had been privateers, we would have had to split with the Crown like they did.) The main difference was that we pirates did not need a war.

Here I ought to say that there were Spanish pirates, too. There were not as many because there was not as much English, French, and Dutch shipping as there was Spanish. But there were some, and they had more ports to operate out of.

I ought to say, too, that both kinds of pirates would turn on their own flag sometimes. An English or French ship was not always safe with us, especially if there was something we needed bad and yesterday. A Spanish ship was not necessarily safe with them, either. The thing was, we never got together much. Mostly we would take Frenchmen, Dutch, and so forth, and of course Scotch, Irish, Welsh, and guys from Africa. The Spanish pirates would take black guys, too, and had a lot of them. (And pretty often they had a dozen Native Americans to keep things interesting.) But that was it. Nothing else. It was a funny setup, when you come to think of it.

I HAVE JUST come back from way out in the country. Fr. Wahl is retiring and will stay on as pastor emeritus. I will be the new pastor, so two of us for as long as he lives. (May it be long!) After that, just me.

Yet the time is coming, and when it comes I am going. I did not tell Fr. Wahl that. I have not told anyone else, either. If I have to betray one age or the other, I would sooner betray this one.

There will be a fete on Saturday. At two, I am to arrive, fetched by Fr. Wahl. We will eat and drink and socialize, and that is all I know. Eventually I will unpack in a new bedroom. I will say mass at seven that night, and at seven and nine Sunday morning. Fr. Wahl will take the last mass, at eleven. I have prayed to be a good priest for as long as I remain.

SUPPOSE I DO not finish this here. Am I supposed to take it to Our Lady of Bethlehem? No way! I have to write more and better, and hurry.

I had made Ben Benson our bosun. That sounds like a joke, but it was the job he wanted. We found his body outside the sail locker. He had been strangled. There was a man on board who said he had been a hangman for a while, and I got him to take a look at Ben.

"We al'ays tries to break the necks, Cap'n. Heavy enough and drop far enough is what does it, but you can't. Not al'ays. So I'd jump up and grab the feet and swing till they died. They'd look like him when I took the cap off. A cap is what we call it, so they can't see the face. But I'd take it off, after, to use again. Then I'd see 'em. So he's choked, but no rope. I'd see the marks."

Pete and I carried Ben's body out on deck. We did that because I thought the sunlight might show us rope marks we had missed. There were none, but we did see finger marks. He had been strangled by somebody with big, strong hands.

We buried him at sea, sewn in his hammock and weighted with a nine-pound round shot. After that I talked to a lot of the men, looking at hands and trying to learn who his enemies were. Just about everybody's hands were bigger than mine and looked stronger, but I could not find anybody who did not like Ben. Most of them had not known him until he came on board. Red Jack had been his friend. Big Ned and Mahu had been his friends, too—not as close as Red Jack, but friends. All three said they wanted to kill the man who had killed him, and it sounded like they meant it.

I made it clear to everybody that on my ship, fighting was one thing but killing was something else. Tell me and I would put them ashore, each with his cutlass. Other than that, I wanted to know who did it and why. That was fine with everybody, but it did not get me anywhere. Somebody had killed Ben. It had not been Mahu or Novia, and it sure as heck had not been me. After that it was up for grabs.

When I had talked to just about everybody and gotten no leads at all, I went into my cabin, closed the door, and prayed. Novia was out on deck sketching, and I guess she knew I did not want to be bothered.

In the beginning I prayed for Ben's soul. After that I prayed for mine. I told God I knew I was a pirate and no better than Ben. Any punishment He gave me would be just. I knew that, and I told Him so. Maybe I would yell and cry and beg and squeal, but I would never say what He had done was not fair. I promised I would never be any worse than I had to be, and begged Him to forgive me for everything wrong I had done and was going to do.

That was the only time in my life that I have heard the voice of God. He answered me, not in my mind or my heart, or in my soul. He spoke out loud, and His voice was wonderful in a way that there are no words for. What he said was *"Love Me, Chris, and all else will follow."*

When I went out on deck again, everybody was talking about the noise they had heard. Even though there was not a cloud anywhere, Novia said it had been thunder. Bouton said no, it had been guns. The *Magdelena* stood north-northwest of us just then, two or two and a half miles away. He thought she had fired her larboard battery. I told them I knew what it was, it had been for me, and they could forget about it.

Before I write about the galleon, there is one more thing I ought to cover—in fact, I should have written about this sooner. You know that when I had turned Estrellita over to Capt. Ojeda, I found Novia waiting for me in my cabin. It was dark, of course, and she was in the bed I had made on the cabin floor (it is a deck, really), hidden under the blanket. We had made love and had not talked much while we were doing it, just things like "Now," and "Do that again."

We did not talk in the morning, either. We were both afraid that one of us would say something that would break us up again, so we were both pretty quiet. When she got dressed, it was the blue shirt and the sailor's pants, and I was afraid she was going to leave like before.

She did not. But after that she dressed like a man a lot more often than like a woman. At first I thought it was so she could go anytime if there was another blowup, but she kept doing it after we put out. Sometimes she wore her gowns. More often, she just dressed like everybody else on board.

Part of it was size, I know. When we first met, she had told me she wanted to be round again, to be womanly. With us she did not have to work nearly as hard and got better food, when we were in port particularly. Some of the gowns she and Azuka had made would not fit at all, and the rest were tight.

The other part was something else. I think I know, but I am not sure I can make it clear. When she wore gowns all the time, and stayed in that tiny little cabin mostly, she had not really been one of us. When I had made her get out, and she—proud as she was, because Novia was always very, very proud—had turned around and come back, she had changed. I was a pirate, so she would be a pirate, too. Right about the time we were running from the *Santa Lucía,* something clicked with me that I had not seen before.

Bouton was first mate, but Novia was really number two on the ship. If one of those shots from the *Santa Lucía* had killed me, Novia would have been captain with Bouton as her first mate. Pages and pages ago I wrote about reading about those women who had been pirate captains. That would surprise a lot of people, but it had not surprised me. It could have happened on the *Castillo Blanco.*

We were headed up the Jamaica Channel with the wind south-southwest, about as good a wind as you can get for that course. When we rounded Lady Marie Cape, there she was. She could not have held the wind close enough to head straight for us, but she did not want to do that anyhow. She went for the place where we were going to be, holding as close as she could with all plain sail set.

When I say now that we tacked east, it sounds like I wanted to commit suicide, I know. I did not, and I will explain what I was doing in a minute. While we were tacking, I made signal to Rombeau on the *Magdelena*: SPLIT. MEET TORTUGA.

He acknowledged and held his course north, which was what I wanted.

Here is how I was thinking. First off, by going east I was going straight for the galleon like it sounds. I was heading between the galleon and the north coast of the Tiburon Peninsula. It meant I was going to have to pass in front of her broadside, sure. But she was heeling quite a bit, and I could see that she was not going to bring those guns to bear. Second, that end of the island was still French from what I had heard in Port Royal. I figured a Spanish galleon was not going to want to get too close to shore. Third, with us hugging the shore, the range was going to be long. And we were fast.

From all that, it ought to be clear I was figuring the galleon would go for the *Magdelena.* She was on course for her already, for one thing, and for another the *Magdelena* was bigger. When she did, I was going to come up behind her and cross her stern. It would mean coming under the fire of her stern chasers, sure. They would be twelve-pounders or about that, and there would probably be two (though there could be four). But while they were shooting at us—probably one shot from each gun—we would be raking her stern with our broadside. If we could not disable her rudder like that, it would be mighty poor shooting and we would try again.

I have gone into all this detail because I still think what I did was logical and good tactics. The problem was that the captain of the galleon was not on the same page. She turned into the wind a lot faster and handier than I would have expected from a ship that size and came after us. What she wanted, of course, was to come alongside us. With thirty guns a side in her main battery, she would have blown us out of the water. All we wanted was to get away.

We were fast, and that was good. But after a bit of racing along and gaining a bit on the galleon if anything, it hit me that all we were really doing was racing for the armpit of Hispaniola, where the land makes a hairpin turn to run northwest. That was where Port-au-Prince was, and there were sure to be shore batteries. If we were lucky, they might protect us. If we were not, they would probably sink us.

What looked practically certain was that once we got under the protection of those shore batteries we would not get out again until they said so, if they ever did. A good big bribe might do it—one that would leave us flat.

We would not *have* to make port there, though. Not unless we wanted to. We could turn north and try to slide past the galleon instead. I figured we would have about one chance in ten.

Up ahead I could see Big Cayemite Island, the little shallow channel between it and the coast, and a finger of land beyond it that would force us to turn north. That looked like a very, very big break to me just then, and I decided to go for it. If the galley followed us in there, she would have to drop back, and there was a good chance she would run aground. That is what I was hoping would happen. If she passed Big Cayemite on the north—which is what she did—I had another plan.

There are no brakes on a ship like my dear quick and slick old slider, but there are ways to stop pretty fast, and we used two of them. As soon as the galleon was out of sight behind Big Cayemite, we loosed the sheets, which spilled the wind from our sails, and we put the rudder over hard.

I think most of the crew thought I had gone crazy, but that is what we did.

If *Castillo Blanco* had been a speedboat with a nice big engine, I would have done a one-eighty and come out the way we went in. With the wind the way it was, there was no way. We would have had to tack, two steps forward and one back. It would have been too slow, and there was no room for it anyway.

What we did instead was sail east again, exactly like we had been going before, then gybe and head hard north so as to come up behind the galleon as she stood out to clear that finger of land. The bad part was that it was not the perfect crossing of her stern I had visualized. We came up at a slant, so our shots were more quartering than raking, and the range was five hundred yards or so.

The upshot—and it was up, we had to elevate our guns as much as we could—was that out of five shots we got three hits and two misses, and the galleon's rudder was not touched. She fired her broadside at us as we made north, too; but by the time her captain got her swung 'round for that, the range was a lot longer. If any of those shots made it as far as we were, they did not come close. We saw an awful lot of splashes, and my guess is that none did.

I was watching her through my glass, looking for hits—you can imagine. Praying for hits was more like it. I saw three, as I just wrote. I also saw all the gilding and carving on her stern, and she was the *Santa Lucía,* the same galleon that had crossed the Atlantic with us when I was on the *Santa Charita*.

After that it was a straight chase up the west coast of Hispaniola. The *Santa Lucía* had a couple bow chasers, and banged away with them. I would guess they were long twelves, or about that. When our stern chaser fired the first time, I was so busy trying to get a little more speed that I had practically forgotten about it. I watched the bow of the *Santa Lucía* through my glass for the next shot and the one after that, and the first hit right at the waterline. The next hit on her foredeck somewhere—I saw the splinters fly.

It was mighty good shooting, and I felt like I ought to run down and give the gun crew a pat on the back. Down I went, and guess who was aiming the gun and touching it off?

It was Novia, and that was when it really hit me that if something happened to me, she would be the new captain. The men swabbed the bore, loaded the new charge and the new ball, and ran the gun out again. She sighted the gun and fired it. I did not see where that shot went, but I saw the men cheer and heard her yell, "That's the way, my braves!"

When they were swabbing the bore for the next shot, I just backed out of the cabin and went up on the quarterdeck again. She was taking care of things down there as well as I could have or better. Anything I said or did was a lot more likely to hurt that operation than help it.

Right here is where there ought to be a desperate sea fight, with the *Castillo Blanco* slugging it out muzzle-to-muzzle with the *Santa Lucía* and me leading a little party of desperate men from our sinking hamburger stand onto the Spanish galleon. I would have a knife in my teeth, but I would shout something thrilling anyway.

Well, sorry. I am writing the truth here, and that is not how it was. We ran north into the Gulf of Gonâve with the galleon in hot pursuit. She lost her bowsprit, and when one of Novia's shots broke her foremast main yard, the Spanish gave up. Rombeau had circled around with the idea of coming up behind her, but by the time *Magdelena* came into sight it was all over.

Here I ought to say something about shooting big guns at sea. It is a whole lot worse than shooting wild cattle with a musket. On land, you can generally steady your musket on a tree or a rock, or lay the barrel in a forked stick you carry. There is no way to steady a big gun at sea.

What is almost as bad is that you cannot be looking through the sights when the gun fires. The recoil would kill you.

Here is what you have to do. First you notice how much the ship is rolling or pitching—most of the time. (Every so often a big one will fool you.) Then you aim the gun. The best aim is to have the base of the enemy's mast in your sights at the top of the roll or pitch. You jump out of the way and grab the slow match. You stick the burning end in the touchhole, timing it so the muzzle will be as high as it is going to go when the gun fires. It will take a quarter of a second or so for your gun to fire after you touch it off.

There is a lot of luck involved. There is also a lot of skill, particularly in knowing the roll or pitch and knowing just how long it will be before the gun fires. A pretty bad shot may get lucky. It is bound to happen now and then. But in the long run, a good shot will beat a bad one hands down.

What I did was to say a Hail Mary, starting at the bottom of a roll or pitch, and notice where the top came, then touch off the gun one word before that. I do not know what Novia did. I only know it worked for her.

21

Good-bye, Old Buddy

———————————

THE LAST TIME I had seen Tortuga I had been paddling a piragua. Now I was captain of the most beautiful pirate ship anybody ever saw, and I had another one, bigger and good-looking too, with her captain under me. It made a lot of difference—the skipper of the *Castillo Blanco* was a heck of a lot more worried than the guy paddling the piragua had been, and had a heck of a lot more things to worry about.

"That's Turtle Island," I told Novia. "See the shape?"

She nodded, still studying it through my glass, then looked up at the gold-and-white French flag we were flying. "They will not shoot at us?"

"Good on you," I said, "you spotted the batteries. So did I. We won't come in range. Rombeau and I are going ashore in *Magdelena's* gig."

"You are no more French than me, Crisóforo. Send Bouton."

I told her I could pass, and I wanted to see those batteries for myself.

When Melind and I had left Tortuga, there had been no shore batteries and the town had been shot up by the Spanish. The town was back now, still shacks mostly but with wider and straighter streets, and not all shacks.

The shore battery Rombeau and I went to had five long guns, probably twenty-pounders, with a furnace for heating shot. There was a stockade to protect the gun crew. We saluted the officer in charge and told him we were law-abiding traders who just wanted to go into the harbor to do a little business.

He winked and asked if we were selling cannon—he noticed we had quite a few gunports. I explained that we had them to fight off the accursed Spanish and said I felt sure there was a small fee to be paid by each ship going into the harbor. We would be glad to pay it. How much? After that we talked about money for a while, Rombeau and I finally getting him down close to half.

We had no sooner tied up at a wharf than a soldier came with a letter saying the governor of the island wanted to parlay with both captains that afternoon.

M. Bertrand d'Ogeron was one of the biggest men I have ever seen. He was fat, sure, but he was tall, too, and there was lots of muscle under the fat. The funny thing about him was that he looked stupid, with his big, wide, fat face and little nose and mouth. Then too, he had a trick of opening his eyes wide that made him look like a real idiot. About the third time he did it, I caught on. He was hoping we would say something stupid he could use if we stuck to our story about being honest merchants. As for him, he was about as dumb as the weather glass.

"You have wine, yes? Good wine from France? I would like a lot."

No, we said, we did not have any.

"A pity, Monsieurs. Oh, a great pity! One cannot get good wine here. Rum. Rum is not wine." He looked like he was about to cry, and shook his head.

We agreed and said we just wanted to buy supplies, and maybe sign up a few sailors who needed work.

"No wine?"

"None." We shook our heads, both of us.

"At home, my mother—oh, my poor mother!—would set before me the best food in Provence, and the best wine." He sighed hard enough to fill the mainsail. "They say she is dead. This I do not believe. My poor mother, my poor, old mother. Dead. She? It cannot be! Think you she is dead, Monsieurs?"

We said it seemed pretty unlikely and brought up the sailors again.

"Honest sailors, Monsieurs? You neglected to say honest sailors." Here he gave us the idiot stare. "You neglected to say it, but you would not want men who would filch your goods. No, no!"

I said, "We need men so badly we'd take any kind, Your Excellency."

"Pirates? You would not accept pirates, surely?"

"They may wish to reform, Your Excellency. We need men very badly." I shrugged. "You comprehend, I'm sure."

"French pirates." He nodded and looked pleased. "Good honest Frenchmen, such as we ourselves are."

Rombeau said, "Any kind. I'd soon teach them how to talk."

I added, "We need them badly, you see."

"Again?" He cupped his ear. "Say it again? I did not understand you."

I repeated what I had said.

"Well, well. It is simple enough, isn't it? You need men. I have it now. Need men. And supplies? Food? Rum? Sailcloth? Rope?"

We nodded.

"I see." He picked up a beautiful china inkstand and stared at it as if he had never seen it before. "Why, look there! It has a tower with a lot of roofs. More roofs all the time!" The quill fell out, and he bent to pick it up, grunting. I thought sure he would spill the ink, but he did not.

He straightened up and put the quill behind his ear. "Monsieurs, I have sad, sad news for you." He gave us the idiot stare. "Are you bound for China? There are fortunes made in the China trade every year."

We said no.

"Silk for the ladies. Tea? Scores of other things. You must go! But there are no honest sailors here—none! I myself have never visited China. Never been there! I am but a poor man, a man exiled from his homeland and his poor old mother, Monsieurs."

I said, "We're poor men, too, Your Excellency. Poorer than you are, I'm sure."

"English sailors? You would not want English sailors, I know. They are pigs, those English."

"Any kind, Your Excellency. We would soon teach them French, as Captain Rombeau says."

M. d'Ogeron shook his head. "They cannot be trusted. You are French, Monsieur?"

I said I was.

"Odd. Odd? Well, well, well! Each time you speak—well, it doesn't matter, does it?" He stared, nodding to himself. "Are we not all children of Adam, Monsieurs? I know I am. My poor mother often explained it. I myself, Monsieurs, am the partner of an English merchant." He nodded again, took the quill from behind his ear, stared accusingly at it as though it had tickled him, and dropped it on the floor.

I said, "I hope your partnership profits you, Your Excellency."

He sighed. If the quill had been on his desk, I think he would have blown it off. "It is not my ship, Monsieur. Only my partner's, and he cheats me. Cheats me abominably! And yet . . . And yet he brings me a little gold from time to time."

I said, "That's good."

"It is, Monsieur. Perhaps you know him, being English yourself?"

"No doubt I might know him, Your Excellency, if I were English."

"Captain . . ." He stared at me again, staring for so long it was hard not to say anything. "Burt? My partner and dear friend Captain Burt?"

I smiled. "Why, yes, Your Excellency. As it happens I have the honor of knowing a Captain Burt. An honest man and a good sailor, just like me."

"I see." D'Ogeron scratched his head. "I am forever dropping things, Monsieur. My, um, crayon. That feather thing. You are not troubled in that way, Monsieur?"

"I am," I said. "Why, I dropped two pistols only this morning." A pistole is a Spanish gold coin, and I figured he would know it.

He smiled. "It is fortunate they were not loaded. Mon Dieu! They might have killed you."

Rombeau said, "Yes, Your Excellency. Or somebody else."

"You have Spaniards on your ship, Monsieur?"

Rombeau looked at me, and I knew he was thinking of Don José and Pilar. I said, "He has only a few, Your Excellency."

"That is well, but there should be more to stop the bullets."

I said, "Oh, I would not wish any harm to the Spanish, Your Excellency. We intend to trade down the Spanish Main, south of Maracaibo."

He smiled again. "I wish you well in it, Monsieurs. But you must be careful they do you no harm either, you adventurous young captains. Fear has its uses! It was a favorite saying of my late mother's, Monsieurs. The braver the mice, the fatter the cats. You are not cats? Un chat regarde bien un évêque."

Rombeau said, "Only now and then, Your Excellency." I do not believe he understood what either of us were talking about, and when we were leaving, he tried to get me to look at the little leather bag I had dropped. I had to grab his arm and hustle him along.

BASEBALL TONIGHT. Fr. Phil does not care about it, so he took the Youth Center for me so that Fr. Houdek would have some company while he watched the game. Pittsburgh is in town, so I cheered for them while Fr. Houdek took our team.

We bet—the winner had to say the seven o'clock next morning. Pittsburgh won by one run, which was probably the way it should be. "Une série vaut bien une masse," I told Father. He must have thought I had gone flat-out crazy.

WE BOUGHT POWDER and shot in Tortuga, filling the magazine again. Watered, of course, and bought a dozen other things. No trouble with the merchants, and before we left I found that d'Ogeron's man had been going around to them, telling them to treat us fairly. Or else. D'Ogeron was an honest politician—when you bought him, he stayed bought.

A clerk told me how he had been threatening the merchants, after swearing me to secrecy. What harm he thought it would do for the matter to become known, I cannot imagine. But I swore and have kept my oath until now.

When we had everything on my list, I bought one thing more: a piragua. We had the longboat—not as big as the *Magdelena's*—and the jolly, but I had a feeling we might need something more. From what some of the men had told me, Capt. Burt took fishermen's boats sometimes. Maybe I could have done that, too, but I would never have felt right about it. We stowed my piragua under the longboat.

From what I had learned on Tortuga, the Spanish had been pushed back, and the French controlled the whole east end of Hispaniola again. I was told that it was a good market for slaves, too, because the supply of indentured servants was drying up. I suppose that was because too many of them were coming back to France and telling people what it was like. I kept the slave thing in the back of my mind, thinking we might catch a Spanish slave ship again. But it did not happen.

We did not have to cruise far along the north coast before we spotted buccaneers on the beach, waving rags on sticks and wanting to sell us dried meat. We put in, both ships, and bought all they had.

When I had handed over the money and everything was nice and friendly, I said, "I used to know a man in your business. He was a good shot, and I'd like to talk him into joining us, if I can. His name was Valentin. Anybody know him?"

All of them laughed, and one said, "You would like to earn the reward, Captain. Who would not? We do not have him, and if we did we could not be cozened out of him so easily as that."

Of course I said I didn't know there was a reward, and how much was it? Was it d'Ogeron who'd offered it?

"One hundred pieces of eight, Captain, dead or alive. Another captain has offered it—no mean offer, as I think you will agree."

He had forgotten the captain's name, but another guy remembered it. It was Capt. Lesage. I wanted to know if this Lesage was captain of the sloop *Windward*. They said no, he had a three-master, the *Bretagne*.

After that I took Jalibert and Pat the Rat and went inland to look for Valentin. I knew where he liked to hunt and where he liked to hang out, and we went to all those places. He was not in any of them, and there was no sign we could see that he had been there recently. We found some ashes where Valentin used to dry meat, but they were cold and had been rained on—once anyhow, and probably more than once.

After three days, I decided we would go up to the cave. It would at least tell me whether he had ever gotten the musket and so forth I had left there for him, and after that we would go back to the ship.

That was where I found him, and Francine, too. Dead. They were not just bones, like all the Native Americans who had been killed in there, but their bodies were pretty dry. They had been shot once, both of them, him through the head. The musket I had gotten for him was there, empty, and he may have killed Francine and himself. It could be. I do not know. It could also be that somebody found them there and shot them both. Two men might have done it, or one man with a musket and a pistol.

I left them where they had fallen, and we closed the mouth of the cave with stones, a lot of them. I do not know whether it has ever been found. I hope not.

Tomorrow I move to Holy Family. Fr. Wahl will come for me. I am all packed, except for this. New people and new duties, and farms and farm animals, which I know I will like. Yet tonight I find I cannot think about much of anything except Valentin and Francine, and the time I spent with them on Hispaniola.

Valentin and Francine, dead in the cave.

When we got back to the ship, Bouton had signed up three buccaneers and was proud of himself. I congratulated him like you have to do. Then I went into my cabin and sat looking out the window without seeing anything. When Novia tried to talk to me, I told her to go away, and by and by we put out without any orders from me.

I sat there drinking rum for most of the night, I think. Not chugging it, just sipping it now and then. The long nine at my elbow was all the company I had, and all I wanted. When I had drunk half the bottle, I threw the rest into the sea and went to bed. I will not do anything like that tonight, although a lot of priests are hard drinkers, and Fr. Houdek hits the bottle now and then.

But I feel like it.

Is Holy Family any closer? I hope so. I have my plan worked out. Every detail. Soon—within a year, I think—the government will change.

22

The Vincente

IT WAS NOT time for us to meet up with Capt. Burt yet, so I told
Rombeau we would split up and meet at Île à Vache. (It means Cow Island.)
I had heard it was a good place to careen a ship, and I wanted to have a look
at the bottom of the *Castillo Blanco,* because there was one time when we
scraped the bottom a little running from the *Santa Lucía.* A merchant at Tortuga had told me it would be a good place to sign up new men, too. There
were quite a few buccaneers there, and the cattle had been shot over so
much nobody could make much hunting them anymore.

    Rombeau and I flipped to see who would get the wind, and he won. He
would head west and go around the Spanish end of Hispaniola, looking for
prizes. I would head east and check out the western end of Cuba before going to Île à Vache. To tell the truth I was glad I had lost, because I wanted to
see Cuba again. I would have liked to go back to Habana if I could, but that
was too far.

That was a pleasant cruise in some ways, although it was not a lucky one. We stopped fishermen a few times. It was mostly to ask for information, but I always bought from them when they had anything, just to break the ice and show we were not out to rob them. That got us some nice fish and crabs, and especially turtles. There is no eating like a green turtle, in my experience. English sailors like Red Jack will not eat fish, but our Frenchmen had more sense, and we were mostly French. I had made Mahu our cook, and he and Ned pitched in like they had been born to it. Mahu said hippo was the best meat in the world, but I got him to admit that green turtle was almost as good.

I have gone off writing about food tonight for two reasons. The first is that I am pastor of Holy Family now, and everybody around here grows food or raises it or both, so everybody is always talking about it—pigs, hams, home-cured bacon, chicken, tomatoes, preserves, and everything else. People bring pies and cookies to the rectory. It is nice of them, but there is too much. Fr. Wahl and I wish there was some way we could share it with poor families.

The other is that it was right after a great dinner that somebody found the second body. I am just about sure it was the day we bought rock lobsters from a fisherman. Mahu had boiled them alive the way you have to, and we had cracked them for ourselves and doused them with salt butter and lime juice.

We were just finishing up, when a guy who had gone down to get more butter came running back. The dead man was French, and that is all I remember about him now. He must have been one of the men we signed in Port Royal. I am almost certain that is right.

It was after sundown, so there was no use carrying him up on deck, but I got more lanterns and had Pete come down and look at him. Novia came, too. Pete said the dead man had been strangled like the other.

"Neck's broke, too, Cap'n. Neat job, that is. I hope the man that does for me does it equal good."

Novia said, "How did he do that, Pete?"

"Twisted it is all. No different than you'd wring the neck of a chicken. Wanted to make sure he was dead."

I said, "He must be strong."

"He is, sir. I could do it, but there's not a lot could."

While I was still trying to think of a good way to ask the question I wanted to ask, Novia said, "How do you know you could, Pete?"

"'Cause I've done it, ma'am. Hangin' don't always break the neck. If the drop's not enough, or he don't weigh enough, it won't. So what I did sometimes is break it myself, after. I ain't a man that likes to see folks suffer unless I'm goin' to get some good out it. Animals the same. I'll kill 'em an' eat 'em, you know I will. But I don't never kill 'em for fun, 'cept rats."

Novia glanced at me and shook her head. I nodded, just a little bit. If Pete had killed them, he was the best actor in the world and we would never get him.

I talked to everybody and got nowhere. There is no point in my writing much about that. Just about everybody had been up on deck eating. And everybody eating had been with a bunch of friends, all ready to swear he had never gone below. If this were one of those crime shows, it would be Novia or me, or maybe Bouton or Pete. It was not, this was real, and it was not any of us.

When I had finished my first lobster, I had taken the wheel so that the man who had been steering could get a bite to eat. Novia had come with me, and she could not have done it anyway. She was not strong enough.

Bouton had taken the wheel from me, and had been eating with me until I took it. The group he and I had been eating in, with him and a couple of others, was just in front of our toy quarterdeck. Okay, maybe somebody could have sneaked off—it was getting dark toward the end—but I was ready to swear nobody had. Novia did not think so either.

What it came down to was that nobody—nobody in our crew, that is— had been below except Mahu and Ned down in the galley. The dead man had left the group he was eating with and gone below to fetch a bottle. He had not come back, but he had not been gone long enough for anybody to get worried about him.

That night I thought a lot about it, and it seemed to me there was only one way it could have happened.

THERE WAS A meeting of all the clergy last night. Fr. Wahl and I drove into town for it. Priests molesting "children" was the big topic. Bishop Scully tried not to show how he felt about it, but it leaked through.

"It has happened," he told us, "and happened right here in our diocese. More than one priest has sinned in this way. What is worse, priests who have confessed and been forgiven have sinned again. Every one of you must unite with me in opposing this sin, and report it to me whenever it occurs. Believe me, you are doing your brother no favor by concealing his sin."

After that, he detailed four cases without revealing the identity of the priests involved. When he asked for questions, those he got were pretty obvious. "How could we know a brother priest's sin unless the sanctity of the confessional were violated?" "Shouldn't a report be made to the police?" "How much was needed to settle these cases?" "Shouldn't a guilty priest be punished as well as counseled?" "Might not some priest be falsely accused?" And so on.

Finally I stood up. I said, "When you began, Your Excellency, I thought I was going to hear about little girls being forced by priests, girls in kindergarten or first grade. That was what I expected. I used to run the Youth Center at Saint Teresa's. All the victims you talked about were boys, and it sounded like they were teenagers. I'm not used to thinking of teenaged boys as children, so it took me a while to get on top of what has really been happening. Isn't it our job to tell boys they shouldn't put up with anything like this? I don't believe there are many priests who would keep trying if the boy he was after yelled and swung a few punches."

After that I caught it from everybody—all right, to be fair it was not, but it seemed like it. I was blaming the victim. That was one of them, and both the priests who felt like that piled it on strong.

I was encouraging violence. That was the other one and the most popular one. I was blamed for encouraging so much violence that I felt like I might be lynched. I never got a chance to defend myself in the meeting, so I am going to do it here. I was not blaming the kids. I was blaming us grownups for teaching them to be victims.

If you teach a girl to act like a sheep, you do her quite a lot of harm. But if you teach a boy to be a sheep, you do a lot more. If the girl is lucky, there will be boys around to protect her. But they have to be real boys, not sheep. A boy who has been taught to be a sheep will not protect himself or anybody else. If he is molested and does not fight, the people who taught him to be a sheep are at least as much to blame as the molester. Maybe more.

As for encouraging violence, I have to wonder how many of those priests who molested boys thought the boys wanted it and enjoyed it, even if they would not say so. Many of them—maybe all of them—must have thought that if the boy did not like it, he would yell and fight. The boys were the victims of those priests, I am not arguing that they were not. But those priests were the victims of the people who had taught the boys that even a little bit of violence is the worst thing in the world. The priests had only one victim, or that is how it seems to me. Those people had two, because the priest was another. The tough kids who came to Saint Teresa's Youth Center would have coldcocked anybody who tried what those priests had done.

AS WELL AS I can remember, it was the week after somebody found the dead man that we caught up to the *San Vincente de Zaragozza*. She was a fine, big ship, and mounted more and bigger guns than you usually find on a merchant ship. As soon as I saw them, I decided I did not want to risk them. If we had just gotten close, run out our guns, run up the black flag, and demanded that she surrender, there was a good chance she would fight and do a lot of real damage.

I kept away from her instead, and basically acted like we thought *she* might be a pirate. Right here was one of the places where the men surprised me, and it was something I liked a lot. I had been afraid they were going to start yelling that we could not let her get away and we should go for her straight off. They did not. They knew right away that I was up to something and took in sail like they meant it while they traded guesses about what it might be.

What I had in mind was nothing very fancy—just what Melind had done when we took the *Magdelena*. I knew that if the *Vincente* was what she looked like, she would heave to at night. If she did not, she was really Spanish Navy or was a pirate, too. The sea had a little chop to it, but it was not too rough, and for a ship as small as ours we had a lot of men. The sun went down, and she hove to like I had expected. After that she did something I did not expect—she ran out her guns. They were hard to see in the dark, but the noise of the trucks carried to us across the water, and there was no mistaking it.

Dirty weather would have helped. We did not get it, but I decided to wait until moonset and go in anyway. I left Boucher a skeleton crew and stuffed as many men into the longboat, the piragua, and the jolly as I could. I had the longboat, Bouton the piragua, and Red Jack the jolly.

We left during the middle watch, with me praying that most of the Spanish sailors were asleep. As I told all the men, the main things were for all three boats to come in at once, and for everybody to holler like a maniac as soon as the fighting started. I took the tiller and Novia sat in the stern with an arm around me, but I got her to promise she would stay right there and take care of the longboat for us. Of course she did not, but I will get into all that later.

The piragua and the jolly took the larboard side, which was closer, and us the starboard. I was going to fire a pistol as the signal to attack.

That was not exactly how it went. Somebody on board sang out, and I could see him against the dark and the stars, leaning over the gunwale yelling and pointing. I fired my pistol at him, and as soon as I did one of the starboard guns went off with a bang. I do not know what they were aiming at, or thought they were aiming at, but she fired. Probably it was just to wake up everybody.

Some of our men had their muskets, and they started shooting through the gunports. That was good, but I had no idea what Bouton and Red Jack would make of it. As soon as we were close enough, I threw a grappling hook, thinking I would be first up.

Novia beat me to it, scrambling up that rope like a monkey the minute the hook caught. I have never been so scared in my life as I was when I saw her do that. I went up after her as fast as I could, but by the time I had started up, she was over the gunwale. I heard shots and figured she was dead. It was as bad a moment as I have had in my whole life.

I went up thinking I would see her body, but by the time I got to the top I did not have time to look for it. The Spanish sailors were all armed and full of fight, and there were naked men and men in nightshirts fighting, too. Our guys were coming over the larboard gunwale yelling and shooting, and bullets were coming in through the gunports, hitting the iron cannon barrels and zinging all over. I fired my other pistol at a naked guy with a long sword as soon as I got on deck. When the smoke cleared, I had my cutlass and an empty pistol, and they were what I used after that.

We won, but it was a stiff fight. It would not be far wrong to say that everything that could go against us had gone against us. To start with, the *Vincente* carried a bigger crew than most merchant ships, and all of them were armed and out on deck when we came over the side—their captain had been even more worried about us than we had been about him. Next, there had been passengers, mostly young hidalgos bound for New Spain to improve the family fortunes. Every one of them had a sword, and most had other stuff, too. There were traveling pistols, fusils, fowling pieces, left-hand daggers, and you-name-it. Some had brought manservants, and their servants fought, too.

One of those had a musket with two short barrels, the kind of gun that my father would have called a lupara. There were two hammers and two triggers. I kept it, and it was the gun I used at Portobello and so on.

The one thing that had not gone against us was that they had not spotted us until we got close. If they had, they would have been shooting cannonballs at us. One good gunner with a little bit of luck would have knocked the longboat to kindling. Fire that shot, and they would have won, not us.

Novia had been hit good and hard with something, maybe the guard of a cutlass. She did not know, and I could only guess from the look of her face. When she came to, she was not sure how long she had been out or what she had done before she had gotten hit. I knelt beside her and talked to her a little bit until she could stand up. She had been lying on a long dagger she had bought in Port Royal, and it was blooded to the hilt. Red Jack and a few of his boys hunted around the deck later and found her brass pistols, both empty.

I had gotten banged up some myself, creased by a musket ball and so on, and quite a few others were hurt worse than I was. If I remember right, we had three dead. They had lost a lot more, fifteen or twenty.

As soon as the fight was over, I ought to have torn into Novia really good for shinnying up that rope like she did. As it was, I said, "You promised to stay in the boat."

And she said, "That was when we did not think we would be seen, Crisóforo. They saw us, and someone must get up most quick. It was I."

Like I said, I should have torn into her really, really good for that. But she was hurt and so was I, and all I did was say, "You're going to get yourself killed someday."

We herded the prisoners together, and I made the usual speech about taking volunteers. Anybody who wanted to join us would be welcome and would get rich. Nobody did.

"All right," I said, "now listen up. You put up a stiff fight. We usually kill anybody who puts up a fight, capeesh? Any fight at all. My guys are itching to get at you, but I'm going to save your bacon if I can. Go along with me, and I'll stick you in the longboat and point you toward Cuba. Give me zulla and you're dead."

I let that sink in while I drew my cutlass. "All right, there's a doctor on board. I want him. Now!"

I had been pretty sure there was because I had spotted a guy at the back bandaging somebody's arm, and he had looked like he knew what he was doing. The others pushed him up front, and I grabbed him. I told him to treat our wounded and do it right or there would be trouble, and gave him a shove.

"A carpenter. I know you've got one. Let's see him."

He came forward, I think just because he knew the rest would make him if he did not.

"Carpenter's mate! Let's see him, too."

Three or four sailors said he was dead and offered to show me his body. I made the carpenter pick him out for me, and he was dead all right.

"One more, and you can go. Sailmaker! Come forward."

They had to shove him, but he came.

We launched their longboat and got the rest of them into it. There was bottled wine in the hold. Giving each wounded pirate a drink, with one for Novia and one for the doctor, emptied two bottles. We filled them with water, and gave the men in the longboat those with two loaves of ship's bread. A few minutes after they put out, I saw the little boat-mast go up and a gaff sail run up and trimmed. There were some pretty good sailors there.

I told the three men I had kept that nobody was going to make them turn pirate. "We're heading for Cow Island," I said. "Do your work and keep your mouths shut and I'll put you ashore there safe and sound, with my thanks. There are three of you, so each of you will have two others to swear that you were forced. Make trouble, and you're dead. We won't fool around with you. We'll kill you, capeesh? For now, you two are doctor's helpers. Do what he tells you."

There is a lot more I could say, how we threw the dead Spanish overboard and buried our own at sea, and who they were, and so forth. But time is getting tight.

Back on the *Castillo Blanco,* I did what I had been planning to do before we sighted the *Vincente*. I had some of our wounded stand guard on our food and water. Back there I said we had a lot of men, but after leaving Bouton on the *Vincente* with enough men to work her, we barely had enough sound men to handle the *Castillo Blanco*. So you could say it was a waste, if you wanted to. The thing was that those wounded men would not be much help at making sail or taking it in, but they could handle sitting in front of a door with pistols in their laps. It gave them something to do, and I thought it might save a few lives before long.

23

Jaime

I WAS WRONG about that. I have been trying to make myself skip this part, but that would be a kind of lie. The day before we sighted the *Magdelena,* we found one of my wounded sentries dead. Searching the ship got us nowhere, so after that I had two watch at a time.

And when we met up with the *Magdelena* at Île à Vache, I did one of the dumbest things I have done in my whole life. Being honest means I have to write about it, but it is not fun and I am going to keep it just as short as I can.

I had Rombeau send Don José over. His hands and feet were tied, and I could have tortured him then and there, but I did not. Maybe I had the guts to do it and maybe I did not, but what was for sure was that I did not want to. I told him I had found one secret compartment on his ship, and I knew maledizione well there was another. I wanted to know where it was, and if he did not tell me, we were going to burn him with hot irons—his face, the soles of his feet, and anyplace else we thought might get him to talk.

He said, "You may burn me, Señor. You may tear my arms off as you threaten. I cannot prevent you, but I cannot produce a second hiding place where none is."

So what did I do? I roughed him up a little, tied him to a timber down in the hold without food or water, and told him he was going to have the rest of the day and all night to think about what we would do in the morning. And I left him there.

In the morning he was dead, strangled just like Ben and the others. That is all I mean to write about this.

WE DID A heck of a lot of work on Cow Island, and I am going to skip over just about all of it. First we shook up the crews, me getting more and Rombeau fewer. After that we really got to work, and ended up careening all three ships. The *Castillo Blanco* was first because I was worried about the scrape. After that we did the same thing with the *Vincente*. She was too good a ship to give up, and I knew—though most of the men still did not—that we would be going around the Horn with Capt. Burt. For a voyage as long as that, you want to start with everything in tip-top shape.

And after both of those, we did *Magdelena* all over again, mostly because we had gotten good at it. She was smaller than the *Vincente,* but carried more and bigger guns, and I have got to say she was the hardest of the whole bunch.

We got a few men on Cow Island, but not a lot. Four, I think it was. The thing was, there were not a lot there. And those who were wanted to sign on after we had careened our ships, not before. I did not want men like that, and I told them so. If they were not willing to work, I did not give a rat's rear end whether they would fight or not. I had more men now (and Azuka, who had come back with Willy when we shook up the crews), so I told Rombeau that if he wanted those guys he could have them. I do not believe he took even one of them.

There is another thing I should say. Okay, maybe a couple. One is that he had taken no prizes. The other is that I turned loose the doctor and the others as soon as we dropped anchor, exactly like I had promised. About the time we had the *Castillo Blanco* up on the beach, they came back, all three in a group. For one thing they had found out that Spaniards were not really popular on that island. For another, they had not been able to find any way to get over to the Spanish side of Hispaniola. They wanted me to take them there, which of course I would not do. A day or so after that, they decided to sail to Jamaica with us. It meant we had the carpenter, which turned out to be a lucky break.

It is not a long trip, but we ran into a calm that made it longer than it should have been. We had been going pretty much nowhere for two or three days, I think it was, when one of the wounded men came running to report that his partner had been strangled. He had left his post to use the head, and when he came back he found the body. I went down and had a look at him, and it was Pete the Hangman. I searched the ship all over again, and had Novia, Bouton, and some others search with me. No dice.

Red Jack came early next morning with a round robin and a committee. The ship was cursed, they said. They liked me and all that. They knew how hard it was to be a good captain, and I had been a good one. But either we sold the *Castillo Blanco* in Port Royal or they would vote me out and put in somebody who would.

I told them I had been thinking pretty much the same way, but I was not going to sell our problem to somebody else and get more people killed. If I was going to stay captain, we would shift everything worth moving to the *Vincente* and abandon the *Castillo Blanco* and its curse. (I said curse because they had. I knew by then that it was a stowaway, and I had a pretty good idea who it was. But if I had told them then, there would have been all sorts of trouble.)

As it was, they just wanted to know whether I meant right now. I said bloody right, istantáneamente.

"Today?" They wanted to be sure.

I said, "Let's start loading the longboat. While we stand around here talking, we're just wasting time."

They were scared, and by that time so was I, a little. If we took the *Castillo Blanco* to Port Royal, they were going to be on board her for another three or four days, and it could have been a week. I was offering to get them off right away, so I won.

"What if we bring the curse in the things we are taking, Crisóforo?" Novia looked like she thought we really might.

"There's another secret compartment on this ship," I told her. "I can't find it, but I know there is one, and that's where he is this minute. He may or may not figure out what we're doing, but he'll have to stay there just the same. He can't hide in one of the boats in broad daylight, and he's not small enough to hide in a cannon barrel or a water cask. We're going, and we're leaving him behind."

Which is what we did. The cannon were the hardest part, as they always are. But we used the sweeps to come alongside and were able to hoist them onto the *Vincente* with ropes running from the mainmast of the *Castillo Blanco* and main yard of the *Vincente*. The Caribbean was as calm as glass just then, which helped a lot.

I was the last to go, in the evening after a little breeze had sprung up. Before I left I went through the whole ship with a cocked pistol in one hand and my dagger in the other. What I yelled to the stowaway, I yelled three or four times in various places. There is no sense my giving it here more than once, because it was all the same. This is pretty much what I said in Spanish.

"Jaime! You win! We're going, and I'm taking your wife. If you'd rather we'd stay, or you want to go with us, come out and we'll talk about it. This is a little ship, but I don't think you can handle her alone." Here I waited two or three minutes.

"No hard feelings if you want to try. Head northwest if you can. That will take you to Cuba or New Spain. East ought to be easy. The first land you sight should be the French end of Hispaniola. We're leaving you a keg of water and half a barrel of salt pork. Good luck!"

I was hoping he would come out and give me his hand. I knew Novia—okay, let's be formal here, I knew that Señora Sabina Guzman—did not want him anymore. She would stay with me, we would set him ashore someplace, and we'd be rid of him.

At the same time, I was afraid he would jump me. In which case I was going to shoot him. Or whatever.

Neither of them happened. Novia and I were the last to leave. She was crying, and I felt pretty bad, too. The *Castillo Blanco* was a beautiful little ship, and she had sailed like a dream. She would be called a schooner now, but we called her a two-stick sloop. When I think of her it is always in one of two ways. The first is outrunning the *Lucía,* jumping around among the rocks of the Canal du Sud, half the time in the surf. The other one I am about to tell you about.

Novia and I were on the quarterdeck of the *Vincente* looking back at the *Castillo Blanco*. She had been a sort of resort hotel for us. I almost said a honeymoon hotel, and maybe I should have. Neither of us was ever going to forget her, and both of us knew that. We were holding hands and wishing things had gone differently, when we saw the first flames. That was when the fire burned through the hatch cover.

Novia looked at me and said, "Crisóforo . . . ?"

"No," I said. "Absolutely not. Did you do it?"

She just shook her head. Later she said she thought one of the crew must have done it before he got into the longboat.

The fire got bigger, and all of a sudden there was somebody standing on the quarterdeck. Novia screamed and pointed.

I said, "Is that him?," and she stared for a second or two, then asked for my glass.

She must have looked at him through it for a minute or more. Finally she took it down, slid the brass sections together again, and gave it back to me. I did not say anything more, but the question was still there, if you know what I mean.

Finally, she said, "Yes." There were tears in her eyes.

Rombeau came over and asked who it was, but neither of us told him anything right then. We were watching Jaime. I figured he would dive overboard any minute and start swimming, but he did not. He did not hold the wheel, or climb the rigging to get away from the fire, or in fact do anything. He just stood there. There was a big puff of flame and a roar we could hear just fine over where we were.

When the flames died down a little, he was gone. What happened, I am pretty sure, is that the fire had burned through the quarterdeck. That was the roar we heard, and the puff of flame. When it did he fell, and it must have been like falling into a furnace.

"I am a single woman now," Novia said, and went below. I knew she wanted to be alone, and I told myself right then that I should stay away from the cabin until pretty late.

The first thing I did after I left was explain things to Bouton. "There are only two or three things I'm sure of," I said. "The rest is guesses. If you've got better guesses, I'd like to hear them."

He nodded, "You will, Captain, if they find any faith with me."

"There was a secret compartment in that ship. I showed it to you the night we got Estrellita to come out of it. There was another one, too, one we never found. One I couldn't find even when I knew I was looking for a secret compartment."

"For what purpose?"

I shrugged. "Smuggling, maybe. Have you got a better idea?"

"I have no idea at all, Captain. What would be smuggled?"

"Gold, silver, whatever would show a profit. The gold and silver the mines produce belong to the Crown, because the king owns the mines. It can't be spent until it's been minted. Suppose a smart Spaniard could get hold of some of it before it left New Spain. What could he do?"

Bouton leaned against the rail and pulled at his nose. "What we would do, I suppose."

I shook my head. "We'd take it to Port Royal or some French colony, or a Dutch or Danish one, and sell it for whatever we could get. If a Spaniard went to one of those places, don't you think his government would notice?"

"Yes, if they knew."

"They'd know, because his crew would talk about it when they got back to New Spain."

Something struck Bouton as funny, and he roared.

When he finally quieted down, I asked what it had been.

"They would not get there, Captain. Not to Port Royal, certainly. What chance would a Spanish ship have there?"

He had a point, and I said, "You're right, but that's just another arm of the argument I'm making. Anyway, look at this. A rich man, a big landowner, has a beautiful little ship he uses for pleasure trips and so on. By and by he loses his wife. There's a lot of disease, and who knows? He marries again and uses his ship to take his new bride to Spain, then on a nice cruise to Italy and France. Maybe all around the Mediterranean. What's wrong with that?"

Bouton rubbed his jaw. "Nothing, I suppose, if he can dodge the corsairs."

"They stop at Naples or wherever, and he gives his crew leave, except for one or two men he can trust—the captain and the mate, maybe. When they sail out of the Bay of Naples, the ship's a bit lighter. But who's going to notice?"

"Low," Bouton told me. "This secret place for gold will be very near the keel."

I nodded. "I think so, too. But I couldn't find it without tearing the ship apart. The thing is, Jaime did. Maybe Don José showed it to him—I don't know. When he found out Estrellita had been cheating on him with Don José, he went down there. My guess is that he just wanted to be alone for a while to think things out. He did, and it drove him a little crazy. Sabina was his wife. I know you know that."

"I comprehend."

"He beat her because he thought she'd fallen for me. He'd beaten her before, but this time he really laid into her, and a few days later he did it again. One day he came home and she was gone, and she never came back. It must have hurt him a lot."

"Any man would be hurt, Captain." Bouton was nothing like handsome. Looking at him in the watery light of a lantern somebody had run up the mizzen, I wondered whether any woman had ever loved him, and whether any woman ever would.

"So Jaime took up with his housemaid, Estrellita. It would be a cinch to blame her for that, but I'll skip it. If she had played it straight, she'd probably have ended up with the second son of a grocer. Jaime was big and strong, and rich. A lot of women have done worse things."

Bouton nodded.

"Only Don José was richer and a lot smoother. She probably thought Jaime might dump her when they got to New Spain, and it would be smart to have somebody to fall back on. Only Jaime found out, and when he did he got a little crazy."

"Yet he did not leap into the sea as Don José recounted," Bouton put in.

"Right. My guess is that Don José really thought he had, though, at least at first. The secret compartment down in the hold can't be very big. About the size of a coffin, if I had to guess. Don José probably thought Jaime wouldn't get in there, and he might have thought Jaime couldn't. Later he must have found out he was wrong."

"His crew suffered, Captain. Not ours alone."

"Exactly. What would you have done?"

Bouton drew his finger across his throat.

"Sure. It would have been easy to kill him. Let's say he could shoot through the wood and into that secret compartment. Then he drags the body up on deck. There's an officer on watch who's awake, and a man at the wheel, even if the rest of the watch is asleep."

"The shots would awaken many," Bouton said.

"I think so, too. They make port in New Spain, somebody talks, and Don José gets busted."

"I am in agreement," Bouton said. "He will not do this. He will take his captain and perhaps one other man. They will open the compartment. If this Jaime fights, they will kill him."

"Swell. Only now Ojeda and the other man know where the compartment is and how it works. Besides, what if they don't kill him? Suppose he just gives up. Or suppose Don José shoots him, but he doesn't die? He was Don José's partner. My guess is that he was originally supposed to be their Spanish connection. He'll talk."

I shook my head. "Don José played it smart. He let Jaime alone. There was a good chance somebody in the crew he tried to jump would kill him. There was also a real good chance he would try to jump Don José. If he did that, Don José would be ready. He'd have weapons, probably a knife and couple of pocket pistols, and everybody would call him a hero. He'd have to act before they made port, sure. But until they did, the smart move was to watch and wait and hope for the best. Which is what he did."

We were quiet for a while after that. Finally Bouton said, "He killed him, Captain. This Jaime who was the husband of Señora Sabina. He strangled Don José. It was shortly after we dropped anchor at Île à Vache, was it not?"

"That's right. Don José pushed his luck too far. He hoped Jaime would come around to see him when we left him alone in the hold. He'd always been able to talk Jaime into just about anything, and this time he'd talk him into cutting him loose. The two of them would sneak up on deck, go over the side, and swim for shore. With luck, they might have been able to lose themselves on the island until we left. Only it didn't work—"

That was when Novia came up and asked when I was coming to bed.

24

Our Pirate Fleet

THE SECRETARY of State was on TV tonight. She said flatly that the PCC is losing its grip. I cannot express the joy I feel.

I will see my Novia again, or die trying. I will even the score—no, that is wrong. Vengeance is a sin. I will forgive him, if I can. May God forgive all his cruelty and betrayal.

LAST NIGHT I was shaken by what I had heard. Today I was joyful, whistling and singing under my breath. Old, old chanteys we sang around the capstan, and songs the men used to ask me to sing after we found the guitar on the *Castillo Blanco*—"Far Aloft," "Ritorna-Me," "Sott'er Cielo de Roma," "Mon Petit Bateau," and on and on.

"Carmela," "La Golondrina," "El Cefiro," and "Flor de Limón." Old Spanish songs the priest in Coruña had taught me or that Novia had taught me. Simple songs we had played in the music class at the monastery. It was all I could do to keep from humming when I said mass. To a congregation of old ladies, I preached on the goodness of God. And was really preaching to myself, and preaching to the choir at that.

What follows will be—must be—summary. I will have time for nothing more.

WE HAD A Spanish carpenter on board. I believe I have explained that. I set him to work making more gunports, and before we made Port Royal we had all the guns from the *Castillo Blanco* in place and ready to fire. It gave us fifteen guns per side, plus the same bow and stern chasers we had on the *Castillo Blanco*. With five twelve-pounders and five nine-pounders per side, we could stand up to anything short of a galleon.

In Port Royal, where a big crane on a barge made things easy for us, we reshuffled the guns as well, putting the twelve-pounders on the lower deck and our old nines on the upper deck where the twelves had been. I knew it would make the ship a better sailer, which it did.

We repainted, too. And when the repainting was almost complete, we renamed our ship, making her the *Santa Sabina de Roma*.

We gilded a lot of woodwork on the stern, too. The idea was to make the *Sabina* look like one of the smaller Spanish galleons. Novia wanted to embroider a cross on the mainsail. That would have taken forever, but she and I laid one out, marking it with charcoal, and painted it in an afternoon.

Port Royal was a very interesting town if you stayed sober and kept your eyes open. There were water hoys all over the place, because the town had no wells. Water had to be fetched across from the Copper River. You could buy a white woman—an indentured servant—there just like you would buy a slave. Novia and I watched it one time, and the best-looking one (she was blond and looked German or maybe Dutch) went for forty doubloons.

The fact of the matter was that there was not much you could not buy there. Prices were the highest you would see anywhere, but whatever it was, somebody had it or would get it.

One of the chores I had there was talking to the merchant—his name was Bowen—who had gotten ransoms for Don José and Pilar for us. I had to tell him Don José was dead.

"What of the woman, his wife, Captain. You have her still?"

I said yes.

"Very well." He rubbed his hands. "You'll turn her over to me? I'll see that she reaches her friends safely."

"Sure," I said. "You'll be doing me a big favor."

"And myself, Captain. The ransoms were for both. We will return half, less—let me see . . . Less twenty percent. I will complain that due to the slowness with which the very modest ransom you asked was paid, Don José perished in captivity. Would you care for a cigar?"

I said no, and he lit one for himself from a little spirit lamp.

"As the ransoms were for both, we have every right to return the wife to her friends and family, and keep half. I will take my commission of ten percent on that. Twenty percent of the remaining half we will retain for our trouble, and to defray the expense of holding the two for so long, of writing and sending letters and so forth. Of that, I will take half, you the remaining half. Is that agreeable?"

I could have argued that he was entitled to ten percent, not fifty. But if I had, he would have reminded me that it was my fault Don José was dead. Which it was.

Could I have gotten ninety percent? Sure. I could have cocked my pistol and cut up rough, and gotten every last doubloon—after which, he would never have worked with me again. Instead, I said half the twenty percent was fine with me and walked out with everything I had coming, in gold. If you do the math, you will find that I got better than fifty-five percent of what I had been hoping for the first time I talked to him. I had gone in there expecting to get nothing. John Bowen could have taken Pilar off my hands and kept everything for himself. He did not, and after that I understood why people had advised me to do business with him.

MRS. TAYLOR ASKED whether I would schedule confession sometime. It made me feel as guilty as I ever get, which is not nearly guilty enough in a lot of cases. Fr. Houdek had not really believed in confession, and neither had Fr. Phil. They did not say it, but you could see it from the way they acted. Talking with Mrs. Taylor made me think about the priests at Our Lady of Bethlehem, and how they went into Havana at least once a week to hear confessions. We had confession in the chapel every evening. You did not have to go, but you could.

I told Mrs. Taylor that I would hear confessions every Saturday afternoon from two to four, for as long as I was at Holy Family. If no one came, I would wait for those two hours anyway—it would give me a fine chance to pray.

It will also mean that I will no longer be tempted to go to New Jersey on Saturday, a temptation that has been growing stronger and stronger in the past few weeks. I tell myself that if I do not speak to either of them it can do no harm. That may be true, but can I control the urge to speak to them when I see them?

What if they speak to me?

It would be so easy. Fr. Wahl would be delighted to take my mass. I would buy a monorail ticket, change trains in the city, and arrive in four hours or so. When evening came, I would beg a night's lodging at some rectory. In the morning, I would return.

Very easy—and it might ruin everything. What if my father decided not to go to Cuba to run the casino? What if he did not enroll me in the monastery school because of something I ("that tall priest with the beat-up face," he would call me) happened to say to him? Novia would be lost. Everything would be lost. *None of it would ever have happened.*

I pray God will put this temptation from me.

HAVE I SET down all the important stuff about Port Royal? I think so, and some unimportant stuff, too. With better ships and more men to crew them, we sailed around the island to Long Bay—that's my two ships, Rombeau in *Magdelena* and Novia and me in *Sabina*.

There was a sloop there flying the black flag. The captain—as small and active as his ship—asked to come aboard and did. When I had talked to him a little I got Rombeau over, too, and called a meeting.

"He says Captain Burt's gone to Portobello instead of Maracaibo," I told everybody. "I have some questions, and I'll bet you do, too. Let's hear them."

Rombeau grinned. It makes him look like a hungry shark—I have probably said that. "How do we know you speak for Captain Burt? Prove that to me, and I believe you."

Harker reached into his pocket and took out a folded paper. "Can you read English?"

Rombeau shook his head.

"Then I can't prove it to you. Can you, Captain?"

I said I could and took the paper. I cannot remember the exact wording, but this is close:

The bearer is Capt. Hal Harker of my sloop Princess. *He will tell you where I have gone, and why; it will be the Devil's own chance, that if fortune favors us should leave all of us rich. Join me as speedily as wind and weather permit, bringing none but sound men.*

Your Comrade and Commander,
Abraham Burt, Captain
Signed aboard my ship Weald
this 12th day of September

I read it aloud in English, then in French, and at last in Spanish as a courtesy to Novia, although I knew she had understood the first two.

Rombeau licked his thin lips. "Do you credit it, Captain?"

I shrugged and asked Harker, "Were you there when he wrote it?"

"I was, Captain, and I watched him write it, sand it, and fold it. After that he passed it to me. He'd already given me my orders."

"He dipped his pen in the inkwell seven times," I said. "I can tell from the writing. You saw him do that, Captain Harker. What did his inkstand look like?"

For a minute Harker looked blank. Novia giggled a little.

"I'll give you time to think about it, but you must have seen it."

"Aye, sir. I did, Captain. It was brass, not one of the big ones. All brass, I believe, and no wood about it. There were shells on it. Not real shells but in the brass, I mean. Scallops, Captain."

I spoke to Rombeau. "I believe him. Do you?"

"It was correct? What he said?"

I nodded.

Novia said, "He has told us he is going to Maracaibo. We are to meet him there. Do you know why he changed his plans, Capitán Harker?"

"I do, madam. Captain Gosling took a Spanish ship, the *Nuestra Señora de las Nieves*. I would say that means 'Snow Lady,' although you may correct me, and welcome. She was bound for Maracaibo and had letters aboard. Gosling opened them and read them."

"He reads Spanish, Captain Harker?"

Harker nodded. "He was a prisoner of theirs for three years, madam. The governor of the prison liked him, and loaned him his books. He didn't

227

know ten words when he was taken, he says, but by the time he was exchanged, he could read it like 'twere English."

Rombeau frowned, and Harker said, "I mean no offense, gentlemen. I can't read Spanish myself, nor your French neither."

There was some arguing here that I will skip. I cut it off by asking what the letters said.

"That we were planning to attack Maracaibo, as I understand, Captain. Somebody had talked, and it had come to the ears of some Spaniard in Veracruz. Gosling told Captain Burt when they met, and Captain Burt got all of us together—as many as were there, is what I intend. He told us and wanted to know who was game to go through with it. I was." Harker shrugged. "The rest were not. The Spanish have been shipping silver from Portobello now—bar silver, we're told, because the mint in Mexico can't keep up. They wanted to go for that, and Captain Cox has made friends with a tribe on the coast. They'll guide us around behind the town, he says, for there's a fort to guard the harbor."

Novia asked, "And that is what Captain Burt has decided to do?"

Harker looked doubtful. "It was decided for him, if you take my meaning, madam. Dobkin and I stood by him, those that sit with us now weren't there, nor was Captain Lesage. The rest were against him, every man. If he had stood out for Maracaibo, they'd have gone at Portobello on their own, and he wouldn't have had force enough to do it."

Novia nodded. "I see."

"So he sent me here," Harker continued. "I'm to speak with you and Captain Rombeau here, and to Captain Lesage, and send you to Portobello—to the Pearls, really, that being where we are to meet."

I said, "On the other side of the Gulf of Mosquitoes?"

"Exactly, Captain. You are to go there straight away, if that's convenient. I'll have to wait here for Captain Lesage. We'll join you directly when he comes. I don't suppose you have news of him?"

I did not, but I asked about his ship. It was the *Bretagne,* which was what I had been thinking.

THE COMMUNISTS HAVE fallen! Or if they have not, they are falling. The reports we get are very confused and none of America's intrepid journalists are sufficiently intrepid to go to Cuba and see for themselves. I have been thinking of going. It might be possible to hire a boat in Miami that would make the run, but I am quite sure it would take a lot more money than I have. It might also be possible to steal one, and to tell the truth I am sorely tempted.

But no. Our Lady of Bethlehem will not have been reopened so quickly. Once in Cuba, I would have to wait. I can wait just as well here, and perhaps do some good.

Until air service is resumed, I will remain. That will be—must be—my yardstick.

A lot of things must have happened while we sailed from Long Bay to the Pearls, but the only one I remember clearly is that Novia and Azuka had a big fight and tried to kill each other. We separated them and told them that when we got to the islands we would set them ashore with whatever weapons they wanted.

I believe I probably said we would do it right away, but Capt. Burt wanted to see me as soon as we got there. So I came, bringing Novia with me. It was something I had never done before.

There were two reasons for that, both good. The first was that she was my real second-in-command, and everyone knew it by then. Taking Porto-bello meant going ashore and marching through the jungle, and I meant to leave her on the *Sabina* to look after things for me. She would need to be filled in as well as it could be done.

The second was pretty obvious. I was afraid she and Azuka would go at it again and the crew would take sides. A big fight among ourselves, with four or five dead and fifteen or twenty wounded, was exactly what we did not need.

I explained my first reason (but not my second) to Capt. Burt, who smiled and paid Novia compliments, and poured wine for all three of us. Then, when we were seated in his cabin and comfortable, he snapped, "Can we trust you, Señora?"

For a minute there I was afraid she would fly off the handle, but she was cool as Christmas. "If you are indeed Crisóforo's friend, Capitán Burt, you may trust me to the death and beyond. If you betray him, I will see you hang or kill you myself."

"Captain Burt won't betray me," I told her.

He chuckled, and put down the pistol he had been oiling. "She had a right to say what she did, Chris. I began it, after all."

He went back to Novia, dead serious again. "You're Spanish, Señora? You did not deny it."

"I am. So was my husband, who was a beast. So was the father who sent me to him and turned the blind eye to my bruises and my degradation. If I had been as I am now, Capitán Burt, I should have killed him by my own hand. I was not so hard in that time, only a silly chit who thought herself a woman. It is now otherwise."

"You'll kill him if you see him, Señora?"

"He is no more, Capitán Burt. I did not kill him, nor did Crisóforo, yet we watch him die."

I said, "I suggested to Novia that you might marry us, Captain. We talked it over and decided we'd like a priest and a wedding in a church. I told her you'd understand, as I'm sure you do."

"I do, of course. I understand, too, that a Spanish woman, a beautiful, educated Spanish woman, may be a great help to us. Will you help us, Señora? Should the occasion arise?"

Novia nodded. "If Crisóforo wishes it. No! Even when he does not. He does not wish me to risk myself. Inquire of him who was first of all to board the *San Vincente de Zaragozza*."

"It was the person we found lying on deck unconscious with a couple of empty pistols," I told him.

"There was the blood on my puñal? You must say this, too."

I nodded. "A lot of it."

"Capitán Burt—you comprehend?"

"Oh, I do indeed, Señora." He favored her with his warmest smile. "Not all beautiful things are treasures, but all treasures are beautiful. You're a treasure."

"Then I, this treasure, ask a question. We come here, not Maracaibo, because they are warned there. Not by me. Did you think that?"

His head bobbed, though so little I might have missed it. "I had to consider it, Señora. I'd have been a fool not to. Would I credit the idea now? Not I, Señora. I wouldn't."

I was starting to relax. It could have been the wine, but I think that what Capt. Burt had just told us had a lot more to do with it. I said, "Let me put another idea to rest before it comes up. We had a prisoner we were holding for ransom, a Spanish lady called Pilar. Her ransom was paid—I'll give you your cut of that and a good deal more before we go. When it was, I handed her over to John Bowen, who'd collected the ransom for us, and I assume he handed her over to her relatives."

"I see." Capt. Burt was watching me, his face expressionless.

"So there are a bunch of questions. Could she have heard about Maracaibo while we had her? Yes, it—"

"That fool?" Novia looked as if she wanted to spit. "She might hear a hundred times and understand nothing."

"It isn't likely," I continued, "but it's possible. I know I didn't spill the beans. But my officers knew—Rombeau and Bouton. I made them swear they'd tell no one, but who knows?"

Capt. Burt nodded.

"I also, Crisóforo."

"Right. Novia here, too. It could have happened. Next question. Could Pilar have gotten to Veracruz in time for her to tell somebody there, who wrote a letter that he put on a ship to Maracaibo—a ship that was taken by Captain Gosling, who told you about the letter? And—oh, yeah, there had to be time for you to have a meeting with your captains and tell them about it, and send off Harker to tell us."

"Right you are, Chris. Was there?"

"Absolutely not. Two days after I turned Pilar over to Bowen, we sailed for Long Bay. We got there the next day. Harker was riding at anchor there when we came into the bay. Say four days tops. I'd bet you a doubloon to a shilling that Pilar was still in Port Royal when we talked to Harker. I'll bet you again—same bet—that Bowen sent her to Spain, not Veracruz. As a gentleman and a friend, I'll warn you before you take my bet that Spain was where he told me he'd send her. It's where her family is."

"Need I say I believe you, Chris? I do. One more question, and we'll leave it. Whom have you told?"

"The people I've already mentioned. Bouton, Rombeau, and Novia here. Nobody else."

"And you, Señora? Whom did you tell?"

"Nadie. No one."

I said, "We should ask you the same question, Captain Burt. Who did you tell?"

He sipped his wine. "Far too many, as is now clear. All my captains. Besides yourself, Gosling, Cox, Lesage, Dobkin, Isham, Ogg, and Harker. All my captains. Add to that Tom Jackson, my mate. You don't have to tell me any one of them may have been indiscreet. I know it already."

"You must indulge me," Novia said, "for I am a woman and we ask many questions. Has someone told them in Portobello? If no, we should act soon, is that not true? If yes, we should not go there at all, I think."

"I agree, Señora. Your Captain Chris has brought us two fine ships. Three more ships would complete our pirate fleet—Isham's, Lesage's, and Harker's."

Capt. Burt drummed his fingers on the table, and his face got hard. "The minute one more arrives, we'll sail. If none in a week, we'll sail anyway with what we have."

THAT NIGHT, AS Novia and I lay naked and sweating in the larger, longer bunk I had made for us in Port Royal, she said, "There is a certain one you did not speak of today, Crisóforo. One more who might know. I did not say her name to Captain Burt, and now I wish you to know I did not."

"I told him the truth," I said, "he wanted to know who I'd told, not who might have overheard me."

"She was listening, you think? In the wall which once was in the *White Castle*?"

"Say *Castillo Blanco*," I told Novia, and kissed her ear to show I was half kidding. "You don't translate ships' names."

"Was she?"

I do not remember just what I said then. Probably it was that Estrellita might have been. If she had been, and had told, who could blame her?

25

The March to Portobello

TWO DAYS AFTER I had reported to Capt. Burt, Capt. Isham's *Emilia* joined us. We sailed the next morning, going wide of Portobello before entering the Gulf of Saint Blaise.

The Native American tribe Capt. Cox had found for us was the Kuna. Nothing I had seen in Veracruz had prepared me for them. The men went naked, or nearly so, and striped their bodies with black paint.

The women touched up their faces and bodies with red paint a lot like ours do. They wore blankets or shawls, draped in various ways and generally slipping in one way or another at any unusual motion. Quite a few were slender, handsome girls, so flirtatious that I wondered if they had learned it from the Spaniards who raided them for slaves. For as long as we were among these women, men disappeared—only to rejoin us, grinning and swaggering, after an hour or two.

Both men and women wore nose rings, and the status of the wearer could be judged by them. The rings of the poor ones were silver and narrow. Wealthier ones wore wider silver rings. For still richer Kunas, the ring was gold. The ring of chief was gold, and so wide he had to lift it with one hand to eat and drink.

There were a number of white women Kunas, blonder women than any American I ever saw. Their eyes were blue, and their hair hardly yellower than ivory. Capt. Cox, who knew the Kuna better, I think, than anyone else, told me once that these white Native Americans could see better in the dark than by day, like owls. They were of all ranks, as far as I could see, some having narrow silver rings, and a few broad gold ones. The women who were better off, both the blondes and the black-haired women, wore necklaces and bracelets of beads.

We gave the chief a good many gifts, which he parceled out among his people. When I heard there was to be an exchange of gifts, I expected junk jewelry, but we did not have any. We gave him steel axes, hatchets, knives and needles, as well as some copper pots that had been polished bright. In return we got gifts of fresh meat, fruit, and cornmeal. That may not sound like much, but you should have seen us eat.

This chief was a tall man, elderly but still strong-looking. He wore a crown of rushes bound with a gold band. We called him the king and said "Your Majesty" when we talked to him. His robe was a loose smock of cotton hardly thicker than cheesecloth that I would think must originally have been a woman's retiring gown. It had been embroidered just about everywhere with red and black thread. The designs were probably significant to him and his people, but to me they were only meaningless shapes of various colors, except for a big red-and-black cross.

He had many wives and what seemed like at least two dozen daughters. Seeing these, Novia informed me in no uncertain terms that she was sticking close to me when we marched. I countered by ordering her to remain on the *Sabina,* and swore that I would flog her if she disobeyed. She said that I could beat her if I liked—she could not prevent me—but she would come no matter how cruelly I punished the love she bore me.

I countered, of course, by saying that if she truly loved me she would trust me with the chief's daughters or any other woman on earth.

She replied to that one by threatening to kill herself if I left her behind. And so it went.

The next day the chief asked that she be undressed for his inspection, as he had never seen "English woman." That decided me.

I took her back to the ship and chained her in our cabin by an ankle, giving the key to Bouton. "Turn her loose three days after we march," I told him. "For as long as she's chained up, you're in command. When you unchain her, she is."

"And she will sail home!" Novia screamed. "Never, never will she lay the eye on you again!" After that she cried. I waited until she had finished crying and would talk sensibly before I left her.

I had expected us to march the next day, but it was spent on plans, preparations, and more eating. Half of each ship's crew was to remain on board. Four days would be enough for us to get behind Portobello. On the fifth, the ships would fake an attack on the fort, drawing any troops that might be in the town to it. We would take the town from the landward side, loot it, and carry our gains east along the coast far enough that they could be loaded onto the ships beyond the range of the Spanish batteries.

LAST NIGHT I dreamed it was all happening again. I was back in the jungle and trying to load my lupara before they rushed us, then wandering drenched with sweat and half blinded by bugs through a battle that never ended, looking for my father and knowing that if I did not find him first we would kill each other.

I do not suppose I dream more often than other men, or that my dreams are more lifelike than theirs. But that dream shook me about as deeply as I can be shaken, and left me so slowly that I wondered whether it would leave me at all. I had eaten lunch and gone out visiting the sick before I was entirely free of it. (If I really am now. It will not be easy to sleep tonight.)

The dream was clearly due to writing about our attack on Portobello. Writing it woke a bunch of memories—the mosquitoes, the screaming of the birds, the big crocodiles with devil eyes, and Paddy Quilligan getting bitten by a snake and dying almost before anybody could ask what was wrong.

TONIGHT I FOUND a Web site that has quotations. I looked for dreams, and this one is so much like mine (and like what we went through) that for a moment I wondered whether Shakespeare could have been along with us.

He was not, and yet he might have been. That, I think, must be why so many people say he is so great. Here it is.

> Sometimes she driveth o'er a soldier's neck
> And then dreams he of cutting foreign throats,
> Of healths five fadom deep: and then anon
> Drums in his ear, at which he starts and wakes,
> And being thus frightd swears a prayer or two . . .

We marched under flags by ship's companies, but all the flags were black. So that each might know his own, differing objects were hung from the flagpoles. Capt. Burt, I remember, used the green bough of some flowering tree, Capt. Cox a Turk's head tied in a rope about thick enough for a halyard, and Capt. Dobkin a dried hand. His men said it was his own hand, that had been cut off when he sailed with Mansveldt. Maybe it was.

I have never been good at thinking up things like that and knew it would have to be something light, so as not to tire the man who carried the pole. I asked Novia, and she said she had colored ribbons for trimming gowns, and I could have some of those. She was still chained in our cabin, so I said I would unchain her if she would swear with God as her witness that she would not try to go with us. She said she could not keep it, and it was better to be chained than to break a promise made to God. So she stayed chained, and I went off with the ribbons feeling a lot worse than she did.

Just a minute ago I wrote that there were not really any drums. Then I remembered that there had been, and I had to cross it out. The drums belonged to the Kuna, and three old men beat them. They stayed in the village and drummed for us while we marched out.

We had almost two hundred Kuna with us, and the king's son to lead them. Each of his men had a spear, a bow, arrows, and a steel knife. I know that there were almost two hundred because I tried to count them. The number kept changing, because one or two would run off or come in. But it was almost two hundred, so call it a hundred and ninety.

I never really counted our pirates, because there were a lot more. But we had eight ships, and half the crew of each of the eight. *Weald, Sabina,* and *Magdelena* were all pretty big, but most of the others were smaller, the two-stick sloops that people who write about Blackbeard and Capt. Kidd call schooners. I am going to take a guess and say the average for each ship was a hundred men. That is fifty men from each ship, or four hundred men in all. I had sixty-seven men under me, and Rombeau and his seventy-two. I would say Capt. Cox had less than forty, and that may have been the smallest. It was probably better than four hundred—four hundred and twenty, or something like that.

Before we left, Capt. Burt made a little speech. I do not think I remember it well enough to quote it for this record, but one of the things he said was that we did not want any man who did not want to be with us. Any man who wanted to could go back to the ships at any time. Nobody would interfere with him.

Another thing was that those who could not keep up would be left behind. Nobody would blame them, but nobody would carry them either. They could go back to the ships or try to catch up. That was up to them.

After the first day, we lost some men both ways.

The main things I remember about the march are how hot it was and how bad the bugs were. I had been down in the lowland jungles of Hispaniola. I have already written all about that. When I was there, I thought that had to be the worst place in the world for bugs. Darien was every bit as bad, and it seemed to me like Darien was a lot hotter. We greased ourselves to keep them off, and we sweated off the grease and got bitten anyhow. (The Kuna greased themselves just like we did, but they never seemed to sweat as much.) There were big snakes, some of them poison and some not. There were places where you could drink the water, and places where you could not. The Kuna told us which water was safe, but some of the men drank bad water. It gave them diarrhea. After a while the diarrhea would make them too weak to march.

Here I ought to say that the Kuna marched in front and we followed them. Capt. Cox marched next, because they knew him better than any of the rest of us, and he knew more of their language than we did. After him, Capt. Burt. And after Capt. Burt, me and the *Sabina* gang, with Rombeau and his *Magdelena* gang right behind us. I had given Rombeau some of the ribbons I got from Novia. His were yellow and white, mine red, white, and blue. They reminded me of home, and after a while I remembered that America had fought Spain once and freed Cuba. It made me feel better about what we were doing.

As far back as I was, it was the third day before I realized the Kuna had women with them. The way I found it out was that when they had found something they thought we ought to know about, good water for example, or a lot of fruit that was good to eat, the chief's son would send a runner back to tell us. This time the news was that they had a Native American from another tribe who had been a slave in Portobello and run away. Only this time the runner was one of the white Native American girls. She spoke enough English, and was good enough with signs, for me to understand that there was somebody new up front the captains might want to talk to.

I told her she was going to get hurt going to war like this, and she said she was as brave as any man, thumping her chest above her breasts and pretending to draw a bow. It might even have been true. I told her good luck and gave her Paddy Quilligan's little gold cross. (One of the men had taken it off his body before we buried him. We had kept his weapons, but we had not searched his body and I did not think it was right to do it. When I found out that Marais had his cross, I said we did not loot our own dead and took it away from him. It had been too late then to give it back to Paddy.)

I had only started up the column when one of Capt. Burt's men came. He said I had to come, and I told him I was coming already.

The thing was that this was a Moskito Native American and the Moskitos did not speak the same language as the Kunas. So he was trying to make himself understood to the chief's son, and the chief's son to Capt. Cox, who told Capt. Burt. But he had picked up quite a bit of Spanish while he had been a slave, so Capt. Burt wanted me.

This Moskito was a tough-looking man without an ounce of fat on him. Capt. Burt had what they called a barber-surgeon with his gang, and this doctor was putting soldier salve on the Moskito's ankle, which looked just awful.

The first thing he asked me was whether I was Spanish. I said no, English, but I had lived in Cuba awhile. It was the sort of lie that is not a sin, because I was not trying to deceive him, just trying to make it clear where we stood.

He told me there were many soldiers in Portobello. They stayed mostly at the fort, but now they would send some out to look for him because he had run. I said how many, and he held up five fingers. Capt. Burt and the other captains all agreed that did not sound too bad.

After that, I asked him about the other soldiers who were not at the fort. Where were they? There was a "wall of logs," he said, to watch the road. They were in there. Many soldiers. He opened and closed his hands to show how many, and if he was right about that it was about fifty. He had gone around this stockade through the jungle. He would show us the way.

Of course I asked about other defenses, and he said there were not any. The big questions, naturally, were whether the townspeople would fight? And how hard? There were going to be more of them than us, and if they had guns and were willing to use them, we would have a tough time of it. We were counting on their running when we beat the soldiers.

I talked to Capt. Burt then, mentioning that we could go around the stockade. He said we would have to take it. If we did not, they could hit us from in back when we were looting the town. I said, "Let's leave a couple of dozen men to watch it and shoot at anybody who opens the gate. They won't know how many there are, and I'll bet doubloons to shillings they'll stay in there."

He shook his head. "We can't risk it. They might fight their way out, or our men might run off to get in on the looting." Which I suppose was right.

After that I asked the Moskito how he had escaped. He showed me his ankle, which I had seen already. To keep him from running, his owner had kept him chained to a log he had to drag around. After years of that, his ankle had gotten so bad his owner had taken the chain off to put medicine on it. When he did, the Moskito had knocked him down and run, bad ankle and all. If I could write down how bad I felt about Novia when I saw his ankle, I would. I felt like I was the lowest thing on earth, even though I chained her up because I did not want her to get killed.

To get back to the Moskito, he had seen that some of our men had axes, and he said that if we would lend him an ax he would cut a club and help us kill the Spanish. I told him to come with me and I would give him something a lot better than a club.

There was a lot more talking before we got moving again, but I will not try to give it all. The important thing was that nobody was sure how far we were from the stockade. It was less than a day's march, but still a pretty good way. We talked about it a lot, and asked questions of the Native Americans, but in the end that was all we really knew. We probably would not get there today, but we might. If we did not get there, we might be pretty close by the time we camped. It bothered me.

Before I say more about that—I took the Moskito back with me and gave him Paddy's cutlass. He was crazy about it, and we parted about as friendly as a white and a Native American can ever get.

We camped and ate a little, and lay down hoping the bugs would bother somebody else. I was swatting some and swearing under my breath when it hit me that I was not going to get much sleep anyhow, and it might be better to have a look and see where the stockade was.

I got up as quietly as I could, told Boucher that Rombeau was in charge while I was gone, and off I went. The Kuna stopped me like I knew they would. When I told them what I was doing, the chief's son said he would send a man with me. I said no, let them get some sleep. I would not go far, and I would be right back.

After that I was alone. There were certain animals that were dangerous, and you could always step on a snake that had fallen asleep, but the worst danger was getting lost, and I knew it. I went slowly and carefully, trying to notice bends in the path and trees that might help me on the way back. I kept hoping for a clearing that would let me look up and take my direction from the North Star, but no luck with that.

When I felt a hand on my shoulder, I about jumped out of my clothes and spun around ready to kill somebody. It was the white Kuna girl I had given Paddy's cross. She sort of flattened herself against me the way girls will sometimes. "Happy see me?"

I should have said it was too dark to see anything, but I said yes instead.

"Me show. Keep safe. Come me."

I swear we crossed the same little creek three times before we got to the Spanish road. After that, we did not have to worry about losing our way anymore because it was too plain for that. The worry was that they would see us before we saw them.

That did not happen either. We got to the stockade and crept all the way around it. Twice I saw sentries behind the pointed logs. I could have shot one pretty easily, too, and I was tempted to. But it would have been the worst thing I could do. We did not want them to know we were anywhere in their neighborhood until we rushed them.

I counted my steps when we went back. It was seven thousand two hundred and something. The blond Kuna girl and I kissed twice because she wanted it. She would not tell me her name, saying I had to give her an English name. I said all right, your name is Pinkie.

I swear, that was all we did.

26

Portobello and Santa Maria

ONE OF MY jobs here is to teach religion in the school—I have been doing it to the best of my ability. Perhaps I have mentioned those classes before, but I may not have: the basis of Christian faith is well known, and all the concepts I have taught our children are quite elementary. Their many questions are usually easy and predictable.

Today we discussed the nature of saints. I emphasized that while all those the Church names as saints are indeed saints, there are many, many others who are saints, too.

"Saints," I said, "are the friends of God. Everyone who gets to Heaven is a saint. Whose grandparents are dead? Anybody?"

Several hands went up.

"If your grandparents are in Heaven—it's quite possible they are—they are saints."

Tim waved his book. "I don't understand, Father. It talks about Saint John here and what he did. He wasn't in Heaven when he did those things."

Peggy said, "He was a saint afterward, so they call him that."

I held up my hand. "What did I say a saint was?"

Several voices: "God's friend."

"Exactly. I did *not* say a friend in Heaven. Anyone who is truly God's friend is a saint. He may not know it—that doesn't matter. If he or she is God's friend, that's all it takes." After that I talked about some saints, the Saint John who baptized Jesus, Saint Lucy, Saint Ignatius Loyola (always a favorite of mine), and Saint Catharine of Alexandria.

Donald wanted to argue. "If I was to be a saint, Father Chris, would God do stuff for me? Miracles?"

"He might, but He probably wouldn't."

"I'd be doing stuff for Him, so why wouldn't He do stuff for me?"

I said, "He's already brought you into being, Donald. He maintains you in being, and has given you free will. That means He made you free in a profound way that this desk of mine is not, and in a way that no animal can be. He died for you."

I paused. "Perhaps He might consider that He has already done enough."

Of course I was asked then whether I was God's friend. I explained that I try to be—and often fail. When I go back to Cuba, will they think that I was not God's friend after all? That is what Bishop Scully will think, I know. Let it not be what I think.

Yet none of those things are important. What matters is what He thinks. What He thinks is so.

IN THE MORNING I told Capt. Burt—how many steps along the trail, and how many along the Spanish road.

We had only just gotten on the Spanish road when we heard the drums. They were not Native American drums, but snare drums, beaten to keep soldiers walking in step. We hid in the jungle, whispering that nobody should shoot until they were all in front of us.

It would have been a good idea, but somebody saw a chance to kill the officer and took it. He shot, the officer was bowled over like a rabbit, and the fat was in the fire. After that it was just a wild fight.

We won, I would have to say, mostly because we had more men. There were probably about a hundred fifty Spanish. Maybe two hundred, but it could not have been more than that. We had about six hundred, counting the Kuna. The Spanish bugged out before long, the men who had been at the back of their column forming up, firing a volley, and retreating for all they were worth. The Kuna were after them like hounds, but we held up and tried to get our men back together. It would have been fun to chase those Spanish soldiers, sure, and we would have gotten quite a few. The thing was that if we had we might have run into more, which would have been bad.

Some of our guys did chase them, actually. For an hour or so, as we got organized again and tramped on down the road toward the stockade, we could hear shots in the distance. Some of that was the Spanish shooting at our Kuna, but not all of it was. Our buccaneers were dead shots with a musket or a pistol.

Naturally the Spanish in the stockade knew we were coming after that. They had a couple four-pounders and three or four swivel guns, and everything loaded and ready. There were various things we could have done if there had been time, but there was not. The town would hear the shooting—had probably heard it already—and tell the fort, and the fort might send more soldiers.

Capt. Burt and I went out, with me carrying a flag of truce, and I called on the officer in charge to surrender. If they did, I said, everyone would be spared. But if they did not, we were going to massacre every man. The officer showed himself above the pointed logs and said no way, which was what we had expected. I dropped the flag, three dead shots we had told off to do it killed him the moment my flag hit the ground, and we charged.

Eight of the strongest men I had tried to smash the gate with a log. That gate held, but our guys were jumping up, grabbing the points of the stockade, and pulling themselves over. By the time the log had hit the gate twice, we must have had a hundred men inside the stockade, including me. Each of the four-pounders got off one shot. I do not think all the swivel guns fired, and I know most of the soldiers who tried to shoot between the points died before they could pull the trigger.

Here I ought to say how brave I was, killing Spaniards left and right and fighting it out cutlass-to-sword with a Spanish officer.

Only none of it happened. I am a whole lot prouder of what I really did, which was save the lives of the slaves. Those Spaniards had eight slaves in there to do the work, five Native Americans and three blacks. Our guys were killing everybody, and they would have killed them if I had not stopped it. The Native Americans were Kuna and Moskitos. I freed them straight off, and they grabbed muskets and bullet boxes right away—there were plenty of those lying around by then.

I found Big Ned and showed him to the black slaves. It turned out that they spoke the same language, all four of them having come from the same part of Africa. We told them they could join us and be pirates like Ned, or they could go with our Kunas, if the Kunas would have them. Or if they did not like either of those, we would take them as slaves. They would have to work then, but they would not have to fight. All three decided to join us.

There are a lot of bad memories when I look back on my pirate days. I have already written about some of them, and there are more coming. Just the same, there are good memories, too. Sailing the *Windward,* and a lot of times with Novia when I knew I loved her and she loved me. Marriage is a good thing. I will never say it is not. But it is God who makes you one flesh, not marriage.

So this is one of the best memories, saving the slaves in the Spanish stockade. There were a lot more slaves in Portobello. I am sure some of them were killed, and we made some of the others be slaves for us. I could not stop the killing or talk Capt. Burt into freeing the black ones. (Most of them were Native Americans, and some were white.) So the stockade was the exception.

That just makes it sweeter.

SOMEDAY I AM bound to figure out why I am always getting into trouble. When I try to be bad, I get into trouble. When I try to be good, it is the same thing. We had a parish meeting this evening. This was because of a letter Bishop Scully sent to all the parishes advising us to get together with any parishioners who might have gripes or suggestions. Fr. Wahl and I talked it over and put an announcement in the bulletin. Tonight was the night, and the first part was pretty dull. People told me they liked my sermons (they are short), and some others said how much they appreciated having regular confession on Saturdays.

When nobody else seemed to have anything to say, I told them I had been thinking about starting Adoration of the Blessed Sacrament. Nobody would have to come, there would be a short prayer service—under half an hour, I said—and after that I would stay there as long as anyone wanted to stay and pray. I warned them that I would not necessarily be praying. I might read or write instead. But I would be there for as long as anyone wanted to stay.

Nobody could believe it. They looked the way those slaves looked when I got Big Ned to come over and they saw him with his cutlass, and pistols in his belt, and the rag around his head where he had gotten hit with something. He talked to them a little in the African language, got out the leather bag where he kept his money, and showed them pieces of eight and some gold doubloons.

Through it all their eyes got bigger and bigger, and they started smiling.

That was how it was when we talked about Adoration and decided Tuesday nights at eight. But when the meeting was over and we were back in the rectory, Fr. Wahl told me I was going to get into trouble with Bishop Scully. He did not like Adoration, Fr. Wahl said.

I said okay, Bishop Scully has a right to his opinion and I have a right to mine. He will not be in trouble with me.

Here is where I did something mean, and I am sorry for it. I whistled as I went upstairs. I knew how Fr. Wahl would take it, but I did it just the same. I will ask him to forgive me for it, and I am sure he will.

The thing was, I knew that Bishop Scully was going to have a lot more reason to be angry with me. I am going to dress like a layman and drive over to the airport one day soon, and he will never see me again. I know he will not like that, and I do not blame him for it. But he will not be quite so angry when he remembers I was the troublemaker who reinstituted Adoration of the Blessed Sacrament and thought boys should stand up for themselves and what is right.

I HAVE JUST read over what I wrote about the stockade, and I do not think there is any reason to write more about that here. We formed up again and marched on the town, with the Kuna running ahead to look for ambushes.

Out in the harbor, our ships were faking an attack on the fort. Tom Jackson was in charge of that, and from what I have heard he managed it pretty well. They would run in toward the fort, then turn away when they came in range.

Then Novia saw smoke coming up from the landward side of the town, where some houses had caught fire. She made another run, only this time she meant it. The Spanish in the fort were short on men because of the party they had sent to reinforce the stockade, and they were expecting her to turn back when she got in range.

Here I have to explain something about hot shot, which all the shore batteries I ever heard of use. You heat the cannonballs in a furnace near the guns until they are bright red but not white-hot. When you load the guns, you follow the powder with a dry wad and a wet wad. The dry is to keep the powder from getting wet, and the wet is to keep the hot ball from burning through.

When you have done that, you have to fire the gun pretty fast. Otherwise, either the hot ball will burn through both wads and fire itself, or it will cool down to the point where it will not start a fire on the ship it hits.

That was why there was only cold shot in the Spanish guns when Novia made her run for the harbor. The other thing that helped her was that the guns were elevated way high to shoot at our ships when they were turning away. They had to be lowered before they would bear.

Two of the Spaniards' five fifty-pounders were fired before they bore. One ball carried off the maintop, but that was all the damage they did. The rest could not be lowered before *Sabina* got off a good broadside. It killed quite a few soldiers and dismounted a gun. One of the other two holed *Sabina* at the waterline. It was serious and had to be fixed, but it did not start a fire or sink her. After that, the rest of our ships came in behind her. They had half crews, but even half of a pirate crew is big. With all hands hoy, there were enough to manage the sails and man the starboard guns.

After that, the fighting in the town did not amount to much. There were too many of us and too few of them who would fight. We looted the whole town and put the screws to anybody we thought might have money hidden away. That could be very rough.

To tell the truth, I did not pay a lot of attention to it just then. I was running through the town looking for Novia, who was running through it looking for me. Finally we found each other and hugged and kissed and all that. And every time we thought we were finished, we did it some more.

Eventually we went off looking for food and wine that was worth drinking and found an innkeeper hiding in his own cellar. We made him fix us a decent meal, telling him that if either of us got sick afterward we were going to shoot him. It was good, and between the two of us we killed a bottle of what he swore was his best wine.

Somewhere in there I asked Novia what had gone on, and why she was not on the ship, and she said, "You think I would wait to watch you die through my glass, Crisóforo?"

We went back to the *Sabina* to sleep, and that was when I found out she had been holed. The hole had been stuffed with hammocks and spare canvas, but she was taking on a lot of water. We rounded up some of the Spanish prisoners and put them to pumping. It was hard work, but better than getting your fingers cut off by somebody looking for money you did not have.

In the morning we had a sort of meeting to talk about the fort—did we want to make another run for it, with the battery shooting at us, or would it be better to take it?

I stood up. "It'll be cheap and easy to call on it to surrender, and if we do maybe they will. If they won't, we can storm it from this side. They won't be able to shift fifty-pounders around in time to use them on us."

Pretty much everybody agreed with that, so that was what we did. Capt. Burt and I went out with a white flag just about like we had at the stockade, what I said was pretty much the same. The officer on the wall said his comandante had been wounded and could not come up there, but he wanted to talk about terms of surrender. Would we come in and talk with him?

We said we would, and they opened the gates—very strong oak gates bound with iron—and let us in. As soon as we were inside, we were grabbed from behind. Our weapons were taken, and we were roughed up quite a bit. It reminded me of the Spanish who had taken my gold back on Hispaniola, and I got madder and madder.

After a while, they carried the comandante out in a chair. His leg had been hit by a fragment of stone. It had laid the leg open, he said, and broken the thighbone. "So you see, Señors, I am quite incapable to fight you. My men, however, will fight to the last drop of blood, and we shall be reinforced within a day or two, as you will see."

Capt. Burt wanted to know about that.

"You have not the gold that was to arrive here. Had you taken it, we should have seen you loading it. Thus it has not arrived. You met with a company of my men in the forest? I think it must be so."

I said that we had met more than a hundred Spanish soldiers before we got to the stockade.

He smiled and nodded. He was middle-aged and beefy, and he needed a shave. I hated him from the minute I laid eyes on him.

I told Capt. Burt what we had said, and he said, "They were going out to meet the gold. I should have guessed it, Chris. The officer in charge of transporting it must have heard the shooting and turned back."

The comandante chuckled, so I knew right then that he spoke some English. Still talking to Capt. Burt, I said, "Our men will be rushing this place any minute, Captain, and when they do, we'll be shot. How can we stop them?"

He must have caught on, because he just shrugged.

"You," the comandante told me in Spanish, "will tell them not to. You will tell them they must surrender. An army is marching on this place to defeat them, and you will die at once if they attack it."

There was more palaver, and the upshot was that I was marched up on the wall by an officer and two soldiers, knowing I would probably die up there. Portobello is one of the most beautiful places I have ever seen. I should already have said that, but I will say it right now. It is a death trap and the Devil's port, a place where healthy men get sick and die in a month. Just the same, nobody could ever imagine how lovely it looked from the top of that fort up on the little hill overlooking the harbor. A west wind was blowing, the sky was blue, and the sun was just getting hot and flashing on the blue water.

I had a good look all around, and waved in case Novia was watching the fort through her glass. After that, I took a couple of deep breaths, and wondered whether they would throw my body outside the fort or down into the courtyard.

The officer poked me in the ribs and told me to start talking to our men.

I said, "They cannot hear me, Señor. They are too far from fear of your guns."

He said to wave to them to come closer.

"You should have brought Captain Burt up here." I was waving as I spoke. "The men are accustomed to obeying him, not me."

"We will bring him here if we must. We will have to, because you will be dead."

Clouds and blue sky are gifts from God, but He gave me something even better just then. He showed me that there was no railing for the inside of the walkway. On the outside there was the top of the wall, with spaces between the stones for soldiers to shoot through. But on the inside there was nothing. If you stepped over, you fell maybe twenty feet onto the stones of the court-yard.

The officer started crowding me the way they will sometimes, wanting to talk right into your face. I kneed him between the legs. He must have gone over—when you knee somebody like that, he generally grabs the place and takes two or three little steps back—but I never saw him because I was slap-ping the musket out of the hands of the nearest soldier. When I had it, I brought the butt up and got him under the chin.

The other soldier might have been bad news if he had stuck me with his bayonet, but he tried to cock the hammer, and I kicked him in the knee and shoved him over, too.

After that I yelled to the men outside to rush the fort and I would open the gate.

I never did, but before I get to that I ought to say something about those spike bayonets the soldiers had. We could have used them, and a few of us did. The main advantages they gave were more reach and a thrust like with a boarding pike. When we camped on shore, they made good candleholders, too. You just stuck them in the ground and put your candle in the socket.

Only they had two big disadvantages. The main one was that even if you killed somebody with one he did not die right away. You could put one into somebody's chest, and sure, he was going to die. But he was going to a minute or ten from now, and not now. He would have time enough to stab you back, or cock a pistol and shoot.

Like I said, I never did open the big gate. It was Capt. Burt who did that. Three people falling off the wall got everybody's attention, and he just went over and took down the bar. He did not let things like that rattle him, and it was one of the qualities that made him such a good leader.

That night, just about everyone was for going after the gold. I could not believe it. I liked money as well as anyone—or I thought I did. But going af-ter the mules and the soldiers who were guarding them? A couple of hun-dred soldiers minimum? When they would have at least a full day's head start?

I thought it was crazy, and I said so.

When the vote was finally taken, my side got maybe two hundred out of the whole eight hundred or so. One of the votes we got was Capt. Burt's, because my side had been his side, too. I am still proud of that. The sensible men voted with us, but there were not enough of us.

At first the thinking had been that the mule train with the gold would head back to Panama. Our Kuna said that it had not. It had taken the road southeast into the San Blas Mountains, probably making for Santa Maria, a little town on the Pacific side of Darien. I never got to talk to anybody who had been with that mule train, but my guess is they thought we would head to Panama, and going east would throw us off.

Nearly everybody wanted to follow the gold. We could march faster than loaded mules, they said, and would catch up to it. If we did not, we would take the town and catch them there. The men who had marched up behind Portobello would stay on the ships this time, and those who had stayed on the ships would march. Only all the captains would march again, just like before. The Kuna had agreed to guide us again. They had never beaten the Spanish before, and they were on cloud nine.

I would have chained Novia up again. Or I think now that I would have or I might have. I never got the chance. She just disappeared. I left Bouton in command of the *Sabina,* telling him that he was to take orders from Novia if she came back to the ship. I knew she would not, but that is what I said. He was going to move some guns to heel the ship over and lift the leak out of the water, then patch it properly.

I am not going to write about the march to Santa Maria. I could not make it sound as bad as it really was. I had thought the march to Portobello had been bad, and that Portobello itself had been bad, which it was. The march to Santa Maria was ten times worse. There were a hundred times when I simply could not believe that the Spanish were stupid enough, and tough enough, to ship gold across Darien to Portobello. Then we would find fresh droppings from the mules, which proved that we were on the right track. The only thing I know about mule droppings is that they are dirty and stink, but people who knew more (or said they did) said they showed that we were only a day and a half behind the mule train.

About the time we hit the big lake and had to go around it, it got to be a day. A map I saw when I was still at Saint Teresa's said that was Lake Bayana.

It was very, very bad. The Spanish must have had mules loaded with water as well as gold. We did not. There was water everywhere, but it made anyone who drank it sick. We tried to boil it, but everything that might have burned if it had been dry was wet. Rain was the only thing that saved us, and the rain made us as miserable as any Spaniard could ask for. When it rained, we caught the water any way we could, including wringing out our clothes into our mouths. It would rain all day and all night, and the whole country would flood a foot deep. Then it would stop, leaving everything dripping with humidity. It was like a steam bath. Sweat poured from us. Everything was wet, and nothing was drinkable. We greased ourselves to keep from being bitten by the mosquitoes, and sweated the grease off. We got leeches on our legs, not just once but again and again and again.

It is a mortal sin to take your own life. I know that, and it was one of the things the monks pounded home to us—do not kill yourself so that your soul can be with God. It will not. You are not free to reject His gift of life.

But I think I would have killed myself if Novia had not been there. She had hidden among the Kuna, as I ought to have guessed. Pinkie brought her to me when we had been marching for almost a week, saying that Novia was my wife, too. I did not bother to explain that we were not married. I just said that I did not have two wives. Novia was my wife and Pinkie was not—not that I did not like her. (The last thing I needed was an enemy among the Native Americans.) I did like her, she was a wonderful woman and very beautiful and smart. Only not my wife.

Pinkie would not hear of it. She was my wife. Novia was my wife. The other woman was my wife, too.

Novia and I just stared at each other. What other woman?

It was Azuka. I am sure it was funny, but none of us could laugh. We could only hold each other and try to bring each other some comfort. Willy was dead. Jarden had tried to kill Azuka, and she had run away from him. It took me a long time to get the whole story, and I never did get all of it. Willy had drowned crossing some little river. Jarden had tried to kill her because she would not stop crying for Willy. I told her I understood, she could cry all she wanted, and if Jarden or anybody else tried to kill her I would stop it quick. Novia said the same thing.

(That was when I found out that the best way in the world to make yourself feel better when you have hit bottom is to try to get somebody else to feel better. There are certain things in life that are truly worth knowing, and that is one of the big ones.)

So Azuka had run away, and I was the only person she could think of who might protect her. She had started asking about me, where was I, when she stopped running. It had made Pinkie think she was another wife.

For the next week or so, I kept telling Novia that she should have let me know she was along sooner. And she kept saying that she had been afraid I might really kill her. I think the thing she was really afraid of was that I would have wanted to take her back, and there would have been a big fight with Capt. Burt.

That is all I am going to say about the march, except that people kept getting sick, day after day after day. Later, Capt. Burt told me there was one day when we lost twenty men.

Anyone would think we would not have had the strength left to attack Santa Maria when we got there, but we did. There were houses to keep off the rain, cisterns full of good water, food, and a navigable river. A Spanish army could have killed us all before an hour was out, but we would have gone for its throat like mad dogs. Which was pretty much what we were by then.

The really crazy thing was that there was hardly anyone in the town to fight. The Spanish settlers just gave up, and there were only about a dozen soldiers. We took the whole town just by saying we had taken it.

There was no mule train, though, and only a little gold. Everybody we captured said that the officer in charge of the mule train had decided that Santa Maria was too dangerous. He had taken the mules and the gold back along the coast to Panama.

We had another meeting the next day—not just the captains, the whole bunch of us. I was starting to hate those meetings. It seems to me that the more people there are at a meeting the more nuts there are, and the nuts are always the loudest people there. At this one, what seemed like just about everybody wanted to follow the mule train again. It was only a day and a half ahead of us, maybe two days, and if it beat us to Panama—it could not by much—we would take Panama and the gold, too.

Finally Capt. Burt stood up and said very sensibly that it was common knowledge that Panama had been rebuilt and fortified since Henry Morgan had taken it and burned it, and we had no more chance of taking it than we would have of taking Mexico.

They did not like that, but he was the senior captain there, and they had to let him talk.

Which he did, pointing out that there were supposed to be about two thousand soldiers in Panama now. Maybe more. If we caught up to the mule train now, it was bound to be close to there, and some of the soldiers guarding it were bound to make it back there. It would mean that we would be crossing the isthmus driving tired mules carrying heavy loads of gold, with a thousand or more soldiers after us.

He sat down, we voted, and it was something like five hundred and ninety for chasing the mule train. Capt. Burt stood up again and said he was not going. He was going to lead a party back to Portobello and the ships. If nobody would go with him, he was going back alone.

I jumped up then and said he would not have to. I would be with him, and so would Novia. By noon, it had all been settled. Capt. Burt would go back, with Rombeau and me, and Capt. Gosling. We would have about sixty men. Both the women would go with us, of course.

Captains Dobkin, Cox, Isham, and Ogg would go after the mule train with the rest, including the Kuna. Capt. Dobkin would be in command of their group. For our part, we promised to tell the men that had been left on their ships what had gone on when we got back to Portobello.

Which we did.

Both groups marched as soon as everything had been decided, Dobkin's because they were hoping to overtake the mule train and knew that one hour might make all the difference. Us, because we were worried about our ships, and most of all because we wanted to put the whole fool enterprise behind us.

We were slower even so. As well as I can remember now, Dobkin's bunch had left a couple of hours before we had everyone rounded up and ready to go. Dobkin's bunch, I said. That did not include the Kuna, even though the Kuna had promised to guide them. The Kuna stayed behind. I was hardly aware that they were still there when Novia and I were rounding up as much food as we could find and filling empty wine bottles with good water.

And of course, stealing anything else we could find that seemed worth carrying back to Portobello. It was a couple of doubloons and a ring—or that is all that I can remember.

Finally we left, after getting together all the men we could find. Jarden went with Dobkin, I am sure. Antonio stayed with us. So did Azuka and Mahu, and various others. There is little point in my trying to write a roster here. I would be certain to make some mistakes.

27

Novia in Council

WE REACHED PORTOBELLO ready to drop. Just the same, we put out the same day. A Spanish pinnace had been sighted the day before, everyone felt the galleons could not be far behind, and the mates left in charge had practically been holding their crews at pistol-point. When they heard that Dobkin, Cox, and the rest were not with us, they hoisted anchor within an hour. We would meet in the Saint Blaise Islands to decide what to do next.

Before we got there, however, Capt. Harker joined us in his sloop, the *Princess.* Novia and I watched him board the *Weald* and speculated a good deal on what news he might bring—a sport in which we were soon joined by Boucher. When I saw signal flags being run up the mizzen of the *Weald,* I felt certain the signal was to be "All Captains." When the flags were shaken out, however, it was only "Capt. Chris" who was asked to join Capt. Burt.

To head off a row I took Novia with me, and Capt. Burt made no objection.

———

TWO DAYS, AND I have written nothing. My passport came, but no one is answering the telephone at the Cuban consulate in New York. None of the airlines I have called is offering service to Havana yet. Nor would I wish to try to make my way to the airport through this snow, to be entirely honest; mono service is not to be relied upon in weather as cold as we have had.

Before I write any more, I ought to explain that I have been generally called Capt. Chris or Fr. Chris because of the length and difficulty of my last name. Few know it, and fewer can pronounce it correctly. As for spelling out my name in signal flags, there is not a signalman in the world who would not abbreviate it.

After mass today, I went trolling for some pirate Web sites and found several. One offered a short biography of a Capt. Cos or Kruss, believed to have been Dutch or German. It was not until I read that he had disappeared after sailing from Havana alone in a small craft that I realized that I was "Capt. Cos," although the detail that Cos was said to have made his wife his chief lieutenant should have alerted me.

WHEN THE FOUR of us were seated in Capt. Burt's cabin, he said, "You two have met Captain Harker before, I know. I left him at Long Bay to speed the bigger vessels to me, and he's done well. I've already given him his company's share of what we got at Portobello and Santa Maria. That was little enough, I'm afraid."

Harker nodded. "Not what we were hoping for, but bad luck can't last forever."

"Exactly. Forgive me now, Hal. I'm goin' to repeat a few things you've already heard.

"Chris, you know what I planned earlier. Maracaibo's a different article from that damned Portobello. Or Santa Maria, either. Portobello may be the most disease-ridden town in the world. Maracaibo's healthy. Portobello's a coastal place. Because it is, the good cits feel exposed and are forever demandin' more protection from the Spanish Crown. Maracaibo's an inland port, at the tail end of the Gulf of Venezuela. Think of jolly old London, up the Thames from the sea. Better still, think of Santa Maria, miles and miles up its river from the Gulf of Saint Michael."

I nodded.

"You say Maracaibo is not like." Novia looked worn and tired, as all of us except for Harker did. "How is different?"

"Santa Maria's little more than a fishing village, Señora. Maracaibo's a city, larger than Portobello and Santa Maria combined."

"A rich city," Harker added.

Novia shrugged. "Ver es creer." I doubt that either Capt. Burt or Harker understood her.

"A damnation rich city. The cacao trade alone . . ." Burt shook his head. "Great fortunes have been made in that. More are bein' made every day. Besides that, the land behind Maracaibo's prime cattle country. Hides, tallow, and dried and salt beef flow like water through the city, tons of 'em."

"What is cacao?" I asked. "I've never heard of it."

Novia grinned. "We say chocolate, Crisóforo. What is your English word?"

Capt. Burt answered for me. "Pretty much the same, Señora—chocolate." He turned to me. "Chocolate's made from cacao beans, and they say the best beans in the world are grown in Venezuela."

"About this I do not know," Novia told him. "Three things only, I know. Of these primero, my first, is that chocolate costs silver in Coruña, where it is drunk at the tables of the most rich. Segundo, my second, is that this Maracaibo has been warned of us. Tercero, my third, is that Crisóforo and I have only marineros sufficient for the work of our sails. Because I know these three things, I listen and listen. But I do not believe."

Capt. Burt smiled. I could not see his hands, but I suspected that he was rubbing them together. "Everythin' you say is true, Señora. As to the price of chocolate, I can only set my seal to your own assessment. It's awfully valuable. Because it is, great sums reach Maracaibo. As to the second—"

Harker interrupted him. "Can we trust her, Captain? She's Spanish."

"I'd trust her," Capt. Burt said slowly, "as far as I'd trust any man I know."

I said, "You can certainly trust Novia—and me—enough to tell us we'll be going back to Port Royal to refit and fill our ship's companies."

"I won't lie to either of you." Capt. Burt smiled again. "We're not. I mean to recruit among the logwood cutters of Campeche and the Cimaroons of Honduras."

Novia looked sidelong at me, and when I did not speak asked, "They are good marineros there, Capitán?"

"They ain't seamen at all, Señora. You and Chris will have to train 'em. Which you'll do, I know, and first rate."

"They're good fighting men," Harker added.

Captain Burt nodded. "That takes care of your third point, Señora. As for your second, I'm fortunate to have a captain who speaks Spanish so well that he can pass as a Spaniard."

He turned to me, and I would swear his eyes twinkled. "I mean to send him to Maracaibo ahead of us to take the lay of the land."

"No! You cannot!" Novia jumped to her feet, knocking over her chair.

I made her sit down again and said, "Yes, he can. I'll go, of course, Captain."

"Knew you would, Chris." Capt. Burt cleared his throat. "Somethin' was said about trustin' a while back. Just to show you two how much I trust you both, I'm goin' to tell you somethin' more. Mum's the word on this. Do you recollect the Spanish pinnace? The one that scared us out of Portobello?"

We nodded.

"Well, shipmates, the captain of that pinnace is sittin' at this table with us this very minute."

I do not know whether Novia's jaw dropped, but I am sure mine did.

Capt. Burt's laughter filled the cabin. "Hal flew Spanish colors, thinkin' there might be a galleon or two about. A good sensible precaution, I call it."

"This you knew, Capitán?"

"Not at first, Señora. I came flash only after I'd talked to Hal here. But think, now. Leaky ships, most shot up a bit by that fort. Foul bottoms on some of 'em. Small crews. But got out without seein' so much as the topsails of a galleon, and why didn't the pinnace shadow us? It's what they do, usually, Señora. Take station 'tween you and the galleons, where the galleons will see their signals."

I said, "Now that you know, shouldn't you send the ships back to Portobello?"

"I will, Chris. Trust me for that. But not yet. Not till they're in better shape, and there's been time for the crews to shake off their fevers. Only tell me now, you were with us, and the señora, too. Is Dobkin comin' back? Honest, now."

"He could," I said. "There's a chance." Somehow I felt that if I said no, I would be dooming him and all the *Sabina* men who had gone with him.

"Odds, Chris?"

"Ten to one, maybe."

Capt. Burt grunted. "You're more generous than Bram Burt would've been, let me tell you. My ten doubloons to your one, hey? If we don't see him within a year, or hear that he got out alive, you'll owe me your one. If we do, I'll owe you my ten. Bet?"

"Bet," I said. "But I've another question—one that has nothing to do with Dobkin. Can I ask it?"

"Fire away."

"It may be for Captain Harker, really. More for him than for you. Where's Lesage?"

Capt. Burt nodded. "That's for Hal, right enough. All I know is what he's told me. Hal?"

Novia said, "We spoke to you at the Long Bay. You say you must wait for this Lesage, but we must go. Now you are come. What has befallen him?"

"An unshipped rudder, madam. No more than that. We set out in company. The second day, it was. He signaled me to proceed with all speed, saying he would follow when practicable. He's senior to me, madam, so I did as ordered, though I offered our assistance first. He thanked me for that, but said it was not needed. So off I went."

Novia turned to me. "We were many days in the forest, Crisóforo."

"We were." I tried to recall the entries I had made in the log, and the ones Bouton and Boucher had made as well. "From the time we went ashore to take Portobello to the time we sailed away from it comes to thirty-three days, I would say. I don't believe that can be off by much."

"So I think, Capitán Harker. A month, I say. We women are given a reason to take note of the moon. You waited long when we had gone?"

Harker nodded. "Those were my orders, madam. I was to wait until your good captain came and Captain Lesage. Not one, but both. Wait I did."

"So may God wait my soul. Long and long, I hope. Capitán Burt, you are our man of wisdom. Where is this Lesage, who was Chris's lieutenant once?"

Capt. Burt spread his hands. "I have no more notion than you, Señora. A thousand things may chance at sea."

I said, "He may be hanging from a Spanish rope right now." The thought cheered me, I admit.

"Aye," Harker put in. "Or his crew may have voted him out and gone elsewhere—he's a hard man, by repute."

"He may be nosin' around Portobello lookin' for us, Chris."

I felt Novia's small, hard hand slip into mine as she said, "You will send this man back to see, Capitán Burt?"

With a slight frown, he shook his head.

"When we come, Chris wish to know. Now I, too, wish to know this. I do not like them, this capitán and his ship which disappear."

"You fear some treachery, Señora. What is it?"

Her hand tightened on mine. "I do not know."

"No more do I, Señora. What could he do? Tell the Spanish we intended Portobello? By the time he learned of that, Portobello had fallen to us. Tell the Spanish we intended Maracaibo? Yes, certainly, and it seems someone did. You'll remember Goslin's letters, eh? So that may have been Lesage. But it may have been any of two dozen others as well."

Novia did not speak.

"We held a meetin', Señora. A council of war. You weren't there, and neither was Chris, nor Lesage for that matter. The rest were. Hal and I were for Maracaibo. Only us. Not Goslin', not Cox, not Dobkin, not Ogg, though I'd counted on Ogg. Not another soul. What does that tell you?"

I said, "I don't know, Captain, and I don't think Novia does either."

Capt. Burt leaned back in his chair, making a steeple of his fingers. For about half a minute, nobody spoke. Then Novia burst out, "We wish to know what it tell *you,* Capitán."

"Suppose that you'd known I meant to raid Maracaibo, Señora. Suppose further that you, famished for gold, had sold your knowledge to the Spanish. Would you want to send Chris here off to help me raid the place?"

She shook her head violently. "Not I!"

Capt. Burt nodded. "What about you, yourself, Señora? You marched with us from Portobello to Santa Maria."

"Back also, Capitán. Who is carry me?"

"Would you want to march on Maracaibo?"

"No! They are warn. I have say this."

"So you have, though I intend Maracaibo even so. If you had been a captain in that council of war to which I referred, wouldn't you say the same? Maracaibo's fly? Let's go somewhere else?"

Capt. Burt looked at each of us in turn. "Recollect now that every captain there, save for Hal and me, said just that."

Harker said, "They won't all have spilled the works, Captain."

"Naturally not, Hal. I'm saying only that if our Judas was there, he'd have spoken as the rest did—and might, perhaps, have suggested Portobello. The ideal result of our meetin'—from his perspective, mind—would be for me and some others to go off after Maracaibo, while he and the rest went elsewhere. He might've asked himself where Bram Burt wouldn't care to go, d'ye see? And been answered Portobello, for saucy Bram knows Portobello to be a hellhole.

"Of them that was at the meetin', who could Bram trust then, shipmates?"

I said, "Only Captain Harker here, I would think."

"Well said, Chris, but there's one other. Besides myself."

I probably looked as blank as my mind was at that moment.

"Hal? Care to have a go?"

He shook his head.

"Señora? You've a long head."

"Capitán Isham, I think. Because you have say nothing of him here."

"Clever." Capt. Burt smiled and leaned toward us, his elbows on the table. "Clever, but not right. No, I ask you, shipmates, if you had played Judas with Spain, and had afterward found letters saying the Spanish had been warned, would you tell Bram Burt?"

Novia shook her head.

I said, "I see."

"So you should, Chris. There's a good reason to trust Goslin', and here's another. When the rest went off to Panama and left me, who stayed by me? Why, it was Goslin' again. You with him, to be sure, and your man Rombeau. So there's four captains I can trust. I suppose everybody'd like a spot more wine?"

When it had been poured, Novia said, "Four to trust, but I do not count four here."

"Correct, Señora. Goslin' spoke against Maracaibo at the meetin'. If I was to say to him what I've said to you today, he'd always think he was not trusted. He is, but he'd think the contrary, d'ye see? I wouldn't want that. You can't trust a man who thinks he ain't trusted, Señora, and you can make book on that. As for Rombeau, I called him Chris's man, which he is. It's my wish he should make fast there, for the time bein'. If he were drinkin' with us now, he'd begin to think himself Chris's equal, and I don't want it. Do you, Señora?"

28

Maracaibo

CAPTAIN BURT HAD told us we would be going to the Bay of Campeche. We did, but first we took a sort of working vacation in the Saint Blaise Islands. They are small and very lush—sort of jungle light—and there must be hundreds of them. Because the sea breezes tend to blow away flying bugs, they are nowhere near as bug-ridden as the lowlands of Darien or Hispaniola. You get beautiful beaches, big trees (mostly cedars), and parrots everywhere. Altogether, it is about as nice a place as I have ever seen.

The people are Kunas, like those we knew in Darien. Our Kunas there had been small, smaller than we were and smaller than the Moskitos. These Island Kunas were smaller yet, but they spoke the same language and seemed to have about the same customs. That was when I really wished Novia had let me bring Pinkie back with us when we left Santa Maria. I do not believe there would have been any trouble about getting her on board, and when we reached the islands she could have interpreted for us and I would have known a lot more Kuna than I did.

As it was, all of us did our best to make friends. The Kuna did not have anything we wanted, and it was pretty obvious that they would be good people to have on our side. We explained as well as we could that we were not Spanish and would not raid them for slaves the way the Spanish did. We were the enemies of the Spanish, who were their enemies, too. We proved it by giving them hatchets, axes, knives, and needles, the same kinds of gifts we had given the other Kuna. The Island Kuna liked them as much as the others had, and repaid us with meat, fish, and fruit.

We careened two ships there and scraped their bottoms, and made some other repairs. We also loafed a lot and ate a lot of fruit, and I taught Novia how to swim. At that time, I do not believe I had gone swimming since I had been on Hispaniola, and it was good to get back into the water. Once we were joined by two Kuna girls who could swim like seals, and anybody who saw the three of them playing would have found it easy to believe there were girls with fish tails right over the next wave. I have had some bad times in my life, but I have had a lot of wonderful times, too, times I would love to go back to. That was one of those.

Another one was just this morning. I bundled up in my sweater, my over-coat, and so on, and unlocked the church so I could go in to say my mass. (We have to say mass every day, whether anybody comes or not.) The furnace had been turned down the night before, and the church was so cold that there was a skin of ice on the fonts. But the warm presence of God was waiting, and He and I were alone in there together. After I had received, I was no longer aware of Him.

But I knew that He had not gone away.

THE LOGWOOD CUTTERS lived in the swamps and cut a kind of wood used to make red dye. They said it pays better than anything else a man can do, but their living conditions are about as bad as living conditions can get. Imagine the march to Santa Maria—the part through the lowlands. Now imagine living like that all the time. Imagine sleeping in a swamp and eating in a swamp. Instead of marching with the hope of getting out, you go off each day to fell trees and haul logs. The Spanish try to drive the logwood cutters out from time to time, just like they did when we were buccaneers on Hispaniola. It comes, and it goes. That is what the cutters say. They fight if there are not too many Spanish, and hide in the swamps if there are.

They fight with Spanish logwood cutters, too.

We signed up a few men—three for my ship—but not what we had hoped.

The Cimaroons were something else. I have seen some tough men, but I never saw any tougher than they were. Most are black—escaped slaves, and men whose fathers were escaped slaves. Some are Zambo Moskitos, some white. (The whites are mostly runaway slaves, too.) We went ashore and talked with them, explaining what we wanted. They said they would talk it over that night and call us in the morning.

Right.

We were keeping a close watch, because we were almost within shouting distance of the Spanish Main, and there was no port. If the weather had looked like it was going to get rough, we would have to get out to sea in a hurry. Novia and I woke up in the middle of the night, and when we were both sweaty and out of breath we decided to go up on deck, look at the moon, and cool off.

Everything seemed to be in good shape. Boucher was officer of the watch, and he was awake and nearly sober. There was a man at the wheel and another at the masthead, both awake, and the moon—one of those thin crescent moons that always look prettier than anything has a right to—was setting behind the trees. Novia and I watched it go down, tangling itself in the branches and shining through the leaves.

Then she pointed, and I saw a piragua putting out, all dark and not making a sound that I could hear. To its left there was another, and another to its right.

I smacked Boucher a pretty good one, yelled, "Are you blind!," jerked the pistol out of his belt, and fired it in the air.

That woke the watch and we had the guns run out and firing before the piraguas had covered half the distance from shore. That woke men on the *Magdelena,* the *Weald,* and Gosling's *Snow Lady.* The piraguas scooted back, and when the sun came up there were twenty or thirty bodies floating in the water.

Pretty soon some Cimaroons hailed us just as nice as you please and said they wanted to join us, and would we kindly come ashore and pick them up?

We said no thanks, just swim on out and we will throw ropes to you so you can climb on board—no more than ten on each ship.

Eventually they paddled out in piraguas, carrying muskets, hatchets, cane knives, and so forth. Twenty-six came aboard *Sabina*. I do not remember how many went to the other ships. I looked them over and sent back all those who had any kind of wound. That left about twenty. After that, I let my officers pick out one man each, telling each officer that he was responsible for that man and was to kill him if he found him plotting with the rest. At that time, we had a quartermaster (Red Jack), a first mate (Bouton), a second mate (Boucher), a third mate (O'Leary), a bosun (Corson), a bosun's mate (Dell), a gunner (Hansen), and a gunner's mate (Maas). So that took care of eight.

After that, Novia and I picked one together, and Mahu, Big Ned, and Azuka did the same thing, making ten.

We told the rest they had to go back. They wanted to fight, but we were too many for them and we were standing all around them. Eventually they went off with no blood spilled.

We had not done as well at either place as we had hoped, but Captain Burt wanted to take a shot at Maracaibo anyway, and Harker, Gosling, and I went along. We all agreed that if it looked too bad we would not do it. Novia was against it, but I felt like Harker—our luck was bound to change sooner or later.

Which it did in about a week. We took a fair-sized ship carrying cacao beans and twelve thousand pieces of eight. As if that were not good enough, four of its crew joined us. Gosling put a few of his men on board and took it to Jamaica, promising to do some recruiting and meet us at Curaçao, a Dutch island that was about as close to the Gulf of Venezuela as we wanted to go before we were ready to move in.

Everybody except Harker and me, that is. He sailed into the Gulf with me on board one fine evening and dropped me off close enough to see the lights of the city. I do not believe I will ever forget standing there with my boots ankle-deep in mud and watching the *Princess* sail away, as dark and as silent as any shadow. I had some money of my own in my money belt, plus a heavy purse of doubloons Capt. Burt had given me. Besides the money, my long silver-hilted Spanish sword, a Spanish dagger Novia had picked up somewhere, and a letter she and I had forged together.

I also had Captain Burt's words ringing in my ears. "You're the best man I could hope to have for this, Chris. I'm countin' on you more than I've ever counted on any man in my life. We've got to know about that fort, first and last. After that, the watchtower. After that, the whole city—where to look for money, and how many soldiers there are. Mark where you're landed, because Harker will come lookin' for you in a fortnight. In one fortnight, mind. That's fourteen days, neither more nor less. If you're not finished by then, come back and report anyway. We sent you in once, and we can send you in again."

I had nodded. "I've got it."

"Good." He was trying to smile, but too worried to make it look right. "I'm countin' on you not to get caught. If you are, keep your chin up, stand mum, and don't lose hope. We'll do everythin' we can to get you out. And good luck."

I knew I was going to need it.

IF I WERE to tell all that happened in Maracaibo, I would be at this for a year. I doubt that I have a month. I hiked into the city, staying out of sight until I was practically there. By the time I got down close to the waterfront, where the action was, it was midmorning. I went from inn to inn looking for a place to eat, and more importantly for a place to stay. There's no better place for a man to listen to gossip and maybe ask a few questions than the taproom of an inn. Eventually I found one that looked clean and decent without being too pricey. The innkeeper had a Native American slave, and on the third day I was there I bought him.

It was the kind of thing I had told myself over and over I should not do, but I did it just the same. That morning, I heard noises like somebody pounding oakum and some pretty fair Spanish cussing in the courtyard and went out to see what was going on. The innkeeper and his sons had their Native American slave down and were beating him with good-sized sticks. He was curled up the way you do, trying to cover his head with his arms. I kept thinking he would yell for mercy any minute, but he never did. He never said a thing until they stopped, and as I watched I started to wonder whether he could talk, and whether they were going to kill him.

Finally they quit, wiping the sweat off their faces and panting. That was when I heard him whisper, "Oh, Jesus . . ."

It was all he said—but it was in English. Our Lord's name sounds a lot

29

Hoodahs

WHAT I DID was mosey up to the innkeeper and ask what the Native American had done. He was stupid, the innkeeper said.

"Yeah," I said—only in Spanish—"me, too. Listen here. You've pounded him to dog food, and pounding won't fix stupidity anyhow. What you've got now is a cripple you'll just have to feed. I'll take him off your hands for . . ." Here I pretended to search in my pockets. "Eight reales. This looks pretty good. Doesn't look like it's been sweated at all." It was one of the new pieces of eight we had gotten from the cacao-bean ship.

The innkeeper just laughed and turned away, and I said, "Okay, stupido, you keep him. He's your hard luck. I hope he dies tonight."

I went to the street gate then and lifted the latch. When I did it, the innkeeper turned back and called, "One hundred, Señor de Messina, because you are my guest. But not one real less."

After that we went back and forth for half an hour or so. I knew I was going to buy him, but I had to keep the innkeeper from knowing it, too. I finally got him for eighteen reales, which showed that the innkeeper really and seriously thought that he and his sons might have lamed him for life.

Once I had a signed bill of sale, I helped him stand up and got him up two flights of stairs to my room. That was about as easy as pulling up a fourpounder. There were a couple or maybe three times when I felt certain we were both going to fall.

Up there, I laid him on the bed, which was way too short for me and too short for him, too, got him to drink a glass of wine, and told him I was going out and he should just take it easy in there until I got back. You are not supposed to give Native Americans alcohol is what all the books say, because they have this big alcoholism problem. But that wine was from the inn, and I swear by Monkey King Jasmine that Novia could have downed a whole bottle of it and never stumbled.

(Confession is good for the soul, and so: Monkey King Jasmine is tea. Mr. and Mrs. Briggs gave us a food basket for Christmas, and there is a package of tea in it—Monkey King Jasmine Tea. Fr. Wahl thinks it is hilarious, and I think it is pretty funny myself.)

When I came back, I brought him some good clean water and something to eat. After a couple of days, he started telling me that I should sleep on the bed and he would lie on the floor. That was how I knew he was well enough for us to change inns. Which we did, because I could see there was going to be trouble about him if we stayed where we were.

A day or so before that, I had asked him what his name was. What he said was Spanish and pretty dirty, so I told him we would have to use another one. I tried to find out what his Native American name was, but he played dumb. That was okay, because I knew by then that your real name was a very personal thing with a lot of Native Americans. Maybe with all of them. The way he had been beaten by the innkeeper and his sons reminded me of Saint Jude, who was beaten to death with traveler's staffs, so I called him Hoodahs, which is how you say that saint's name in Spanish. By the time we changed inns I was Captain and he was Hoodahs, and Hoodahs had gotten over the idea that I was planning to do something horrible as soon as I thought he was strong enough to stand it.

The whole time I was just itching to try English, but I was supposed to be a Cuban officer who was in Maracaibo hoping to get a job with the army in

Venezuela, so there was no way I was going to risk saying a word in English where anybody could hear it.

The day after we moved, I took him to a blacksmith who took the chain off his feet. It had been about eighteen inches long, a chain that would let him walk but not run, and it had galled both his ankles. When he was loose, I said (in Spanish), "I'm freeing you, Hoodahs. If you want to split right now, or tonight, or tomorrow, that's fine with me. I'm not going to stand guard over you. The only thing is, if you go now, from here, you'll probably get picked up by some other Spaniard. If that happens, I'll help you if I can but I probably won't ever know about it. But you can take the chance if you want to."

He shook his head.

"Okay, if you want to stick with me for a while, you can do that. Only you're free to split whenever."

He shook his head again. I was not really sure what he meant by that, but I thought it was probably "Not any time soon." So I said, "Come on, we're going fishing."

One of the things I had been doing when I went out was looking at boats, and the day before I had bought a good one, new, a boat small enough that one man could handle it, but big enough to carry three. (Maybe three men and a kid, in a pinch.) It had oars, a mast a little longer than a mop handle, and a sail a little bit bigger than a blanket. We got a pole, some line that should have been for tying up weeds to burn, a few hooks, a piece of salt pork to cut up for bait, and a bucket. Nothing fancy, because I did not care whether I caught anything or not. As long as we looked like a don and his slave out for a bit of fishing, that was good enough.

Hoodahs rowed us away from the dock. Then I showed him how to set up the mast and spread the sail. When we had sailed a little—there was a pretty good breeze—I went to the bow and let him manage the tiller and sheets. After five minutes or so, I knew he was no stranger to boats. He was not an expert, either, but he had been around boats enough to understand the basics.

We sailed between the fort and watchtower just as pretty as you please, and nobody said boo to us. When we were through the strait and out in the Gulf, and not close to anything or anybody, I had Hoodahs put down the sail. I baited my hook, hoping not to catch anything, and held the pole and pretended to fish. Then I said (just as I am writing it now), "You speak English,

Hoodahs. So do I, and I think it's time we leveled with each other. Where did you come from?"

"North, Chris." He pointed. "My land north."

"America?"

He stared, then shook his head, and right then about ninety percent of my hopes washed down the drain. I had been hoping—I had been praying—that he was from the future, just like me.

When I had pulled myself together, I said, "Who taught you English?"

"Master."

I got a little bit more than that out of him that day, but not much. Later, Novia and I got a little bit more. If I were to space it all out the way we got it, it would drive you crazy. So I am just going to give the gist of it here and let it go at that.

Hoodahs was a Moskito who had signed up with Captain Swan. They had raided down the Atlantic coast of South America, and maybe around the Horn. (Hoodahs's geography was pretty sketchy.) Eventually they had put in at some islands where there were rocks, trees, and goats, and not much else, hoping to shoot fresh meat. Hoodahs had been in the hunting party, and he had been left behind. Our guess was that a Spanish ship had come up, but it could have been no more than a change in the weather.

Eventually, he made a little raft and paddled it to one of the other islands. There had been a white man on it, and they had made friends and joined forces. Hoodahs called this man Master. Master had taught him English, and more or less converted him to Christianity. By that I mean he still believed everything Moskitos do, but he knew about God and Jesus, too, and I think may have liked them better.

They started building a real boat together, cutting little trees, sawing planks, seasoning the wood, and so forth. They had gotten pretty far with it, from what he said, when a ship came. Master went aboard to go back to England, but Hoodahs did not. Part of it was that he did not want to go to England, and part was that he did not trust the men on the ship. Or that is how it seemed to Novia and me.

He stayed on the island and stopped working on their boat. As well as I can figure, he was on the first island for a year or so, then with Master for at least two years and maybe longer. After that he was alone on Master's island for at least another year.

Spanish ships had come from time to time, and he and Master had always hidden their boat and hidden themselves, too. This time Hoodahs hid, but forgot to hide the boat—or maybe could not carry it by himself. These Spanish had dogs, and the dogs hunted him down. The Spanish caught him and made him a slave on their ship. Eventually they had sold him to the innkeeper.

As I said, I got a whole lot less than that when we were out on the boat. I am not sure whether Mahu was the most talkative man I have ever met, but I am absolutely certain that Hoodahs was the most closemouthed. I told him not to speak English to Spaniards, and warned him that he was never to tell anybody I did. At first I worried that he might do it anyway. As I got to know him better, I realized that I had wasted my breath telling him to clam up. Hoodahs was not big on telling anybody anything, and that is putting it mildly.

Nobody had stopped us, or questioned us, or made any other kind of trouble, so the next day we went fishing again, this time south into Lake Maracaibo. It was a funny setup. The eastern shore of the lake was Spanish, with a lot of agriculture and a little town called Gibraltar down toward the south end. The western shore was still wild jungle, with Native Americans there that the Spanish called Indios Bravos. Boats that came too close to their side were likely to be in trouble. I asked Hoodahs whether he wanted to join the Indios Bravos, saying that he could dive over the side and swim, and it would be okay with me. I would not try to stop him. He said no, the Indios Bravos would kill him, he was not of their tribe.

We stopped at Gibraltar, got some wine and something to eat, and I talked about fishing with a couple of men where we ate. The man who sold us our food said that Hoodahs would have to take his outside, then said that Hoodahs would run away when he saw he was not chained. I said he would not, don't worry about it. He got his food, ate outside, and did not run away.

The day after that, we decided to try the Gulf again. It was a nice setup for defense, with a narrow strait that was too shallow for ships anywhere except right down the middle between Lookout Island and Pigeon Island. The watchtower was on Lookout Island, on top of a little hill that was just about the whole island.

Pigeon Island was bigger, maybe twenty or thirty acres. The fort was stone, built so that any ship that went down the strait to Maracaibo had to sail right under the guns. When I had gotten a look at it two days before, I had seen right away that the only way to capture it was to attack it on the landward side. Eight or ten big galleons might have been able to knock it down, but they would have lost four or five ships first.

There was a little cove over on the shallow-water side, pretty well hidden by trees. We tied up there, and I explained to Hoodahs that I needed to have a look at that side of the fort without being seen. He said, "Me first. Watch hands," and faded into the underbrush like smoke. I followed him, trying to move fast without making any noise. Trying, I said. I moved less than half as fast as he did, and made ten times more noise. Or a hundred, because he did not make any noise at all, and I did. I would move ahead as fast as I could for five or ten minutes, then I would catch sight of him waiting for me. He would wait to make sure I had seen him, motion for me to follow, and fade out.

After that had happened twice he did not go, but stayed right where he was, pointing. There was a little clearing in front of us, and he was pointing to the other side. I caught up with him and looked across that clearing as hard as I could. What I saw was more trees and more brush. Nothing else.

Hoodahs motioned for me to follow, and faded off to his left, not going into the clearing at all. I am dumb, but I was not dumb enough to step out there. I followed him, and when we had gone maybe twenty or thirty feet, there was a trench about three feet deep with gravel on the bottom, and a thick wall of dirt not quite two feet high in front of it. There were little bushes scattered along the top of that wall, looking like they had been planted there. In front of it were more little bushes, not high enough to block the view of anybody looking over it.

We followed it around until we were looking across the clearing from the other side. Hoodahs came as close to smiling as I ever saw—by which I mean that his mouth was set in stone, but his dark and narrow eyes were laughing—raised an imaginary musket, and pulled back the invisible hammer. I nodded to show I got it, and we went on to the fort and had a good look at that.

A couple of days after that, I got all dressed up in the fancy clothes I had been buying in Maracaibo, strapped on my long sword and Novia's dagger, and Hoodahs and I sailed up to that fort and tied up at the wharf, all as open and aboveboard as you please. I told the colonel I was a soldier, a captain, who had come to Maracaibo from Havana hoping to get a promotion from General Sanchez.

And I showed him the letter that Novia and I had cooked up, complete with a pretty scarlet ribbon and the smudged red wax impression left by the "official" seal Long Pierre had carved for us. It talked about the good family in Spain I came from (which really was Novia's) and praised me to the skies. I had held the pen that signed it, but the name on it belonged to the governor of Cuba.

When the colonel had read all that, I told him I had been promised an audience with the deputy governor and General Sanchez in a few days, and I wanted to show them I was already familiar with the military situation here.

He stood me a glass of good wine and showed me all over the fort. Which was, I admit, pretty impressive. Impressive from the seaward side, particularly.

I did various other things in Maracaibo after that, sometimes with Hoodahs and sometimes on my own. None of them were important, although some of them were fun.

Then my fortnight was up, and we sailed out to meet Harker in the Gulf and went aboard, tying our little boat on behind *Princess*.

30

Our Attack

CAPT. BURT WELCOMED me with a big smile and a glass of wine. "You're lookin' healthy, Chris. How's everythin' on the *Sabina*?"

I said thank you and "Fine, sir. Novia had to shoot one guy while I was gone and hang another one, but she says it's done wonders to bring the rest into line. So do Red Jack and Bouton."

"I've known it to help, myself." Capt. Burt grinned. "You'll be short two men, just the same."

I shook my head. "You're right, sir, she was down two men. The man she hanged had killed Compagne, so that was two. But the one she shot—it was one of the Cimaroons—is recovering. I brought us another man when I came back, so we've only lost one, really."

"You're sure he ain't a spy, Chris?"

"He was a Moskito slave, sir. They just about beat him to death. He hates the Spanish worse than I hate . . . well, anybody."

"You trust him."

"Absolutely. If you knew him like I do, you'd trust him, too."

"Good enough." Captain Burt leaned back, making the steeple with his fingers. "Tell me about the fort."

"Strong on the water sides, not so strong on the others. The walls fronting the strait are granite, about four feet thick. Landward—"

"How many guns?"

"On the water side? Sixteen. There are ten eight-pounders, four twelve-pounders, and two twenty-fours. They have two furnaces for heating hot shot."

He rubbed his hands together. "You got into the fort, Chris?"

"Yes, sir. It was no great trick."

"I'm impressed. I thought you were a man worth havin' when we met in Veracruz. Remember that?"

"Yes, sir. I'll never forget it."

"I didn't know how right I was. Like some more wine?"

I shook my head and put my hand over my glass.

He poured more for himself. "Now let me count up. Four men for each of the eights, that's thirty-two. Four twelves, you said. Let's say six men for each of them, which is another twenty-four—fifty-six so far. Two twenty-four-pounders. They could be worked by eight, but let's allow ten—another twenty men. There will be officers, men to tend the furnaces, and so on. I'd say a hundred at least. Does that square with what you saw?"

I shook my head again. "It's more like two hundred, Captain. I'd guess about a hundred and sixty. Maybe a hundred and eighty, but at least a hundred and sixty."

He nodded, I would say to himself. "Stand against a fleet. L'Olonnais took the place, you know. Got a fortune out of it and scared Spain half to death. They've made it a lot stronger than it was in his day. Tell me about the watchtower. Is it part of the fort?"

"No, sir, it's not. It's on a different island on the other side of the strait— Isla de la Vigia. It means Lookout Island. It's a stone tower on a hill. I'd guess the tower must be about fifty feet high, but the top of the tower must be close to a hundred feet above sea level. Whenever a ship comes into the Gulf, the tower signals to the fort. I tried to crack the code, but I couldn't."

"I take it the strait's narrow? That's how it looks on every map I've seen."

"Yes, sir. Really narrow, and the channel down it is worse. Narrow and crooked. There's a famous sandbar called El Tablazo about ten feet down. A lot of ships get hung up on it."

"I've got the picture." The steeple came back. "What would prevent our taking the tower, Chris?"

"Fire from the fort. Soldiers from the fort or from the barracks outside the city."

"There are more soldiers there to defend the city, then."

"Yes, sir. About eight hundred, from what I saw of them."

"Good soldiers?"

I shrugged. "About average, I'd say. I don't know a lot about soldiers."

"Good soldiers stand straight and keep themselves as clean as possible. Like marines." Capt. Burt rose as he spoke, walked to the big stern windows and looked out at *Snow Lady*. "I don't imagine you know much about marines, either."

I said, "No, Captain. I don't."

"I wish I had some. I wish the Navy would lend me a couple of hundred. Or more." As he walked back to his chair, I noticed that the deck beams just cleared his head. I had to crouch in that cabin, just like I crouched in our cabin on *Sabina*.

"I've got two plans to propose, Chris. Maybe they're both workable. Maybe neither one is. I'd like your frank opinion of both."

"Sure," I said. "You'll get it, Captain."

"Good. Here's the first. We land on the western shore of the Gulf, march along the coast staying out of range of the guns of the fort, and take the city."

"Sure." I nodded. "That's what I was thinking when I got there. It might be done, sir, but it carries some big disadvantages."

"Which are?"

"A tough march, to start with. The men won't like that. We'd have to leave half our force on the ships, just like Portobello, but Maracaibo's a lot bigger."

"And we've fewer ships. Go on."

"We'd be seen landing by the watchtower. That would give General Sanchez—he's in the city now—two or three days to arrange a defense outside the city. Not just soldiers, but cannon."

"No element of surprise," Capt. Burt murmured.

"Exactly, sir. It would also give General Sanchez time to call for more soldiers from Caracas. He'd get them, too. He's the highest-ranking officer in Venezuela, from what I hear."

"We might beat him before they got there, Chris. Or so I'd hope."

"Yes, sir. We might, but we'd have to get our hands on the gold fast, and they'd have had lots of time to hide it. If we hadn't gotten it, we'd have to fight the fresh soldiers, too. If we beat them, we'd still have to carry everything out to the ships the same way we came in. And if Caracas sent ships instead of troops marching overland—"

Capt. Burt cut me off. "Exactly. That's the great objection. Our ships'd be trapped in the Gulf like so many rats. They'd have to fight their way out, with their crews at half strength."

"Leaving us," I added.

"Right. I take it we agree my first plan's workable but damnably risky. Here's my second. Don't be afraid to get rough with it. All the guns in the fort are directed toward the strait?"

"All but two eight-pounders, sir. Those are pointed inland."

"Good. We could bombard the watchtower without being shot at by the fort, from what you say. We'll knock it down, blinding them. When there's a good stiff wind on a dark night, we'll run through the strait. We'll take the city and threaten to burn it and kill our hostages if the fort doesn't surrender."

I said, "I like that one a lot better than the first, Captain. The strait would be the tricky part. The longer we wait for a favoring wind, the longer the Spanish will have to send for ships and soldiers. And to get them."

Capt. Burt nodded. "I agree, of course. We'll have to act within the next few nights."

"It's narrow, too, and we'll have to feel our way with sounding poles. Any ship that runs aground will be knocked to pieces as soon as the sun's up."

"I understand."

"What's worse is that any ship that runs aground may block the channel for the others. If they've entered the strait, they'll have to kedge to get out. May I tell you how I'd do it, sir?"

He nodded, and I did.

WE CAME INTO the Gulf in broad daylight, proudly flying our black flags. *Sabina* was in the lead, and the man at the masthead called down, "Tower's makin' signals, Cap'n. I can't read 'em, though."

I grinned at Novia and said, "I imagine it is." I remember that so well that I cannot resist putting it in.

She insisted on going with me in the longboat. We landed—all our boats landed—on the west side of the Pigeon Island, the side away from the strait. Putting it another way, we landed just about opposite the fort, which put us behind the ambush that Hoodahs and I had found. I had hoped to catch the soldiers as they beat it back into the fort, but nobody had warned them. We came up behind them while they waited in their trench. We drove them like sheep to the northern end of the island, where our ships' guns did for a hundred or more before they could surrender.

After that we jumped the fort from behind, took it, and drove iron spikes into the touchholes of the guns. There was hardly anybody left inside, and I doubt that more than a dozen shots were fired.

So I had been wrong about the soldiers. I was wrong about the city, too, because I had expected street fighting with the civilians and General Sanchez's soldiers. He used his men to cover the evacuation instead. That might have been good if the civilians had stuck together. As soon as they were clear of the city they scattered like chickens, and he could not have covered them all with five thousand men. We sent strong parties pretty much wherever we wanted to, and rounded up a lot of them, with the gold, silver, and jewelry they had been trying to save from us.

That was when I really found out why Capt. Burt rated buccaneers as highly as he did. Our buccaneers could load and fire twice in the time it took a soldier to load and fire once, and they could bowl over a running man at fifty paces. There were days when it seemed like the only time anybody was hit by one of those soldiers was when the soldier was aiming at somebody else. Hand-to-hand was liable to be pretty even—the side with the most men won. (That was just about always us.) But the way to win with the fewest losses was to follow a party of civilians who were hot to get away from us and pick off the soldiers who were trying to protect it. In half an hour they would have hardly one man left.

I would be lying to you if I said there was no rape and no torture, but I did not do it and did my best to stop it. As well as I can remember I succeeded twice.

Here I ought to say more about torture. I have been skipping over things, I know, and I would like to skip over that. I am not going to do it here because I understand very well how useless it is to make a confession that does not confess.

Besides, I know that a lot of things are considered torture now that would just be punishments on a ship. A sailor would be keelhauled, for instance. It meant that he was tied to rope looped around the ship's waist and dragged under water, beneath the keel, and up on the other side. When he came up he would be half drowned, and half skinned by the barnacles, too. If he did not die, he might be given a week or two in chains to recover. When he was a little stronger, he would be returned to his duty, and nobody called it torture.

We burned our prisoners, dropping live coals onto their faces and roasting them over fires. We cut off men's private parts and raped their wives before their eyes. We tied ropes around people's heads, stuck a stick through the ropes, and turned that stick until their eyes came out and hung down on their cheeks—all this to get them to tell where they had hidden money, or where somebody else had.

We did all that, and while we did it we knew that if we were captured by the Spanish we might be treated the same way. The Spanish often tortured a Native American slave just to make their other slaves fear and respect them.

When I was looking for Hoodahs—it was the third day we were in Maracaibo, and we were getting ready to sail—I went to the inn where I got him, thinking he might have gone back there because he knew where something would be hidden. I did not find him—or any gold either—but I found the bodies of his old master's sons. One's head had been split with an ax or a hatchet. I think it was the only time I saw a human face divided like that. The other had been dismembered, it seemed while he was still alive—his arms and legs hacked off, and the rest left to bleed to death.

Let me say something here about the Spanish and their king that most people today do not know. Not even most pirates knew it. When a Spaniard got a land grant from the King of Spain, he had to swear that he would protect the Native Americans whose land he was getting and teach them Christianity.

Hardly any of them did it. The Native Americans were taught Christianity, yes. But it was not done by the men who got their land. It was done by priests and brothers, Jesuits, Franciscans, and Dominicans. They protected the Native Americans, too, as much as they could. Mostly that meant protecting them from Spanish laymen.

After reading this, you are bound to judge people like Capt. Burt, Hoodahs, and me pretty harshly, and I am not saying we do not deserve it.

No doubt God will judge us with severity. But God will not forget that the times in which we buccaneers plundered the Spanish Main were not like these times, and that the men we tortured for gold would have tortured us for sport.

All of us had known that Maracaibo was rich. It turned out to be richer than any of us had expected. We loaded our ships and two Spanish ships that had been in the harbor, and headed off to Jamaica with so much gold and silver, and so many tons of cacao beans, that I expected Capt. Burt to give up his plan and head home to Surrey.

He did not, but before I get into that, I want to say something more about Maracaibo. The Spanish made two mistakes there (in my judgment) that were characteristic of them, the kinds of things that let us operate as freely as we did.

The first was being too confident of their defenses. They envisioned one kind of attack and defended against it. When somebody does that, his enemy sees he has done it and adjusts his plans. It is not enough to guard against the obvious move and let everything else slide. If the colonel I talked to in the fort had patrolled the shore of Pigeon Island, he and his men would never have been caught like they were.

The other is that the loss of the city was not one man's fault. It was the fault of just about every Spaniard there except the soldiers under General Sanchez. (They were the ones who died, more than any of the rest; but at least they were not tortured.) General Sanchez had eight hundred soldiers left after we took the fort. There had to be at least five thousand men capable of bearing arms in Maracaibo, and a lot of them had muskets, pistols, or swords. I doubt that there was even one who did not have a knife or an ax. If those men had been organized and led against us, we would have had to get out and get out quick. They were not. I doubt that as many as a hundred of the five thousand fought us. They depended on the soldiers to defend them instead, and the soldiers tried to do it when they should have been attacking us. If they had hit us hard when we were drinking and looting, they would have driven us back to our ships in short order.

Was that colonel at the fort stupid? Maybe he was—I fooled him, after all. But I spoke his language at least as well as he did, and he had no reason to suspect me. The north end of the island was the obvious place to land, and that ambush he had planned was well thought out. If we had walked into it the way he expected, we would have been wiped out. He was not stupid, he was careless.

As I write this, it is Christmas Eve, and that is what I plan to preach about at midnight mass.

BEFORE I GET back to Maracaibo, I should say that my homily seemed to go pretty well. I began by explaining that intelligence in God's service is a great blessing, but that we are not judged by it.

"It is innate. For God to favor you because you're smart would be as unjust as it would be for Him to favor me because I'm tall. We're all born with certain talents—His gold, that the Master has left with us—and without certain others. If we are wise, we use our talents in His service. Every member of our choir was born with a good voice, and has wisely chosen to honor God with it. You can think of many other examples, I know.

"Saint Thomas Aquinas was a genius, and Saint Francis of Assisi reminds us of Jesus more than any other saint. I would not be surprised to learn that Saint Teresa of Avila was the most extraordinary woman since the Holy Mother. Have any of them gone to a better Heaven than Brother Juniper? I promise you, they haven't—and they wouldn't want to. Many saints were just children when they died—Saint Agatha is the one I think of first, but there are a lot of others. Bernadette was a plain village girl, and so was Saint Joan.

"Examples like the ones I just gave could be trotted out all day, but you saw much better ones when you came into church. Wise men from the east were called to witness the Incarnation. So were shepherds. Shepherds and wise men, both called as witnesses.

"So am I called. So are every one of you, or you wouldn't be here. Many of you are smart, I know. I know, too, that I'm not. I'm a plain man and not always a good man, a man who in a rougher age might've been a pig farmer or a pirate. Knowing it, I'm very happy in the knowledge that God does not put me down because I'm not a genius. He asks me to be careful— something every one of us can do. If I'm careful to learn the will of God for me and careful to do it, then I'm one of the witnesses Jesus wants.

"You see, it doesn't matter whether we're captains or just ordinary sailors. The wise men went away and told others that Christ had come into the world. The shepherds did the same, spreading glad tidings of great joy.

"You and I can do it, too. If we know what Christmas means and where true happiness lies, then all we have to do is to wish others a Merry Christmas. And mean it.

"I wish you a Merry Christmas, you good people of Holy Family. A Merry Christmas to us, one and all."

HERE I SIT, tapping my teeth with the end of my pen. I feel sure I have forgotten half the things I wanted to write about Maracaibo. No doubt that is for the best.

In Maracaibo I understood why Capt. Burt had wanted two hundred marines. He could have held them together and kept them from looting until the Spanish had been beaten, not just driven from the city. General Sanchez could have held his Spaniards together, too, and hit us hard that evening. I have already said what would have happened if he had. Was he a bad general? I doubt it. He had known, I think, what he ought to do. But he had worried much too much about what people might say if he left the civilians to escape—or be captured—on their own. Some of those civilians had been men of wealth and position. (I know they were, because we captured some of them.) They would have yowled like cats to the governor in Caracas that Sanchez had not protected them. From his viewpoint, he had been smart.

A plain general, one who thought of his men on the battlefield and not of the governor and what the governor might say and do, would have beaten us. Year in and year out, the Spanish thought too much about governors and about Madrid. In the end it cost Spain an empire that covered a quarter of the world.

31

To the Pacific

THIS TIME WE went to Port Royal to refit. Now Capt. Burt had a major win for us to talk about, and we were turning men away by the second day. Each ship was to sail when ready. We would meet again at the Pearls.

The *Weald* was the first to put out. At the time, I thought nothing of it. Somebody had to be first.

We were keeping the Spanish ships we had taken at Maracaibo, and Red Jack was made captain of one of them, which meant I lost him. It also meant the crew got to elect a new quartermaster, and they picked Red Knife, a Zambo Moskito. I thought I was probably going to have to shoot him before the year was out. In a day or two, I found out that he and Hoodahs were great buddies, so I relaxed quite a bit. I never did shoot him, or have a reason to, either. Red Knife was as steady as they come, and as tough as they come, too.

Perhaps I should say here that it takes a while to find out that two Native

Americans are friends. It is when one looks at the other and they both understand. If they are friends, they are a team, and you do not hear their signals.

The Pearls are beautiful islands. I have probably said that already. There are Native Americans there, but we never did find out what tribe they belonged to. They hid, and if there were any on an island we landed on, they would be gone in a few hours. At first I thought they had been raked over good by Spanish, and perhaps they had been. Later it came to me that they might have been raked over just as hard by people like us. They had learned that whites had guns, and that a lot of whites would shoot them just for practice. That was all they needed to know. When the last ship got there, we set out.

If I were to tell everything that happened as we sailed south, I would never be through. Our policy was not to rob any ship that did not look big and rich, and not to take any town, no matter how small it was. We followed those rules all the way south to the Strait of Magellan, and followed them even more strictly for a long time after that. We watered where nobody was, if we could. If we could not, we said that we were English merchants come to trade. We traded for supplies or bought them. All this was so nobody would get alarmed, not from any reformation. We wanted water and supplies, and no trouble. By and large, that was what we got.

People who have not done it talk loosely of going around the Horn. It means rounding Cape Horn, the south end of South America. The good thing about the Cape Horn Passage is that it is not tight. You have a lot of gray water between you and the Cape, and between you and the ice. The bad things are that it is hundreds of miles longer, and the icebergs are even worse. The Strait was worse still, or that was how it seemed. Ice and storms and contrary winds. Novia and I had a big fight, and she said she would kill me if she were not so tired, and I said I would kill her if I were not. In another minute or two we were in each other's arms, me laughing and she crying.

In five more we had forgotten what our big fight was about. All this was on a deck that seemed like it was dead set on throwing both of us into the sea.

I know we lost men in the Strait. Some fell from the rigging, and some were washed overboard. I should know how many we lost and what their names were, but I do not. It is all a long nightmare that passed while I was awake. Six men, at a guess. Or eight.

When a ship has gone into the Strait four times and been blown back out three—which is what happened to us—the Pacific Ocean looks like paradise. Everyone on board expects more storms. Everyone expects to be wrecked, and sees the wrecks of other ships on rocks. There are fires at night on Tierra del Fuego, and everyone knows those fires have been lit by Native Americans who are following the ship, hoping to loot a wreck. It is a cold Hell.

One morning the sun rises over a different sea to light a new sky. The storms are gone. The wind is warm and gentle. The sea is blue, the sky is blue, and the distant land shows blue mountains higher than anyone on board has ever dreamed of, mountains like the walls of giants.

Wet bedding and wet clothes are spread or hung in every conceivable place. A topgallant mast is hoisted and lashed into place, and a Spanish flag run up it. The men off watch have their breakfasts on deck, take their time eating them, make jokes, and sing.

And Novia, lovely delicate Novia with her dark eyes and irresistible smile, hands me a guitar I had almost forgotten I owned. I grin and strike up a lively tune while the whole crew cheers, and soon Pat the Rat has his fiddle. Novia whirls, a skirt I have not seen in months swirling about her flashing legs while her fingers snap like firecrackers—popping like little whips in place of the castanets she does not have.

Red Knife is drumming an empty water butt with two belaying pins. Hoodahs chants, shuffles, and stamps. Big Ned swings Azuka in a wild reel he must have learned in Port Royal, for there is nothing of Africa in it—or else it is all Africa, about which I know nothing. My guitar and O'Leary's fiddle, Red Knife's drum and Novia's dance while the bare feet of fifty of the toughest men who ever pushed a boat into the water smack the planking in fifty hornpipes.

I shout, "Down the middle, Jake!" and Jake touches his forehead without the least alteration of his flying steps. Dear, dear Lord!

Perhaps, someday, in Heaven, you will consent. . . .

THE SADDLE ISLANDS lie off the coast of Ecuador. We had scurvy aboard by the time we put in there, and water was short. It is a place remarkable for turtles of great size. We feasted on them, on sea lizards so big they rivaled crocodiles, and on wild turnips and other greens. (There are seals there as well, but we had eaten seal in the Strait and had no stomach for more.) The shores of these blessed islands are nearly as barren as those of any place we saw in the Strait, but the mountains inland are covered with lush green jungle and ring with the sweet music of flowing water everywhere. It is said that two weeks ashore will mend any scurvy, and Capt. Burt was determined to remain for two weeks at least, so as to catch the treasure ships off Callao with a healthy crew in sound ships. I agreed wholeheartedly, and I believe that every other captain felt as I did.

Here I should say that we did not know the precise date the treasure fleet would sail, only that it put out every six weeks or so, and that its sailings were never more than two months apart.

We were seven vessels: Capt. Burt's *Weald,* my own *Sabina,* Rombeau's *Magdelena,* Gosling's *Snow Lady,* Harker's *Princess,* Red Jack's *Fancy,* and Jackson's *Rescue.* The last two we had taken at Maracaibo, renamed, and refitted at Port Royal. *Weald* was the largest of the seven, *Princess* the smallest, and *Sabina* the fastest in most weathers.

These details are of no great importance. Yet I know that Capt. Burt must have thought long on them, and many others. Now I find my own mind clothed in his blue coat, and plan, consider, and suppose as he must have through many a long hour.

The great matter now was to keep our crews usefully occupied and so out of mischief while our sick regained their strength. We careened the *Fancy,* scraped and tarred her, and made some small repairs to her hull. We drilled our crews at the sails and practiced turning on the heel and suchlike maneuvers. We drilled at the guns, as may be imagined, and took some target practice, too, though I for one begrudged every pound of powder we spent.

Far better, so far as Novia and I were concerned, we sailed from island to island, sightseeing and exploring. This took some time, required a good deal of ship handling, and was, to us and I believe to most of our crew as well, endlessly fascinating. There are fifteen islands of considerable size in the Saddles, and so many small ones that I never succeeded in charting them all. We saw a turtle that must surely have weighed six hundred pounds, found places so lovely and so lonely that it seemed certain each was the loveliest spot on earth and the most isolated, and discovered a spring that rose in soil so barren that nothing—absolutely nothing—grew around it.

At no time did we glimpse another human being, or even see any trace of one. At no time did we see or find the tracks of any four-legged animal other than the turtles and sea lizards I have mentioned. Hoodahs assured me that there had been goats and wild swine on the island he shared with Master. There was nothing of the kind in the Saddles, though there were many birds.

One night I woke and could not sleep. A list of all the things that worried me that night would make dull reading, and I doubt that I could remember all of them now if I tried. Fretting and afraid that I would wake Novia, I went up on deck. The moon was full, and the warm night so calm no sail could have been of the least use. Boucher was awake and yawning, but every man of his watch slept.

I stood at the gunwale, looked at the moon, and thought how easy it would be—how very easy and delightful—for me to quit the ship and not return. I could return to our cabin and get my musket and bullet bag, and with it a couple of pistols and my dagger. When I returned to the deck, Boucher and I would wake two of the watch and have them row me ashore. I would tell them to return to the ship and walk away. No one would question me or try to stop me.

I felt sure that Capt. Burt would search the island for me, but I had seen enough of the high jungle by then to know that I could evade any number of searchers there. Soon the flotilla would set sail, and I would be alone. Alone in a climate that was too hot only at midday, and never too cold. Alone on an island that would have provided meat, fruits, and greens enough for a hundred men indefinitely. No more fighting and no more storms. No ship and crew to worry about. No more fear of hidden rocks, hanging, and mutiny.

Later Novia told me she had felt the same way the whole time we had been there. If I had ever proposed that we leave the ship and hide, she would have agreed at once. Now I wonder whether Hoodahs's shipwrecked Master ever regretted boarding the vessel that had returned him to England. It seems to me that he must have, and often. Did he ever try to get back, I wonder?

And did he succeed?

IN THE END, we remained among the Saddle Islands for a little over two weeks. Before we left we caught hundreds of turtles of manageable size to take with us. Laid on their back they must stay where they are put, and they can live for weeks (for months, some sailors say) without food and water.

They provided us with fresh meat that lasted until—but I must not jump ahead.

We lay ten days off Callao. *Princess* stayed near enough to shore that no ship could put out from the port without being seen. The rest of our ships were scattered to the north, none so far from the rest that she could not read the signals of some other. When the treasure ships put out—several large ships, strongly armed—*Princess* would make signal. As they sailed north, they would encounter us one by one, and by the time there were enough of us to alarm them, the passage back would be a long one. That was Capt. Burt's plan, and I still think it was a good one.

32

The Sea Fight

MOST OF THE numbers in this account have been guessed at. They are good guesses for the most part—when I said that there were four unmarried men on the *Santa Charita,* for example. There could have been only three, or there might have been five. But I am fairly sure it was four. These are exact numbers: we had waited ten days off Callao when the treasure ships put out, and there were three of them.

The ten days have stuck in my mind because of the awful suspense of the wait. You cannot stay in one place in a ship unless you are tied to a wharf. If there were no currents and no wind, you might try. But even a toy boat set in the middle of a tub of water will drift to one side of the tub or the other, given time. A ship at anchor is held by its cable, but moves even so, now here, now there. We made a sea anchor, drifted downwind for three or four hours dragging the sea anchor, then took in the sea anchor and tacked slowly back to our original position. We did that so often that all of us, I think, began to hope for a storm. None blew.

At night, and sometimes by day, Novia and I talked about what we would do with our share of the gold. We would buy a hacienda in New Spain. Or a big farm in the New Jersey colony Capt. Burt had told me about once. Or a fine house in Madrid. Or Havana. A sugar plantation on Jamaica.

We would have the yard that had built the *Castillo Blanco* build a ship like that for us, hire a crew, and sail it around the world.

As time wore on we talked about what Novia might do if I were killed, and what I might do if she were. I am not going to go into that here. Some things are too personal, and that is one of them.

The tenth day was clear and warm, just like the first nine. It was about halfway through the forenoon watch when the *Weald* signaled ENEMY IN VIEW. After that, we followed *Weald,* in accordance with orders.

I did not get a good look at the three treasure ships until the day was more than half gone. There was a big galleon (later I learned she was the *San Felipo*), and two other ships that were only a little smaller (the *Socorro* and the *Zumaya*). So far, we had not worried them enough to make them turn back, which was what we wanted.

What we did not want was for them to keep going after sundown. Most Spanish ships hove to after sundown, and that was what we were expecting and hoping for. These kept going. That may have been SOP for the treasure ships, or it may just have meant that the captain of the *San Felipo* was getting a little concerned.

If it had been up to me, I would have gone for them that night. Capt. Burt decided to wait until morning. Having said that, I should also say that he had good reasons for it. First, we might wear down the Spanish crews a little if they were made to stand to their guns as long as we were in sight. Second, and more important, they could have put out their lights and scatted. If they had done that, we would have had a good chance of getting one, but not much chance of getting all three.

All three were what we wanted.

I slept on deck that night, which was no great hardship. About the time I was yawning and stretching, the *Weald* made signal: CROSS BOW OF LEAD SHIP GOOD LUCK CHRIS.

We crammed on as much sail as *Sabina* would carry in that wind, which was pretty much everything. The Spanish ships were strung out, as I saw when we got closer. The big galleon was in back to protect the smaller ships. One of those was about a quarter mile in front of her, and the other out in front of that one by about half as much.

I stayed west out of range of the galleon's guns. She fired anyway, throwing up fountains a hundred yards to starboard. It is a trip to be shot at and missed. It gets the old heart pumping and brightens up the eyes something wonderful.

When we got out front and put the wheel over, all that torment we had gone through in the Strait of Magellan paid off. This was fair weather, just a good stiff following wind. We put the helm over, brought the yards around, and had everything drawing again faster than any diesel-engine sailor would have thought possible.

The Spanish captain was ready for us and began his turn the moment he saw us go about. We fired as soon as our guns bore and got off the first broadside. *Zumaya* answered before the echoes had died away. Counting her guns was easy—she carried eight per side, five in the main battery and three on the weather deck. I guessed them twelve-pounders. If I was right, we were throwing a little more metal.

What really counts, though, is how much metal hits. The general rule with guns like we had is to aim at the base of the mainmast and pray to hit something. We were aiming a little higher and firing chain shot, because the last thing we wanted to do was to sink her. Novia was running up and down our weather deck checking aim, and Boucher was doing the same thing down below. But chain shot is slower to load and less accurate than round shot, and we were taking some punishment.

It looked bad until the Spanish captain tried to get fancy. His idea was to lag a little, then turn north again and rake us. It was the kind of thing I have seen a lot of guys do in fights—a good idea for somebody faster. We swung *Sabina* north again, it was our broadside to his bow, the same thing Capt. Burt had wanted originally.

I do not know how much damage altogether it did to *Zumaya*'s rigging, but her foremast went down and there seemed to be a good deal more.

"Shall we lay alongside, Captain?"

That was Bouton, and I told him I was not ready to die quite yet.

"But, Captain—"

"How long for the rest of them to catch up?"

He had not thought of that. I could see it in his face.

There was more fencing. One of our ships—usually the *Weald*—would engage the big galleon broadside-to-broadside. While the galleon was busy with whoever it was, somebody else—*Snow Lady, Rescue, Fancy,* or us— would cross her stern.

Or try to.

A minute can be forever when there is that kind of fighting. All afternoon (and we did it all afternoon) takes a year. There would be an hour or more of jockeying for position. Then hard shooting for five minutes or so, and then another hour or two of tacking, turning and edging around. I had musket men in the rigging, and Nazaire swore he hit the captain. If he did, I did not see any sign of it.

We did our best to keep track of them during the night and lost them anyway. Capt. Burt thought they had gone back to Callao. I did not get to speak to him, but I know he did from the orders he gave. *Sabina* was to look north, with *Magdelena* and *Princess.* I was in command. If we found them, Rombeau and I were to engage, and send Harker south. *Weald, Snow Lady, Rescue,* and *Fancy* would look south and send to us if they found the chase.

So what he thought was pretty plain. *Sabina* and *Weald* had taken more punishment than the others—*Weald* most of all, I would say, but it was the biggest we had and so was more able to take it.

The other thing was that I had the three fastest ships. The prevailing winds are north along that part of the coast, and he must have figured that if the Spanish had taken off north, they would make good time. It would be no use to send any ships but the fastest we had after them. On the other hand, running home to Mama would mean a lot of tacking. Our ships could prob- ably out-tack the Spanish even if they were in good shape, and *Zumaya* had no foremast and would have trouble tacking even with a good captain and a handy crew.

Anyway, off we went with six men at the pumps and a dozen more trying to plug shot holes. That sounds like we were limping along, but actually we were not. I had the log cast three times, and one of those readings was six- teen knots. That was flying for a ship like *Sabina,* and I knew darned well that the Spanish were not going to make that kind of speed.

The thing was that I had thought about the same things Capt. Burt had, and had come up on the other end. There were three things they could do: go back to Callao, go west into the Pacific, and go north to Panama.

I tried to put myself into the head of the galleon captain: *"Callao is close,"*

I said to myself, *"but it's upwind. It might take us every bit as long to get there as it would for us to get to Panama. So that's strike one. My orders don't say a thing about going back there, and everybody in town will say I'm a quitter. Strike two. Worst of all, it's what they'll expect. So strike three and out.*

"Heading off into the Pacific is something they'll never expect, so that's a point in its favor. Ball one. But just look at all the problems. The farther we go, the longer it will take to get back. Strike one. We're not carrying enough food and water—water especially—to sail west for a week or so and then come back, angling north for Panama. Strike two. When we get back, we'll likely find the pirates hanging around near Panama waiting for us, and have to fight them anyway. Strike three. But none of that is the worst. It's against orders. If I do it, people may think I'm running off with the gold myself. Those people could include the captains under me and even my own crew. So that's absolutely out. No way!

"That leaves Panama. Sure, it's farther—strike one—but look at all the good stuff. It's what my orders call for—one base. Nobody's goin' to talk about cowardice or stealing—two bases. They won't expect it—I'm rounding third. It's downwind—home run! 'Well, Admiral Valdes, sir, God and all His saints were with me, and Captain Burt hung his curve.'"

I told everybody to get ready. We had drawn the long straw, and they were ours.

Which they almost were. We caught up with them about noon, *Princess* scooted off to tell Capt. Burt as ordered, and Rombeau and I got out in front and turned broadside-on. The idea was to keep them dodging and tacking until *Weald* and our other ships showed up. It worked twice, and then they caught on.

I had expected them to scatter, but they came at us in a line ahead, the *San Felipo* in the lead. It meant she was heading into our broadsides, and as long as she was bow-on we really pounded her.

She pounded us a little bit, too. She had six bow chasers, and they looked like four twelve-pounders and two twenties to me. We had the upper hand and did some real damage, but it was no picnic.

We wore ship as she came on, turning so as to keep our broadsides toward her. I kept hoping she would veer off. But hit or missed, or maybe replaced, her skipper had guts.

And big guns on the lower deck, probably thirty-two-pounders. She got it from both sides as she passed between us, but she gave as good as she got, and better. *Socorro* and *Zumaya* followed her. All I can say about them was that they pounded us some more. Maybe we pounded them a little, too. I know we tried, and tried hard.

This gets painful. Fr. Wahl keeps a bottle of Scotch in his bedroom, or so he says, and has invited me to join him whenever. Tonight I am going to knock on his door and take him up on it. If things go as I hope, I will get a drink or two—no more than two—and an hour's good talk.

Then go to bed. More tomorrow.

33

Gold!

A LOT OF men were dead, and a lot more were hurt so badly that they died in the next couple of hours. When a wooden ship is hit by a cast-iron cannonball, it throws splinters every which way. It throws them hard, and some are big. We did the best we could for our wounded, but our best was not much.

I am not going to list all the men who died here. I will list the one woman—otherwise you will feel sure it was Novia. It was Azuka. As for the rest . . . Well, a lot of the names I have mentioned over and over in telling my story will not be mentioned anymore.

Novia and I were not hurt, or at least not badly. I would say that there were about thirty of us who were not. Why God ruled that we were to be spared, I cannot say.

His mysteries lie beyond our comprehension.

The Spanish might have turned around and sunk both our ships. Or maybe *Magdelena* could have gotten away. What I know for sure is that we could not have. Anyone's guess is as good as mine as to why they did not. Mine is that their assignment was to carry the gold to Panama, not to fight pirates. They may also have seen *Princess* run off to fetch *Weald* and the rest of our ships.

Magdelena chased them, and we did our best to keep up. After six hours or more of that, Novia came up from the hold and said, "She sinks tonight, Crisóforo. It is best, perhaps, if we go before the sun. No?"

It was, and we did. I signaled Rombeau, and he hauled wind. Our longboat was stove, but we got a few men into the jolly and the piragua. *Magdelena*'s longboat took the rest, the sound and the wounded.

The dead we left on board.

No. I did not go down with my ship, but I was the last to leave. That night, when we were alone in the cabin Rombeau gave up for us, Novia and I held each other and she cried. I did not, but I wanted to. I would have felt better, I know, if I had. I could not.

I WOULD NOT want to go back to the three or four days that followed, but I must write about them here for the record to be complete.

For you to understand, and for me to understand, too.

The Spanish ships reached Panama. We thought of raiding the harbor, but by the time *Weald, Snow Lady, Rescue, Fancy,* and *Princess* joined us, a lot of the gold had been unloaded. Capt. Burt knew the route the mule train would follow if it headed north to Mexico or Veracruz and we decided to cut them off. I say we. Even though I did not get to vote, Capt. Burt let me sit in on the captains' meeting. Having no ship, I did not count.

How would I have voted if I could? To tell the truth, I am not sure. But probably as they did.

We sailed west along the coast to a village of eight or ten houses called Rio Hato, where the road turns inland. Half of each crew was to stay on each ship, as before. I got Novia alone and said, "Now listen to me. I'm not going to lose you. I've already lost a lot of people I liked, and I'm not about to lose the one person I love. I want you to swear to God Almighty, right here and right now, that you'll stay on this ship."

She raised her hand and said, "I, Sabina María de Vega Aranda Guzman, do swear as I live that I will remain behind until this good man who is my husband before you, O Lord, returns for me. I shall not follow him, save he permits me."

I knew she meant it. I could hear that in her voice and see it in her face. I did not ask her any questions, but she knew me better than anyone else ever has, and she knew. Almost whispering she said, "I have in me a child, Crisóforo."

Half the crews were supposed to stay behind. That was not how it was, although I did not realize it until that evening, when we had laid out our ambush and camped. Novia had not followed, but a lot of men who were supposed to stay with the ships had. Some of them were probably afraid that we would never come back to the ships. (Most of us never did.) Some just felt that this was going to be the biggest thing in their lives and wanted to be in on it, saying, "I was with Burt at Rio Hato," the way people said, "I was with Morgan when he burned Panama." Later I found out that there had been only five men with Novia on the *Magdelena*.

For most of the morning we tramped up the road until we found a good place, with some big trees back from the road and a lot of brush alongside it. We set up our ambush a hundred paces or so after that. Men were stationed every yard or so on both sides, with twenty good musket men to block the end once the soldiers and mules had gotten between the rest. I was in charge of that group; and Mahu came with me, although he did not have a musket. Nobody was to fire until we did.

It seemed like a good plan and would probably have worked. The trouble was that when the mule train ambled into it late that afternoon, somebody got spotted. A soldier shot at him, his friends shot back, and in less than a minute every barrel was hot. We moved out into the road and started shooting the way we were supposed to, but the nearest soldiers were still forty or fifty paces away.

They were shot to rags just the same, but half the mules and mule drivers ran hell-for-leather back toward Panama. We were running after them, yelling for all we were worth, when something happened that just then seemed like a miracle. There was more shooting off to the east, and a terrible pileup when the men and mules who had been at the back of the column turned around and tried to bug out toward us. We shot, and the guys who had been east of us shot, and the soldiers who were left did not stand a chance.

The new pirates—the ones who had been east of us blocking the way back to the coast—turned out to be Lesage and the crew of the *Bretagne*. We were happy to see them, and they pretended to be happy to see us. I hugged Lesage and got to talk to him a little bit. He said he had missed us at Portobello, but he had known what Capt. Burt planned to do so he had gone after us as fast as he could, and had finally found our ships at Rio Hato.

Maybe I should save what happened after that for a big surprise—which it was to us. All right, I will, but there was a big hole in Lesage's story that I should have thought of right away, and I am going to say that here. I should have seen through him. So should Capt. Burt. We trusted him and so we did not.

Did I think of Valentin? Yes, I did, but that did not seem to be the time to bring it up. Everybody was pulling gold off dead mules, and yelling, and marveling at the weight of the ingots: one dozen to a mule, and solid gold. If Capt. Burt had been right about a mule carrying three hundred pounds, each of those ingots weighed about twenty-five pounds.

For the rest of the day, we were all rich.

The killing started that night when most of us were asleep. I was lying awake. Maybe it was because I had not had anything to drink, but I think it was mostly because of what Novia had said.

I was going to be a father. I had never expected it or thought much about it. Novia had been married to Jaime Guzman for thirty-four months and had never been pregnant, so it had seemed to us that there was a good chance she never would be. Now I knew it had been him. Maybe he had known it, too, and that was why he had been so jealous. All I know is that when I was lying there thinking about the kid who was on the way and money that the three of us would have, I was not jealous of anybody in the whole world.

Somebody started screaming and there were three or four shots. I jumped up, felt around for my belt and pistols, and yelled for Mahu.

He was not there, just a guy with a cutlass coming for me. I could barely see him in the moonlight filtering through the trees and what was left of our little fire: a big guy with a dead-white sling for his pistols that jumped out at you. That, and I saw the gleam of his cutlass.

Just about then, I found mine. If this were TV or a movie he and I would have a big cutlass fight that would last long enough for somebody to go for popcorn, and for sure I would not kill him the same way I killed Yancy. This is real, and that is what happened. I grabbed a burning stick and stuck it in his face, and cut him down when he dodged it. I have never been really sure, but I think my blade must have caught the side of his neck.

After that four guys came for me, and I dropped my cutlass and ran away like a rat.

If I had been a hero I would have fought them and died. If I had been a superhero, I would have killed them all. I am not a hero and have never claimed to be. As for superheroes, that is a sandwich. I have no idea how far I ran, but it must have been a good long way. After that I should have gotten myself under control and gone back to the fight.

Right.

You bet.

I did no such thing. When I was certain I had shaken them, I went to my knees and thanked God for preserving my life. I did not try to go back to where the fight had been, either. There had been a fight, people had died, and my side had lost. That was all I knew, and all I needed to know just then. For as long as it was dark, I stayed there on my knees, trying to make some sort of deal with God. When I could see my shadow, I stood up and went looking for the road, knowing it would take me back to Rio Hato.

Sometimes it does not matter what you set out to do. You do what you are fated to do. I did not find the road. I found the battle—where it had been at least, because everybody who could leave was gone by the time I got there. I saw dead mules and dead men, quite a few of them men I knew. Somebody had gone around killing the wounded, I think. Or maybe only killing those hurt so bad they could never recover.

What was for sure was no one had looted the bodies. (No, I did not try to loot them either.) But that was how it had to be. I could see that there had been so much gold on those mules that no one had bothered to turn out pockets or cut off fingers to get rings.

"Chris . . . Chris . . ."

It was so faint I thought for a minute I had imagined it. The voice came again, like the sighing of the wind, and I found Capt. Burt.

He had been shot at least twice. Maybe more, I do not know. I started trying to help him, but I could see it was no use, so I stopped when he told me to. A modern ER, with plasma and whole blood and an expert surgeon, might have saved him, though I doubt it. For me, kneeling in the jungle and tearing strips off my shirt, it was as hopeless as trying to sweep away the sea.

"*I'm dead man, Chris. Dead man breathin'* . . . *Knew you'd come.*"

I said I was there, I would not go until he died, and would have masses said for his soul.

"*You like maps, Chris. Take my maps.* . . . *In my coat.*"

Nodding, I reached into the big blue coat he always wore and pulled them out.

As I did, he died.

He died smiling, still the big boss pirate and still confident. Confident of what? I would love to know.

I was able to fold his hands over his chest in a way that hid one of his wounds, but that was all I did. I thought of burying him or trying to, but I was worried sick about Novia and left him lying there among his men. Now that I have had time to think about it, I know that is how he would have wanted it.

34

Afterward

I AM GOING to end this tonight. If I have to sit up all night writing, that is what I will do. Yes, and catch a plane in the morning. There is not much more to tell, nor any reason that I should not finish before midnight.

Back to Darien, a place I am very glad to be out of.

THE *MAGDELENA* WAS a mile or so out to sea when I reached Rio Hato. That is the important point, and the only thing I remember accurately. *Weald* had gone already, I feel sure. Perhaps the rest had, too. Or perhaps they were actually closer than *Magdelena*. I cannot be certain. One of the ships I saw may well have been *Bretagne*. If so, I can remember nothing about her rig.

This, although I stood on the little quay and watched them go until

Magdelena was out of sight. I thought then of buying a fishing boat, stocking her, and chasing them. But nothing could have been more hopeless, and Novia was almost certainly dead.

When the last sail was out of sight I went to the village's tiny inn, bought a bottle of wine I did not particularly want, and asked the innkeeper what he had to eat.

It was bread and cheese, but the first bite reminded me that I was ravenously hungry. After that, I found no reason to complain of it. The first glass of wine soon reminded me, too, that I had fought twice, had been awake all night, and now had been up another half day. I asked the innkeeper whether he rented rooms.

He shrugged. (He was a stocky, cheerful-looking man about ten years older than I was back then.) "One room, Señor. Only one room, and it is occupied already." He leaned a little closer. "A distressed lady, Señor."

"A lady?" I could not believe my ears.

Leaning closer still, he whispered, *"A lady who escaped the pirates!"*

I think I had found the room and started pounding on Novia's door before he had finished.

We hugged and kissed and did it all over again, and went to bed in the middle of the day—a siesta, with a little foreplay to begin with. The funny thing is that neither one of us said a lot—we were too happy to find each other alive. Words cannot cover things like that. It takes kisses and hugs, laughter and tears. Eventually we got up, got the innkeeper's wife to feed us, and went back to bed.

Here is what I learned the next day. Lesage had come into the bay with four ships, as friendly as could be. When he saw how few men there were on our ships—Novia had five—he said it was too dangerous. What would they do if the Spanish came? He put twenty men on the *Magdelena,* telling Novia they were a loan, not a gift. She did not know how many he had put on the others, but it was probably a hundred men all told.

As soon as the introductions were over and Lesage and the rest had gone, those men seized the ships. They were going to rape Novia. Or perhaps they did, or some did. She said they had not, only torn off her gown. I believe her, knowing that not everyone would.

Whether they did or not, she got away from them, jumped over the side, and hid under the overhang of the stern until dark. We had both seen enough of pirates by that time to know that hardly any of them could swim.

My guess is that when she did not come up after a minute or two they decided she had drowned.

While we were fighting Lesage, she had swum to shore, penniless and pretty nearly naked. Almost everybody had left the village by then, or else they were hiding in their cellars and keeping quiet. Finally she heard a woman's voice, went to the window, and begged for help. The woman, God bless her, had let her in.

That woman was the innkeeper's wife. When she had given Novia an old gown, Novia had told them both that she was a reputable Spanish lady (naming her father and a bunch of distinguished relatives) who had been kidnapped by pirates. (All of which was true, as a matter of fact.) She had promised that if they let her hide in their house and helped her, they would be repaid ten times over. I had enough gold in my money belt to make good on that promise before we left, giving them as much as the room would have brought if they had rented it for a month.

Together, we explained that we were husband and wife. I had thought that Novia had been killed by the pirates, and she had thought I had been. And that was true, too, except that we were not technically married any more than Adam and Eve were.

From that point on, everything we did was dictated by two things. The first thing was the maps I had gotten from Capt. Burt. One was a general map of a part of the Pearl Coast, showing the Pearl Islands and Pearl Lagoon, with a lot of other things. Another one was a not-terribly-detailed map of the Pearls themselves, with the islands marked on which Capt. Burt had buried the money he meant to take back to Surrey.

The last map was on the back of the island map, and it was a sketch map that he had drawn himself. It showed both those islands, and how to find the places to dig.

The second thing was that Novia was pregnant. We knew that even if we made it to the Caribbean just as fast as we could, she was going to be showing a lot by the time we got there. After that we would have to get a boat, fit it out, and so forth. It was bound to be dangerous for her, and might be terribly dangerous. A girl in Port Royal had told me once that rough sailing in a small boat is about as good a way to get a woman to miscarry as there is. She said some of her friends had done that on purpose, and I still get sick just thinking about it.

What it came down to was that Novia wanted to go after the treasure and I wanted to park her in a good safe place, a place where they had good people and good midwives, and go after it by myself.

In the end, I won—I think mostly because she really wanted me to.

There is not a lot more to tell, and I have not a lot of time left in which to tell it. Eventually we were able to buy horses and a lot of other things. When Mahu joined us (I think two days after we left Puntarenas) we bought him a horse, too. By that time I was Don Crisóforo de Vega, and Novia was Señora de Vega. Mahu became our servant, Manuel. I was pretty worried then about his talking addiction, but need not have been. In the first place, he did not know a whole lot of Spanish. And in the second, we had rescued him from slavery on a pirate ship. The story changed every time he told it, and nobody who took the trouble to listen believed it no matter which version they heard.

If you want to point out that Puntarenas is not on the way to the Pearls, you will be dead right. It is not. I did not want to go anywhere near them for fear that I would give in to temptation, get some kind of a boat, and go off treasure hunting.

There was also the chance we would run into somebody else who had known me when I was Capt. Chris, just like we had run into Mahu. Somebody from Santa Maria, say, or Portobello. Every time I went into an inn, I was scared half to death that somebody who had been drinking in the taproom would set down his glass and stare.

It never happened. We just kept traveling and trying to look like we enjoyed it, asking about the safest roads and taking those, and wondering if so much riding was good for the baby. If there had been good roads and a chance to buy a good coach with decent springs, we would have jumped at it. The roads were all bad, and there was nothing but wagons and farm carts. Neither of those had any springs at all.

We stayed at private houses when we could, because they were generally cleaner and had better food. As soon as the siesta hour was over, we started looking for one. The bigger it was and the richer it looked, the better we liked it. Good clothes and good horses helped, so we bought better ones every chance we got—and always apologized for what we were wearing and riding. Travel, you know. We were thinking of buying a hacienda and settling down in the New World, we told our hosts, and were looking for the right place. Novia's maid had fallen ill and been left behind in . . . Whatever town seemed most credible at the time. Thinking about what had really happened with

Estrellita could make it tough for me to say that without laughing, but I generally managed.

Somewhere in here I ought to say that I had a nice Spanish sword, a couple of pistols on the pommel of my saddle, and a musket in a boot I had a saddle-maker fix up for it. Novia had a dagger and two guns—not the brass ones she had used for so long, but silver-trimmed iron ones she had found in Managua. All that hardware stayed hidden under the big, full skirts she wore. "Manuel" had a short musket and a fancy machete, partly because he might need them and partly because they established straight off that he was a paid servant, not a slave. That got him better treatment and may have saved a couple of lives. Guys who have crewed on pirate ships awhile are a certain way, and that is something nobody but God can do anything about.

We stayed a week in Mexico. Everybody calls the country "Mexico" now, and the town is "Mexico City." Back then the country was New Spain, and Mexico was just the capital of New Spain. It was nice, but all three of us wanted to be nearer the sea.

I had a special reason for picking Veracruz. If you read this far, you will have guessed it already.

It did not take me long to find the priest who had carried water to the slaves. "Padre," I said, "I know you won't remember me, but . . ."

He was nodding and smiling. "You are the sailor who showed me how to tie my jug to the hook, my son. An angel of God. How could I ever forget you?"

I shook my head. "I'm not really an angel, Padre."

"God may think otherwise. You have sinned. Did you think angels never sinned? If that were true, my son, they would stand as high in the sight of God as Our Lord. They are not, but are mere servants, even as we."

"There's this girl, Padre. We loved each other and wanted to marry, but we couldn't. We were in a place where it couldn't be done right, just to start with, and there were other problems."

"I see. Is she with child?"

I nodded. "You're going to say I ought to marry her. That's what I want to do. Those other problems aren't around anymore, and we're both right here in Veracruz. We want to be married here in this church, and we want you to do it."

After that he asked about impediments. Were we sister and brother? Cousins? Was either of us married already? And so forth. I explained that we were not related at all, that I had never been married and that Novia was a widow.

"You're certain of that, my son?"

I was, naturally, and I told him so. He married us the next day.

My guess is that Novia thought I would get a boat and go after Capt. Burt's treasure right after the ceremony, and she liked it a lot when I did not. The truth is that I did not want to, because I was so worried about her. I could leave her quite a lot of money, and I would. Still, I knew that I would be worried sick as soon as I cast off. If waiting until our child was born was all it was, I would have done it, and been glad to. It would only have been a couple more months, so that would have been okay. The trouble was that I could not risk taking our child out on a boat for weeks and maybe a month or more until he or she was a lot older, eight at least, and ten would be better. So I would have to leave Novia alone with only Mahu to look after her, and it scared me half to death.

Then one day I was walking down the street and I saw a tall, thin man with a beat-up face. I stared and stared, and he just grinned at me.

"Brother Ignacio! Goombah!" I yelled it so loud everybody must have thought I had gone crazy.

"Hello, Chris." He stopped grinning, but he could not stop smiling. "How are things with you?"

I brought him back to meet Novia and heard his story while the four of us ate and drank a little wine.

"There really isn't much to tell, Señora. I was a lay brother at the monastery in which Chris was educated. The students had to work as well as study— working is one of the most important things a boy must learn—and Chris used to help me, hoeing the garden and pruning our vines and orange trees. Minding our pigs. I came to love him like a son, and I know he looked up to me."

I said, "He still does."

"Thank you, Chris." Grinning from ear to ear, he went back to Novia. "When he left our monastery, I realized I didn't want to stay without him. I followed him, hoping to help him."

He tried to stop grinning but could not. "You owed me this chicken, Chris. I'd paid for one, and you stole it."

"That was you!" I could not believe it.

"It certainly was. So you owe me one, but I'm being repaid tonight. Might I have another helping?"

Novia passed the chicken to him.

"I lost sight of you after that," he said, "and there is not much left to tell. I found honest work, confess often, attend mass when I can, and here I am. You've done well for yourself, Chris, as I always knew you would."

"In some ways I have," I told him, "and in some ways I haven't. Maybe someday we'll have to talk about that. Now I have to ask my wife something. Novia, do you remember what I said about Brother Ignacio when we were on Virgin Gorda?"

She nodded. "You said he was the second father to you, Crisóforo. I have remember what you say of him ever since, and you speak of him many times."

"Right. I also said I'd trust him further than I'd trust myself."

She nodded again. "This I remember also."

"Do you trust him, too, Novia? Now that you've seen him?"

"Oh, sí!" She gave Ignacio a warm smile. "He is very like you, though more old. A good man."

She had lifted a load from my shoulders, and I could not have stopped myself from smiling if I had tried. I asked Ignacio what he was doing now.

"Little enough, Chris. I left my ship when it got here, wanting to stay awhile. Since then I've had a few odd jobs. If you're thinking of hiring me, I'll work cheap."

I named a salary, about twice what a sailor usually earns and the same as what we were paying Mahu.

"Fine, if I can do the work. What is it?"

"Looking after Novia while I'm gone. The midwife we've lined up says another six weeks, and I'm hoping to be back before then. But meanwhile I'd like to be certain there's somebody with her who has a good level head and a Spanish background—most of all, someone who'll have her best interest at heart."

"And the baby's," he said.

So that was how we worked it. Novia got most of the gold left in my money belt. She would pay Ignacio and Mahu, and could fire either or both of them if she thought that was the best thing to do. I bought a fine little sloop that I could manage alone, stocked it with supplies, and put out.

I hit the storm on the fifth day out, and lasted in it maybe five hours tops. Probably it was not even that long. My guess is that it was a hurricane, although it was early in the season for them.

I stayed afloat by holding on to a ringbolt I had mounted on my beautiful little sloop so I could rig a jib on her. It had stayed attached to the biggest piece of wreckage, and after a while I was able to climb up on it. I was about dead when some Mexican fishermen took me on board.

They had a little radio so they could listen to the weather forecasts, and that was when I knew when I was.

I AM WRITING this on the plane to Miami. I will have a three-hour lay-over there, then catch a plane for Havana. I plan to mail this to you before I go. I know you will not believe it, but I cannot help that.

There will not be time enough for me to write about all the things that happened to me after that, and I would not want to anyway. I worked on Mexican boats awhile, then crossed into the U.S., which was pretty easy. This happened and that happened, and twice I was nearly sent to jail. I got into the seminary by explaining that I had grown up in Cuba. With the communists in power, they could not look for records there. They made sure I was not in the FBI's files and took me.

Now I am a priest. Let me repeat that: NOW I am a priest. But when the monastery is reopened, I will not tell them. I will come in as a lay brother, able to read and write because all Cubans can, and able to speak a little English because I worked in a hotel. Pious in the good sense, and willing to turn my hand to any kind of work.

Soon a young I, called Christopher, will come as a student. We will work together sometimes, tending the pigs and the other livestock, planting cucumbers and harvesting okra and peppers. I will stay close to him, and when he drifts back, I will drift back with him.

When he needs someone in Veracruz, I will be there. I will look after Sabina and our child as if they were my own—because they will be.

As the years pass, she will come to know the truth. You may say I will violate my vow of chastity then, but you will be wrong if you do. God will not hold me to a vow I have not yet taken. I know Him, and He is just. No just judge holds a man to a vow to be made in the future.

The maps I carried aboard the sloop have been lost forever, but I studied them a thousand times and recall every detail. When the time is ripe, Sabina and I will claim Capt. Burt's treasure.

Then she and I, and our child, will sail around the world. Today, as you sit reading this, we have been dead three hundred years.

We are the people of your past.

Glossary

All persons of importance in the text are listed here, with many lesser persons. Persons and places are limited to those not apt to be familiar to the average reader. It is assumed that such a reader will have little difficulty with "Shakespeare" and "South America." A few technical terms, etc., are included as well.

ACADIA   A French colony in eastern Canada.

AGATHA, SAINT   An early Christian martyr.

ALVAREZ   Captain Ojeda's lieutenant.

ANTILLES   The island chain separating the Caribbean Sea from the Atlantic Ocean.

ANTONIO   A Portuguese sailing master turned pirate.

AQUINAS, SAINT THOMAS   A great medieval theologian.

ARNOLD, MARY ANNE   A woman who posed for years as a male seaman.

This sort of thing happened much more often than is credible. Deborah Samson became a private in the Continental Army during the Revolutionary War. Dressed as men, Rachel and Grace Martin were American partisans in the same war. Other examples might be given.

AZUKA   The slave mistress of the captain of the *Duquesa de Corruna*.

BARBARA, SAINT   The patroness of gunners.

BENSON, BEN   An English sailor in the prize crew put on the *Duquesa de Corruna*.

BERNADETTE, SAINT   A visionary to whom the Virgin appeared repeatedly in 1858.

BIG CAYEMITE   An island off the north coast of the Tiburon Peninsula.

BIG NED   A slave freed to reinforce the crew of the *New Ark*.

BLACKBEARD   Real name Edward Teach. His death in 1718 may be said to have ended the great age of piracy.

BONNEY, ANNE   A woman seduced by Calico Jack Rackam who joined his crew. She is believed to have borne his child in prison; neither its fate nor hers is known to history.

BOUCHER   Under the narrator, second mate of the *Castillo Blanco*.

BOUTON   Under the narrator, first mate of the *Castillo Blanco*.

BOWEN, JOHN   A trustworthy merchant of Port Royal.

BRENDAN, SAINT   A patron of sailors. He is said to have reached the New World.

BRETAGNE   Lesage's ship.

BULL, BILL   An alcoholic pirate.

BURT, CAPTAIN BRAM (ABRAHAM)   The commodore of a pirate flotilla.

CALLAO   A seaport of Peru, near Lima.

CAMPECHE, GULF OF   The southern arm of the Gulf of Mexico, bounded on the east by Yucatan.

CANAL DU SUD   The passage between Île de la Gonâve and the Tiburon Peninsula.

CARACAS   The capital of Venezuela.

CARTERET, SIR GEORGE   The proprietor of New Jersey.

CASTILLO BLANCO   Don José de Santiago's ship.

CATHARINE, SAINT   A Christian martyr who forgave her executioner.

CHENG, MRS.   Cheng I Sao. Arguably the greatest pirate of all time. Those who may have sought the original of Milton Caniff's Dragon Lady need look no further.

CHIN   One of the narrator's crew. (Presumably a nickname.)

CHRIS (CHRISTOPHER)   The narrator.

CIMAROONS   Escaped slaves living in the jungle. (From the Sp. *cimarrón*—"wild beast," "fugitive.")

CLÉMENT   A buccaneer turned pirate.

COLE, FATHER ED   A missionary.

COPPER RIVER   A Jamaican river emptying into Kingston Harbor.

CORSON   Bosun aboard the *Sabina*.

CORUÑA   A seaport at the northwest corner of Spain.

COX, CAPTAIN   One of Captain Burt's subordinates, friendly with the Kuna.

CROMWELL   The English revolutionary who made himself Lord Protector. (Born 1599, died 1658.)

CUSTOM OF THE COAST   The usages of buccaneers.

DARIEN   A Spanish colony roughly congruent with present-day Panama.

DELL   Bosun's mate (that is, assistant) aboard the *Sabina*.

DOBKIN, CAPTAIN   One of Captain Burt's subordinates.

DOMINIC, SAINT   The founder of the Dominican Order.

DOMINICANS   The monastic order founded by Saint Dominic.

DRAKE, SIR FRANCIS   An Elizabethan hero who plundered the Pacific Coast of South America and helped defeat the Spanish Armada. He is the father of naval strategy.

DUBEC   Apparently, the third mate of the *Magdelena*.

DUQUESA DE CORRUNA   A Spanish slaver. Later, the *New Ark*.

EMILIA   Captain Isham's ship.

ESTRELLITA   The Guzmans' housemaid.

FANCY   Red Jack's ship.

FAT VIRGIN ISLAND   Its official name is Virgin Gorda, q.v.

FRANCINE   Valentin's dog, stolen from Lesage.

FULGENCIO, BROTHER   An elderly lay brother at Our Lady of Bethlehem.

GAGNE   A buccaneer with whom the narrator quarrels.

GIBRALTAR   A village at the end of Lake Maracaibo.

GOLDEN HIND   The ship in which Drake raided the Indies and circumnavigated the globe.

GOSLING, CAPTAIN   A subordinate of Captain Burt's who captures a ship carrying letters of importance.

GROMETTO   An armed servant. This interesting word is said to be derived from an East African language. The gromettos found on sailing ships were slaves or freed slaves.

GUADELOUPE PASSAGE   A corridor (between Antigua and Guadeloupe) through the Leeward Islands and into the Atlantic. It is wide and deep enough for large vessels.

GUZMAN, JAIME   A merchant of Coruña.

GUZMAN, SABINA MARÍA DE VEGA ARANDA   A Spanish lady who wished to buy a parrot.

HANSEN   Gunner aboard the *Sabina*.

HARKER, CAPTAIN HAL   One of Burt's subordinates.

HISPANIOLA   An island of the Greater Antilles, now divided between Haiti and the Dominican Republic.

HOLY FAMILY   A rural parish.

HOODAHS   A Moskito slave.

HOUDEK, FATHER   The pastor of Saint Teresa's.

HOY   As a noun, a work boat or barge. The expression "all hands hoy" (that is, to work) is equivalent to "all hands on deck."

IGNACIO, BROTHER   A lay brother at Our Lady of Bethlehem.

IGNATIUS LOYOLA, SAINT   The ex-soldier who founded the Jesuits (the Society of Jesus).

ÎLE À VACHE   An island just south of the western end of Hispaniola.

INDIOS BRAVOS   Any unconquered tribe. (Sp.)

ISHAM, CAPTAIN   A subordinate of Captain Burt's.

ISLANDS OF KING PHILIP   The Philippines.

JACKSON, TOM   First mate on the *Weald*.

JAMAICA   A large island one hundred and fifty miles south of Cuba. It was a British possession.

JARDEN, PAUL   Second mate on the *Magdelena*.

JERSEY   One of the Channel Islands.

JIB   A usually triangular sail set on a forestay.

JOAN, SAINT   A teenager in armor, one of history's most successful generals. The English burned her alive.

JOHN, SAINT   The apostle whom Jesus loved is probably meant.

JUDE, SAINT   The apostle who asked the New Testament's most famous question. He is the patron of hopeless causes.

JUNIPER, BROTHER   A foolish Franciscan.

KIDD, CAPTAIN   A privateer who turned pirate.

Kuna   A Central American tribe prone to albinism.

Lady Marie Cape   Presumably Cape Dame Marie, at the western end of the Tiburon Peninsula.

Lake Maracaibo   A large freshwater lake near the coast of Venezuela. It receives the waters of the Catatumbo River and empties into the Gulf of Venezuela through a narrow channel.

Languedoc   A region of France bordered to the southeast by the Mediterranean.

Lesage   First mate on the *New Ark*.

Lisboa   Lisbon, the capital of Portugal.

L'Olonnais, François   Also Francis L'Ollonais. A pirate leader most famous for his cruelty. These may be pseudonyms.

Long Bay   A pirate rendezvous on the southern coast of Jamaica.

Lucy, Saint   A martyred Sicilian girl.

Luis, Father   A monk at Our Lady of Bethlehem who taught mathematics.

Maas   Gunner's mate aboard the *Sabina*.

Macérer   A ship commanded by Captain Burt.

Magdelena   The naval vessel captured by Melind.

Mahu   A slave freed to reinforce the crew of the *New Ark*.

Mansveldt, Edward   Henry Morgan's mentor in piracy.

Maracaibo   A city on the channel linking the Gulf of Venezuela with Lake Maracaibo.

Melind   A buccaneer leader.

Mexico   The Aztec capital, captured by the Spanish.

midshipman   An aspirant to an officer's commission. Midshipmen slept between the crew in the forecastle and the officers in the stern.

Morgan, Henry   Later, Sir Henry. After other daring exploits, Morgan assembled an army of pirates, crossed Darien, and looted and burned the city of Panama.

Moskitos   A Central American tribe.

Mosquitoes, Gulf of   An arm of the Caribbean bordered to the south by the western end of Darien.

Mzwilili   A slave aboard the *Rosa* who joined the narrator's crew. He is usually called Willy.

New Ark   The new name given the *Duquesa de Corruna* by the narrator.

New Spain   A Spanish colony in North America. It is now the Republic of Mexico.

Novia   The narrator's pet name for the woman he loves.

Novice Master   The monk in charge of postulants at Our Lady of Bethlehem.

d'Ogeron, Bertrand   The governor of Tortuga. He was later captured by the Spanish, but escaped.

Ogg, Captain   A subordinate of Captain Burt's.

Ojeda, Captain   The Spanish master of the *Castillo Blanco*.

O'Leary, "Pat the Rat"   Under the narrator, the third mate of the *Castillo Blanco*.

O'Malley, Grace   An Irish pirate queen. Writing to Queen Elizabeth I, she called herself Grany Ne Mailly of Connaught.

Our Lady of Bethlehem   A newly reopened monastery outside Havana.

Patmos   An island in the Mediterranean.

Pearl Coast   The eastern coast of Nicaragua opposite the Pearl Islands.

Pearl Islands   A group of small islands off the eastern coast of Nicaragua.

Pearl Lagoon   A sheltered bay on the eastern coast of Nicaragua. It is extensive. A section of the Pearl Coast may be said to form its eastern boundary, and the mainland its western boundary.

Pete the Hangman   One of the narrator's crew on the *Castillo Blanco*.

Phil, Father   An associate pastor at Saint Teresa's.

Pinkie   An albino Kuna girl.

Portobello   A beautifully sited city on the Gulf of Mosquitoes.

Port Royal   A city at the mouth of Kingston Bay. Twice destroyed by earthquakes, it has been rebuilt each time.

Princess   The sloop commanded by Captain Harker.

Provence   A region of southeastern France.

Quilligan, Paddy   A member of the *Sabina*'s pirate crew.

Rackam, Calico Jack   A pirate captain who is said to have maintained a harem somewhere on the Cuban coast. Anne Bonney and Mary Read served in his crew.

Read, Mary   An extraordinary woman who was successively a footman, a sailor on a British warship, a soldier, a merchant sailor, and a pirate, all while disguised as a man. She died in prison.

Red Jack   An English pirate who volunteers for the prize crew of the *New Ark*. Later, quartermaster of the *Castillo Blanco*.

RED KNIFE   One of the Cimaroons who joins *Sabina*'s pirate crew.

RIO HATO   A Spanish colonial town on the Pacific Coast of Darian, west of the city of Panama.

ROMBEAU   The buccaneer who takes command of the *Magdelena*.

ROSA   The narrator's first capture.

SABINA   In full, the *Santa Sabina de Roma*. A pirate vessel commanded by the narrator. Formerly the *Vincente*.

SADDLE ISLANDS   The Galápagos Islands. A Pacific island group lying on the equator six hundred miles from the mainland of South America.

SAINT BLAISE, GULF OF   The body of water containing the San Blas Islands, q.v.

SAINT TERESA'S   A city parish.

SAN BLAS ISLANDS   An archipelago on the Atlantic coast of Darien, between Portobello and the Gulf of Darien.

SANCHEZ, GENERAL   The commander of Spanish troops in Venezuela.

SAN FELIPO   A Spanish galleon, the largest of the treasure ships attacked by Captain Burt's flotilla.

SAN MATEO   A Spanish merchant vessel.

SANTA CHARITA   A Spanish merchant vessel. Captain Burt renames her the *Weald*.

SANTA LUCÍA   A Spanish galleon.

SANTA MARIA   A Spanish colonial town at the mouth of the Tuira River; this river flows into the Gulf of San Miguel, an arm of the Pacific.

DE SANTIAGO, DON JOSÉ   The owner of the *Castillo Blanco*.

DE SANTIAGO, PILAR   Don José de Santiago's wife.

SCULLY, BISHOP   The head of the narrator's diocese.

SEÑOR   Usually, the first mate of the *Santa Charita*.

SNOW LADY   Captain Gosling's ship.

SOCCORO   A treasure ship attacked by the narrator and his friends.

SOLDIER SALVE   Ferric chloride ointment, used at this time to treat every sort of wound, cut, bruise, and abrasion.

SPANISH MAIN   The mainland of Spanish America. (Often misused and misunderstood.)

STRAIT OF MAGELLAN   A narrow and contorted passage between the South American mainland and the island of Tierra del Fuego.

SURREY   An English county, south of London.

SWAN, CAPTAIN CHARLES   A pirate who sailed across the Pacific to raid the Philippines and Spice Islands. He was eventually marooned by his crew.

EL TABLAZO   A notorious sandbar at the southern end of the Gulf of Venezuela.

TIBURON PENINSULA   A long, mountainous finger of land at the southwestern corner of Hispaniola.

TIERRA DEL FUEGO   A large island at the southern tip of South America. Cape Horn is on a small island south of Tierra del Fuego.

TOLEDO   A city in Spain famous for cutlery.

TORTUGA   A smaller island on the north coast of Hispaniola.

TROY (WEIGHT)   A system used by jewelers in which a Troy pound is divided into twelve Troy ounces.

VALDEZ, ADMIRAL   A Spanish naval hero.

VALENTIN   An indentured servant who has fled his master.

VANDERHORST   A merchant on Virgin Gorda.

VASCO   A sailor aboard the *Santa Charita*.

VENEZUELA, GULF OF   A sea at the northernmost extremity of South America, open to the Caribbean to the north.

VERACRUZ   A port on the east coast of New Spain.

VINCENTE   In full, the *San Vincente de Zaragozza*. The Spanish name of the ship that becomes the *Sabina*.

VIRGIN GORDA   One of the Virgin Islands. It lies due east of Tortola, from which it is plainly visible.

WAHL, FATHER   The pastor emeritus of Holy Family.

WEALD   Earlier the *Santa Charita*. Captain Burt's flagship.

WEST INDIES   A vague term covering the Bahamas and all the islands of the Caribbean, including the Antilles.

WILLY   Mzwilili, q.v.

WINDWARD   The sloop the narrator bought in Port Royal.

WINDWARD PASSAGE   A wide channel between Hispaniola and Cuba.

YANCY   A pirate with whom the narrator duels.

YUCATAN CHANNEL   The channel between Cuba and the Yucatan Peninsula. It connects the Caribbean Sea with the Gulf of Mexico.

ZAMBO MOSKITO   A member of the Moskito tribe of Native American and African ancestry.

ZAVALA   The oldest man on the *Santa Charita*.

ZUMAYA   A treasure ship attacked by the narrator and his friends.